THND THE GLORY

By

H A Culley

Book four about the Anglo-Saxon Kings of Northumbria

Published by Orchard House Publishing

First Kindle Edition 2017

Text copyright © 2017 H A Culley

The author asserts the moral right under the Copyright, Designs and Patents Act 1988 to be identified as the author of this work.

All Rights Reserved. This book may not be reproduced in any form, in whole or in part, without written permission from the author.

Cover Image: © Sergiyi Patalakha | Dreamstime.com

TABLE OF CONTENTS

List of Principal Characters 4

Place Names 6

Glossary 8

SYNOPSIS OF THE FIRST THREE BOOKS 10

CHAPTER ONE – THE STAGE IS SET 12

CHAPTER TWO – THE BATTLE SHIRKER 32

CHAPTER THREE – PEACE AND WAR 43

CHAPTER FOUR – INTO THE LAND OF THE PICTS 54

CHAPTER FIVE – MERCIA RESURGENT 67

CHAPTER SIX – THE PLAGUE OF JUSTINIAN 83

CHAPTER SEVEN – PEACE AND RECONCILIATION 102

CHAPTER EIGHT – STRATHCLYDE 132

CHAPTER NINE – THE BATTLE OF LOCH KATRINE 148

CHAPTER TEN – THE SUBJUGATION OF DALRIADA 170

CHAPTER ELEVEN – THE SYNOD OF WHITBY 183

CHAPTER TWELVE – ALCFRITH'S REVOLT 198

CHAPTER THIRTEEN – THE FALL OF ARDEWR 206

CHAPTER FOURTEEN – THE RETURN OF WILFRID 234

CHAPTER FIFTEEN – BROTHER AGAINST BROTHER 251

Author's Note 275

Other Novels by H A Culley 281

About The Author 283

List of Principal Characters

(In alphabetical order)

Historical characters are shown in bold type

Alchfrith – Oswiu's son by Rhieinmelth. Sub-king of Deira 655-664. *(NOTE: Spelt Ehlfrith in earlier books but changed to the alternative spelling of Alchfrith in this book to save confusion with his brother Ecgfrith)*

Aldfrith – Oswui's eldest son (illegitimate)

Aldhun – Member of Oswiu's gesith, later its leader

Alaric – Catinus' elder son

Alweo – Son of Eowa and nephew of the late King Penda of Mercia

Ælfflaed – Oswiu's daughter by Eanflæd. Later Abbess of Whitby

Ælfwine – Oswiu's younger son by Eanflæd. Later Sub-king of Deira

Bruide – Son of the King of Prydenn and later High King of the Picts

Beornheth - Cuthbert's younger brother and heir presumptive to the Eorldom of Dùn Barra

Cadafael – King of Gwynedd (North Wales)

Cadwalladr – King of Gwynedd after Cadafael

Catinus – Briton born in Mercia who became Ealdorman of Bebbanburg

Ceadda – Oswiu's hereræswa (army commander), later an ealdorman

Chad – Monk at Lindisfarne, later Bishop of Northumbria in competition with Wilfrid

Colman – Bishop and Abbot of Lindisfarne after Finan

Conomultus – Catinus' younger brother, chaplain to Oswiu

Cuthbert – A member of Oswiu's gesith, later Prior then Bishop of Lindisfarne

Domangart – King of Dalriada until 660

Domnall Dhu– King of Dalriada after Domangart

Drest – High King of the Picts after Garnait

Eadstan – Leader of the garrison at Bebbanburg, later the captain of Catinus' gesith

Eanflæd – Oswiu's second wife. Daughter of his uncle, Edwin of Northumbria

Eata – Novice at Lindisfarne, later Abbot of Melrose, then of Lindisfarne

Ecgfrith – Oswiu's son by Eanflæd. Sub-king of Deira 664 – 670

Elfin – King of Strathclyde after Guret and Mermin

Ethelred – Penda's third son. Later King of Mercia. Also spelt Æthelred in some sources

Finan – Bishop and Abbot of Lindisfarne

Fergus – King of Ardewr and Ròidh's younger brother

Garnait – High King of the Picts after Talorgan

Guret - King of Strathclyde

Hereswith – Catinus' daughter, later wife of Alweo

Kyneburga – Daughter of Penda of Mercia and wife of Alchfrith

Leoflaed – Wife of Catinus and mother Hereswith, Alric and Osfrid

Leofric – Catinus' body slave

Lethlobar – Son of Eochaid, King of the Ulaidh in Ulster

Mael Duin – King of Dalriada after his brother, Domnall Dhu

Morleo – King of Ardewr after Fergus

Osfrid – Catinus' younger son

Osthryth – Oswiu's daughter by Eanflæd. Later married King Ethelred of Mercia

Oswiu – King of Northumbria and Bretwalda

Redwald – Hereræswa after Ceadda

Rægenhere – Wilfrid's younger brother and chaplain to Alchfrith

Ruaidhrí – The bastard son of King Eochaid of the Ulaidh and half-brother of Lethlobar

Talorgan – Oswiu's nephew. High King of the Picts

Tuda – Bishop of Lindisfarne after Colman

Wigmund – Alweo's cousin. Prior of Whitby

Wilfrid - Abbot of Ripon. Later Bishop of Northumbria, initially in competition with Chad

Wulfhere – Penda's second son, later King of Mercia

Utta – Former warrior in Eaochaid's gesith, later chaplain to Oswiu and then Bishop of Prydenn

Place Names

(In alphabetical order)

I find that always using the correct place name for the particular period in time may be authentic but it is annoying to have to continually search for the modern name if you want to know the whereabouts of the place in relation to other places in the story. However, using the ancient name adds to the authenticity of the tale. I have therefore compromised by using the modern name for places, geographical features and islands, except where the ancient name is relatively well known, at least to those interested in the period, or else is relatively similar to the modern name. The ancient names used are listed below:

Austrasia – A part of Frankia (see below) centred on the Meuse, Middle Rhine and the Moselle rivers, with a coastline opposite that of southern Kent

Bebbanburg – Bamburgh, Northumberland, North East England

Bernicia – The modern counties of Northumberland, Durham, Tyne & Wear and Cleveland in the North East of England. At times Goddodin was a subsidiary part of Bernicia

Berwic – Berwick upon Tweed, Northumberland, North East England

Caerlleon – Chester, Cheshire, England

Caer Luel – Carlisle, Cumbria, England

Caledonia - Scotland

Cantwareburg – Canterbury, Kent, England

Dalriada – Much of Argyll and the Inner Hebrides

Deira – Most of North Yorkshire and northern Humberside

Dùn Add – Dunadd, near Kilmartin, Argyll, Scotland. Capital of Dalriada

Dùn Barra - Dunbar, Scotland

Dùn Breatainn - Literally Fortress of the Britons. Dumbarton, Scotland

Dùn Dè – Dundee, Tayside, Scotland

Dùn Èideann - Edinburgh

Dùn Phris - Dumfries, south-west Scotland

Eoforwīc - York

Elmet – West Yorkshire

Frankia – The territories inhabited and ruled by the Franks, a confederation of West Germanic tribes, approximating to present day France and a large part of Germany.

German Ocean – North Sea

Gleawecastre – Gloucester, England

Goddodin (later Lothian) – The area between the River Tweed and the Firth of Forth; i.e. the modern regions of Lothian and Borders in Scotland

Gwynedd – North Wales including Anglesey

Kinneddar – Lossiemouth, Moray, Scotland

Loidis – Leeds, Yorkshire

Lundenwic – London

Maserfield – Oswestry in Shropshire

Medeshamstede – Peterborough in Cambridgeshire

Mercia – Roughly the present day Midlands of England

Neustria - The region of Frankia between Aquitaine and the English Channel, i.e. the north of present-day France

Northumbria – Comprised Bernicia, Elmet and Deira. At times it also included Rheged and Goddodin (Lothian)

Orcades – The Orkney Islands, Scotland

Pictland – The confederation of kingdoms including Shetland, the Orkneys, the Outer Hebrides, Skye and the Scottish Highlands north of a line running roughly from Skye to the Firth of Forth; made up at this time of seven kingdoms

River Sabrina – River Severn

River Twaid – The river Tweed, which flows west from Berwick through northern Northumberland and the Scottish Borders.

Rheged - A kingdom of the Ancient Britons speaking Cumbric, a Brythonic language similar to Old Welsh, which roughly encompassed modern Lancashire, Cumbria in England and, at times, part of Galloway in Scotland

Strathclyde – South east Scotland

Yr Wyddfa – Mount Snowdon, North Wales

Glossary

Ætheling – Literally 'throne-worthy. An Anglo-Saxon prince.

Birlinn – A wooden ship similar to the later Scottish galleys. Usually with a single mast and square rigged sail, they could also be propelled by oars with one man to each oar

Brenin – The Brythonic term by which kings were addressed Wales, Strathclyde and the Land of the Picts

Bretwalda - In Anglo-Saxon England, an overlord or paramount king accepted by other kings as their leader

Ceorl - Freemen who worked the land or else provided a service or trade such as metal working, carpentry, weaving etc. They ranked between thegns and villeins and provided the fyrd in time of war

Currach - A boat, sometimes quite large, with a wooden frame over which animal hides are stretched and greased to make them waterproof

Custos – A guardian or custodian, the word was used in a variety of contexts including to mean one left in charge in the absence of the lord or king

Cymru - Wales

Cyning – Old English for king and the term by which they were normally addressed.

Ealdorman – A rank of noble that came into use at this period. A high-ranking royal official and chief magistrate of an Anglo-Saxon shire or group of shires. He also commanded the army of the shire on behalf of the king. He ranked between an eorl (later earl) and a thegn

Eorl – A noble originally ranking between thegn and members of the royal house. In the seventh century it meant the governor of a division of the kingdom. Later replaced by ealdorman, the chief magistrate and war leader of a county, and earl, the ruler of a province under the King of All England; for example, Wessex, Mercia and Northumbria

Gesith – The companions of a king, usually acting as his bodyguard

Hereræswa – Military commander or general. The man who commanded the army of a nation under the king.

Mormaer – Literally great steward, title accorded to a sub-king or ruler of a province in Scotland; equivalent of an earl or eorl.

Seax – A bladed weapon somewhere in size between a dagger and a sword. Mainly used for close-quarter fighting where a sword would be too long and unwieldy.

Thegn – The lowest rank of noble. A man who held a certain amount of land direct from the king or from a senior nobleman, ranking between an ordinary freeman and an eorl/ealdorman.

Ulaidh - A confederation of dynastic-groupings that inhabited a provincial kingdom in Ulster (north-eastern Ireland) and was ruled by the Rí Ulad or King of the Ulaidh. The two main tribes of the Ulaidh were the Dál nAraidi and the Dál Fiatach

Uí Néill – An Irish clan who claimed descent from Niall Noigiallach (Niall of the Nine Hostages), a historical King of Tara who died about 405 AD

Settlement – Any grouping of residential buildings, usually around the king's or lord's hall. In 7th century England the term city, town or village had not yet come into general use

Síþwíf - My lady in Old English. The term used to address a queen

Weregeld – In Anglo-Saxon England, if property was stolen, or someone was injured or killed, the guilty person would have to pay weregeld as restitution to the victim's family or to the owner of the property

Witan – Members of the witenagemot, the council of an Anglo-Saxon king. Usually it included the eorls and the chief priests (bishops and abbots in the case of a Christian kingdom) and, later, the ealdormen, but for the selection of a king or other important matters, it might be expanded to include the more minor nobility, such as the thegns

Villein - A peasant (tenant farmer) who was legally tied to his vill

Vill - A thegn's holding or similar area of land in Anglo-Saxon England which might otherwise be described as a parish or manor

SYNOPSIS OF THE FIRST THREE BOOKS
WHITEBLADE, WARRIORS OF THE NORTH & BRETWALDA

Woken in the middle of the night to flee the fortress of Bebbanburg on the Northumbrian coast, the twelve year old Prince Oswald escapes his father's killer, Edwin, to establish a new life for himself on the West Coast of Scotland. He becomes a staunch Christian on Iona and trains to be a warrior.

He makes a name for himself in the frequent wars in Ulster and in a divided Scotland, earning himself the nickname of 'Whiteblade' and establishing himself as the greatest war leader in his adopted homeland. However, he is beset by enemies on all sides and is betrayed by those he should have been able to trust the most.

After playing a leading role in deposing the treacherous Connad, King of Dalriada, he helps his successor to extend Dalriada to include the Isles of Skye, Arran and Bute. When King Edwin is killed in battle and those who try to succeed him are also killed by Cadwallon and his invading Welsh army, Oswald decided that his moment of destiny has arrived; he sets out with his brother, Oswiu, and his warriors to confront Cadwallon and win back Northumbria.

Once secure on his throne, he enlists the aid of his friend Aidan to convert his pagan subjects to Christianity and establishes the monastery on the Holy Island of Lindisfarne that will become the focus for the spread of the faith throughout the north of England.

Oswiu marries the heiress of Rheged and becomes its king. Gradually he overcomes the ancient enemies of Rheged and allies himself to them to become the dominant force in Caledonia (Scotland) as well as North West England.

Meanwhile Oswald uses a mixture of force, diplomacy and threat to become the most powerful ruler in the whole of England. However, his enemies lurk in the wings and he is betrayed by his allies and killed in battle by the pagan King of Mercia.

After Oswald is killed and his corpse dismembered, Oswiu rides deep into enemy territory to recover his brother's body. Despite his efforts to keep it together, the Kingdom of Northumbria is split into two but Oswiu vows to reunite it.

However, he is forced to concentrate on securing his northern border first. Once he becomes overlord of the North he fends off an invasion by

Penda, the powerful pagan King of Mercia, before he resorts to underhand tactics to kill his cousin, the King of Deira, and unite Northumbria once more.

Having overcome rebellion by the Picts and another invasion by the Mercians he survives, only to be betrayed by his nephew who he had raised up to be King of Deira. Matters come to a head at the Battle of the Winwaed where he must win or see Northumbria torn apart once more. Against all the odds he prevails and Penda is slain. Oswiu is now Bretwalda of England as well as overlord of Caledonia (Scotland). His greatest challenge will now be to hold his vast realm together

CHAPTER ONE – THE STAGE IS SET

656 AD

Bedwyr sat on his pony just below the skyline and watched the column wend its way along the valley path below him. The air had that clean feel to it that only comes just after recent rain has washed the dust out of it. The moderate breeze blew his long, matted hair across his eyes and he impatiently brushed it away.

He was only a boy and he wasn't very good at estimating numbers, but even he realised that there must be at least a thousand, maybe even fifteen hundred, men on the move, mainly warriors with quite a few boys and servants leading packhorses loaded with supplies. He headed around the side of the hill so as to remain in shadow from anyone who happened to glance up. He sniffed at the change in the air and glanced up at the crag above him. Birds flew in and out of cracks in the short pitch of vertical rock which was streaked with guano. That explained the acrid tang in his nostrils.

He rode on, glad to be away from the stench. Once out of sight he started back through the hills to where Cadwalladr currently had his base. He was so excited by what he'd seen that he failed to watch his surroundings as carefully as he should have done. He had entered a shallow valley before he noticed the six riders below him. He saw with alarm that they weren't men he knew; in all probability they were scouts from the army he'd seen.

He pulled his pony to a halt, then yanked her protesting head around to head off up the side of the valley to the north. Initially he left the startled scouts behind but, once they'd collected their wits, they started up the slope to try and intercept him.

They too were mounted on sure-footed mountain ponies, but larger and more powerful beasts than Bedwyr's. However, this advantage was somewhat negated by the heavier weight of their riders; all except one. He was no more than fourteen and therefore only two years older than the boy they were chasing. His pony drew ahead of the others and, as their quarry darted a look over his shoulder, it was obvious that the leading scout would overtake him before he was able to reach the ridge up ahead.

Bedwyr started to sweat, despite the chill in the air rushing past him, and his tongue licked around his dry lips. He dug his heels into his pony but it was tiring. He tried veering to the left but this was only postponing the inevitable. He managed to get to the crest first but the older boy was only ten yards behind him now, and was closing the gap quickly.

The smaller pony stumbled and Bedwyr went flying over her head. He landed with a thump, unhurt but too badly winded to move. His chest felt as if it had been crushed and he struggled to breathe. The other boy rode up and, grinning triumphantly, he pulled a dagger from its sheath as he jumped off his pony.

He grabbed Bedwyr by his long hair and pulled his head back, exposing his throat. Bedwyr was spent, all the fight having been forced out of him along with his breath. He was resigned to having his throat cut when one of the other scouts reached them.

'Don't kill him. He's more than likely one of Cadwalladr's whelps and he'll know where his camp is.'

The boy with the dagger gave an evil smile.

'Can I cut off bits of him until he talks then?'

When the other man nodded he grasped the younger boy's hand and put his dagger against the bottom knuckle of his little finger and sawed it to and fro.

'You can do what you like to me, I'll not talk,' Bedwyr spat at him, grimacing as the somewhat blunt blade cut into his skin.

Suddenly the face of the boy with the dagger crumpled in disbelief as an arrow struck his chest. Bedwyr looked on uncomprehendingly as his assailant fell to the ground in a heap and lay still. Although something in his brain was telling him that he was saved, he didn't believe the evidence of his own eyes. His was still in shock, waiting for death, and he couldn't move.

The other five scouts looked around in alarm, seeking the archer. They saw two men standing in front of their ponies on top of the ridge fifty yards away. Before they could react, a second arrow hit one of the mounted men in the thigh. With a yell of fury the other four kicked their horses into motion and headed up the grass covered slope whilst the wounded man pulled the arrow from his leg.

It was a mistake. Blood spurted from the severed artery, which he frantically spent some time trying to staunch with his hand. In agony, and now faint from loss of blood, he toppled to the ground. Bedwyr calmly bound a dirty bit of cloth torn from the dead lad's tunic around his bleeding finger and picked up the dagger. With a grunt of satisfaction, he plunged it into the neck of the wounded man, although he would have been dead soon anyway.

Meanwhile, two more men had been killed by the archers as they cantered towards them; the remaining two hastily changed their minds and started to head away from the two on the ridge. It was futile. One was hit in the back and crashed to the earth with a thud and the last one had his pony killed from under him. Two minutes later all the scouts were dead.

'You're a bloody fool, Bedwyr,' one of the men told the boy. 'I'm sorry we teased you about the size of your manhood when we all stopped for a piss but we meant no harm by it. Riding off like that in a sulk nearly got you killed.'

The man who'd spoken cuffed the boy around the head, partly because he was angry with him and partly in affection.

'More importantly, you were captured by Cadafael's men. You may think you would've stayed silent whilst that sadistic lad cut bits of you, but you wouldn't. Never go off on your own again,' the other man added quietly.

He had the sense to know that if you shouted at a boy of Bedwyr's age he'd merely get resentful and wouldn't listen. The message was more likely to hit home if delivered in a calm voice. The boy nodded dumbly, trying hard not to cry.

'Right, let's get back to camp.'

The boy sobbed, more in relief than anything, and told them about the army on the move. At first they didn't believe him, but eventually he convinced them he wasn't spinning a yarn.

'Right, let's get you back to the prince. He'll want to know about this.'

'And you're sure that this was an army you saw, not just some chieftain and his retinue?' Cadwalladr asked.

'I can't count very well, Brenin, but this was a mighty host.'

The boy had accorded the prince the title of king in Welsh. Though he had never succeeded his father, Cadwallon, his followers regarded Cadafael as a usurper and Cadwalladr as the true King of Gwynedd.

'Very well. It would seem that Cadafael and his warriors are moving south east for some reason. We'd better go and see for ourselves.'

Bedwyr took them to the spot from where he'd spotted the army and they followed the wide valley until they caught up with the stragglers. Cadwalladr and a handful of his men then followed the slowly moving army, keeping just below the skyline along the tops of the hills as they did so, not that the men below spent much time looking around them. A light rain had started to fall and that was enough to discourage them from taking much of an interest in their surroundings.

'It looks as if they are heading for Powys, but I thought that he and their king, Manwgan ap Selyfin, were in alliance against the Mercians at the moment,' the prince said to his chieftains once the army below had stopped for the night.

'Perhaps the slaying of Penda has changed things,' one of them suggested.

'I doubt it. It's more likely that they have agreed to use the present chaos to launch a joint attack on the western part of Mercia,' another said, shaking his head.

It had been twenty four years since Oswald had slain Cadwalladr's father, Cadwallon, in Northumbria and sent the invading army of Welshmen fleeing back to their homeland. He had been twelve at the time, the same age as Bedwyr was now, and too young to become king. Instead a proven warrior named Cadafael had been given the throne in the interim. The expectation was that he would hand over to Cadwalladr when the boy grew to manhood. That had never happened, of course, and Cadafael had sought to kill the rightful heir ever since.

Cadwalladr had fled into the bleak mountain fastness around the mountain called Yr Wyddfa and had lived the life of an outlaw. He was now thirty six and the usurper was in his mid-forties. Despite his advancing years, Cadafael hadn't slowed down and now he was on his way to invade the region of Mercia known as Salop.

That night Cadwalladr led his men on a raid into the enemy campsite. The moonless night was particularly cold for the time of year. The rain had ceased but raindrops still pattered from the trees onto the rotting foliage that covered the forest floor. Cadwalladr's scouts had to brush the leaves aside with their feet before taking each step so as not to alert the sentries with the sound of crunching.

The sentries were few and had gathered around fires to keep warm. The forest around them wasn't silent; nocturnal animals scurried hither and thither and from time to time the hungry nocturnal predators sprang on their prey. It was nothing to alarm the men, even if they had heard the sounds above the crackling of the fires.

Cadwalladr's scouts were experts at their task and made less noise than the wildlife around them as they crept towards their prey. The sentries all died silently with slit throats. They retraced their steps as silently as they'd come and reported back to Cadwalladr, using gestures not words. He waved his men forwards and they advanced as quietly as they could into the camp.

Cadafael was fast asleep with a girl in his arms – one of a long line of bed mates. His affairs were always brief as he soon tired of even the prettiest. He had sired a number of bastards but had never acknowledged any of them. When the alarm rang out he leapt out of bed naked, grabbed his sword and a small round shield called a targe, and rushed outside. The sight that greeted him was confused. Men were running about, seemingly aimlessly, whilst sounds of fighting came from the darkness to his right.

'Grab your weapons and stay in your groups,' he bellowed at those nearest to him.

Taking the torch mounted on a pole outside his tent, he stalked off in the direction from where the clash of arms was coming. Sound is deceptive at night and it took him a few minutes to find its source. The area illuminated by his torch wasn't large but he could just make out a few mounted men herding his ponies away from the horse lines. He later found out that the ten men guarding the ponies had all been killed. He was about to turn around and return to his tent when several men ran at him out of the darkness.

'To me, to your king,' he roared out in the hope that some of his men were in earshot. As the first man reached him he brought his sword down towards the king's bare head. His assailant was wearing a leather jerkin and a simple round helmet so he was able to see his face clearly. It had been well over twenty years since he'd last seen Cadwalladr and then he'd been a half grown boy, but he knew it had to be him. He threw up his targe to ward off the blow and swung his own sword around in an arc aiming to cut into his rival's side. However, the blade was deflected by a spear and all it succeeded in doing was to chop the shaft in two near the point.

By now he was surrounded by six men and he started to sweat. He was a brave man but only a fool wouldn't be afraid when outnumbered. He pushed all such thoughts from his mind and concentrated on taking as many with him as possible. He backed up against a tree and crouched down waving his sword to and fro, waiting for his enemies to make the first move. Two men went to attack him at the same time, but suddenly a dozen of his men arrived and his assailants vanished back into the darkness before a blow was struck.

He chased after them, exultant at his narrow escape from almost certain death, and tried to make contact with them again, but it was hopeless. After a couple of his warriors had been killed by men hiding in the woods he called them off and returned to the camp.

Once dressed, he gathered his chieftains together to find out what the damage had been. A few dozen men had been killed or badly wounded in the attack, but the most serious loss was that of their ponies. It was bad enough that one of the scouting parties that had been guarding his flank hadn't returned yesterday; now he was completely blind. He wondered whether it was wise to continue. An army without scouts could easily walk right into a trap. Reluctantly he came to the conclusion that they would have to slow their progress so that scouts on foot were able to reconnoitre the flanks and the land ahead of them.

However, Cadwalladr hadn't finished harassing his enemy. For a reason no one understood, the rearguard always seemed to have to march faster than the main body and, even then, an inevitable gap developed between them. Now, despite the slow pace set by those in the lead, the same gap was developing, not helped by the absence of the pack ponies and the consequent need for the men to carry Cadafael's tent and the rest of the equipment between them.

Suddenly several dozen men attacked both sides of the straggling rear guard and another twenty interspersed themselves between them and the rest of the column. The rearguard struggled to divest themselves of the panels and poles of the heavy leather tent and the other equipment, but the enemy were too quick for them. By the time they were ready to fight their assailants had disappeared back into the woods that lined the slopes of the valley, leaving behind nineteen of the rear guard as casualties.

The man in charge sent a runner to tell Cadafael what had happened, but shortly after he left there was a second attack and twenty four more of the rear guard were cut down. They had had enough by the time that their attackers disappeared into side valleys once more. They abandoned the cumbersome tent and the rest of the equipment and supplies before running down the track in an effort to catch their comrades up.

'Now,' Cadwalladr yelled and once more his men emerged. This time to block the path ahead of the rearguard. More men cut off their retreat and arrows ripped into them from the flanks. They never had a chance and ten minutes later there wasn't one left alive.

Cadafael had sworn when he heard the runner's report and he sent one of his best subordinates back with fifty men to find out what was going on. They found the slaughtered remains of the rearguard some five hundred yards behind the last of the main body.

These new arrivals were not farmers and shepherds, as the rear guard had been, they were trained warriors and Cadwalladr had no intention of sacrificing his followers needlessly. So he confined himself to occasional volleys of arrows. They caused few casualties because the new rearguard had been trained to keep together and crouch down behind their interlocked shields as soon as they heard the thwack of a bowstring.

That night Cadafael cursed long and loudly when he realised that his tent had been lost. It was especially tough on his current bed mate as he took his rage out on her. His mood wasn't helped by the torrential rain that started to fall at midnight. His men, even his chieftains, were used to sleeping wrapped in their cloaks in all weathers, but their king was not.

The next morning most woke up sopping wet, disgruntled and hungry. Those who had slept near the periphery of the camp didn't wake up. Cadwalladr's men had killed the sentries during the night and then crept into the camp and slew forty of the sleeping men.

Even worse for morale, the severed heads had been piled in the middle of the path leading south for the army to encounter as they set off the following morning. Cadafael's men were terrified of further attacks and most slept badly the next night, but by then they had made it into Powys and Cadwalladr didn't pursue them across the ill-defined border.

~~~

Alweo was surprised when King Oswiu sent for him. He had settled down as a member of the Bernician warband and now the former Mercian ætheling had accepted his lot. He was the son of Eowa, Penda's turncoat brother, who had supported Oswald and been murdered by his own men in consequence. The Mercian king would undoubtedly have killed Alweo had Oswiu not rescued him. Now Penda was dead and Oswiu ruled Mercia. Perhaps he wanted to reward Alweo by appointing him to an important post in Mercia? He could only hope.

Alweo looked around the small chamber off the king's hall in Eoforwīc as he entered. It was built of timber, like the rest of the hall, with one open window through which the cold wind whistled. The brazier in a corner did little to heat the room but it did fill it with acrid smoke. He was surprised how spartan the room was. Apart from a large coffer and a sleeping platform covered in furs, the only other furniture consisted of a chair, a bench and a stand on which the king's byrnie, helmet and weapons hung. The floor was of beaten earth covered with dried rushes, the same as in the meanest hovel, and there were no animal skins, shields or other decoration on the walls.

Then he noticed a small table in a corner with a plain wooden cross on it. The earth in front of it was bare of rushes and had two small indentations, presumably made by the king's knees when he prayed. Alweo thought that Oswiu must do that a lot to have worn the hard packed soil away.

'Ah, Alweo. Come in and sit down.'

The young man sat on the edge of the bench and Oswiu took the chair. The king's body servant, Ansgar, brought in two goblets of mead and a tray of sweet biscuits and then quietly withdrew.

'How old are you now? The king asked, nibbling on a biscuit.

'Twenty six, Cyning.'

The young man was holding a flagon of mead in one hand and a biscuit in the other, but he was too nervous to sample either.

'They tell me that you're a good rider and you know your horseflesh.'

'Dunstan was training me at the request of Catinus. He wants me to take charge of his horsemen and their mounts at Bebbanburg.'

'Well, I'm afraid that I'm going to disappoint Catinus. As you know, Dunstan was killed at the Battle of the Winwaed and I need someone to replace him. Everyone tells me that no-one is better qualified to be my master of horses than you.'

'I'm, er, I'm not sure what to say, Cyning.'

'Well, do you want the job or not?'

'Yes, of course. I'm honoured. I'm just not sure that I can fill Dunstan's shoes adequately.'

'If you're worried because he was a shipmaster as well, don't be. I'm not asking you to take that on, just breed my horses and train my men to ride.'

'Thank you, Cyning. Of course, I accept with pleasure.'

'Good.' He paused. 'If you were hoping to become an eorl in Mercia or something like that don't be dissatisfied. I have no illusions about how difficult it's going to be to keep Mercia subjugated. After all, your uncle didn't manage to hang onto Wessex for long after he'd conquered it. In any case, many Mercians haven't forgiven your father for betraying Penda and you'll be tarred with the same brush.'

Alweo nodded, acknowledging the truth of what Oswiu had just said. Then he stood, put down his untasted mead and biscuit, inclined his head briefly in farewell and made his way to the stables. He knew the king was correct, but he couldn't help but cherish a dream that one day he might return to Mercia as a noble. He shook off his malaise and thought about the future. He realised with surprise that he was actually eager to visit the farm where Dunstan had bred his horses and get started and there was no time like the present.

Oswiu had smiled to himself as Alweo left. He sensed that the young man was disappointed, despite what he'd told him about Mercia, but whatever he'd been hoping for when he'd entered the room, he should be pleased with the role that Oswiu had picked out for him. Once he'd settled in he'd talk to him about training fifty more of his warband to ride. With the vast domain he now ruled it would be useful to have a sizeable mobile force available to patrol it and nip any trouble in the bud.

Two days after Alweo had departed Oswiu started to muster the army he planned to take with him to settle matters with Powys and Gwynedd. He moved his base from Eoforwīc to Towcester and then west to the border between Mercia and Powys. Once the army was fully assembled he intended to attack the capital of

Powys but then a messenger arrived to say that the Welsh were attacking the Mercian settlement at Elles' Mere.

'They've caught us unprepared,' Oswiu said, banging his fist the table in front of him in frustration.

'The scouts are watching them and so far they've failed to take the settlement,' Ceadda replied. 'The palisade is higher than normal and the Welsh haven't got any siege equipment. Not yet at any rate. However, they are beginning to construct a battering ram and make ladders. That'll take them time and, with any luck, the Mercians inside will be able to hold out for a day or two.'

'Hmmm. How many horsemen do we have at the moment?'

'About thirty plus your gesith, sixty in all. Catinus' men returned to Bebbanburg with him.'

'In retrospect it was mistake to let him go. Ah well; we'll have to make do with what we've got. I want the horsemen to make for Elles' Mere as quickly as they can and attack the men who are cutting down trees to make the ram and ladders. I don't want to lose any of them needlessly, so they are to pick their targets carefully. My aim is to delay things until we can get there with the army. Now, who's the best man to put in charge?'

'I would have said Redwald but you surely don't intend to leave yourself without a bodyguard?'

Oswiu nodded. 'Yes, this is more important. The leader of my gesith is resourceful and clever. You'd better send for him so we can brief him. Don't worry about my protection, I'll keep a few of my gesith with me. They and Ansgar will suffice.'

'Are you sure? There are a lot of Mercians with our army. They were our enemies not so long ago; are you sure they might not take the opportunity to assassinate you.'

'They may have been our foes in the past but they are leaderless. Besides they will want revenge on Cadafael for deserting them at the Winwaed.'

'Penda and Peada may be dead and Ethelred a prisoner, but don't forget Wulfhere is still at large.'

'He's taken refuge with Eorcenberht of Kent, who's an ally. I don't think I need worry about him.'

'I think you're mistaken. Eorcenberht is as slippery as an eel. I've heard a rumour that he's betrothed his daughter Ermenilda to Wulfhere.'

'A rumour? From where? I thought I could count on his support.'

'James the Deacon. He heard it from the archbishop.'

'A bit more than a rumour then. He should know.'

Ceadda nodded and Oswiu sighed.

'Well, I can't worry about that now. We need to concentrate on removing the Welsh threat.'

~~~

Catinus had fallen in love. He'd lost his virginity to a village girl when he was barely thirteen, before Oswiu had plucked him and his brother from obscurity as shepherd boys to be his guides though the black peat bogs of the High Peak. Since then he'd enjoyed sex with a succession of women, latterly with Sunngifu, the sister of his body servant, Leofric, but he'd not thought about settling down. Now he was in his late twenties, an age when many men had already been married for years and had sired several children.

However, he wasn't consciously seeking a wife at the time. He was happy enough as it was. There were plenty of willing girls around the fortress who were eager to share the bed of the handsome new custos. The fact that he had an olive-skinned complexion added to his allure compared to the pale Angles and Saxons.

He had seen the girl who was to change his life when he went to visit the Thegn of Bebbanburg. He was lord of the vill that shared a name with the fortress and his villeins and slaves farmed the land to the west and south of it. Consequently they sold their excess produce to the garrison and both the thegn and his ceorls had grown prosperous over the years.

The thegn, an elderly man called Gamanulf, had two sons. The elder helped him to manage the vill and would succeed him in due course; the younger was a member of Oswiu's gesith. He also had a daughter called Leoflaed who had come as something as a surprise to her parents as she put in an appearance some ten years after their younger son. At the time that Catinus first saw her she was fourteen. She was lissom and moved with a grace that excited him sexually. He couldn't help but wonder what she looked like under her clothes. In contrast to his slightly swarthy appearance and black hair, she was blonde with a peaches and cream complexion. Her face was not exactly pretty - except for her pert, upturned and rather small nose - instead it had character.

Gamanulf knew that he should be thinking about her betrothal – indeed many fathers would have started to do so before this - but ever since his wife had died three years ago Leoflaed had looked after him and managed his hall. He couldn't bear the thought of losing her, despite knowing that he was being unfair to her. Secretly he hoped that she would stay with him until he died. Of course, by then it might well be too late to find her a worthy husband. She wasn't an heiress and, although she was very pretty, men who were in a position to choose wanted a nubile young girl to bed, not a grown woman. Her options later on in life would be to marry a ceorl who wanted to improve his status or become a nun.

Catinus had first seen Leoflaed when she brought in some bread and mead when he, Gamanulf and his elder son were discussing hunting and fishing rights. Normally a slave would have served the refreshments but she wanted to see this man who the other girls kept giggling over. Catinus couldn't take his eyes off her and she felt a strange lurch in her belly when she demurely cast a quick glance his way. She could tell that he was interested in her and she realised with a start that the feeling was mutual.

She hurried out of the hall and leant against the wall breathing heavily. She knew that her father wanted her to stay with him but she was beginning to feel stifled. Life was slipping away and her resentment was growing. She told herself that Catinus' interest was a fleeting fancy and that he wouldn't want to marry her, but from that moment on she allowed herself to hope.

She was therefore encouraged when Catinus came back two days later on the pretext of wanting to clarify a few points from their earlier discussion. This time when she entered he asked to be introduced. With a frown Gamanulf did so and she sank to her knees, glancing up at Catinus with a smile.

'How old are you child?' he asked her directly.

This worried Gamanulf even more, and it annoyed him. Such a question should have been directed at him, not directly to his daughter.

'Fourteen, my lord.'

'Your daughter is very pretty, Gamanulf. She must take after her late mother,' he said with a grin.

That annoyed the old man even more.

'Go back to your duties, Leoflaed,' he told her gruffly.

'Yes father.'

But she gave Catinus a lingering glance over her shoulder as she left the hall.

'Is she betrothed?'

The new Custos of Bebbanburg was not a man to beat about the bush.

'Um, er, no. I need her here. My wife is dead and she looks after me; I'm not looking for a husband for her,' the thegn told him bluntly.

His elder son, a man of Catinus' age who was married with three children of his own, shifted uncomfortably in his chair. He tried hard not to upset his father but he'd told him some time ago that it was time that he found a husband for Leoflaed. His wife was impatient to move out of the cramped hut in which they lived and take over the running of the hall; but the old thegn knew that, if he allowed them to move in, his son and his wife would take charge and he'd become a doddering old grandfather sitting by the fire waiting to die. He was anxious to avoid that at all costs.

A week later Catinus received a visit from the elder son. He gazed around him in awe as he entered, impressed by the hall at Bebbanburg. His father's hall was no more than an overgrown hut. Where Catinus lived was imposing by comparison. Not only was it much bigger and taller, but its roof was supported by large, straight tree trunks all along its length. These were set some distance in from the outer walls so that they created two separate areas either side of the main hall. Part of these side areas had been partitioned off to provide separate sleeping quarters, Catinus' being the largest. In Gamanulf's hall everyone slept together. The only privacy for the thegn was provided by a tattered curtain around his corner of the communal space.

    He was also used to some rain coming in through the hole in the roof above the central hearth. Here there were two hearths and above them, instead of a simple hole, there were twin hatches, hinged at the apex of the roof, which could be closed by ropes when there was no fire and which, when opened to the horizontal, kept most of the rain out whilst still allowing the smoke to escape. This hall also had windows at intervals along its length with shutters which let in the light whenever the weather was fine, and kept the rain and wind out when it wasn't.

    Catinus greeted his visitor courteously but loudly to attract his attention and he stopped gawping at his surroundings. After the usual greetings he got down to business with no further preamble.

    'My father will never let Leoflaed marry whilst he lives. He's frightened about what will happen to him if my wife moves into the hall to replace my sister. He's right to worry too. She's a bit of a shrew and she'll make his life hell, as she does mine.'

    'Sounds to me as if it'll be in all our interests if you replaced your wife with someone more biddable and pleasant. I make no secret of the fact that I want to get to know Leoflaed better, but I can't do that very easily if Gamanulf opposes the match.'

    'I've tried to talk to my wife about becoming a nun but she attacked me like a screaming banshee as soon as I suggested it. I can't think of any other way of getting rid of her.'

    'Have you applied to Bishop Finan to divorce her on the grounds of adultery?'

    'But she hasn't committed adultery.'

    'No, but you could.'

    'She'd kill me!'

    'Then I can only suggest you go back to your wife and stand up to her. Are you a man or a frightened little boy? Oswiu won't let you become thegn after your father if you don't show a bit more backbone than this.'

The man sighed. 'You don't know her.'

'Then perhaps I should become acquainted. Bring her here tomorrow afternoon.'

Gamanulf's son appeared shortly after the midday meal accompanied by a truculent looking woman. They waited, impatiently on her part, whilst Catinus dealt with a dispute between the blacksmith and the chief huntsman over an unpaid bill. As the two left, one grumbling and the other smiling broadly, the custos greeted the couple with a welcoming smile.

Two servants brought in a bench for the couple to sit on and Leofric served them bread and ale. He went to offer the refreshments to Catinus but he declined.

'Thank you for coming. I think we need to talk privately.'

He waved the others in the hall away and they withdrew out of earshot; all except the commander of the garrison, a man called Eadstan, who remained standing by his side.

'Now, as you know, I intend to ask Thegn Gamanulf for Leoflaed's hand. However, I understand that he is loath to lose her services as the mistress of his hall. Normally he would ask you two to move in and your wife would take over Leoflaed's duties. For some reason Gamanulf isn't prepared to allow that to happen.'

Confronted by his unblinking regard the woman glared back at him for a minute; then her gaze faltered and she lowered her eyes to the floor.

'Why do you think that is?' he asked. The man looked panic stricken so he added, 'I'm asking your wife.'

'You have no right to ask me these questions,' she retorted, glaring at him once more.

'Perhaps not, legally speaking, but you are obstructing my desire to marry your husband's sister. That makes it my business. Now I'm a warrior and warriors tend to see things in simple terms.'

He paused and, still keeping his eyes fixed on the woman, he asked the man beside him a question.

'Eadstan, what would you advise me to do in these circumstances?'

'Well, I could make this shrew disappear one dark night, I suppose.'

'You mean kill her and quietly dispose of the body? Yes, that's one solution I suppose.'

Both the man and his wife were now staring at him in horror.

'I'll bear that in mind if I can't find another solution, thank you Eadstan. Very helpful. On the other hand there are less drastic solutions to our little problem. If you became a nun it would automatically release your husband from his marriage vows or, if he committed adultery it would be grounds for divorce.'

He had fixed his eyes on the woman whilst he was speaking and she swallowed hard, having seemingly lost her belligerent attitude; indeed she was now looking a little fearful.

'Which would you prefer?' he asked with an insincere smile.

The woman seemed unable to talk, opening and closing her mouth like a fish. Catinus sighed and then winked at the husband - who was still looking worried - when his wife wasn't looking.

'Come now; it's a simple choice. Divorce, in which case you would be a free woman and your dowry would be returned to you, or become a nun. Of course, there is also the other option Eadstan mentioned.'

'Free woman! He's spent my dowry and I'd be left destitute!'

Some of the fire had returned to her eyes.

'You might be able to find a new husband, perhaps.'

She gave him a withering look. Everyone knew her reputation; men would try and kill a maddened boar with their bare hands rather than marry her.

'Very well, would you like to speak to Bishop Finan to see if he can find a monastery to accept you, perhaps the new one at Whitby?'

She pursed her lips and was about to say something, but evidently changed her mind and merely nodded dumbly. She knew when she was beaten.

'I'm sorry. I need to hear you say it.'

'Yes, damn you to Hell. I'll become a nun.'

Catinus laughed. 'I rather think that your husband is the one who has been in Hell for the past few years. Go and see the reeve. He'll make the necessary travel arrangements.'

When she left the man looked at him with a mixture of gratitude and awe.

'Would you really have had her killed?'

'If necessary, yes. Now, down to more practical matters. You'll need a good slave to look after your children and to manage the thegn's hall. Do you have someone in mind?'

'There's an old woman who's the children's nurse, but she has no experience of managing a hall.'

'Good. I've a slave, a young girl, who's been trained to look after my hall here. Her name is Sunngifu. When Leoflaed marries me she'll want to look after my household herself. In any case, for reasons I won't go into, it might be better if Sunngifu wasn't here when she arrives. I'll give her to you as part of Leoflaed's dowry.'

~~~

Cadafael was getting nervous. Elles' Mere should have fallen quickly and he and his allies from Powys should have been well away from there by now. Instead the wretched place had resisted his assaults and now his men were being picked off in the woods when they went in search of timber for the siege ladders and the battering ram. Initially he'd suspected that Cadwalladr had followed him into Powys but the two men who'd been killed attacking one of his forage parties yesterday had been dressed like Angles or Saxons.

To make matters worse he'd had an argument with his fellow king, Manwgan, who was getting impatient to move on and find more profitable pickings. Cadafael knew deep down that he was right, but he was an obstinate man and he took their failure to take this place personally. He'd just decided to launch an assault at dawn on the morrow and to withdraw if that failed when several of his chieftains arrived, clearly excited about something.

'Oswiu's army is less than five miles away,' one of them burst out, omitting the usually form of greeting when coming into his king's presence.

'What? Why didn't our scouts find them long before this?'

'Because they're frightened to go too far from the camp. Too many have disappeared,' another chieftain told him bluntly.

Cadafael glared at him and was about to utter an angry retort, but he stopped himself just in time. Recriminations would have to wait; the immediate problem was Oswiu.

'Do we have any idea how many men he has?'

Something between two and three thousand, they think.'

'They think? Is that the best they can do? How many trained warriors and how many men of the fyrd?'

'About half and half, or so they say.'

Cadafael snorted impatiently whilst his fellow king, Manwgan, who had just joined him, looked nervous.

'Perhaps we should retreat into the mountains?' Manwgan suggested.

'We have over three thousand warriors between us. Do you want to scuttle away like a timorous mouse or do you want to remove this so called Bretwalda of England? With Oswiu dead we can take back the land our ancestors lost to the Anglo-Saxons.'

Manwgan drew himself up and glared at Cadafael.

'My ancestors were kings of Powys when yours were poor shepherds,' he reminded Cadafael. Take back what you just said or you can fight the Northumbrians and the Mercians on your own.'

Cadafael bit his lip. He had a poor opinion of Manwgan, both as a king and as a warrior, but he needed his men; and he was in his territory.

'I'm sorry,' he said after a short silence. 'Of course we are in this together and whatever we decide will be a joint decision. Where do you suggest that we fight Oswiu?'

'The hill fort at Maserfield, the place that men are beginning to call Oswald's Tree. Let's make a martyr of Oswiu there as I did his brother.'

Cadafael smiled inwardly. Manwgan was embroidering the truth somewhat. It was Penda who had defeated Oswald there fourteen years previously; the men of Powys had merely made up the numbers.

'Yes, that would be fitting. Tell the men we are moving back to Maserfield,' he told his chieftains.

Manwgan nodded triumphantly. By getting Cadafael to accept his plan he felt that the battle was already won. He couldn't have been more wrong.

CHAPTER TWO – THE BATTLE SHIRKER

656 AD

Oswiu grunted in satisfaction when he heard that the Welsh had withdrawn to the hill fort near where his brother Oswald had been killed. There would be a poignancy in defeating Cadafael and Manwgan there. Now that they were committed and awaited his attack, he could afford to delay whilst the rest of his army assembled.

More Mercian eorls answered his summons than he had dared hope for and even some from Middle and East Anglia joined him. Additional men from Rheged and Goddodin also arrived, admittedly they were mainly from the fyrd, but he now had over four thousand men under his command. Once Alweo and Catinus joined him, making the number of mounted warriors up to eighty, he moved.

'I've no intention of letting Cadafael shirk this battle and I want Manwgan killed or captured in retribution for the part he played in the martyrdom of my brother,' he told his assembled war leaders.

His tent was large but it was filled to overflowing by the eorls and other leaders who had crammed into it. The wind was getting up outside and the tent flapped making a noise that make conversation difficult. The king climbed onto a table so that he was visible amidst the throng and now he paused whilst his eyes engaged their upturned faces. Satisfied that he had their attention, he cleared his throat and raised his voice so that he could be heard.

'Our horsemen and a thousand of the lightly armed fyrd will travel around the fort near Oswald's Tree and take up position to the west to cut off their escape. We know that they are short of supplies and so we will sit at the bottom of the slope and wait for them to make a move.'

He eyes roved around those looking up at him until they lit upon his two sons. The eleven year old Ecgfrith was about to start his education at Lindisfarne with the novice monks. His father had brought him along to let him experience warfare for himself, albeit at a distance. His other son, Alchfrith, was nearly seventeen and the experience of command would be good for him. However, he would need someone with experience to advise him so that he didn't make foolish mistakes.

He considered the options and then he searched amongst the assembled throng for Catinus and his friend Alweo.

'The blocking force will be commanded by my son, Alchfrith, with advice from Alweo in charge of the horsemen and Catinus as leader of the fyrd,' he announced.

One or two of the eorls were surprised at the king's choice; not at putting Alchfrith in command - after all he was an ætheling who had just been made the ruler of Deira under Oswiu – but at the choice of the two Mercians as his deputies. Admittedly Alweo was still officially an ætheling in Mercia, but Catinus was a Briton who had been born a villein. Murmuring against Oswiu's choice started to swell inside the tent until it could be heard above the flapping fabric of the tent. The king scowled and pointed his finger, shouting spoke above the hubbub.

'Arthius, you have something to say? Spit it out man.'

The Eorl of Elmet seemed uncomfortable at being singled out but looked Oswiu in the eye as he replied.

'You have favoured Catinus above your Anglian nobles time and time again. He has been raised up from his origins as a shepherd boy and made custos of your most formidable fortress. Now he is to lead the fyrd as your son's deputy. You do too much honour to a humbly born Briton, Cyning.'

'Did any of you recover my blessed brother's head? Catinus risked his life to do so. Many have served me loyally, but none more so than this man. He may have been born a Briton and the son of a poor shepherd in Mercia, but he has proved himself time and time again in battle. He has a wise head on his young shoulders and he is a skilled tactician.

'Look back at your own ancestors. You may have been born the sons of eorls but where did they come from? My great-grandfather was Ida, a minor Anglian chieftain until he landed on the east coast of what was then Britannia and built a fortress there. Eoppa, his father, was a fisherman. How was his social status different to that of Catinus' father?'

There was silence in the tent now. All the eorls were proud of their nobility but they knew that they owed their present standing to their grandfather's or great-grandfather's emergence as leaders of the settlers who left their original homeland. None of the Anglian nobles across the sea had given up their land to come and settle in Britannia. The men who had carved out the new kingdoms had been farmers, shepherds and fishermen.

Arthius nodded. 'I apologise to you and to Catinus. I acknowledge that he has proved himself a courageous warrior and a good leader in battle.'

A few of the others muttered agreement but most remained silent. They had yet to be convinced that Catinus deserved his place amongst them.

'Good.' Oswiu smiled. 'Let's go and besiege Cadafael, and this time make sure he doesn't escape.'

As he watched the last man leave his tent he wondered why he kept favouring Catinus. When he had first come across him and his brother fourteen years ago he had nearly agreed with Ceadda's demand that they be killed once their usefulness as guides had ended. He was glad he hadn't listened to him, but he could have left him as an ordinary member of his warband. However, something about him convinced Oswiu that the young man was destined for greater things. His recent betrothal to the daughter of a thegn meant that his sons would be born noble and, although he had slightly belittled Eoppa's standing by calling him a common fisherman, there were parallels between the history of his own family and that of Catinus.

The man's brother, Conomultus, had done well too, rising in the church until he was now the king's chaplain. He would be very surprised if he didn't become an abbot or a bishop in due course. Conomultus was a devout Christian but he was also politically astute; a quality that the saintly Aidan and the present head of the Northumbrian Church, Finan, lacked, but which the Roman churchmen like John the Deacon and Archbishop Deusdedit, the leader of the church in the south of England, possessed in abundance.

The next morning was dank and miserable. Drizzle permeated everything as Alchfrith led his contingent around the hill fort well to the north to block the route between it and the rest of Powys. The young king was proud of his elevation to the throne of Deira, despite being only a sub-regulus under his father, and even prouder to have been given his own command. The weather hadn't dampened his spirits, even if it had that of his men.

Unfortunately, he seemed to think that Alweo and Catinus were just there to follow his orders and not to advise him. He'd obviously turned a deaf ear to that part of his father's briefing.

He started his advance without sending out scouts and when both of his deputies advised him to do so, he ridiculed the idea, saying that all the enemy were shut up in the hill fort.

'They will have sent out forage parties, Cyning,' Alweo said tactfully.

'Well, they are hardly likely to pose a threat to us are?' he joked.

'No, but he needs to force them to abandon the fort and attack him. If we can stop them taking back supplies to the hill fort that would starve them out that much sooner,' Catinus pointed out.

'That wasn't what he told me to do. We are to form a blocking force to stop supply columns from Powys reaching them and to kill them when they flee,' he said stubbornly.

'But can't you see, locating and eliminating any foraging parties is all part of that strategy,' Catinus said in exasperation. 'That's why he sent Alweo and the horsemen with us.'

'Mind your tongue, peasant!' Alchfrith snapped at him. 'The eorls don't understand why you are in command of my footmen and neither do I. One more outburst like that and I'll replace you and you can take your rightful place in their ranks.'

Catinus seethed with rage and was about to make an intemperate retort when he saw the warning look that Alweo gave him. He bit his tongue and, muttering sotto voce about stupid, arrogant boys, he dropped back to join his men. When he'd calmed down he decided that he and Alweo would have to employ a little more subtlety to make a success of this task.

Alchfrith picked a place to make his stand which was a poor choice for a number of reasons. It was a shallow valley so fleeing Welshmen could get around his force easily; even worse, if the enemy retreated in good order, they'd be able to push in his flanks and trap him.

'Doesn't he understand anything about military strategy,' complained Catinus.

'Apparently not,' Alweo replied, not making any attempt to keep his disgust out of his voice.

'Is there any point in remonstrating with him?'

'I wouldn't have thought so; the obstinate little sod will just dig his heels in.'

'So what do we do?'

'I'll send my men out early tomorrow to find a better position to the west of here. Then, as soon as the routed Welsh appear, we can withdraw before they reach us.'

'He's bound to ask where you and your scouts are.'

'Then you can tell him we are watching the hill so we have advance warning if the routed army are coming this way, and also watching the approach from the west so we can intercept any supply carts.'

'Thanks. Where will you be whilst I'm having to deal with the little brat?'

Alweo grinned. 'Looking for a good defensive position to the west, of course.'

'He had no right to go off without my orders,' Alchfrith bleated. 'And he certainly had no authority to take his men with him. Now I have no horsemen to act as my eyes and ears.'

'That's exactly what Alweo and his men will be doing,' Catinus said soothingly, resisting the temptation to cuff the petulant youth around the head.

'But he should be following my orders, not acting on his own initiative.'

'Cyning, Remind me again how many battles you have won.'

'What do you mean? You know that this is my first.'

'Do you think your father was born with the experience needed to defeat his enemies, or do you think it's conceivable that he learned his trade as war leader from listening to those with more experience than he had at the time? Even now he consults his senior eorls and leaders before making his mind up.'

Alchfrith's face turned crimson and Catinus prepared himself to receive a tirade of abuse; instead the young king's shoulders slumped and he appeared to be on the verge of tears.

'So you think I'm being arrogant?'

Catinus was astounded at how quickly the young man's bravado had turned to self-doubt. It had obviously all been a defensive screen to hide his insecurity. He considered a diplomatic reply but decided being honest would be more productive.

'The thought had occurred to me, yes.'

'I just want to make my father proud of me. He's spent most of his life ignoring me; this is my chance to prove to him that I'm worthy of his regard.'

'You won't do that by failing in the task he has set you, Cyning. Why do you think he sent two of his best leaders with you?'

'Not so you could tell me what to do; I'm not a child!'

'No, of course not. But you might at least listen to our advice before making your mind up and giving us your orders,' Catinus said patiently.

The young king looked doubtful, but then reluctantly decided that Catinus might have a point.

'So what is your advice?'

'To find a place which is more easily defendable and where you can't easily be outflanked. Don't forget we are assuming that we'll be dealing with routed men. Cadafael might just as easily decide to give your father the slip and withdraw into the mountains of Powys and Gwynedd; he's done it before. You do know that his nickname is Battle Shirker? In which case we'd be facing the whole Welsh army.'

A horrified look crossed the youth's face and Catinus grunted in satisfaction. It seemed that, at long last, he was getting through to Alchfrith.

'We must get Alweo back at once so that he can find a proper defensive position.'

'His scouts know their business, Cyning. I wouldn't be at all surprised if he returned with a choice of suitable places for you to decide between.'

~~~

Oswiu emerged from his tent as dawn broke the following day. Thankfully yesterday's incessant drizzle had been replaced by a mixture of clouds and sunshine.

'They've gone Cyning. The hill fort is deserted,' Ceadda told him as the king relieved himself of the ale he'd consumed the previous evening.

'So it seems that Cadafael has once more lived up to his nickname,' he replied.

Then he realised what the overnight departure of the Welsh army meant. They were marching back into Powys and straight into the blocking force commanded by his son. Alchfrith would be outnumbered by well over two to one and most of his men were from the fyrd.

Ten miles away Alweo's scouts rode back to report that the Welsh were on their way, marching in a column, a disorganised column to be sure, but evidently this was a planned withdrawal, not a hasty retreat. Catinus had decided to keep tactics simple. The fyrd weren't capable of any complex movements; they had barely known how to form a shield wall before he'd started to train them two days ago. Now at least they could keep a steady formation with the best shield bearers to the fore and the bulk of the men pushing against their backs to hold the front two ranks firm.

They were lined up along the far bank of a river which no-one seemed to know the name of. It wasn't a case of holding a ford this time, unfortunately, as the water was knee high at its deepest. However, it would slow men down and there was a steep, muddy – and therefore slippery – bank on the far side where Catinus' men had formed up. The area on both sides of the stretch of river bank that Alweo had found was marshy and so the flanks were secure.

He had some one hundred archers and he stationed them at the rear of the spearmen from where they would be able to fire at high trajectory into the Welsh. They were all skilled with the bow, but they were hunting bows, less powerful than war bows, and the fyrd weren't well enough trained for the bowmen to engage the enemy from in front of the shield wall and then retreat through it when the enemy got close.

Alchfrith sat on his horse surrounded by the twenty five men of his gesith some four hundred yards behind the river from where he could see what was going on. Catinus and his own warband were in the centre of the fyrd to stiffen them. Of Alweo and his horsemen there was no sign. The young king had fretted about having no reserve but eventually his two commanders had convinced him that a reserve would make no difference to their plan; either it would work or they were doomed.

The first Welshmen to arrive at the river didn't wait for the two kings and the rest of their army to arrive before launching an attack. It was sheer stupidity. A third were hit by arrows whilst they were still crossing the river and the rest were easily repulsed by the spearmen manning the shield wall. Not only did it cost them over a hundred casualties needlessly, but it gave encouragement to the men of the fyrd. Most were unsure what to expect and were very fearful in consequence. Now they were much more confident – overconfident in some cases.

As more and more Welshmen arrived on the opposite bank that confidence evaporated as they realised that they were facing over twice their numbers. Furthermore, a good proportion of the enemy would be seasoned warriors. Catinus yelled out to his men, assuring them that they had repulsed the Welsh once and would do so again. Then he gave the order for the archers to fire another volley.

He watched as the dense cloud of arrows arced high in the air and came down amongst the milling foe some fifty yards away on the opposite bank. It was long range for a hunting bow but the Welsh suffered about thirty more casualties. Their own archers replied in a ragged volley but most of their arrows struck the shields of the first rank of the fyrd.

The casualties inflicted on the Welsh enraged them and another wave started across the river without orders. This time there were many more of them, perhaps three hundred in all. A second volley from Catinus' archers disabled or killed about ten percent or more of them but the rest kept coming. This time it was more of a close run thing. The Welsh concentrated on the centre of the shield wall where Catinus and his men stood. Even they were forced back a couple of paces before he managed to get some rear rankers in from the flanks to add their weight to the centre. Slowly the Welsh were pushed back into the water.

This time the fyrd had quite a few casualties but the Welsh had suffered many more. When they withdrew they left over a hundred behind. Many were only wounded but boys darted out to slit the throats of those on the bank and the river carried the other wounded away to drown.

At that moment Cadafael arrived and quickly assessed the situation. By the time that Manwgan had joined him he'd already decided to move further along the river to find another crossing place. The Welsh formed up to move off when Alweo appeared with his horsemen on the east bank – the same side as the Welsh. They cantered up to the rear of the column and threw their spears into the packed ranks before vanishing as quickly as they had appeared.

This panicked the rest of the Welshmen at the rear and they started to run to get away from a second attack. The men in front of them became unsettled and their anxiety communicated itself to the middle of the column. Their mood wasn't improved when they saw that the fyrd on the opposite bank had marched around the marshy ground and were now shadowing them on the far bank.

At one point the river narrowed and the two armies moved closer together. Catinus seized the opportunity to order his archers to halt and send another cloud of arrows over towards the Welsh. A couple of dozen were killed or incapacitated but that wasn't important. The fact that one of the dead was Manwgan was pure chance. The arrow had struck the neck of his byrnie and had been deflected upwards into his throat, nicking one of his two carotid arteries on the way. He fell from his horse and his life blood spurted out of him as he lay on the ground.

The men of Powys were now demoralised and leaderless. Manwgan's only son, Eiludd, had been killed in the second attack across the river and his own son, Beli, was still a boy of fifteen. He and his chieftains did their best to rally their men but some had already started to slip away. The few gradually became a flood as Alweo pressed home a second attack on the rear of the column.

Seeing this Cadafael decided that his only chance lay in making a stand and wait for nightfall. It was a fatal mistake. Alchfrith was all for making an attack across the river once he saw that the numbers were now more evenly matched but Catinus managed to dissuade him.

'Cyning, the Welsh have made an error in stopping. That gives your father the chance to catch them up and together you can destroy them. If you attack now you will lose men and Cadafael may decide to continue his retreat. Our job is to hold them here until the main army can join us.'

When Oswiu did appear with his vanguard an hour before dark Alchfrith wanted to charge across the river to join his attack. However, Catinus suggested another plan to him and Oswiu was puzzled to see his son march his men off upstream whilst more and more of own men arrived to join in the fight.

Alweo had seen Alchfrith and Catinus march off and he immediately guessed what his friend's plan was. He managed to stop his excited horsemen from joining in the fight and led them around the battleground and headed further along the river.

Twenty minutes later he found Alchfrith and Catinus on his side of the river with the rest of the fyrd in the process of crossing.

'What now?'

'We make our way back towards the battle and I'll wager ten pounds of silver that we'll meet Cadafael and his gesith fleeing the battle, having deserted his men. It's what he did last time as soon as he saw he was losing.'

As Catinus had predicted Cadafael and the remaining twenty men of his bodyguard rode straight into Alchfrith's army. He tried to turn away from the river to escape that way but this time it was Alweo's horsemen who blocked his retreat. He was trapped and neither he nor any of his gesith escaped.

An exultant Alchfrith greeted his father just as night was falling and presented him with Cadafael's head.

CHAPTER THREE – PEACE AND WAR

656 AD

Catinus returned to Bebbanburg a hero. Of course, Alchfrith had claimed all the glory for his men's part in the destruction of the Welsh army and the death of the two kings, but Oswiu wasn't a fool. Later he'd sent for Alweo and Catinus and asked for their version of events. Neither wanted to explain how Alchfrith had so very nearly led them to disaster but they answered the king's questions truthfully. What they didn't know was that Oswiu had asked Ceadda to talk to some of the men of the fyrd and to those of the Bernician warband who were with Alweo and so he already knew exactly what had happened.

'I suspect that you two are being very modest and that you prevented my son from making a fool of himself. Of course, that's why I sent you with him in the first place. Catinus, your main reward already awaits you back at Bebbanburg. I regret not being able to attend your wedding but I need to make sure that neither Powys nor Gwynedd give me a problem in the future.

'You are already custos of Bebbanburg but I intend to raise you even higher. There is no Eorl of Bebbanburg; that function has always been associated with the King of Bernicia. However, I intend to base myself at Eoforwīc in future. Both Yeavering and Bebbanburg are too far north now for me to spend too much time there.

You will take over the government of the area from Berwic in the north across to the Cheviots and south as far as Morpeth. However I'm not making you an eorl. Mercia and Wessex have introduced a new rank of noble called an ealdorman to act as tax collector, judge and military leader in a new administrative division called a shire. I intend to do the same. You will therefore become the Ealdorman of Bebbanburg.

'Thank you, Cyning. I am most grateful, as ever, for your trust in me. I assume from what you have just said that I'm free to return to wed Leoflaed?'

'Yes, I think we can manage without you. Wait until you have my charter appointing you as ealdorman before you go though. My scribes should have it ready by tomorrow morning.'

When Catinus had left them, Oswiu turned his attention to Alweo.

'You too will become an ealdorman, this time of the area from Morpeth down to the River Tees. Unlike Catinus, you will report to an eorl, rather than directly to me, so you'll be part of the Eorldom of Hexham. I'm making Ceadda ealdorman of the other half of the earldom. He's no longer young and he's earned his retirement as my hereræswa. His place will be taken by Redwald and Aldhun will become leader of my gesith.'

'You know how grateful I am to you, Cyning. Do you still want me to remain as your Master of Horse?'

'Yes, you are to move the stud and training centre for my horsemen to Morpeth as soon as possible.'

'Yes, Cyning. I'll do it as soon as this campaign is over.'

Oswiu smiled. 'Unlike Catinus you have no blushing bride to rush home to wed; I need you with me until I've pacified Gwynedd and Powys.'

To the king's surprise Alweo looked uncomfortable. He knew it was time he was married and had children but he had yet to find a woman who he could visualise spending the rest of his life with. He certainly wasn't going to marry just for the sake of it. He went to leave but then asked one final question before he did so.

'It's not my place to ask, Cyning, but if your capital is to become Eoforwīc, where will Alchfrith be based?'

'I don't mind you asking, it's a good question. Obviously two kings in one place isn't going to work so my son will move to either Ripon or Loidis.'

'Ripon?'

'Yes. A monk called Wilfrid is building a new monastery near a settlement called Inhrypum for me and that's what he's decided to call it. Already a settlement has sprung up for the masons, other workers and their families, and now merchants are joining them.'

Alweo's heart sank. His cousin, Wigmund, had told him of Wilfrid's arrival at Lindisfarne as a novice and of the arrogant boy's rapid departure after a fight with Conomultus and another boy called Eata. Now it seemed that the obnoxious Wilfrid had returned to Northumbria and was to be an abbot. The abrupt change in Alweo's facial expression hadn't gone unnoticed by Oswiu.

'You know Wilfrid?'

'Only by reputation. He arrived at Lindisfarne as a novice shortly after I left. He had an argument with my cousin and Catinus' brother as soon as he arrived and he was sent elsewhere to train. By all accounts he was an arrogant, argumentative prig then. The last I heard he was in Frankia.'

'Well, he's back and is reputed to be one of the greatest scholars of his age. We're lucky to have him in Northumbria,' Oswiu said with a frown, somewhat displeased by Alweo's comments. 'I'm sure that he's changed a great deal since he was a boy.'

The other man had his doubts but he said nothing more. He bowed to Oswiu and left the tent.

~~~

The October day on which Catinus was to be wed didn't start in the most propitious manner. There had been a storm the night before and part of the thatched roof of the little church inside the walls of Bebbanburg had been blown away. Leoflaed's father and brother had gone down to the fishermen's huts first thing to see assess the damage and found that several fishing boats had been lost.

The wind was still whipping the waves into a frenzy and there was no way that the small boats used to travel up and down the coast would be able to put to sea in the prevailing weather. This was a serious problem as Bishop Finan was conducting the ceremony. It normally took an hour or two at the most to cover the six mile journey across the bay to Bebbanburg in one of the monastery's fishing boats; by land it was sixteen miles. And that was always assuming that it was low tide so that the route across the sands to the mainland was feasible. Finan didn't possess a horse and the donkey he used to travel on land had one speed – plodding. It would take the best part of a day for him to reach the fortress.

Catinus was almost in despair and had resigned himself to postponing his nuptials when the lookout yelled something that was whipped away on the wind. The ealdorman ran across to the tower and climbed up to find out what the man had spotted, but when he got there he didn't need to ask. There was a large birlinn out at sea. One minute it appeared cresting a wave before surfing down and disappearing in the trough. It was flying along under bare poles with the oarsmen straining to keep it heading towards the fortress.

He hurried back down the ladder, out of the sea gate and onto the beach.

'Do you need your sword and armour, lord?'

Leofric was standing behind him weighed down with his byrnie, leather cap, helmet and sword. He smiled at the boy.

'No, thank you Leofric. I'll stay dressed in my wedding robes for now. I suspect that the birlinn contains friends.'

Catinus was dressed in red leggings with yellow ribbons tied from ankle to knee, a dark blue overtunic with silver embroidery around its V neck, hem and at the bottom of the three quarter length sleeves. This was worn over a long sleeved white linen under-tunic and secured by a leather belt stained black and decorated with silver studs. Over the tunic he wore a crimson woollen cloak pinned in place by an intricate gold broach studded with a large ruby and several opals. He had to smile at the thought of trying to put his chain mail byrnie on over the top of that lot.

He looked out at sea again. The birlinn, instead of running ashore below the fortress as was normally the case, had headed for the calmer waters of the bay to the north of Bebbanburg. The tide was in so the ship would have to beach some distance from where he stood.

'Go back to the fortress, Leofric, and get them to saddle my horse, your pony and a couple of horses for our guests.'

Ten minutes later the two set off with the boy leading the two spare mounts and rode up the hill that rose inland from Bebbanburg. From the top they watched the birlinn approach the beach below them. As they cantered down the long slope to the edge of the bay two figures were helped off the deck of the birlinn into the spume laden waves that crashed onto the shore. They were dressed as clerics and both displayed the distinctive Celtic tonsure. Unlike their Roman Catholic counterparts, their foreheads were shaven from ear to ear making them look bald from the front but leaving them with a full head of hair at the rear.

As they drew closer Catinus recognised one as Bishop Finan. He breathed a sigh of relief that his wedding could now go ahead as planned, but at first he didn't recognise the other man. Then he realised that it was Utta, Oswiu's chaplain immediately before his brother Conomultus. Utta had gone on to be consecrated as the Bishop of Prydenn. Presumably Talorgan, High King of the Picts, had sent him as an emissary. Catinus had a sinking feeling that his presence didn't bode well.

'God's greeting, Bishop Finan, I'm relieved that you've made it. I had a feeling that the storm would prevent you coming.'

'It wouldn't have been possible had Bishop Utta's ship not taken refuge in the lee of Lindisfarne last night. He kindly gave me passage as he's on his way to Eoforwīc. However, I've told him that the king is still in Gwynedd.'

'Is aught amiss in Prydenn then?'

'Greetings Catinus, you seem to have risen in station somewhat since the last time we met.'

'Indeed Bishop Utta, I'm now the Ealdorman of Bebbanburg.'

'Ealdorman?'

'A noble who ranks between a thegn and an eorl; it was introduced in Mercia first, then in Wessex.'

'I see. Finan told me that you were now custos of the fortress but not that you had risen further up the slippery slope of ambition.'

It was evident that Utta didn't approve, but he himself had been an ordinary warrior before becoming a monk, priest and now bishop in turn.

'You seem to have managed to stay at the top of that particular slope yourself, Utta,' he said, slightly more curtly than he had intended.

The bishop laughed, exposing teeth that were filed to a sharp point; something he had done when he was a member of the Bernician warband.

'Well said, ealdorman. Much as I'd like to stay for your wedding and the feast afterwards, I must sail on to Eoforwīc. Finan will tell you the dire tiding I carry.'

With that he turned, bade farewell to Finan, and started to trudge back to the birlinn whose crew stood ready to push her bows off the sand before the tide receded any further and they became stranded. He waded through the waves to the ship's side, hoisting his robes high to keep them dry and exposing his spindly shanks. Once he was back on board Finan looked at the big horse doubtfully. It was over twice the size of the donkey he normally rode.

'Take my pony, bishop,' Leofric said as soon as he saw Finan's hesitation.

'Thank you, my son.'

To Catinus' surprise the eleven year old Leofric leapt into the saddle of one of the spare horses without difficulty, despite his small size, and, leading the other horse, he followed the other two, trying not to laugh at the comical sight of Catinus mounted on his big horse leaning over to listen to the small, rotund bishop on his pony. What the bishop was saying was not comical, however.

'Talorgan is in trouble. Garnait and his brother, Drest, have managed to turn several of the other Pictish kings against him because they regard him as a creature of his uncle, Oswiu.'

'This couldn't have come at a worse time. Oswiu was facing unrest in Mercia and he still has to conclude a treaty with Cadwalladr, the new King of Gwynedd. Having to divert his attention to the north is the last thing he needs.'

'He wants me to travel to Mercia next. With the pagan Penda out of the way he believes that it is ripe for conversion to Christianity.'

'Are there no other churchmen there already?'

'Yes, but they are an idle lot, Romans to a man and more interested in their own comfort than the spiritual well-being of the general population. They seem to think that their job is done once they've baptised the nobles.'

'Who is their bishop?'

'A man called Diuma. He was a monk who was appointed by Peada after his conversion. He served the Middle Angles, after a fashion, before Oswiu made him Bishop of Mercia. He's based at the abbey at Lichfield, though he is not its abbot.'

'What will happen to him?'

'Apparently he is to submit to my authority as Bishop and Abbot of Lindisfarne. Once my work is done as a missionary I understand from Oswiu's letter that he will be left to manage things on his own.'

'Will he accept the teachings of the Celtic Church having been brought up a Roman?'

Finan sighed. 'I very much doubt it, but my duty is clear. Enough of that, today is your wedding day. Let's concentrate on that, and on not getting blown away before we reach the safety of the fortress,' he said as another strong gust of wind hit them.

~~~

Oswiu sat on his horse with two of his sons on either side of him watching as Cadwalladr rode towards him. He was accompanied by thirty of so mounted warriors and a small army of men on foot, waving various weapons and farming implements and shouting their new king's name.

The Welsh horde stopped four hundred yards from the crest of the hill on which Oswiu had lined up his men. The fyrd had gone home but he had kept most of the warbands from Northumbria and Mercia with him until peace was assured. The Welsh king trotted forward accompanied by two warriors and a boy bearing a banner depicting a red dragon on a black field. The lad who had been given this honour was Bedwyr; the same boy who had first spotted Cadafael's army moving towards Powys.

The last time that Oswiu had seen Cadwalladr had been fourteen years ago when he and Oswald had defeated his father at Heavenfield. The boy had grown to manhood as a fugitive and an outlaw. Now he had claimed his rightful place as Cadwallon's heir. Oswiu couldn't help thinking that he looked a little like Catinus; both were dark haired and had a swarthy complexion and both were smaller than most men, but broad shouldered.

'Greetings King Cadwalladr, I'm pleased to see you in your rightful place.'

'Are you, King Oswiu? The last time we saw each other you had just killed my father and no doubt I'd have met the same fate had you been able to catch me.'

'Not so. My brother Oswald gave the order that you were not to be pursued. We had no dispute with you; it was your father who ravaged Northumbria. You were only a boy.'

The Welshman sighed. 'It all seems a long time ago now. I can scarcely remember my father to be honest.'

'Yes, it was. I'm willing to let it lie in the past if you are. I hope that now we can be, if not friends, at least allies.'

The young man laughed. 'If we sign a treaty, who will you have left to fight?'

'I don't enjoy warfare. It is a means to an end, and that end is peace. I want to lead my kingdom forward to prosperity and build new churches and monasteries to the glory of God and his Son, Jesus Christ.'

'That at least we can agree on, but it is a dream, Oswiu. Even I have learnt that today's ally is tomorrow's enemy.'

'Somewhat cynical, but unfortunately too often that is true. Let's pray that at least between us the truce will last.'

'What about Powys?'

'Powys?'

'Beli is a boy so his chieftains will rule until he is older. They have often made a truce with Mercia and just as often broken it.'

'In my experience a boy ruler means that his nobles will be too busy struggling for control to be much of a threat externally.'

'Perhaps, but boys grow up quickly. It won't be long before Beli is old enough to seize the reins of power.'

'Well, at least we have a few years when Powys won't be a factor.'

Privately he didn't expect to be able to maintain his rule over Mercia indefinitely. Its nobles were too powerful and it was too large and influential for them to accept incorporation into his kingdom. If he kept Northumbria inviolate for the rest of his life he would be satisfied. By the time that Powys started being a problem for Mercia he might even welcome an enemy on its borders. His main concern today was to keep Rheged and the rest of his kingdom safe from Gwynedd.

'That aside,' he continued, 'are you prepared to sign a treaty of friendship?'

'Yes, of course. I have a lot to do now to sort out my own kingdom and if my warriors grow restless I can always raid the Isle of Man or Ireland.'

This last remark was said with a grin. Oswiu began to warm towards Cadwalladr and he smiled back.

'Fine. I'll send my clerics to meet yours and they can draw up the treaty in writing.'

Oswiu went back to his camp feeling pleased with himself but the grin was wiped from his face when Cuthbert, now one of his gesith, came into his tent.

'Cyning, there is a messenger from Bishop Utta, who has apparently arrived in Eoforwīc looking for you.'

'Do you know what the message is, Cuthbert.'

The latter looked uncomfortable.

'I fear it is not good news, Cyning. There is civil war in the land of the Picts.'

'I see.' Oswiu had been looking forward to a wash in the river followed by a few hours of well-earned sleep. It seemed it was not to be. 'Well, you had better show the messenger in then.'

Oswiu read Utta's letter with a sinking heart:

Cyning,

I fear that I'm the bearer of ill tidings. Your nephew, King Talorgan, has sent me to inform you of the perilous situation he finds himself in. Two months ago Bran, the King of Cait, renounced his allegiance to Talorgan as high king. As Cait covers a colossal area of largely uninhabited land in the north of Caledonia, Talorgan didn't feel that he could effectively contest Bran's decision but he sent an emissary, one of my priests, to ask him to reconsider. Bran sent his head back in a basket.

Immediately two of the other kings, Garnait and Drest, started to pressure Talorgan to attack Cait and depose Bran. Of course, it was merely a ploy and, when Talorgan sensibly ignored their advice, they accused him of cowardice.

Fergus of Ardewr, whose kingdom is the only one which physically adjoins Cait, backed Talorgan's stance but the King of Uuynnid sided with Drest and Garnait. Maelgwn of Penntir, surrounded as he is by Ardewr and Talorgan's own kingdom of Prydenn, has remained neutral so far.

When I left Talorgan was being besieged by Drest and Garnait in his fortress of Stirling. He has sent messengers to Domangart of Dalriada and Guret of Strathclyde asking them to come to his aid. I beg you to send as many men as you can spare to support your nephew before it is too late.

With Christ's blessings,
Utta.

Oswiu groaned in despair. Just when he had killed his arch-enemy Penda and subdued the Welsh, now the north was in flames again. Privately he thought that an invasion by the men of Dalriada and Strathclyde, both ancient enemies of the Picts, would only turn all of Talorgan's subjects against him. He wished now that he had killed Drest and Garnait when he'd had the opportunity after Talorc had been deposed as high king.

He would have to go north to see if it was possible to resolve the dispute peaceably. After thanking the messenger he sent for his Hereræswa.

'Redwald, I'll need to send messengers to Domengart and Guret asking them to come and meet me at Caer Luel. Oh, and I'll need a birlinn to take me there. It'll be much quicker by sea than on horseback. Only my gesith need to come with me but warn the warbands to be ready to join me as soon as the treaty with Cadwalladr is signed. You had better stay here for now.'

'Who will sign the treaty if you're not here, Cyning?'

'My son, Alchfrith.'

CHAPTER FOUR – INTO THE LAND OF THE PICTS

657 AD

Catinus was making love to Leoflaed when the messenger from Oswiu arrived in the middle of February. His new wife had proved to be everything he wished for, in bed and out of it, and now she had given him the greatest present of all. She had confided to him that she was fairly certain that she was expecting their first child. It had been less than four months since they had wed, but she said all the usual symptoms were present. He wasn't sure what she meant, and didn't want to know, but he had been concerned recently when she kept vomiting for no apparent reason. He assumed that had something to do with it.

His idyllic life came to an abrupt end when he received the order to muster his fyrd and bring them, with as many members of the garrison as could be spared without leaving the fortress vulnerable, and join the king at Dùn Èideann as soon as possible.

Catinus hadn't been idle over the winter. Once he'd become Ealdorman of Bebbanburg Oswiu had withdrawn his garrison to join his main warband based at Eoforwīc. A few married men had elected to stay and these formed the nucleus of Catinus' own warband. Over the past four months he'd been recruiting hard but he'd been careful who he selected. He'd rather have a boy of fourteen eager to train as a warrior than a man who seemed untrustworthy or idle.

In consequence he now had twenty men who were able to both ride and fight dismounted to a reasonable standard and another twenty youths under training. Eventually he hoped that they would all be able to fight on horseback as well. He decided to leave the trainees behind with two instructors to defend his fortress, together with a few archers who had been called up with the fyrd. He left Leoflaed in charge, assisted by the reeve.

As ealdorman he'd been given ten vills but not all had a thegn. Lindisfarne and another vill on the mainland belonged to the monastery. However, Finan was still obliged to furnish ten armed men to join the fyrd. These were ceorls who farmed their own land but paid rent and taxes to the monastery. They brought with them two boys to act as servants, as did the contingents from the other vills.

Catinus hadn't been readily accepted as overlord by all the thegns and one, in particular, had resolutely refused to pay him homage. Now his muster of the fyrd was ignored and Catinus had to act or lose the respect of both the other thegns and his own men.

He left the rest encamped at Bebbanburg and took his warband over to visit the rebellious thegn in his settlement at a place called Wooler. Like most thegns, Eboric kept a few warriors who lived in his hall. They collected his taxes, protected him and trained his ceorls to fight as members of the fyrd. When Catinus and his twenty men rode into the settlement he found himself confronted by Eboric supported by six warriors and a dozen other armed men, several with hunting bows.

He dismounted and walked up to Eboric. The thegn was a big man, both in girth and height, and was at least a decade older than Catinus. Two of the men wearing padded leather jerkins beside him looked like younger versions, presumably his sons. The other four warriors were elderly and they looked distinctly uncomfortable. Catinus ignored Eboric and spoke instead to the men around him.

'Your thegn is in rebellion against King Oswiu and must pay the price for that rebellion. If you support him you too will face the king's justice; you will hang, your homes will be destroyed and your families will be enslaved. Is that what you want?'

'You are no noble, Catinus, merely a Mercian serf who has become Oswiu's pet. I refuse to bend the knee to you, but I am a loyal servant of the king's.'

'Let us be clear about this,' he continued, looking each of the men behind Eboric in the eye one by one. 'The king has made me Ealdorman of Bebbanburg and the Witan of Northumbria has approved my appointment. Anyone who refuses to obey me as their lord is refusing the orders of the king and the Witan. Are you prepared for the consequences? Are your families?'

All except Eboric and one of his sons were now looking at each other uncertainly.

'I am loyal to my thegn but I will not rebel against the king,' a man with muscular arms and a powerful body said, throwing down his sword and shield.

Later Catinus learned it was the blacksmith; a man of influence in the vill. Several other men followed his example and they withdrew to one side. More followed until just Eboric, his sons and his warriors remained facing him. The thegn looked at his ceorls in disgust and spat in their direction.

'Would you let this dog, a Mercian, a Briton and a serf, order you about. You disgust me.'

With that he drew his seax and went to stab Catinus in the stomach. He never reached him. His younger son grabbed hold of him to restrain him but the elder went to his father's aid, grabbing hold of his brother. Both fell to the ground and there was a nasty crack as the younger man's neck broke.

The thegn cradled his dead son for a moment, tears running down his face, then arose with a cry of fury and went to jab his seax towards Catinus again.

Before Catinus was able to react an arrow flew out of the ranks of his men and pierced the thegn's byrnie, shattering the links of chain mail and entering the man's heart. He died instantly.

The ealdorman looked to see who had saved his life and nodded at Leofric, who had nocked another arrow to his bow ready to kill anyone else who threatened his master. It was just as well. The surviving son looked down in horror at his dead father. He'd never liked his brother so he regarded his death as unfortunate but little more. However, he had worshipped his father. With a bellow of fury he drew his sword intending to kill Catinus, but the latter was too quick from him. His own sword was in his hand in time to block the blow and he counter-attacked.

It was evident that Eboric's son, although a large, well-muscled man, had little or no skill with a sword. Within a minute he was on the defensive as Catinus' blade feinted and jabbed at him. The man didn't come anywhere near touching the ealdorman but Catinus relentlessly drew blood in a series of small cuts to his face, legs and arms. Leofric had lowered his bow. If he tried to use it now he was just as likely to hit Catinus.

Catinus sensed the big man was tiring and decided to end it. He feinted again at the man's abdomen and, when he dropped his sword to block the move, Catinus suddenly changed the direction of the thrust and aimed at his neck instead. The third male member of the thegn's family dropped dead to join his father and brother.

The ealdorman wiped his blade clean on the man's clothing and sheathed his sword.

'Where's the reeve?'

A small man, still armed with a spear and shield, stepped forward.

'Give these three a Christian burial. Until I appoint a new thegn, you will manage the vill on my behalf. You had better stay here for now.'

The man nodded, relieved that he wouldn't be going to war. Catinus' eyes swept over the four warriors.

'Who is the senior?'

'I am, lord.'

'Gather what you need. I expect you and the rest of these men to join the muster at Bebbanburg by noon tomorrow.'

'Yes, lord. We'll be there.'

At that moment two women, presumably Eboric's wife and daughter, came running out of the hall and threw themselves on the bodies of the three men. Catinus hadn't considered that there might be other members of the family and for a moment he was at something of a loss. Then his eyes lit on a young boy, perhaps eight or nine years old, standing wide-eyed and nervously wringing his hands, outside the hall.

'Who's the boy, reeve?'

'The thegn's youngest son, Octha, lord.'

Catinus thought for a moment. He didn't want the boy to grow up hating him and nursing a desire for revenge. He had a choice. He would either have to ask the king to disinherit him or accept him as his father's heir. He beckoned the boy, who hesitated but then reluctantly approached him. Catinus noticed with surprise that he walked with a pronounced limp. He led the lad away out of earshot.

'Octha, do you understand what just happened?'

'Yes, lord,' he answered in a soft voice. 'My father and brothers are dead because they opposed you.'

'Not just me, the king as well.'

'Yes, lord. I know they were wrong to do so.'

Suddenly he broke down and started to sob.

'Is it wrong of me to be glad that they are dead?'

'Glad? Why?'

'My father and the others belittled me because of my limp, saying that I'd never be of any use to anyone. My leg was broken in a fall when I was four and it never healed properly. I tried to love them as it says I must in the Bible, but I grew to hate them. My mother is no better, she always sided with my father.'

'What about your sister?'

'Sister? Oh, she's my bastard half-sister. She's my mother's maid. My father took one of the laundry maids as his mistress and she disappeared shortly after the baby was born.' He shrugged. 'Everyone said that my bloody mother was responsible.'

Catinus was a little surprised at such language from a young boy, but no doubt it came of being brought up in an atmosphere where there was no love, only hate and discord. He made his mind up then that he would take Octha to Finan on Lindisfarne to be educated. Perhaps the infirmarian might be able to do something about the limp as well. In due course Octha could either become a monk or return to the vill as its thegn, provided he was prepared to swear allegiance to him of course. In the meantime the reeve would manage it for him. If the boy became a monk, then the vill would be given to the monastery.

'What will happen to my mother?' Octha asked diffidently.

'She will become a nun. I'll send her to the king's sister at Coldingham, and your half-sister can go with her.'

The boy's normally handsome face was disfigured by a look of grim satisfaction that reflected the hate he felt for them.

'And me?'

'I'm taking you to Bishop Finan. You'll become a novice monk for now. When you reach fourteen you can decide whether you wish to remain as a monk or train as a warrior and later return here as thegn.'

'Me? The thegn?'

'Provided you swear to be loyal to me.'

'Of course, lord. You've saved me from a life of misery. I'll always be grateful to you.'

~~~

When Catinus rode into the encampment beneath the fortress of Dùn Èideann he was followed by eight thegns, twenty five other horsemen, forty other trained warriors on foot and another ninety men to supplement the fyrd. The baggage train contained a number of carters and servants leading packhorses. However, Leofric wasn't amongst them. Catinus had freed him for saving his life and, although the boy remained as his body servant, he now rode behind his master carrying his new banner of a stylised Celtic beast in yellow on a red background.

The journey had taken six days, rather longer than he'd expected. However, it had rained almost incessantly for the first three so that, when the sun put in a very welcome appearance on the fourth day, he decided to stay at the overnight camp to allow everyone to dry out their clothing and clean the rust from their armour and weapons.

It had rained again on the last two days but this time the showers were interspersed with periods of fine weather. As the Firth of Forth came into sight they emerged from the trees and the incessant drip of water from leaves, even when the sun was shining, to see Oswiu's army encamped outside the settlement under the dominant fortress on top of its rock to the west.

Catinus was surprised by the vastness of the camp; at a rough guess there must have been at least three thousand men there. He reported to the king's tent and was welcomed by Oswiu and the other nobles already there – or at least by most of them. A few of the eorls were still not reconciled to his elevation, or that of Alweo come to that. Their hostility wasn't only due to his lowly birth status and the fact that he was a native Briton born in Mercia, they also objected to the whole idea of ealdormen.

There were some thirty eorls in all, some ruling large territories like the former kingdoms of Elmet, Rheged and Goddodin, and others only presiding over a score or so vills. The latter were little different to the new ealdormen in that respect and therefore they were concerned that they might lose their status as eorls in due course.

In fact that was exactly what Oswiu intended. Gradually, as they died off, their replacements would be termed ealdormen and the number of eorls would be reduced to four – for Goddodin, Rheged, Bernicia and Elmet, with Deira being ruled by one of his sons as sub-king. Of these, only Bernicia and Deira had a plethora of small eorldoms at the moment and Goddodin had three. But all that would have to wait. The priority for now was to bring the Land of the Picts back under his influence and nip the incipient civil war in the bud.

The current situation was a worry but it wasn't that which really depressed him. It was his estrangement from his wife. He simply couldn't understand why she was so upset. He had six children, three of them by Eanflæd, and dedicating one of them to serving Christ seemed entirely understandable, even obligatory, to him. Of course, Alchflaed had also become a nun after her disastrous marriage to Peada, but that had been her choice, not his.

In his mind sending their daughter Ælfflaed to Hild when she was still a baby had been sensible. Eanflæd would only have become more attached to her had he delayed. In any case, he needed to express his gratitude to God by doing something tangible at the time for his victory over Penda, not at some time in the future.

Eanflæd had said that she couldn't continue to live with him and had only agreed to stay at Eoforwīc after Oswiu had announced his intention of taking the army north. His one hope was that they could be reconciled when he returned. He still loved her deeply and the thought that she might retreat to a monastery worried him every waking moment.

He tried to put his grief at her hostility towards him to the back of his mind. It was distracting him from the current problem. Talorgan was trapped in the fortress at Stirling, besieged by Garnait and Drest. Cait, Penntir and Uuynnid had remained neutral whilst Ardewr and Prydenn, Talorgan's own kingdom, had mobilised to go to Talorgan's help. However, before anyone was able to lift the siege rumours circulated that Talorgan had been killed.

It later emerged that he had led a night time raid on the besieger's camp. It had been successful but Talorgan had been separated from his men in the darkness and killed as the others were withdrawing back to the fortress. His body had been displayed the following morning to encourage the garrison to surrender to Garnait.

The high king had had the sense not to infuriate Oswiu and the people of Prydenn further by mutilating the body, though he would dearly have loved to exhibit his head on a pole, and it was given a Christian burial. By the time that the news reached Oswiu at Dùn Èideann the summons had already gone out for a meeting of the six remaining kings to elect a new high king and to decide who should rule Prydenn now as Talorgan was the last of his line.

On the day appointed for the meeting Oswiu arrived with his war host having marched through Uuynnid and Hyddir to reach Stirling. The Picts had discussed resisting Oswiu's advance but in the end they decided to wait and negotiate with him.

The Picts were drawn up on the plain below the fortress when Oswiu appeared at the head of his army. The six kings rode forward and Oswiu did the same, taking Redwald, Aldhun and the Eorls of Rheged, Dùn Èideann, Elmet and Dùn Barra with him.

'What are you doing here Oswiu?' Bran challenged him as soon as he was within shouting distance.

Oswiu didn't reply but continued walking his horse towards the now stationary Pictish kings. When he was five yards away he stopped and contemplated the six men silently.

'I am here because I am the nearest relative by blood to Talorgan and I am therefore now King of Prydenn,' he said quietly.

This resulted in an animated discussion amongst the six kings until Oswiu held up his hand.

'Does anyone here dispute my right to Prydenn?'

'Yes, I do,' Drest almost spat at him. 'You are not a Pict and you already rule vast tracts of England. Prydenn would be neglected under your rule.'

'Descent is through the female side under Pictish law,' Fergus of Ardewr stated calmly, giving Drest a disgusted look. 'Therefore, as there are no longer any descendants of Bebba still alive, the royal line of Prydenn is extinct. We need to elect a new king of Prydenn – the start of a new dynasty. It doesn't matter to me that Oswiu is a Northumbrian. I, for one, think it would be sensible to ally ourselves with the Bretwalda of the North.'

There were several murmurs of agreement and both Drest and Garnait felt the support of their fellow kings slipping away from them. Even Bran, who had precipitated this crisis, had remained quiet. They were also very conscious of the large army which had accompanied Oswiu.

'If your claim to Prydenn is accepted, Oswiu, how will you rule there as your capital is hundreds of miles away?' Garnait asked him.

'In the same way that I rule Rheged, of which I am also king; by appointing an eorl to represent me when I'm not there.'

This provoked another round of heated discussion. Oswiu waited with the appearance of patience for them to come to a decision, though inside he was getting more and more exasperated.

'We will need to retire to discuss matters amongst ourselves,' Bran told him eventually.

'I'll be back at noon tomorrow, with my men, to hear your decision.'

The next day dawned cloudy and chilly. During the morning light rain started to fall which gradually got heavier. Oswiu had no intention of sitting on his horse conducting interminable negotiations in a downpour, so he sent his men to erect his tent at the place he had met the six kings the day before. He made do with sharing Redwald's tent in the meantime.

Once the six kings were seated Oswiu offered them refreshments. This time he was accompanied by Bishop Utta of Prydenn; his son, Alchfrith of Deira, and the three eorls from Goddodin. As usual his son sat at his right hand and the leader of his gesith, Aldhun, stood behind him.

'Have you reached a decision?' he asked without preamble as his servants handed around tankards of ale and sweet biscuits.

'In part,' Garnait replied. 'First you should know that my fellow kings have elected me as high king.'

'Without Prydenn having a say?'

'It would make no difference. Only Ardewr apposed my election,' he said giving Fergus a venomous look.

'I would advise you to adopt a more conciliatory attitude towards King Fergus if I were you; that is if you wish to stay high king for very long.'

'Are you threatening me?'

'Yes. But you have nothing to fear if you behave in a fair and just manner.'

Garnait muttered something under his breath but didn't pursue the matter.

'Have you reached a decision about Prydenn?' Oswiu continued.

'The people would never accept you as king, let alone rule by a foreign eorl.'

'I beg to differ.' Bishop Utta spoke for the first time and smiled, showing his alarming row of teeth filed to points. 'They accept me and I'm an Irishman. In contrast they detested it when Drest ruled them a few years ago.'

Drest gave him a look of hatred but said nothing.

'Very well. Let's be clear. You have murdered my nephew and I would be within my rights to slay his killers.' Oswiu's eyes lingered on Garnait and Drest for a moment. 'However, to avoid conflict I am content to accept weregeld in compensation, provided I am recognised as King of Prydenn and Bretwalda of Caledonia.'

Weregeld was an Anglo-Saxon concept and meant 'man price', but it was understood by the Picts. It meant payment by the perpetrator to the man's family for his injury or death. Oswiu was gambling that would they would regard it as a better alternative to entering into a blood feud.

'How much weregeld?' Garnait asked cautiously.

'If you agree to my other conditions, shall we say a ton of silver?'

There was a collective gasp in the tent. They had expected him to say something like a hundred pounds.

'That's far too much,' blustered Drest. 'I doubt there is that much silver in the whole of Pictland.'

Oswiu smiled. He knew that the Picts were a poor people, but not that poor.

'Very well. How much do you suggest? What price would you put on a high king's life?'

'Perhaps a hundred pounds of silver?' Drest tentatively suggested, then added 'apiece' when he saw the look in Oswiu's eyes. He ignored the strangled protest from Garnait sitting next to him.

'I accept. It is to be delivered to me here within the week and you can have the pleasure of feeding my men in the meantime. I'm sure you'll find it preferable to having them forage for their own sustenance. Oh, and I will, of course, retain ownership of the fortress of Stirling.'

~~~

Catinus rode back to Bebbanburg feeling pleased. He hadn't lost a man and, as Oswiu had distributed half of the weregeld to his army, he'd been able to give a coin or two to each of his men as well as retain a pouch for himself. He was surprised that the coins were all Roman and portrayed a man wearing a laurel wreath on one side and a woman seated on some rocks on the other. The worn writing indicated that they were issued in the reign of Antonius Pius and presumable they'd been plundered during the time that the Romans had occupied Britain.

Some of the coins were silver and some bronze. The latter hadn't been part of Oswiu's demand but he'd accepted a few chests of bronze in lieu of the equivalent value in silver. He'd even received some gold.

Not all the weregeld was in coinage but coins were a lot easier to distribute. Catinus wondered why Oswiu didn't produce his own. Some gold coins, called shillings, had been produced in Lundenwic for the past decade or two and, more recently, the King of Kent had started to produce them as well. He'd even seen a few silver coins called pennies that had come from Ludenwic, so he supposed that it was just a matter of time before they came into common usage.

He arrived back at Bebbanburg on a beautiful summer's day to find that Leoflaed's baby was now beginning to show.

'Does the wise woman from the vill say when our child will be born,' he asked her in bed that night after making love rather carefully to her.

'In September, she thinks. You don't have to treat me as if I'm fragile, you know. Obviously we mustn't squash it but there are other positions.'

'Other positions?'

'Yes, lie on your back and I'll show you.'

'I rather like that,' he told her when they'd both recovered. 'For a start you do all the work for a change.'

She giggled. 'It also makes the best of your rather short member,' she told him with a twinkle in her eye.

'Short member! What do you mean short.' His eyes narrowed. 'Who have you been comparing me to?'

'That new stallion in the stables.'

He laughed. 'If I had one that size you'd run a mile.'

He leaned over and kissed her before he thought of something.

'Where did you get the idea of sitting on me from?'

'The wise woman of course. Where else?'

Catinus kissed her again to avoid replying. The thought had crossed his mind that his formerly innocent wife suddenly seemed to be much more sexually aware. Then he was ashamed of himself for thinking that she might have betrayed him with another man. He supposed women talked about that sort of thing, just as men did. He rolled over to go to sleep but it was some time before he drifted off.

CHAPTER FIVE – MERCIA RESURGENT

658 AD

Catinus was playing with his five month old baby daughter when Oswiu's messenger arrived. He handed Herewid back to her wet nurse, smiled apologetically at Leoflaed, and followed the servant who'd told him of the messenger's arrival into the main hall. The snows had melted and the fine early spring weather had dried the ground out so the man hadn't arrived as mud splattered as messengers often were.

He greeted Catinus formally, bowed and handed him a leather cylinder.

'Go and get yourself cleaned up and have something to eat and drink whilst I see if this needs a reply.'

The man nodded his thanks and went outside to wash in the horse trough. Catinus unrolled the sheet of parchment he'd pulled from its leather container and started to read. The letter was in English and he cursed. He'd been educated at Lindisfarne Monastery and was far better at reading Latin than he was English, which wasn't even his mother tongue. He'd been born of British parents in Mercia and his first language had been Brythonic until he was fourteen. He spoke English like an Anglo-Saxon now, but he still found reading and writing in the language difficult.

To my loyal servant Catinus, Ealdorman of Bebbanburg, greetings,

Having been quiescent for the past three years I had hoped that Mercia had accepted my rule, but it seems that hope was a vain one. Three of the leading Mercian eorls, Immin, Eafa and Eadbert, have joined together with Wulfhere, Penda's eldest surviving son, and risen in revolt, killing the Eorl of Tamworth, who I placed there to govern Mercia in my name, and seizing the town and the king's hall.

As if these grave tidings were not enough, word has just reached me that my friend, Guret of Strathclyde, has just died, possibly poisoned. He has been succeeded by his cousin Mermin, a man I don't know, but who I'm told is younger than Guret by some five or six years, which would put him in his middle to late twenties. At thirty two, Guret was young to die of natural causes and the fact that he had just married makes the circumstances even more suspicious. The rumours are that he was killed before he was able to sire an heir.

Obviously my priority is to deal with the insurrection in Mercia but I need someone to go and meet this Mermin and sound him out. Hopefully he is amenable to continue the agreement reached with Guret and will recognise me as his overlord. If not, I will have to prevail upon Dalriada and the Picts to help me to bring pressure to bear on him.

I have written to the Eorl of Prydenn to ask him to enlist Garnait's support. Likewise the Eorl of Rheged will sail north to Dùn Add to see Domangart. Normally I would ask the Eorl of Dùn Èideann or the Eorl of Dùn Barra to travel to Dùn Breatainn on the River Clyde to visit Mermin but the former is ill and Kenric is now a frail old man. Two of his four sons are dead and the third Cuthbert, who you know well from your days together in my gesith, has recently announced his desire to return to the life of a monk. I hope to change his mind but he seems determined.

Kenric's fourth son is Beornheth but he is a boy of nine. I have gone into some detail in order to explain why I would like you to travel north-west to Dùn Breatainn as my emissary to Mermin. Enclosed with this letter is one addressed to him. It is full of elegant phrases and flattery but says little of importance. It is written in Latin as no-one here can write in Brythonic so I hope that he has been well educated. If not, I'm sure that you, of all people, can translate it for him.

Take those of your warband who can ride with you but don't make it look as if you are invading, just enough to protect you.

God speed you on this important mission,

Oswiu,
King of Northumbria and Bretwalda of Britain.

Catinus finished reading the letter with mixed emotions. He was honoured to be sent as the king's representative to another king, but he was well aware how perilous his mission might be. If this Mermin proved hostile he might send his head back to Oswiu in a basket. It wasn't unknown.

If Catinus was concerned, Leoflaed was positively frantic with worry when he told her.

'If this Mermin had Guret poisoned then he's hardly likely to support his predecessor's ally, is he?'

'He can hardly feel secure on his throne at the moment, though, can he? He won't want to antagonise Oswiu, surrounded as he is by Rheged, Dalriada and the Picts.'

'He might make an ally of Garnait. He has no cause to love Oswiu; he only accepts him as overlord because he has no choice.'

Catinus sighed. 'Don't worry, I'll be careful; and I'll take a sizeable escort with me.'

However, Catinus wasn't able to set out straight away. The early spring conditions changed as cold weather swept down from the north. At first it was just very cold with hard frosts overnight, but then black clouds filled the sky and the snow started. A week after the messenger had arrived the ground was covered by a foot of snow with drifts as deep as eight feet in places. He wouldn't be going anywhere until the weather broke, and he didn't imagine that Oswiu would be able to achieve much in Mercia either at the moment.

~~~

Eanflæd had stayed on at Eoforwīc in the expectation that Oswiu's visit there would be a short one but when the snowstorm hit it was evident that he wouldn't be able to move against Mercia for a while. She tried to avoid her husband as much as possible and even moved into a separate hut with her women and her daughter – the eleven year old Osthryth. Her son, Ecgfrith, was now nearly thirteen and had left a year ago to become a novice on Lindisfarne. However, unlike his half-brother Aldfrith, he was no scholar and couldn't wait to start training as a warrior.

His other half-brother, Alchfrith, was almost a stranger these days. He avoided Eoforwīc and, at nineteen, tried to rule Deira with as much autonomy as his father would allow him. Having established his new capital at Loidis, he got to know the new abbot of the monastery that was slowly taking shape at Ripon, some twenty miles to the north. He admired Wilfrid and, after a while, the monk established himself as Alchfrith's closest confidant.

This didn't please his eorls or the new ealdormen who Oswiu had appointed. As Wilfrid's influence with the sub-king increased, so theirs decreased. It was a situation that Oswiu was aware of and he now regretted appointing Wilfrid. However, the man had given him no justifiable cause to remove him, so there was little he could do.

Eanflæd was a woman who was slow to anger but equally slow to forgive. The loss of her baby daughter to the Church had infuriated her, especially as Oswiu hadn't seen fit to discuss it with her before making his commitment. She had fancied herself in love with her husband but that love was slowly turning to hate as resentment festered inside her.

To make matters worse, Oswiu didn't know what to do to make amends and so he did nothing. If she avoided him, he too avoided her and slowly bitterness at their estrangement festered inside him as well. He was now in his mid-forties but he was still a virile man and he missed making love to Eanflæd. Many another man might had sought solace elsewhere, but Oswiu was devout and, apart from Fianna, Aldfrith's mother, he had only slept with his two wives. He considered asking Eanflæd to become a nun so that he could marry again but there were two problems with that. It would upset her relatives in Kent - and he needed Kent as an ally now that he was confronted with a resurgent Mercia - and deep down he was still in love with her.

When the weather improved and the snow eventually melted the roads were a morass of mud. The warm dry spell that followed eventually made travel possible again and Eanflæd promptly left to go and stay with her stepson in Loidis. This would turn out to be a significant move as there she came under the influence of Abbot Wilfrid.

Oswiu meanwhile marshalled his forces and set off for Leicester which, according to the latest reports, had been captured by Wulfhere and his supporters.

'The Mercians have massed their army on a ridge about a mile ahead of us, Cyning,' Redwald told him as they approached Leicester.

'It seems the reports were true,' Oswiu said, with some relief.

Redwald gave him a strange look. Oswiu seemed almost happy that he was confronted by an enemy. In a way he was. He was very cautious about committing himself unless he had reliable intelligence about both the enemy he faced and the terrain. He had brought every warband he was able to muster, not only his own but those of his eorls and his ealdormen from Bernicia and Deira. Those of Rheged and Goddodin had stayed behind, partly because he wanted to move swiftly but also because he didn't trust either Garnait of the Picts or the new King of Strathclyde. He hadn't brought the fyrd either; it would have taken too long to muster them and his aim this time wasn't to defeat the Mercians in battle.

He led his army towards the ridge where Wulfhere was waiting with some two thousand warriors and men of the fyrd. When they reached the top of the other side of the valley Oswiu halted but remained mounted, his gesith beside him. The warbands fanned out to either side of him and formed up in ranks five deep under the dull, grey sky waiting patiently for something to happen.

'How many do you estimate?'

Redwald clicked his tongue repeatedly as his eyes scanned the enemy host. It was an annoying habit but he said it helped him to count.

'No more than eight hundred warriors and perhaps twice that number in the fyrd to the rear of them. They're standing eight deep. He has few horsemen and archers.'

Oswiu grunted before turning to the rider on his other side.

'Well, Ethelred, what do you think Wulfhere will do now?'

Wulfhere's younger brother was a hostage for the good behaviour of the Mercians. He was thirteen and was being educated as a novice at Lindisfarne. His brother's revolt against Oswiu's rule had, unsurprisingly, caused him to fear for his life and he sat there looking nervous and unsure how to reply.

'Don't worry. I won't execute you, not because I'm fond of you, but because I suspect Wulfhere would welcome your death. It would remove a rival for the throne.'

Ethelred smiled grimly. 'We were never close and, after Peada, I was father's favourite son. Wulfhere hates me as a result. However, I don't know him very well. He has the reputation of being unpredictable: impetuous one minute and cautious the next.'

'Hmm, that's what I've heard. Unfortunately, it doesn't help me very much.'

Oswiu continued to sit and regard the Mercian host. The only things he knew about Wulfhere were that he had led an expedition to recruit mercenaries from the continent when he was fourteen and he'd been outwitted at the Battle of the Winwaed by Catinus. Eventually he signalled to the man holding his banner aloft and he waved it to and fro. Wulfhere's banner bearer repeated the action after a minute's pause and Oswiu cantered down the slope to the valley floor accompanied by Ethelred, Redwald, Arthius of Elmet and five of his gesith.

Wulfhere had been standing in the middle of his men but now he mounted and he rode to meet the King of Northumbria with a similar sized escort.

'Greetings, Wulfhere.'

The other man nodded cautiously.

'I think you know Redwald and Arthius and, of course, your brother,' Oswiu continued.

Wulfhere spat a globule of phlegm into the dust.

'He's not my brother, or he wouldn't be dressed like a lickspittle of the White Christ,' he said, referring to the coarse brown novice's robe that Ethelred wore.

'So you are a pagan like your father? I understood that many Mercians were now Christians?'

Wulfhere grunted but didn't respond to the question; instead he changed tack.

'Are you prepared to recognise me as King of Mercia or do I have to fight you for my right to succeed my father?'

'That rather depends.'

'On what?'

As they'd been speaking a light rain had started to fall, now it was changing to sleet and the wind had picked up.

'We can sit here negotiating all day getting wet and cold, or we can agree a temporary truce, withdraw our forces by a mile or so for the night and agree to meet here again tomorrow. By then my servants will have erected a tent where we can discuss matters in a more civilised manner.'

Wulfhere sucked his teeth, glared at his brother for a moment - receiving an equally cold look in response – then nodded.

'Very well. Two hours after dawn with no more than four men.'

'Agreed.'

The cold weather of the previous day had changed overnight, but it was raining quite heavily when the two sides met again, so they were glad of the protection afforded by Oswiu's tent. The two men sat on chairs whilst the others stood behind them. Nerian, Oswiu's body servant, and two other men served ale and bread to the negotiators before withdrawing to seek what shelter they could find under the cart that had transported the tent.

Wulfhere studied Oswiu whilst he took a drink of the indifferent ale and chewed on the tough bread. Evidently Oswiu wasn't a lover of good food. The king was of average height, well built with fair hair and pale blue eyes. He face was hidden behind a bushy beard but Wulfhere had the impression that it hid a strong jaw. In contrast, Oswiu saw a young man with an oval face, green eyes and a hook nose. The jaw was slightly receding, which gave him a weak appearance; something that Oswiu suspected was far from the truth. He was beardless but wore a moustache that was a little darker in hue than his fair hair.

'You asked me yesterday if I would be prepared to recognise you as King of Mercia,' Oswiu said without preliminary. 'The answer is perhaps, but it would depend on you agreeing to certain conditions.'

'Such as?'

'I have no desire to rule Mercia but I'm not prepared for Northumbria to be raped and pillaged as it was so many times in your father's day. I have brought peace to my northern border by making enemies into allies and I seek to do the same in the south. However, you word is not enough, I fear.'

'What would satisfy you that I don't share my father's dream of a Greater Mercia encompassing all of England?'

'Your conversion to Christianity and marriage to a princess who is also a Christian.'

'I suppose you have some old harridan in mind?'

'Perhaps Eormenhild of Kent? I'm afraid that she is neither old, being but ten years of age, and she is certainly not a harridan. I am told that she is positively pretty. Of course, it would be a betrothal only at this stage with marriage in three or four years' time. I'm sure you are nothing like your brother Peada, but you'll understand that I and her father, King Eocenberht, want to play safe.'

'Anything else?'

'A treaty, of course, and Ethelred remains under my protection.'

Just when Wulfhere thought that Oswiu had finished he added one last stipulation.

'I nearly forget. I also require you to surrender the eldest sons of Immin, Eafa and Eadbert to me as hostages for their good behaviour.'

Oswiu hadn't forgiven the three Mercian eorls who had instigated the revolt that had put Wulfhere on the throne of Mercia, nor did he trust them not to talk Wulfhere into some act of folly. Holding their sons should, he hoped, keep them in check.

The three men were amongst the Mercian delegation and they started to protest loudly.

'Silence!' Oswiu thundered. 'The alternative is for you to risk everything on one turn of the dice. If you think you can win, go ahead, but be warned; if you lose there won't be any more cosy little negotiations like this. Your head will be struck from your body, as will the heads of those three,' he said, gesticulating towards the three eorls. 'Your decision. We'll retire and leave you to deliberate.'

Three hours later a messenger rode into Oswiu's camp to let him know that Wulfhere had decided to agree to his conditions.

~~~

Whilst Oswiu was heading into Mercia, Catinus was leading his gesith south west towards Caer Luel, the capital of Rheged. He knew that its eorl would have already departed by sea for Dùn Add too but he hoped that he would be able to borrow or hire a few ships to transport him and his gesith around the Rhins, the bow shaped peninsular at the western extremity of Strathclyde, and up into the Firth of Clyde. Dùn Breatainn, the fortress of the Kings of Strathclyde, lay on the northern bank of the firth where the estuary began to narrow before it became the River Clyde.

His journey was uneventful until he reached Caer Luel. Being early in the sailing season, the few ships that had already been put into the water had been needed to take the eorl to seek Domangart's support. There were a number of knarrs, birlinns and currachs beached and propped up on stilts but they were all being repaired, having the weeds scraped off their bottoms and, in the case of the currachs, having some damaged skins replaced before new lanolin was rubbed into them to make the leather waterproof.

He was faced with two unpalatable alternatives: either he would have to wait until enough ships were ready or they would have to ride north through Strathclyde to where there was a ferry over the river and then approach Dùn Breatainn along the north bank of the firth. The problem was he didn't have a safe-conduct and sending a messenger to obtain one would cause even more of a delay to his mission.

It was Leofric who came up with a solution to his dilemma.

'Lord, I've found a fisherman who is willing to transport you to King Mermin's fortress.'

'A fisherman? Have you gone mad, boy? It must be all of two hundred and fifty miles by sea from here to Dùn Breatainn. How on earth is a fishing boat going to take me and my escort all that way? We'd never make it. Quite apart from the fact that most fishing boats aren't large enough to take more than a few men. The owner must be a fool to have made the offer.'

'More like he's got no idea where Dùn Breatainn is,' Eadstan commented dryly.

Leofric gave the leader of Bebbanburg's garrison a pained look.

'He was born in Ayr on the coast of Strathclyde and he knows the way to Dùn Breatainn well. His vessel isn't a normal fishing boat. He and his sons like to venture further afield where there are better and bigger catches to be had. He bought a pontos a few years ago; one of the ships Eochaid captured when he rescued Aidan from the hinterland of Strathclyde.'

Catinus had heard the tale, even if Eadstan hadn't. Over twenty years ago, when Oswald had first come to the throne of Northumbria, he'd sent his friend Eochaid to save Aidan and Ròidh from the clutches of the then pagan King of Strathclyde. In the course of doing so he'd captured several pontos – a craft that had existed since Roman times. They were usually made of leather over a wooden frame but they were also constructed with thin wooden planks as the outer skin. They had a prow and a stern and were much larger than currachs.

In this case the pontos was thirty five feet long with single mast and was it sheathed in wooden planks. It had four oars a side, but they were primarily designed for manoeuvring in port and to propel the craft slowly in narrow rivers. The normal crew was nine but, with an empty fish hold, it could carry another twenty men; though most would have to travel below decks and suffer the residual stink of dead fish.

Catinus had brought forty men with him but twenty of those had to return to Bebbanburg as there wasn't room for them on the pontos. The first part of the journey was uneventful, if tedious as they had to beat into the westerly wind until they rounded the southern tip of the Rhins. After that they sailed with the wind on their beam. They had almost cleared the northern end of the Rhins on the second day when the ship's boy, sitting on the yard that secured the top of the mainsail near the top of the mast, yelled down that a strange sail was approaching from the west.

Catinus looked at the owner of the pontos in alarm.

'Can we out sail it?

'I doubt it. From the sail that's just appeared over the horizon I'd say it is probably three or four miles away and closing on us.'

A quarter of an hour later the ship was close enough for them to make out the hull from the deck.

'It's an Irish birlinn by the look of her, but I can't make out the device on her sail yet. You'd better get your warriors ready for a scrap.'

Catinus nodded. Not all his men were in their best fighting form. The stench in the fish locker had made half of them seasick. They felt better once they were allowed on deck and, once they'd taken a few breaths of fresh sea air, they donned their chainmail byrnies and helmets. Some believed that fighting in armour at sea was madness. If you fell into the water you'd sink like a stone. However, Catinus didn't hold with that. Most of men couldn't swim so they'd drown anyway; it would just take longer.

As the birlinn drew closer Catinus breathed a sigh of relief. He had never met King Eochaid of the Ulaidh in Ulster but he recognised his device. The pontos he was sailing on had once been captured by him from the men of Strathclyde. He had been a great friend of Oswiu's brother, Oswald, and he was a Scot, the same tribe who inhabited Dalriada, one of Northumbria's allies.

'Run up Oswiu's red and gold banner,' he told Leofric, who ran away to do as he was bid.

'Who are you?' a fair haired young man standing on the prow of the birlinn called across.

'I'm Catinus, Ealdorman of Bebbanburg and the emissary of King Oswiu of Northumbria. Who are you? From the device on your sail I presume that your birlinn belongs to King Eochaid.'

'I'm his son, Lethlobar mac Echach. Where are you bound?'

'To Dùn Breatainn. I'm sent to negotiate with King Mermin.'

'Mermin? Is Guret dead then?'

'Yes. The rumour is that Mermin killed him and took the throne. However, King Oswiu doesn't want war in the North again. My mission is to prevent that if at all possible.'

Although the two craft were now sailing abreast about ten yards apart Catinus found that shouting across the waves was making him hoarse.

'Why don't I come aboard so we can talk face to face instead of shouting?'

'Are you agile enough to jump up onto my birlinn? Perhaps I should come aboard your little pontos instead?'

A minute later Lethlobar was standing on the deck beside Catinus. The latter was shorter than most men but, in contrast, the Irishman stood six inches taller than the average. When he greeted Catinus by giving him a bear hug he lifted the ealdorman off his feet. Had he not done so Catinus would have found his nose pressed against the young man's chest.

'Tell me about this Mermin. We Dalriadans are at peace with Strathclyde now and I share your desire to keep it that way. We have suffered grievously at their hands in the past.'

Catinus was interested to hear Lethlobar describe himself as a Dalriadan. Decades ago the Ulaidh were part of Dalriada; indeed the Dalriadans in Caledonia had come from Ulster originally.

However, the link had been broken a long time ago when the two parts of the kingdom had both been struggling for survival.

The two ships beached side by side in a deserted bay south of Ayr for the night and the Northumbrians and the Ulaidh held a friendly drinking competition that ended with both comatose. That night a six year old child could have killed the lot of them whilst they slept.

They woke the next morning with sore heads until Catinus and Lethlobar ordered them into the sea to wash and clear the cobwebs away. A little later than either would have liked the two ships set off again heading north. Lethlobar had insisted on accompanying his new found friend and seeing him safely to his destination. For his part Catinus didn't think that it would do any harm for Mermin to see him arrive in the company of an Irish prince. The more isolated Mermin felt the better.

The pontos and the larger birlinn edged into the shallow bay below the fortress sitting high above them on its truncated cone of rock. As they approached the shore a large warband massed at the top of the beach.

'It doesn't look as if our arrival is particularly welcome,' Lethlobar called across to Catinus.

'I'm going to land without armour, helmet or shield so that they know that we come in peace.'

'I'll be ready to avenge your death if your peaceful intentions aren't reciprocated,' the Irishman replied with a grin.

Catinus jumped down onto the sand followed by Redwald and his banner bearer. They trudged through the sand towards the warband, who were now talking in increasingly agitated voices amongst themselves. When the Northumbrians were fifty yards away from them three men stepped forward to meet them. The leader handed his shield and helmet to one of his men but the other two remained fully armed.

'Who are you and what do you think you are doing coming here with a warband?'

To Catinus' surprise he spoke in English. Lethlobar looked puzzled. He spoke both the Gaelic spoken in Ireland and the

Brythonic tongue prevalent in Caledonia and Rheged but his grasp of the language of the Angles, Saxons and Jutes was rudimentary.

'I'm Catinus, Ealdorman of Bebbanburg and the emissary of King Oswiu. My friend, Lethlobar, is the son of the King of Ulaidh who is kindly keeping me company in case of pirates.'

'Pirates? There are none in the Clyde.'

'No, but we have come from Caer Luel and the waters off Ulster are patrolled by the Uí Néill who prey on other ships.'

'Conceivably you are right, but I still dislike so many armed men arriving uninvited.'

'Did King Oswiu's messenger not arrive informing you of my intended visit?'

'Yes, but I expected you to come from the east, along the north bank of the Clyde.'

For a moment Catinus wondered whether, had he done so, he would have arrived safely at Dùn Breatainn. He was fairly certain that he would have disappeared somewhere along the way. If Mermin denied that he had ever arrived in Strathclyde he would have been spared making a decision about his loyalty to Oswiu, at least for now. As it was, he either had to acknowledge him as his overlord or risk finding himself at war with the kingdoms surrounding his territory.

'What's he saying?'

Lethlobar, who hadn't followed much of the conversation so far, was getting increasingly impatient.

'He didn't expect me to come by sea. He had an escort waiting for me, supposing that I would come by land.'

'More like an execution squad,' the Irishmen grunted.

Catinus glanced at Mermin quickly but it was evident that that the king didn't understand Gaelic.

'My thoughts exactly.' Turning back to Mermin he asked pleasantly whether they might continue their discussions in more comfortable surroundings.

The man's eyes lit up. 'By all means. Come up to my hall. You can bring a couple of men but no more.'

'No need to trouble yourself, I'll have a tent and some chairs brought ashore. We can conduct our negotiations here.'

Catinus had no intention of finding himself a hostage. Mermin scowled at him but had little option but to acquiesce. An hour later both men sat on comfortable chairs with their immediate advisers behind them. Catinus had taken the opportunity to change and he appeared wearing a crimson tunic which came down to just below his knees, blue trousers tied around the calves with white ribbons, and a thick blue cloak secured around his neck with a large broach made of gold with a ruby at its centre. He was bareheaded.

He wished that he'd brought another chair for Lethlobar but his presence was unexpected and space was at a premium on the small pontos.

'My king was saddened to hear of the sudden death of his friend King Guret. How did it come about?' Catinus asked once refreshments had been served.

'Who knows? The gods decide to strike a man down and there is nothing anyone can do about it.'

'Gods? You are not a Christian then?'

'The White Christ is no true god. I worship the gods of my ancestors and respect the druids, like any good Briton should.' He glared at Catinus before continuing in Brythonic. 'You are said to be a Briton, like me, but you have betrayed your people and your gods.'

'There are many more Britons who believe in God and His Son Jesus Christ than there are pagans like you,' he retorted angrily.

Mermin's face burned with fanatical zeal.

'My uncle, Eugein, followed the true faith. Guret betrayed his father and our people so he had to die. Now I'm king I'll continue the work of Eugein and cleanse Strathclyde of scum like you.'

So saying, he jumped up from his chair, drawing his seax as he did so. He thrust it upwards intending it to enter Catinus' chest below his rib cage and tear upwards into this heart. The latter was wearing a leather belt around his waist to which was attached his own seax. Otherwise he appeared to be unarmed. However, he was wearing a short chainmail byrnie under his tunic and the blade slid upwards damaging the expensive tunic beyond repair but leaving Catinus unharmed.

The blunt tip of the seax snagged in the material of the cloak and, before Mermin could withdraw it and try to cut his throat instead, Catinus struck the would-be assassin's arm aside and punched him hard on the nose.

Everyone else standing in the tent was taken completely by surprise when Mermin attacked Catinus; all except Leofric. The boy had helped his master dress in the confines of the small cabin under the aft deck of the pontos. Catinus had told him that he didn't trust Mermin and so the boy was half expecting the attack. When it came he pulled a small knife from the sheath at his waist and, choosing his moment carefully, he threw it with unerring accuracy. It struck the King of Strathclyde in the neck and blood spurted out of his carotid artery, splashing Catinus and those standing nearby. A coppery smell quickly pervaded the air in the close confines of the tent.

The king sunk to the floor as his life ebbed away. The stunned silence in the tent continued for a second before it was replaced by uproar. Swords were drawn and a carnage seemed inevitable when a commanding voice yelled 'halt' in Brythonic. Mermin's followers paused uncertainly, warily watching the Northumbrians and the Irish until Catinus drew enough breath into his lungs to cry 'hold' in English and then in Gaelic.

Warily the two sides stood, swords drawn, watching each other until a large man stepped forward and kicked Mermin's dead body. 'Usurper,' he said angrily and then spat on the corpse.

'I'm Elfin, this piece of shit's cousin. He poisoned my half-brother, Guret, and his men seized Dùn Breatainn. Before we knew it he'd declared himself king. We were too disorganised to oppose him but he wouldn't have held the throne for long, even if you hadn't come along. Nevertheless, I'm grateful.'

Behind him Mermin's small escort had been seized and disarmed by the other nobles of Strathclyde who'd accompanied their late king.

'These men will be tried as accomplices for the crime of regicide and will doubtless hang. However, we have a problem. Your servant is also guilty of regicide.'

'But he was saving my life!'

'Even so. You are a noble and you had a right to defend your life against Mermin's unprovoked attack. The boy is a servant and must die for what he did.'

CHAPTER SIX – THE PLAGUE OF JUSTINIAN

658/9 AD

Catinus was dumbstruck for a moment, but then his anger grew.

'Elfin, he's my servant, not a native of Strathclyde. He was defending me, as was his duty. You have no right to try him for killing your cousin. If you accuse him of a crime, I will try him for it and I will make judgement, though I think you know what my verdict is likely to be.'

'Be very careful, ealdorman. I am likely to be the next king now that Mermin is dead. You antagonise me at your peril.'

'No, it's you who need to tread carefully, Elfin. I came here with instructions to ascertain whether the new king will support the status quo. If not, I am to warn him that he risks war.'

He knew that he was treading on dangerous ground. His task was to sound out Mermin, and now presumably Elfin. Oswiu had mentioned applying pressure if Catinus failed to secure the new king's recognition of Oswiu as his overlord, but that was for him to do, not his emissary.

Elfin looked grim for a moment, and then he relaxed.

'You've got balls, Catinus, I'll say that for you. I'm sure you're clever enough to know that I need to establish my own position and unite Strathclyde behind me before I go looking for any trouble. Very well, I'll allow you to deal with your servant as you see fit. Only those nobles who Mermin has already rewarded are likely to condemn me for letting his killer go. As to acknowledging Oswiu as Bretwalda, I'm content to do that provided he doesn't try to interfere with my freedom to rule as I wish.'

'I'm sure that will be acceptable. He has neither the time nor the inclination to get involved in the internal policies of the kingdoms of Caledonia. His only desire is to ensure that there is peace in the north.'

'Good, now if you'll excuse me I have to deal with a small problem. The fortress is held by Mermin's men and I don't suppose they will submit to me without a fight. The place is unassailable and well stocked with provisions.'

'Won't they surrender now that he is dead?'

'No, Mermin has a brother and they may well transfer their allegiance to him in the hope that he will come to their relief.'

'Would it be helpful if I and my men supported your attack?'

'Of course. How many men do you have?'

'It depends on whether Lethlobar will also help; I have twenty warriors and they're well trained.'

'Yes, I'll support you,' the latter replied with a nod, 'but I'll not throw my men's lives away foolishly. We need a good plan of attack.'

Catinus thought for a moment. 'What do the garrison do with their rubbish?'

~~~

Oswiu returned to Eoforwīc content that, for the moment at least, he had re-established peace on his southern border. He had never imagined that he would be able to keep Mercia subdued for ever. He just hoped that Wulfhere would prove to be more trustworthy that his father and elder brother had been.

Then his heart sank. Eoforwīc meant Eanflæd. She had stayed at Loidis for a while after he set out to confront Wulfhere but the last messenger he'd received from the clerks who dealt with the administration of the kingdom had told him that the queen had now returned. Her treatment of him ever since he had given Ælfflaed to the Church to be brought up as a nun had hurt him deeply. As the town came in sight he made a decision. He hoped that it might heal the rift between them but, even if it didn't, it was something that he'd wanted to do for some time.

As soon as he arrived his wife started to pack to return to Loidis. When he heard this, Oswiu took a deep breath and went to her chamber.

'I hear you are leaving again, my dear. That's a shame; I was about to invite you to come with me to visit my cousin Hild at Whitby. You would, of course, also be able to see Ælfflaed.'

Eanflæd stared at him. Her immediate reaction had been to tell him that she wouldn't go anywhere with him. However, she would dearly love to see her daughter again. She would be four now; no longer a baby but a small child. Her resolve weakened. The slight softening of her attitude towards Oswiu had been helped by the time she had spent in the company of Abbot Wilfrid at Loidis, where he was a frequent visitor, as he had urged her to become reconciled with her husband.

Of course, the abbot's motivation was to ingratiate himself with the king. He had already wheedled his way into a position of influence with Alchfrith of Deira and now the queen was rapidly coming under his spell. If he became the confidante of Oswiu, then perhaps he might persuade him to make him Bishop of Eoforwīc. At the moment the spiritual leader of all of Northumbria was Finan, who Wilfrid despised. Wilfrid had been educated at Cantwareburg, in Rome and in Frankia and he fervently believed that the Celtic Church was an anathema. He was determined to replace it with the Roman Church, at least in Northumbria.

Eanflæd thought of all that Wilfrid had said to her. He had convinced her that hating her husband for dedicating their child to the Church was wrong. It had been an act of piety and her reaction had been the work of Satan. She had difficulty in accepting this but gradually she had come to accept what he said was true and she had been selfish.

When she saw the piteous look on Oswiu's face, her heart melted. He was such a strong man and yet here he was looking weak and vulnerable. She would never forget what he'd done but she decided that she had to try to forgive him. She nodded in acquiescence.

'I would like that, husband. Thank you.'

Repairing the rift between them would take time, but they had taken the first steps down that road.

~~~

Offa lay in his coffin before the altar in the church at Melrose. His death had been unexpected but not suspicious. During the midday meal, such as it was, he had clutched at his heart and collapsed. Within a few minutes he'd stopped breathing.

His prior, Eata, was the obvious choice as his replacement. In recent months Offa had handed more and more of the administration of the monastery over to him and spent his days in quiet meditation. However, although the election of the abbot was the prerogative of the monks, it was prudent to obtain the approval of the bishop and the king before Eata could be sure of his appointment.

The messenger returned from Lindisfarne with Finan's agreement fairly quickly. That of the king took longer. The monk sent to him went to Eoforwīc first, only to be told that the king and queen had gone to Whitby. It was therefore over a month before he returned to Whitby but he was not alone. He was accompanied by Cuthbert.

'Welcome, Cuthbert. I'd didn't expect to see you again, unless it was in the company of the king.'

'Greeting Father Abbot. Your messenger carries a letter from Oswiu but I know the contents. He approves your appointment and commends my unworthy self to you as a supplicant who wishes to return to monastic life.'

'You, unworthy? False modesty doesn't become you, Cuthbert. I welcome you back as a monk most wholeheartedly. Are you sure that you wish to enter Melrose? For someone of your abilities and high birth wouldn't Lindisfarne suit you better?'

'I have no desire to use either my status or connections for personal advantage. I have had enough of this world and wish only to prepare for the next.'

'I see. That's a pity. I am looking for a guest-master and you would be ideally suited to the task.'

'Are the duties onerous? I wouldn't have thought that you would have to host too many high-born visitors.'

'You would be surprised. Many who are travelling from the south of Northumbria to Goddodin or to one of the kingdoms in Caledonia come this way. Melrose doesn't attract many high born novices and so my monks are in awe of their betters. Consequently they hesitate to insist that they follow our rules whilst they are here. You would have no such problem.'

'What do these visitors do that upsets you, Father Abbot?'

'Drunkenness and debauchery. Some have brought whores with them to entertain them at night and there have been fights between men in their cups, even two deaths.'

'And this is commonplace?'

'Well, no. But far too often for me to accept it.'

'I wasn't seeking an appointment as an officer of the monastery, but neither will I stand by and witness that sort of behaviour. If I can prevent it, then I accept.'

His first test came a week later when a thegn from near Dùn Èideann arrived with his two sons, the new wife of one of his sons, five of their friends and four servants. Night had fallen and the gates had been closed when the porter came to find him to tell him of the party's arrival. He added that the thegn was none too pleased when he was told he'd have to wait whilst the guest-master was fetched.

'Welcome to Melrose.'

Cuthbert smiled at the party as they rode into the muddy area in front of the guest hut. The monk in charge of the stables and two boys came running up to take the horses as soon as the servants had unloaded what they would need for the night. The thegn didn't reply to Cuthbert's greeting but stalked up to him and prodded him in the chest.

'What do you mean by it, eh? We're tired, hungry and in no mood to have to wait for some snivelling monk to decide to open the gates.'

'Don't prod me with your finger, thegn, if you know what's good for you. You are the abbot's guests and you'll behave appropriately or find somewhere else to spend the night.'

'Why, you impudent oaf! Do you know who I am?'

'If I remember correctly, your name is Iestyn and you hold a small vill between Dùn Barra and Dùn Èideann.'

The man took a step back as his two sons came to join him.

'How do you know that?' he asked suspiciously.

'Because you are one of my father's vassals. My name is Cuthbert, Eorl Kenric's eldest son. You came to Dùn Barra to settle a claim in the eorl's court when I was about ten. You lost and you took it badly. No doubt that's why you stuck in my mind. You were arrogant then and you haven't changed.'

'Cuthbert? The eorl's son? But I thought you were in the king's gesith?'

'I was; now I'm here as the guest-master. I'm afraid that your son's wife and her slave will have to sleep in a separate hut. I'll show them the way. This hut is yours for tonight; there's no other travellers staying. As to food, I'm afraid we have eaten but I'll get someone to bring you bread, cheese and water.'

'I'm not being parted from my wife!' the elder son suddenly spat out. 'We were only married two days ago.'

'Of course you may enjoy your marital rights, but not in the confines of this monastery. Do you wish to leave again?'

'Drop it, boy. You've the rest of your life to hump your pretty little wife.'

'But father...'

'But nothing! Do as you're told. Thank you Brother Cuthbert. Be sure to remember me to your father when you next see him.'

'I will. I'll bid you good-night and show the lady over to her hut.'

He had a feeling that the horny young bridegroom would try and follow him to his wife's hut to visit her during the night, so he took a circuitous route in the hope that the young man would have difficulty in finding it. At least he'd done his best to maintain the proprieties.

The stupid young man didn't have the sense to return to the guest hut before dawn and emerged from the women's hut just as the monks were making their way towards the church for Prime, the first service of the day. Even worse, his bride followed her husband out of the hut to give him a lingering kiss. The passing monks muttered angrily amongst themselves and one of them went over to remonstrate with the man.

He didn't get very far before the young man punched him hard in the face and he fell over backwards with a broken and bloody nose. Cuthbert strode over to him and told the young man to stay where he was before sending for the infirmarian to deal with the injured monk. Then he grabbed the thegn's son and marched him over to the guest hut. He tried to break away but Cuthbert twisted his arm so far up his back that he howled in agony and his whole body was forced upwards. He had to walk on the balls of his feet for a few yards before the irate guest-master relented and let him walk normally.

Meanwhile the man's wife screamed at Cuthbert to release her husband but an angry crowd of monks surrounded her and prevented her from following them until Eata appeared to find out what the commotion was about.

'You may return and join the rest of your party, girl, but you will behave in a demure and appropriate manner until you leave these precincts. Someone please tell Brother Cuthbert that I would like to see him as soon as he is free. The rest of you should make your way into church where Matins is about to commence.'

The occupants of the guest hut were awake and preparing to walk over to join the monks to break their fast after the short service. The guest-master soon disabused them of that idea.

'I'm sorry that your son couldn't keep his cock in his trousers last night, Iestyn. To make matters worse he kissed his wife in a lewd manner in front of the monks and nearly caused a riot. When one of them remonstrated with him he struck the monk, breaking his nose. I would be grateful if you'd leave immediately. You will not be welcome here again.'

'I apologise on my son's behalf, brother. I hope that you won't feel the need to report this?'

'I don't run to my father with every bit of tittle-tattle, if that's what you're worried about. I cannot say, however, what line Father

Abbot will take. His hospitality has been abused and one of the monks he is responsible for has been assaulted.'

'Perhaps if my son made confession and did penance for his sin?'

'I suggest you don't delay your departure any longer. We endeavour to forgive those who trespass against us but not all of us are as successful as we might be. It would be better if you weren't here when Matins ends.'

At that moment the wife appeared and sulkily mounted her horse. Cuthbert watched the dejected party depart but he wasn't convinced that the thegn's apparent contriteness was genuine. He thanked the monk who came to tell him of the abbot's summons and followed him back to the church.

'That was a bad business, Brother Cuthbert. I had hoped that by appointing you as guest master I had put an end to problems with travellers.'

'I agree, Father Abbot, but I don't see how I could have handled matters differently. I regret laying hands on the young man, naturally, but at the time I feared that our brothers were so incensed that they might well have attacked him and that would have been a far worse mess. I had to get him away from there.'

'Yes, I understand that. However, I cannot let the matter pass. I believe that I should make a complaint and seek weregeld for the monastery for the injury done. Perhaps I should write to your father?'

'You are welcome to do so, of course, but the eorl is frail and bedridden. I came here by way of Dùn Barra to visit him and I was shocked by his appearance. My mother now runs the eorldom. My younger brother is barely ten and it is by no means certain that King Oswiu will let Beornheth inherit, given his young age and the importance of the position. He might, however, let him succeed when the time comes, but with my mother as regent until he is old enough.'

'I see. Perhaps I should write to her then?'

'You would be within your rights to do so, though I doubt she will welcome a claim for weregeld. The eorl's situation, and therefore hers, is vulnerable and she needs the support of the thegns. They won't like it is one of their number is made to pay compensation to us.'

'What do you suggest then? I cannot let this pass. An attack on one of us is an attack on all.'

'I suggest that I write privately to King Oswiu and ask for his advice.'

'Thank you Cuthbert, I'm grateful to you.' He paused. 'Oh, look, I'm sorry if I seemed critical earlier. You handled a difficult situation well.'

~~~

Catinus spat out a mouthful of filth and wondered, not for the first time, whether he shouldn't have just sailed away and reported the changed situation in Strathclyde to Oswiu. The garbage chute was a stone channel cut at forty five degrees through the rock on which the fortress was built. It emerged near the top of a cliff, from where the detritus from the fortress dropped two hundred feet straight into the waves pounding at the base of the cliff below.

It had taken him and six other men, all of whom were good climbers, three hours to quietly edge around the base of the palisade until they were above where the chute emerged. In some ways they were helped by the incessant rain that fell. It kept the sentries out of the way, sheltering in the dry, but it made the foot wide area between palisade and cliff edge quite slippery. Their progress wasn't helped by the strong gusts of wind what would suddenly whip around the rock, threatening to pluck them from their precarious perches at times.

However, he reached the chute exit safely and he climbed up into it. For a moment he thought that he'd slide out again and plummet to his death as he couldn't get a grip on the slimy bottom of the chute. Just in time he managed to get a handhold on the roughly cut rock surface at the sides of the chute. He whispered a warning to the man behind him and then started to haul himself up the tunnel towards the dim circle of light at the far end.

By the time he reached the end he calculated that it must be about the middle of the night. However, he was exhausted and he lay there breathing in the fresh air whilst he recovered. He felt the man behind him tap his foot and he forced himself to clamber out of the hole in the ground. He found himself in a small area surrounded by a low fence, presumably to stop people falling into the chute. There wasn't room for all seven of them behind the fence so he eased his seax out of its scabbard and slipped over the fence and into the shadows.

Once the other six had joined him, he led them along the inside of the palisade towards the gates. They passed by the backs of several huts and they heard the sound of snoring and the occasional fart faintly through the timber walls. Catinus kept looking up at the walkway above him for sentries but it wasn't until they neared the gatehouse that he saw anyone.

A platform had been constructed above the gates. It consisted of a walkway, three foot high walls front and back and a roof to keep most of the rain off the sentries. In the poor light he could just make out two heads looking out towards the path that led up from the beach where the combined forces of Elfin, Lethlobar and himself were camped.

To the left of the gates there was a hut built against the palisade. Catinus assumed that this was where the rest of the men guarding the gate slept until it was their turn on watch. There was nothing to do now but wait until the sentries changed.

Meanwhile, in the camp on the beach men were making their way quietly to the bottom of the defile. The fortifications that guarded access to the path that led up to the fortress had been captured earlier that day and the gates stood wide open. Unlike Catinus and his half a dozen men, who were dressed in tunics and were only armed with seaxes, these men were fully armed.

They settled down just inside the entrance to the defile and waited for Catinus' signal. If the plan was to work they would have to ascend the steep path to the gates as quickly and quietly as they could. If the alarm was sounded before they reached the gates then they would have failed and their men inside the fortress would be killed.

Catinus tensed as he heard movement and two men came out of the hut cursing the lousy weather. When they got to the base of the ladder leading up to the walkway above the gates two silent figures stepped behind them and, putting one hand over their mouths, they drew their seaxes across their throats. They pulled the bodies into the shadows beside the gates.

'Come on you two, what's keeping you?'

The voice calling out in Brythonic startled Catinus and he signalled for two of his men to ascend the ladder. The Britons had been dressed in tunics with oiled woollen cloaks. One had a helmet but the other was bareheaded. The two men quickly donned the cloaks, grabbed the helmet and the dead men's swords and started to climb the ladder, the one in the helmet leading.

'About time too,' one of the sentries grumbled as the first had appeared at the top of the ladder, though Catinus' man didn't understand what he'd said.

The warrior kept his head down so that the helmet hid his face until he was at the top of the ladder, then he plunged the sword in his hand through the mouth of the surprised sentry, cutting off any sound. The point pierced his brain and he slumped onto the wooden planking. The second man had been waiting impatiently behind him and was initially paralysed by shock when he saw his friend killed. The man in the borrowed helmet was having difficulty pulling his sword out of the dead sentry's head and so he abandoned his efforts and pulled out his seax.

The second Briton had opened his mouth to cry out a warning as he scrambled to pull out his own sword. Before he uttered a sound, his attacker thrust the point of his seax into the man's throat. The blow didn't kill him immediately but it prevented him from shouting out. The second of Catinus' men finished the job by thrusting his sword through the man's heart.

Meanwhile the five men outside the hut were dealing with the rest of the gate guard. Catinus quietly opened the door and glanced inside. There were six palliasses filled with straw on the floor, four of which were occupied by sleeping men. Leaving Leofric outside to guard the door, Catinus and three of his men slipped silently inside and, when each was kneeling over their chosen victim, Catinus nodded and they cut the four throats as one. The gate was now secure.

'Leofric, there is a torch burning outside the king's hall. Go and fetch it.'

The boy ran off but returned empty handed a few minutes later.

'There are two sentries outside the hall, lord.'

Catinus cursed. The agreed signal was a torch being waved to and from in the open gateway. The rest of the attackers would then ascend the defile and secure the fortress.

'Right, run down the track and tell Elfin and Lethlobar that we've captured the gateway but there are no torches. They are to come up here as fast as they can. Off you go.'

He waited on tenterhooks for them to appear, praying fervently that no-one would come to check on the gate guard. He was also far from certain that there weren't other sentries around the parapet at the top of the palisade. He hadn't seen or heard any, but that didn't mean that they weren't there. He couldn't believe that anyone who knew that there was an enemy at his gates wouldn't have posted a strong watch, whatever the weather.

Suddenly he spotted someone who had evidently been sleeping getting up and stretching on the parapet a hundred yards from the gateway. He must have pulled his cloak over his head to keep the worst of the rain off and settled down with his back to the top of the palisade. Now the man was pissing down into the mud below him. Once he'd finished he looked up and his gaze swept over the fortress. Catinus imagined his forehead furrowing as he noticed the absence of anyone standing guard above the gates. He could have kicked himself. He should have left his two men up there. Perhaps it wasn't too late.

'Get back up on duty, you idle sods,' he called out in Brythonic, just loudly enough for the sentry to hear him.

The two men who had killed the original sentries clambered back up the ladder to resume their supposed vigil. Seemingly satisfied the sentry sat down again and pulled his cloak over his head. Thankfully he hadn't bothered to look outside the palisade or he might have spotted the shadowy mass of warriors struggling up the steep path to the gates.

When he got the signal from the two posted on the walkway, Catinus and the rest unbarred the gates and swung them open. Something must have alerted the sleeping sentry because he climbed to his feet and was alarmed to see armed men pouring into the compound below him. He called out a warning but by then it was too late. Lethlobar led his men towards the warriors' hall whilst Elfin made for the king's hall.

The rest of his gesith joined Catinus. He posted the men who had originally accompanied him to close and guard the gates to prevent escape, sending the rest along the walkway to deal with any sentries. In the event they only found two. The man who had been sleeping under his cloak and another who'd been in the lookout out tower at the north-west corner of the fortress. He too had been asleep.

Half an hour later it was all over. The garrison were either dead or had surrendered. Whilst Elfin was arranging the disposal of the dead on both sides and making what was now his hall habitable again, Lethlobar walked over to talk to Catinus.

'God in Heaven, you stink!'

The smaller man grinned at him.

'You try climbing up a slimy chute full of rotting debris and come out smelling all fresh and clean. Besides, the stench of blood and sweat on you hardly gives you room to talk.'

'You're right. I suggest we leave Elfin to it for now and come back up later this morning. A dip in the sea down there looks quite inviting to me.'

'Good idea. Bathe, eat and sleep in that order I think.'

'I'll let Elfin know. Then I'll race you to the beach.'

Catinus shook his head.

'I'm too weary to run.'

'You're getting old.'

It was the wrong thing to say. Catinus was very conscious of the fact that he'd just turned thirty. He looked at the other man and guessed his age to be twenty or thereabouts.

'Right you're on. Get someone else to tell Elfin.'

With that he ordered his men to open the gates again and sprinted through them. A stunned Lethlobar watched him go; then, with a laugh he followed his new friend down the steep path. Leofric watched them go, leaping down the track like goats and shook his head. They'd survived the capture of Dùn Breatainn unscathed and now they risked breaking a leg or smashing their brains out on a rock, and for what? However, they reached the bottom without injury and with Catinus still in the lead. As Lethlobar was still clad in his chainmail byrnie, the older man had a distinct advantage; nevertheless the boy was proud that his master had won the stupid contest.

~~~

Eanflæd rode her small horse next to Oswiu as they reached the last crest before Whitby. They halted and gazed across at the new monastery taking shape on the other side of the estuary. The stone walls appeared to be half built with men hauling up cut stone onto the top of the wooden scaffolding whilst others chose pieces of it and mortared it in place. Others were sawing stone to produce the cut blocks from a pile of rocks whilst carters urged their horses to drag more stone from the quayside, where it had been unloaded, up the hill towards the site.

The place bustled with activity. In contrast the wooden huts in which the nuns and monks lived in their separate compounds seemed almost bereft of life. Then she saw them in a nearby hollow on their knees whilst Hild led them in prayers. She scanned the crowd for sight of her daughter but couldn't spot her. Ælfflaed was old enough to attend services now and so her absence worried her. She prayed that she wasn't ill.

She had been excited by the prospect of seeing her daughter again ever since they had set out. She hadn't forgiven her husband for depriving her of Ælfflaed but relations between them weren't as frosty as they had been. Perhaps, once she'd seen her daughter she would be able to forgive him, but she was far from certain about that.

For his part Oswiu seemed content that his wife was once more at his side. He wasn't a patient man but he knew that restoring their relationship to anything like what it had been would take time – lots of it – and he was resigned to taking things slowly.

'I'm sorry, Síþwíf, but your daughter is ill.'

Abbess Hild had taken Eanflæd aside as soon as the formal greetings were over.

'What's wrong with her? Is it serious?'

'She's got a fever and usually children get over that in a day or two, but she's had it for three days now and doesn't seem to be able to keep anything down, so she's growing weaker.'

'Take me to her now please.'

Eanflæd tried to keep the panic out of her voice but she feared she had arrived just in time to see her child die. Hild looked uncomfortable.

'I don't think that would be wise, Síþwíf.'

'Why ever not?'

'She has developed swellings on her neck and in her armpits,' she said at last.

The queen was puzzled for a moment and then something she had heard about as a child surfaced in her mind.

'What sort of swellings?' she asked with a sinking feeling in the pit of her stomach.

'They are quite large and have started to darken.'

'The plague,' she almost whispered.

'It's possible yes, though we don't know much about it or its symptoms. The last outbreak was a long time ago on the west coast.'

'Has anyone else gone down with the same symptoms?'

'Yes, a merchant, three of the monks and five nuns.'

'Did the merchant contract it first?'

'Yes, how did you know?'

'He must have brought it with him. How is he?'

'He died yesterday.'

'Burn his body, his clothes and his bedding. Abbot Wilfrid told me about the plague of Justinian amongst the Romans. No one knows how it's spread, but so many people died of it a century or so ago that the depopulated empire was unable to resist the barbarian hordes.'

She paused deep in thought before continuing.

'We must send for Abbot Wilfrid. He's the only person who knows anything about this dreadful disease. Meanwhile we must keep those who have contracted the plague isolated from the rest. I will nurse my daughter myself; you must find volunteers to look after the rest. They mustn't come into contact with anyone else until the outbreak is over.'

'If you're sure.'

'No, I'm not but these are sensible precautions until Wilfrid arrives. Now I had better let the king know.'

Oswiu took the news badly. At first he was incredulous, then he blamed himself for giving his daughter to the Church. Had he not done so Ælfflaed would not be ill, possibly even dying; she would have been safe at Eoforwīc.

At first he wouldn't be persuaded to return to Eoforwīc, leaving his wife behind to nurse their daughter, even when Redwald, Aldhun and Hild joined Eanflæd in telling him that he was putting the future of Northumbria at risk by staying. It wasn't until Abbot Wilfrid arrived and took charge that he finally made him see sense and he left.

By then Ælfflaed had been ill for a week and the lumps had turned black and spread to her groin as well as her neck and armpits. Mercifully she was unconscious for much of the time and when she was awake she was delirious. During her few moments of lucidity she screamed and complained that her head and body hurt. All Eanflæd could do was to comfort her daughter as best she might and to keep bathing her fevered body in cold water.

Wilfrid worked tirelessly with the hard pressed infirmarian and the volunteers, both male and female, to tend the other victims. Over the next week the numbers grew until fifteen had caught the plague. Of them eleven died but the other four slowly recovered. Ælfflaed's fever broke on the tenth night but she was still in agony. Her mother stayed with her day and night until she collapsed with exhaustion.

'Put her in one of the huts that has been cleansed,' Hild told the two monks who came to help her.

'But she might infest the others,' one protested.

'Is she displaying the symptoms of the plague? No? Well then, do as I ask.'

Eanflæd slept for the next twenty seven hours without waking. Ælfflaed had been a favourite amongst the nuns, none of who would have children of their own, ever since she had arrived with her wet nurse as a small baby. The wet nurse had lost her own baby shortly after birth and consequently she had developed a strong relationship with the royal baby. When the time had come for her to leave she had ignored the pleas of her husband and had become a novice. Now she was overjoyed to take over as the child's nurse.

By the time that her mother woke the little girl had got rid of the plague, but it had left her very weak. Not only had she had no nourishment but fighting the disease had taken everything out of her. She didn't even have the energy to move and it would be two months before she returned to normal. During that time the nun and her mother took it in turns to wash her, feed her, take her to the toilet, and get her muscles working again.

By the time that Ælfflaed was able to walk again without assistance, the two women had developed a deep bond and Eanflæd was loathe to leave. If Oswiu hadn't returned to Whitby at that time to visit her and to check on their daughter's progress, she might well have decided to become a nun. As it was, she realised that the ordeal she had been through had changed her – and in more ways than one.

Wilfrid was about to return to Ripon now that the epidemic looked as if it was over and came to say farewell to the queen.

'Your daughter has made an excellent recovery, Síþwíf, thanks be to Almighty God. The recuperative powers of the young never fail to amaze me.' He smiled at her and she smiled back. 'I presume that you will be returning to Eoforwīc and the king soon?'

Eanflæd's bright smile vanished.

'Oh, I don't know, Wilfrid. One thing I have learned over the past month or two is that I do love Oswiu, but I also love my daughter. She is even more precious to me since I nearly lost her; and I like the life here. It is so peaceful and I feel contentment in a way that I don't when I have to play the queen.'

'What about Ecgfrith? He's also your child.'

Wilfrid was panicking slightly, though he took care not to show it. He had taken a great deal of trouble to cultivate Eanflæd. As queen, especially once she was back at Oswiu's side, she would be a most useful ally. Alchfrith was already a strong supporter but he was only Sub-king of Deira and had little real power. Wilfrid was ambitious, not only for himself, but he yearned to replace the Celtic Church in Northumbria with the Roman Church. The odds were heavily stacked against him but Eanflæd had been brought up in Frankia and Kent so she was already in favour of Rome. He knew he needed her help.

'Ecgfrith?' She was puzzled for a moment. 'He's fourteen now and will soon become a warrior.'

'Yes, but in the king's gesith, no doubt. At least you will see him often. You won't if you become a nun.'

'So you want me to return to my husband's side rather than devote the rest of my life to Christ? That's a strange attitude for a churchman to take, isn't it?'

Wilfrid had to think quickly. Not only would he lose the queen's influence if she stayed at Whitby but Oswiu might well blame him for her loss.

'Síþwíf, I honestly think you can better serve God as Queen of Northumbria than you can as a nun. After all you have a unique position to help the Pope in his struggle to unite the Church in the west, whereas there are many nuns. You are young yet and there will be plenty of time later for you to enter a monastery, if that is what you desire.'

She was not a fool. She knew what Wilfrid was saying. Few kings lived long enough to die of old age, and she was a lot younger than Oswiu. She was not unaware of the struggle between the Celtic Church and the Pope; she had argued enough with Oswiu over the differences in doctrine and other contentious issues, like calculating the date of Easter, to know that the polarisation between Rome in the south and the Celtic monks in the north was unsustainable.

It wasn't just that either. The Roman Catholic Church was a hierarchy with the Pope as its leader supported by bishops and priests. In the Celtic Church the monastery was the pinnacle on which all else depended. There were bishops and priests, of course, but they had all been monks first and the abbot was seen as superior to the bishop.

Bishops and abbots under Rome were also acquiring secular power and wealth, which was anathema to the Celtic monks. Wilfrid was honest enough to admit to himself that he hated the ascetic lifestyle of Finan and the Celtic monks. He enjoyed luxury, eating well and the other trappings of wealth.

In the end Wilfrid managed to persuade her to return to the arms of her husband. Eanflæd set off on a cold, icy morning in February not altogether sure that the welcome she would get from Oswiu wouldn't be as frosty as the weather.

CHAPTER SEVEN – PEACE AND RECONCILIATION

659/661 AD

Catinus was euphoric one minute and full of concern the next. Leoflaed had just told him that she was almost sure that she was pregnant again. It certainly explained the sudden bouts of sickness she'd been experiencing lately. For a dreadful moment she thought she might have fallen victim to the plague but it seemed to have passed Bebbanburg by.

But it wasn't the plague that bothered him. Oswiu was making a tour of the north of his kingdom and planned to stay at Bebbanburg for several days. It wasn't the presence of the king that bothered Catinus; it was the size of his entourage and, to add to his problems, that of the queen who would be accompanying him.

The days when Oswiu would travel around with just his chaplain, his gesith and a few servants were gone. Now he was accompanied by several nobles and their retinues, a horde of administrators and clerks, several priests in addition to his chaplain, Conomultus, and Abbot Wilfrid, who seemed to have attached himself to the king like a leech. Furthermore, the queen would be accompanied by her chaplain and her own servants.

All in all he would have to find accommodation for some one hundred and twenty people in addition to the seventy who normally lived there. Even if he only housed the king, his gesith, his servants and the queen and hers in the fortress, he would have to move most of his own people out. They and the rest of the court would have to camp elsewhere. However, there was no source of fresh water nearby for the camp. The fortress had a well, as did the vill, but the latter was some distance from the flat land near the fortress that was otherwise the most suitable for a camp. The nearest fresh running water was a couple of miles away.

It was Leoflaed who came up with the solution. The northern section of the palisade was built around the high ground where his hall and the warriors' hall were located. She suggested that they extended the fortress to encompass the area to the north. It consisted of two reasonably flat areas divided by a slope. They would build a large hall of wattle and daub with a thatched roof fairly quickly on the nearest area of flat ground, which they would occupy with their family and gesith pro tem. The king and queen would be housed in their hall, which was the old king's hall in any case, and his gesith and some servants would be accommodated in the warriors' hall. The clerks and the rest of the entourage would have to camp in the lower of the two flat areas inside the fortress.

It would, of course, be expensive but Catinus decided that he had little choice. When he had the time and more money he would extend the palisade to enclose the new buildings and improve them as suitable guest accommodation for the next royal visit.

Oswiu was surprised at the new extension and told Catinus that he hadn't expected him to have to move out. He added that he would have been happy to camp to the west of the fortress.

'But there's no water there, Cyning.'

'No, but it would have been far cheaper for you to get your cooper to make some water barrels and hire some carts.'

As it was, the well inside the fortress had problems coping with the demand and Catinus still had to resort to buying a few barrels and hiring carts to bring water in from the river a few miles away.

The following morning Oswiu left with Conomultus and six of his gesith to travel to Lindisfarne. Wilfrid had asked to accompany the king but he had told him in no uncertain terms that to do so wouldn't be appropriate. He wanted a private conversation with Finan and Wilfrid's presence would have made that impossible. He did, however, invite Catinus to accompany him.

It was a fine day, sunny with a gentle breeze off the sea, which put everyone in a good mood. Apart from the noise of the horses in motion, the only sounds were the distant bleating of sheep on a distant hillside and the cry of seagulls.

'I haven't had the opportunity to thank you for sorting out the situation in Strathclyde for me,' the king told him as they rode along, side by side.

'Thank you, Cyning, but it was more luck than anything, especially running across Lethlobar.'

'Sneaking into the fortress and capturing the main gate wasn't luck. It was clever and bold.'

'Perhaps. Hopefully Elfin will now remain an ally and rule for some time.'

'Have you heard that Domangart of Dalriada is ill?'

'Yes; I gather he is likely to die. Who will succeed him?'

'Domangart's only son died last year so I suspect it will one of the two sons of Connal; either Máel Dúin or Domnall Dhu. Neither are likely to prove friendly considering that Oswald and I helped to depose and kill their father.'

'Where will that leave King Eochaid and his son Lethlobar? They are still allied to Dalriada, even if they are no longer subject to the high king.'

Oswiu looked at Catinus in surprise.

'Are you a mind reader? I want you to go to Ulster and sound out your friend Lethlobar for me. Eochaid is in his late fifties now and somewhat frail. His son is the real ruler of the Ulaidh.'

Catinus' heart sank. He had hoped to remain at Bebbanburg, at least until his second child was born. However, there was nothing to be done about it. He owed everything to Oswiu and he would just have to put a brave face on it.

'At least I don't have to worry about the south for now,' Oswiu went on. 'You know that Wessex have pushed the Britons back across the River Sabrina?'

'Yes, at last they seem to have a defensible border with the Welsh.'

'Quite; but that hasn't pleased Wulfhere. He is obviously worried that Cenwahl of Wessex is becoming too powerful.'

'Won't you have to support King Cenwahl if it comes to war?'

'No, I promised Wulfhere I would no longer come to the aid of Wessex when we reached the agreement by which he became King of Mercia. Cenwahl is aware, of course, even if he doesn't like it much. However, I've arranged a betrothal between my son Ecgfrith and Audrey, Anna's daughter. I want East Anglia as an ally in the east as insurance just in case Mercia ever thinks of invading Northumbria again.'

At that moment they arrived at the beginning of the strand that separated Lindisfarne from the mainland. The tide was halfway out but coming in fast. This didn't deter Oswiu and he galloped across the sands with his escort trailing behind him. By the time he reached the far side and climbed up into the dunes his horse's hooves were splashing in the incoming waves. Catinus looked at his king with disbelief. Such recklessness in a youth he could understand, but not in a mature, almost elderly, man. Oswiu's face shone with pleasure at beating the tide and Catinus realised that here was a man who delighted in taking risks and winning, even now when he was in his late forties. He looked quizzically at his brother who just shrugged and grinned. He was used to Oswiu's sudden whims and nothing the king did surprised him now. By the time that the last man had struggled to safety the sea was fetlock deep.

They rode across the island to the monastery where Abbot Finan awaited them, together with the prior, a monk called Colman. As it was such a warm day, Finan suggested that he and the king should take a walk as they chatted. Catinus, Conomultus and Colman followed them out of earshot.

'Do you know why the king has come?' the prior asked them.

Catinus shrugged, eager to avoid such a loaded question from a man he didn't know. However, after an uncomfortable silence Conomultus answered him.

'Only that he seeks Finan's advice.'

He paused, then decided to answer more fully. After all, the Prior of Lindisfarne could prove to a valuable ally.

'My guess would be that, having become reconciled with the queen, he is troubled by the fact that he was brought up on Iona and espouses the faith preached by the Celtic Church whilst his wife resolutely follows Rome. The situation is not helped by the influence of Abbot Wilfrid of Ripon. He has recently converted the king's son, Alchfrith, to the Roman Church.'

'Wilfrid! That snake in the grass!'

'You know him?'

'When I arrived as a novice the year after you left I was told of the problems that you and Eata had with him.'

Conomultus only grunted but Catinus replied for him.

'My brother probably wants to forget him. I heard that Wilfrid ended up at Cantwareburg before forging a reputation for himself as something of a scholar in Frankia and in Rome. I seem to remember also that he was the ill-fated Eorl of Hexham's son.'

'Yes, Oswiu may have forgotten, but Wilfrid has no cause to love him after what happened to his father,' Conomultus replied.

'He was banished to Iona wasn't he?' Catinus asked.

'Yes. His other son, Rægenhere, is a monk here on Lindisfarne. Thankfully he's nothing like either his father or his brother,' Colman replied.

'You seem to think that this Wilfrid is likely to pose a problem for the king?' Catinus asked his brother.

'He has every reason to hate Oswiu, and his influence with the queen and with Alchfrith of Deira means that he's in a position to tear the family apart if he wanted too. However, he is a vain and ambitious man so he may have some other goal in mind.'

~~~

Cuthbert was rather surprised when Eata told him that Wilfrid had asked for him to move to Ripon as his guest-master. Melrose had its fair share of passing travellers but Ripon was rapidly becoming a much more important monastery and, being just off the old Roman road to the north, it was now a major staging post for travelling nobles and merchants. Somehow Wilfrid had heard of Cuthbert and, as a man who always wanted the best, he'd evidently decided that he had to have him. No doubt being an eorl's son helped.

'I'm not sure I should go, father abbot.'

'I loathe Wilfrid but Melrose is a mere daughter house of Lindisfarne and a poor one at that. Ripon is Oswiu's foundation and boasts a stone church built in the fashion of the grand churches of Frankia and Italia, or will do when it is eventually complete. It will be important in due course and this is a real opportunity for you, Cuthbert.'

'Father Abbot, you know very well that I detest grandeur and pomp. There is nothing that I've heard about Wilfrid that makes me admire him, except perhaps his scholarship.'

'That is the reason I think you should accept. You will learn much more from him than you ever will from me.'

'But I don't seek to become a theologian. I merely want to serve Our Lord to the best of my ability.'

'And do you think you can do that better here than at Ripon.'

Cuthbert thought for a moment. Eata's encouragement for him, an aesthetic Celtic monk, to join the haughty and ambitious Roman cleric at Ripon had puzzled him and first; now he understood why.

'You want a friend at court?'

Eata laughed. 'I can't fool you, can I? Yes, Wilfrid is a real threat to the authority of the Celtic Church in the north. Oswiu is under pressure from his wife and son as well as the odious Wilfrid to accept the supremacy of Rome. Only Bishop Finan and his confessor, Conomultus, are on our side. This isn't a battle in the sense that you understand it, but it is a fight nevertheless. I'm thankful that Deusdedit of Cantwareburg is busy consolidating his own position in the south as the first Anglo-Saxon archbishop to be overly concerned with us. I thought that the absence abroad of Rome's greatest advocate in the North, James the Deacon, might have led to a respite in the struggle between the two churches in Northumbria, but Wilfrid is proving to be an even more formidable foe.'

'And that's how you regard him, as our enemy?'

'Yes, Jesus never intended us to be powerful in the secular sense or to be rich. We are the servants of even the poorest in the land, but Roman clerics seem to covet the trappings of the nobility. The Pope is their monarch and the bishops their princes. It's wrong.'

'So what is it you expect of me, Eata? Am I to be your spy at Ripon? I don't think I would be very comfortable with that.'

'No. You should know me better than to think I would ask that of you. I do hope, though, that you can use your influence to keep the monks there true to their calling.'

'I see. You want me to earn their respect and persuade them to follow a life of poverty and devotion only to God and to eschew the lures of Mammon?'

'Precisely. You will have an ally in the prior – a man called Sebbi - but he is not a strong enough character to resist Wilfrid. Fortunately the latter is rarely there; he is too busy currying favour with and seeking funds from his royal patrons.'

'And you think I'm the man to lead them in resisting their abbot?'

'I wouldn't have put it like that exactly but, yes; I think you have the force of personality to lead the monks along the right path.'

A fortnight later Cuthbert arrived at the new monastery at Ripon to find Wilfrid was still away – once again staying with King Alchfrith at Loidis. He soon realised that Alchfrith's advocacy of the Roman Church posed a far greater danger than the disloyalty of the monks to their Celtic heritage. Almost universally they wore the Celtic tonsure and followed the Celtic rites, including the celebration of Easter on the date of the Jewish Passover. Diplomatically they also celebrated it on the date laid down by the Roman Church - that is the first Sunday after the first full moon following the Vernal Equinox. Wilfrid had tried to forbid their observance of the Celtic Easter but they had ignored him.

Cuthbert first met his new abbot after he had been at Ripon for three weeks. He rode into the courtyard in front of the new church that had now reached the stage where the timber rafters were being placed on the top of the side walls. Wilfrid was mounted on a horse that was more suited to a noble than a cleric and was dressed in a soft woollen habit died a light brown, quite a contrast to the rough homespun ones worn by the rest of the monks. Over this he wore an oiled red cloak pinned at the neck by a gold broach fashioned as an intricate pattern of intertwined snakes.

Cuthbert fingered his plain wooden crucifix as his lips curled in distain when he saw the heavy ornate gold one embossed with several jewels worn by the abbot. He studied his face surreptitiously and saw a face that would have been angular if the sharp bones hadn't been hidden by plump flesh. It was in keeping with the slightly rotund body. Obviously the good abbot liked his food and drink.

When he dismounted a boy ran up and took the reins to lead the horse away to the stables. Wilfrid lowered the cowl of his cloak revealing his Roman tonsure. Even this was dissimilar to that of other Roman monks that Cuthbert had met. They had the hair shaved from the crown of their head to a diameter of four inches. That on Wilfrid's head couldn't have measured more than an inch and a half across.

The abbot looked at the monks standing outside the nearly completed church and smiled, but it didn't reach his eyes and Cuthbert thought he detected a hint of a sneer before he greeted the prior. His eyes then lit on Cuthbert and he walked towards him, hand outstretched.

'You must be our new guest-master. Welcome Brother Cuthbert. Welcome to Ripon. I trust you had a good journey from, where was it? Ah yes, Melrose.'

He said Melrose as if it left a nasty taste in his mouth. Cuthbert shook the proffered hand and a surprised frown disfigured the abbot's fleshy face. It was only then that Cuthbert suspected that Wilfrid had expected him to kneel at his feet and kiss his ornate gold ring studded with gems. The man's next words confirmed it.

'It is normal for monks to kneel and kiss my ring,' Wilfrid said with some asperity, whipping his hand away from the other man's grasp.

'Not in the Celtic Church it isn't, father abbot. We kneel only to God and to His Son, Jesus Christ.'

For a moment he thought that Wilfrid was going to strike him. It took a little time for the abbot to regain his composure before he hissed his displeasure at the new guest-master.

'I was told that you were a devout and obedient monk and I had expected you to treat me with the respect due to my position. I see now that it may have been a mistake to have appointed you to a position of responsibility here. I shall make sure that our patron, King Alchfrith, knows of my displeasure with you, as it was his idea to send for you.'

'You must do as your conscience dictates, abbot, and I will do the same. I am happy to return to Melrose, or to go wherever else God needs me. Perhaps to Eoforwīc? Father Conomultus tells me that the king – that is King Oswiu, not his son and vassal – would welcome me as a member of his administration.'

A look of alarm appeared on Wilfrid's face. Cuthbert was evidently going to be an enemy and the last thing he wanted was for him to become close to Oswiu.

'You have a clever tongue, Cuthbert; too clever. You have evidently been with that, arseling Eata, for too long. You will stay here and learn proper humility and obedience. As a start you will keep a vigil on your knees in front of the altar for forty eight hours without food or water whilst you contemplate your many failings, including the sin of pride.'

Cuthbert was shocked at the word Wilfrid had used to describe the pious Eata and he had to bite back the rebuke that came unbidden to his lips. It was something he expected warriors to say, but not churchmen. He paused to compose himself before continuing.

'If you so desire, father abbot, I will of course comply; but perhaps you might wish to join me? I'm sure I'm not the only one who is guilty of the sin of pride.'

'How dare you! Get out of my sight before I have you whipped.'

Without another word Cuthbert walked into the half built church. The inside was bare apart from the wooden table that served as a temporary altar and the simple wooden cross sitting on it. He knelt before it and bowed his head in prayer, shutting his mind to everything else to concentrate on meditation.

Outside the prior regarded his abbot with unconcealed distaste.

'That was undeserved, father abbot. Only a petty minded man would inflict such a penance on a senior monk for standing up for his beliefs.'

'Do you want to join him?' Wilfrid replied with a snarl.

Without a word the prior went in to kneel by Cuthbert's side. Wilfrid realised that he was beginning to look like a fool and his temper grew worse as a result.

'Is my new hall finished?' he spat at the unfortunate monk who supervised the building work.

'N-no, father abbot,' the man stuttered. 'We are concentrating on finishing the church, working on the roof first, and then there's the chancel and the apse to...'

His voice trailed away as he recoiled from the thunderous look Wilfrid was giving him.

'You mean that you haven't even started work on it?'

'N-no. I thought that the church should be the priority. Is not the house of God more important? Your hut is ready for you, of course.'

His voice faded and he swallowed hard.

'You expect me to live in a hovel?'

'We have to, abbot,' one of the other monks called out. 'Why shouldn't you? Other abbots lead by example and share the privations of their monks.'

There was a loud murmur of agreement.

'It is also normal for monks to elect their abbot,' another said. 'We didn't elect you, you were imposed on us. Perhaps it's time we had a proper election.'

Wilfrid couldn't understand what was happening. The humble and obedient had suddenly risen in revolt and he was now seriously alarmed for his safety. The two warriors who had escorted him there were about to return to Loidis but Wilfrid yelled at them to dismount and protect him. The two were members of Alchfrith's warband; they might be prepared to die for their king, but they felt little loyalty to Wilfrid, especially after what they had just witnessed. However, they had been charged with his protection.

'I think you had better ride back to Loidis with us, abbot. You'll be safe there,' the senior of the two said, not without a hint of derision.

Wilfrid flushed but nodded. Once his horse had been brought back he, his servant and the two warriors trotted out of the gate and back onto the road south.

'You can get up now, Brother Cuthbert,' the prior said as soon as he was told of Wilfrid's departure.

'He ordered me to do penance for forty eight hours and he is my abbot, whatever we may think of him, so here I stay for two days.'

'Well, my old knees won't stand for it so, if you'll excuse me I'll leave you to it.'

Cuthbert nodded and remained on his knees, only changing position to lie prone with his arms outstretched before the altar at times to prevent his knees locking up. He didn't like doing it but he was sure that God didn't want him to cripple himself.

~~~

Oswiu hadn't wanted to push things with Eanflæd. He was thankful that they were back on speaking terms at last and, although their relationship had improved considerably since the return from Whitby, it was still early days. When they had stayed at Bebbanburg they had gone riding together, talked animatedly as before and had even cavorted in the sea like a couple of children. However, they still slept in separate beds. It had been a little awkward whilst they had stayed with Catinus because he had given them the screened off part of the hall normally occupied by him, Leoflaed and their children. Oswiu had used the small bed where little Hereswith and her nurse normally slept, leaving his wife to occupy the main bed. At least they had shared the same chamber once more, if not the bed.

'Don't you think it's about time we started to act like man and wife again?'

Oswiu was taken by surprise, both by the statement and by the sultry way it was said. They had been back at Eoforwīc for over a month by then and the nights were drawing in as Christmas approached. They had been sitting in front of the fire blazing in the central hearth of the king's hall talking about nothing in particular when Eanflæd had suddenly whispered in his ear.

He grinned at her and, scooping her up in his arms, he carried her through the doorway into the chamber where he had slept alone for so long. Placing her on the bed he gently started to disrobe her but she responded by pulling his clothes off more urgently. It was evident that she had missed him in her bed just as much as he'd missed her.

They made love three times that night, at first like a couple of wild animals and then more gently. The next morning Oswiu woke with a sore back and grinned when he realised that she had clawed at him with her nails and drawn blood in the throes of her passion. He entered her whilst she was still asleep and she woke looking alarmed before smiling at him when she realised what was going on.

'You've no idea how much I missed this,' she murmured.

'Not as much as I have,' he whispered back.

'You remained faithful?'

She thought that he had but not many men, let alone a powerful king, would have gone without having sex for very long. There were many women who would have readily shared Oswiu's bed.

'Of course. Didn't you think I would?'

'Yes, but it shows how much you must love me.'

Nothing more was said as he finished what he'd begun. She sighed in contentment and pulled him to her as he shuddered in pleasure. Three months later, as the snow lay on the ground, she told him that she was pregnant once more.

~~~

A hundred and fifty miles to the north Leoflaed had just given birth to a son. Catinus was in Ulster at the time. He had ridden across the country to Caer Luel in Rheged and sailed from there to Larne in Ulster, Eochaid's capital. As the birlinn he was on approached the port two smaller ships came out to ask their business.

'I'm Ealdorman Catinus and I'm known to Prince Lethlobar. I'm here as the emissary of King Oswiu to his friend King Eochaid,' he called out across the water.

'I remember you from Dùn Dè, Catinus. Men are still talking about how you managed to sneak into the fortress and take it,' the man standing in the prow of the leading ship called back. 'Follow me in.'

'Have you come to aid us in our fight against Dúngal?' the man who had greeted him asked as soon as they were ashore.

'Is he the leader of the Uí Néill?'

The man, who had introduced himself as Fiachra, shook his head.

'The Uí Néill are too busy fighting amongst themselves again to bother us. No, unfortunately so are we. Dúngal Eilni mac Scandail is a distant cousin of King Eochaid and he fancies himself as something of a war leader, so he's trying to gather support amongst the Ulaidh to seize the throne as soon as Eochaid dies. Lethlobar is doing the same; trying to gather as much backing as possible I mean.'

'I assume that, in the current situation, the Ulaidh are in no position to get involved in the struggle for the throne of Dalriada?'

Fiachra looked at Catinus sharply, then shook his head again.

'The days when we were one kingdom divided by the sea are long gone, Catinus. It doesn't matter to us who sits on the throne at Dùn Add.'

Dùn Add was the fortress on the west coast of Caledonia where the High King of Dalriada was based.

'Unless they intervened to support one contender for the throne of the Ulaidh against another?'

'Why would they do that?'

'To gain an army to help in their struggle for the throne, perhaps?'

'What have you heard?'

'Only rumours. Look, I think I need to find Lethlobar. Where is he at the moment?'

'I'll take you to meet him, but first come and meet King Eochaid.'

He wasn't what Catinus had expected. He knew that he was nearly a decade older than Oswiu but the man who watched him enter his hall had bright, alert eyes and appeared little older than his own king. It wasn't until he tried to shift his position on the ornately carved throne that Catinus realised that Eochaid suffered from pain in his joints and could hardly move without assistance.

'Welcome Ealdorman. Any friend of Oswiu's is a friend of mine.'

He had spoken in English so Catinus replied in the same language.

'Thank you, Cyning. My king sends his greetings and wishes to thank you for your son's help in resolving the problems in Strathclyde.'

For a moment Eochaid looked puzzled and Catinus wondered whether Lethlobar had told him about the death of Mermin and the capture of Dùn Breatainn. If not, he wondered what else his son had kept from his father.

'Did he now; yes well. My son is a most resourceful young man.'

Eochaid invited Catinus to come and sit on a stool by his side. It was only then that he noticed a young boy sitting on a smaller stool on the king's other side. The child smiled brightly at him and Catinus smiled back politely, wondering who he was. When he had been with him in Strathclyde Lethlobar had said nothing about having a younger brother.

'I don't suppose that Oswiu sent you all this way to a man he hasn't seen for over twenty years to enquire after my health. Why don't you tell me why you're here?'

Catinus thought for a moment before replying, but decided there was little to be lost by being honest.

'As Bretwalda of Caledonia he is concerned about the current situation in Dalriada. I'm sure that you are well aware of the situation. Oswiu is determined that it mustn't be allowed to disrupt the fragile peace that has existed throughout Caledonia in recent years.'

'You haven't heard then?'

'Heard what,' he said more sharply than he had intended, then added 'Cyning' to soften his reply.

'Domangart is dead and Domnall Dhu is now on the throne. I fear he is no friend of Oswiu's; or of mine. I was close to Oswald, who he blames for his father's overthrow and death.'

'When did this happen?'

'A month ago I believe; I only heard about it recently so I'm not surprised that the news hasn't reached Northumbria yet.'

'No, it hasn't. I must return and let Oswiu know as soon as possible.'

'It's far too late to set out today. At least stay tonight and keep an old man company.'

'Yes, of course. Thank you.'

~~~

'Sail in sight.'

The bellow from the ship's boy up the mast of his birlinn didn't improve Catinus' headache. He'd stayed up drinking with Eochaid, listening to the stories of his and Oswald's exploits when they were young until it was nearly dawn. He had only just fallen asleep on the hard packed earthen floor of the hall when one of the boys had woken him to tell him that the shipmaster was about to leave to catch the tide.

He had tried to catch some more sleep on the birlinn's deck but its motion soon had him lurching to the gunwale to say goodbye to the food he'd eaten the previous evening. Thankfully he'd spewed over the leeward side of the ship. He'd only just started to feel a little better when the boy's call awoke him.

'Whose ship is it?' he asked the shipmaster when he reached where he was standing.

'Not ship, ships. There are three of them, which is not good news in these waters.'

'Irish then?'

'Or possibly Mercian pirates from Man.'

'Are they birlinns?'

'Their sails are only just coming over the horizon so I can't tell from here. Jared, can you make out what size they are?'

The twelve year old up the mast, whose name was evidently Jared, looked hard with shaded eyes for a moment.

'Difficult to tell as yet, but there are only three; no that's wrong. There are more behind them. They look to be smaller than us; perhaps pontos or currachs, but I can now see five of them.'

'Can we outrun them?'

'Probably; the wind is from the west so they are on a broad reach and they'll have to tack soon. We are larger and better built so we should be able to get away from them if we turn about onto the same course. The trouble is, we need to head south east to get home and that's straight towards them. If we head away from them, it'll take us into Dalriadan waters.'

'Should we not head back into Lough Larne in that case?' Catinus asked the shipmaster, alarmed by Jared's report.

'If we try they may be able to head us off before we get there, as we'd have to turn directly into the wind and row. We've barely got one man for each oar and they may have more. That means ours will tire quicker.'

Catinus thought quickly. The last thing he wanted was to head north into the numerous islands that were part of Dalriada. If Domnall got hold of one of Oswiu's nobles he would probably send him a present of his head in a basket. If the approaching ships captured him they'd ransom him if he was lucky, or kill him out of hand if he wasn't. No, he decided, heading back to Larne was the safest course of action.

It was a close run thing. The birlinn's rowers tired as they approached the headland that marked the entrance to the lough and the leading pontos was closing fast, but then Catinus swapped six of his men for the most exhausted members of the crew and the other four took their bows out of their oiled leather sheaths. Two minutes later three volleys of arrows sped across the sea, one after the other, and half a dozen of the enemy rowers on the side nearest to them were hit. It was enough. The pontos slewed through ninety degrees as the power died on one side and the ship nearly broached.

This time when Catinus stepped ashore at Larne he was greeted by the quiet boy who had sat beside Eochaid in the hall when he'd arrived. At some stage before the feast the boy had disappeared. Now he was flanked by four of the Ulster king's gesith.

'Welcome back, Catinus. We didn't expect to see you again so soon. Was the sea a little rough for your delicate stomach?'

He looked at the boy sharply, not expecting to be teased by someone so young. The boy grinned at him and he couldn't help smiling back, despite the twinge of annoyance he'd felt. The boy wasn't as young as he'd first thought in the dim light of the king's hall. He was probably eleven or twelve and had bright red, almost orange, hair that came down to his shoulders.

'You know who I am but I've no idea who you are, apart from being an impudent brat, that is.'

'I'm Ruaidhrí, the king's bastard. Lethlobar hates me because he thinks our father prefers me to him. He doesn't, but he finds me amusing, so I play the fool and keep out of the way as much as possible when my brother's around.'

His name meant *the Red King*, which suited his hair but was probably not the best name for someone who might be viewed as a rival for Eochaid's throne.

'You surprise me. I only met Lethlobar once but we liked each other straight away. I got the distinct impression he was fair-minded though. Are you as insolent to him as you were to me just now? If so, I can understand why that might turn him against you.'

'Oh! Perhaps I was a little too disrespectful to you just then. I apologise, but I didn't mean to offend you. I just can't help trying to make people laugh. That way I hope they don't regard me as a threat and that I'll live a little longer.'

Catinus thought he was being flippant again but he saw that the boy was being deadly serious.

'You really think that your life is under threat?'

'I've probably said too much, especially to a stranger. Forget I said anything.'

With that Ruaidhrí stood aside and let Catinus enter the king's hall first.

'Ruaidhrí told me that he's also your son,' Catinus said to Eochaid quietly when the boy had left them alone.

The king sighed. 'Yes, presumably he also told you that he is illegitimate? But it's not as simple as that.'

Eochaid was silent for a moment as he debated whether to tell Catinus the full story.

'Can I trust you, Catinus? After all, I know nothing about you.'

'What do you want to know?'

'Well, Catinus is hardly an Anglo-Saxon name, is it? And yet you are an ealdorman, the equivalent of a chieftain or a petty king in Ireland.'

'I was born a Briton in Mercia and entered Oswiu's service with my brother as scouts when we were boys. I think he was going to kill us when our task was done but he didn't and we've managed to serve him well over the years. Now my brother is his chaplain and I'm an ealdorman.'

'I suspect that there is a great deal more to your story than that, but I'll let it go. I take it, therefore, that you are loyal to him?'

'Of course. My brother and I owe him everything.'

'Very well. His brother Oswald was my greatest friend but I parted from him on bad terms, something I've always regretted. Oswiu and I have never been that close but he was Oswald's favourite brother and I admire him for what he's achieved. A few years after I returned to Ulster to become King of the Ulaidh I was challenged for the throne by the chieftain of one of the most powerful clans that make up our nation. We fought and I won. In the course of sacking his main stronghold I rescued a very pretty girl from being raped. My wife, Lethlobar's mother, was still alive then but I was enchanted by the girl and I brought her back here to Larne with me.

'Needless to say my wife was less than happy about this and our son Lethlobar took her side. Nevertheless I couldn't give her up, so I established her in a hut with two slaves to look after her. I learned later that she was the only daughter of the chieftain who had rebelled but by then she was pregnant by me. I kept it quiet but the old woman who helped her give birth couldn't keep her mouth shut. When he found out about it Lethlobar was sixteen and beginning to make a name for himself as a warrior. He decided that both the girl and her baby son must die.

'Her father demanded her return as part of the terms for peace and, as the Uí Néill were getting restless again and I needed the Ulaidh to unite against them, I reluctantly agreed. The girl and her baby were returned to him and she was sent off in disgrace to become a nun. I never saw her again.

'In time I forgot about her but, when my wife died, I decided not to marry again. I did want Ruaidhrí back though, and I paid a great deal of silver to get him, much to Lethlobar's disgust when he found out.

'Ruaidhrí had been raised by a shepherd and his family and I hardly recognised the smelly, filthy eight year old who was brought to me as my son. Even his hair was matted with dirt and grease so that it looked black. At first I thought that I might have been deceived but, when he was scrubbed clean and his hair was washed properly he didn't look like the same child. He looked like his mother and I knew that, whatever Lethlobar said, I wanted the boy by my side. That was four years ago. He has the common sense to keep out of sight when my elder son is around but Lethlobar is often away and then I can enjoy Ruaidhrí's company.'

'Why are you telling me all this? You must have a reason.'

Eochaid sighed. 'I'm getting old and frail and I don't know how much longer I'll live. Lethlobar thinks he'll succeed me, but he doesn't have the support of enough of the Ulaidh to do so. They'll probably choose Dúngal Eilni mac Scandail of Clan Fiachna as he's the most powerful. He's Ruaidhrí's uncle and the brother of the girl I abducted. However, Ruaidhrí could be a double threat to him when he's older, being descended from both me and the leader of the Fiachna.

'So if Lethlobar doesn't kill him, Dúngal will?'

'I fear so.'

'How can I help?'

'I was going to send him to Iona to be educated with the novice monks in a few months when he turns twelve, but I no longer feel that he'd be safe there, especially with Domnall as King of Dalriada.'

'He would never violate the Holy Isle of Iona surely?'

'He might prevail upon the abbot to give him up though. After all, Iona is in his domain.'

'So, you want me to take him to Lindisfarne?'

'He should be safe there, yes.'

'Very well, provided you can give me a birlinn as escort back to Rheged.'

~~~

Ruaidhrí proved to be an entertaining companion. Once away from Ulster his whole personality changed. He no longer played the fool or tried to be impudent. Instead he became more respectful and his conversation became witty and quite erudite for one so young.

A messenger rode to meet him with the news that he had a son who had been christened Alaric. Immediately Catinus increased the pace but soon left the baggage horses behind, so he was forced to slow down again. He wondered idly what his new son would be like and whether he'd be a warrior like his father when he grew up. When Ruaidhrí caught up with him again he realised that he hadn't thought about the boy's future.

'What do you want to become when you're man, Ruaidhrí, a warrior or a cleric?'

'The life of a scholar has a certain appeal, as well as eliminating me as a threat to anyone, but I think I would find life in a monastery claustrophobic; and the dreary routine would drive me mad.'

'You could become a priest, like my brother.'

'Perhaps, but I want more out of life; even if it means that life is cut short.'

'So, you want to train as a warrior?'

'As soon as I can, which I suppose means fourteen, yes. However, that means finding a lord who will train me and employ me in his warband in due course. I don't suppose...'

He gave Catinus a cheeky grin, the first since leaving Ulster.

'You know full well the answer is yes.'

When they crested the last ridge before Bebbanburg Ruaidhrí whistled in appreciation.

'That makes Larne, or anywhere else in Ulster that I've seen, look like a hovel. That's your home?'

'Strictly speaking it's King Oswiu's but he rarely visits it now. I'm the custos and live there with my family so, yes, it's my home.'

'But you're more than the custos?'

'Yes, I have a number of thegns who owe me loyalty as their lord. My land stretches from the River Twaid in the north to the River Aln in the south.'

'Thegns?'

'Yes, there's no equivalent in Ireland. They are lords of one or more vills, which are areas of land occupied by freemen called ceorls – most farmers, but some artisans as well – the villeins, who are free but tied to the land and, of course, slaves.'

'Do these ceorls and villeins and their families live separate from each other then? Doesn't that make them vulnerable to attack?'

'Most live in settlements but some also live in isolation, especially in the Cheviot Hills over there.'

Catinus pointed to the dark hills topped by low cloud some fifteen miles or so to the south west of them.

'Your land stretches into those distant hills?'

'Yes, as far as the junction of the Rivers Twaid and Teviot, all except for Yeavering, which is a royal possession. Beyond that the land belongs to the Eorl of Dùn Èideann and the Abbot of Melrose.'

'And in the south?'

'Another ealdorman, Alweo.'

'Alweo? Penda's nephew?'

'You are remarkably well informed.'

'Is he your friend?'

'Perhaps not like Oswald and your father were friends but, yes, he's my friend. Now, enough talking. I want to see my son.'

With that, Catinus dug his heels in and galloped the rest of the way to the fortress. As soon as he entered the gates he jumped off his horse, leaving a startled stable boy to chase after the snorting stallion and calm him after the hectic race to the fortress, and ran into his hall.

He found Leoflaed suckling the baby in their bed. He paused at the door, his chest heaving until he steadied his breathing, and watched them until she looked up; a brilliant smile lighting her face when she saw her husband standing there.

'Thank the Lord that you're safe, Catinus. I was worried about you.'

He crossed the room and gently kissed her on the mouth before stroking the few strands of dark hair on the baby's head.

'Do you approve of my choice of name?'

'Alaric? It means noble ruler, doesn't it? A fitting name for my son and heir.'

At that moment a hesitant Ruaidhrí appeared at the door, unsure whether to intrude or go and find somewhere to wait until Catinus remembered him. Leoflaed noticed him first.

'Who are you and what do you want? Do you have a message for my husband?'

'I apologise for disturbing you at such a time, lady. I didn't release that you were, er, um.'

'Not like you to be lost for words, Ruaidhrí. Go and wait in the hall, I'll come and find you shortly.'

'Who is he? He's too well dressed to be a servant.'

'He's the son of King Eochaid of the Ulaidh in Ireland. It's a long story which I'll tell you later. I said that I would escort him to Lindisfarne to be educated in the monastery.'

'He's to be a monk then?'

'No, I promised him a place in my warband when he's older. Look, forget about him, are you fully recovered?'

'Enough for you to make love to me again, you mean?'

He blushed. 'I had better go and sort Ruaidhrí out,' he stammered and made a hurried exit. It was exactly what he'd been wondering about but he'd been embarrassed when his wife had guessed.

~~~

Catinus had invited Ruaidhrí to stay for the Christmas celebrations and a few days later he rode northwards with him toward Lindisfarne. As soon as he'd landed at Caer Luel he'd sent a messenger to Oswiu at Eoforwīc to acquaint him with the situation, both in Dalriada and Ulster, but he intuitively felt he should report to him in person as well. He intended to set out as soon as he'd taken the boy to meet Finan but, as they entered the gap in the hawthorn hedge that formed the perimeter of the monastery, he knew that something was wrong.

Finan was dead. The abbot was elderly but quite spritely the last time that Catinus had seen him. Apparently he'd died suddenly in his sleep. The ealdorman went to pay his respects and found the old man in a simple wooden coffin on the floor in front of the altar. He looked at peace but his face displayed the pale grey pallor of the dead. Catinus crossed himself and said a swift prayer before exiting the church. Unheated stone buildings were cold in winter at the best of times but today it seemed ten degrees colder than the air outside.

The monks had already elected the prior – Colman – as their next abbot but they wanted the king's blessing on their choice. Furthermore they needed a bishop to ordain Colman as the next

Bishop of Northumbria. Catinus therefore offered to escort Colman to Eoforwīc.

There remained the problem of Ruaidhrí. A monastery in mourning was a gloomy place and, unsurprisingly, the boy didn't want to start his education at such an inauspicious time. In the end, Catinus, said that he could accompany him and Colman to Eoforwīc and then start his schooling on Lindisfarne upon his return.

'I congratulate you on your election, Brother Colman. Naturally I'm more than happy to accept the monks' choice as abbot,' Oswiu said warmly.

Finan and he had disagreed on a number of subjects and secretly he wasn't sorry he was dead. He only hoped that he would get more support from Colman.

'Of course, we will have to find another bishop to consecrate you,' he went on.

Wilfrid, who was standing off to one side with Oswiu's son, Alchfrith of Deira, frowned at this. He had been trying to persuade Oswiu to move the seat of the bishop to Eoforwīc; Lindisfarne was such a remote place in his opinion and he was doing his best to get himself chosen as the next incumbent. He saw no reason why it should be tied to the abbacy of Lindisfarne.

He was also making progress with his scheme to replace the Celtic Church with that of Rome in Northumbria and he now saw the chance to make a little mischief.

'There are several suitable bishops you might ask to conduct the ordination, Cyning. Perhaps Bishop Boniface of the East Angles would be a suitable choice in view of the marriage of your son Ecgfrith to their king's niece?'

Oswiu scowled. Although Audrey was King Æthelwold's niece, she was twenty five and had already buried one husband. She hadn't appealed much to the virile fifteen year old Ecgfrith, especially as she was reputed to be a virgin. Oswiu needed the alliance and wanted it sealed through a union of their two families.

It was unfortunate that they were the only two available candidates for this.

His son had agreed, albeit very reluctantly, to the match, but he reproached his father about it every time they met. The situation wasn't helped by Audrey's refusal to share her new husband's bed. He gave up after a while and took a mistress instead.

Before Oswiu could respond to Wilfrid's suggestion Colman replied with some vehemence.

'No, Boniface is a Roman Catholic. If I am to be consecrated it must be a bishop of the true church, the Celtic Church.'

Oswiu sighed wearily. It looked as if Colman was going to be as difficult as Finan had been.

'Very well. Who do you suggest?'

'Bishop Utta of Prydenn is probably the nearest.'

'A Pict?'

Wilfrid looked horrified.

'No, not a Pict. He's an Angle, like you. He used to be my Chaplain,' Oswiu almost snapped at him.

He was getting tired of the continual bickering between the churchmen belonging to one or other of the two Churches. He'd been brought up in the Celtic faith but his wife, Alchfrith and Wilfrid, who were all Roman Catholics, were beginning to wear him down.

'I could take Abbot Colman north by sea once the season for winter gales has passed,' Catinus offered helpfully, earning himself a dirty look from Wilfrid and a venomous glare from Alchfrith.

'Yes, good idea. Thank you Catinus. Helpful as ever.'

The smile that Oswiu gave the ealdorman of Bebbanburg was warm and friendly, something that wasn't lost on either Alchfrith or Wilfrid.

At noon Catinus and Colman were invited to sit with the king for the main meal of the day. Eanflæd was noticeable by her absence and Catinus wondered whether she and Oswiu had fallen out again until his brother explained that she was expecting another baby and suffering from the sickness that often seemed to be a feature of the early stages of pregnancy. Colman, Wilfrid, Alchfrith, his wife Kyneburga – sister of Wulfhere of Mercia, Ecgfrith and Ethelred, Kyneburga's brother, made up the top table.

Ethelred had remained at Oswiu's court, not so much as a hostage but as a possible alternative king to Wulfhere should Mercia become a problem again. In any case, it was an open secret that the two brothers didn't get on and Wulfhere was likely to either imprison him or kill him if Ethelred fell into his hands.

Alchfrith's recent wedding to Kyneburga had been another political move to strengthen the truce between Northumbria and Mercia. However, unlike Ecgfrith's marriage to Audrey, Alchfrith and Kyneburga seemed to have a happy relationship. Catinus wondered about Audrey's absence but Conomultus explained that she was on retreat to the monastery at Ely, something she was wont to do from time to time. Ecgfrith didn't seem to mind and, from the way that he kept looking at a young girl sitting at one of the other tables, Catinus surmised that she must be his mistress, Eormenburg.

When the main course, a spit roasted pig, was being served the main door into the hall was opened, letting in blast of icy air and a flurry of snow. Evidently winter was making itself felt for one last time before giving way to spring. The man who entered was dressed like a cleric but he had no tonsure, either above his forehead like Colman or on the crown of his head like Wilfrid. He looked to be in his late twenties or early thirties and carried himself with a certain authority.

'Aldfrith. What's he doing here?' Conomultus said quietly to his brother.

'I thought he was a scholar on Iona?'

'He was, or so I thought.'

'Aldfrith!' Oswiu exclaimed getting up from his seat. 'What brings you to Eoforwīc?'

'You do, father. How long is it since we last saw each other?'

Aldfrith was the illegitimate son of Oswiu and Fianna, the daughter of a farmer on Bute that he had taken as his mistress when she was thirteen. When he had fallen in love with

Rhieinmelth, the daughter of the last King of Rheged, he quickly forgot about Fianna and their son. Although Oswiu had made sporadic attempts to improve the relationship between them, Aldfrith had become alienated from his father. The last thing he was likely to do was to travel all the way from Iona to visit him.

'Many years, to my regret. Come, sit by me. Bring another chair for my eldest son.'

Both Alchfrith and Ecgfrith looked askance at their half-brother. They were well aware that they were both rivals for their father's throne when the time came, but they had always discounted Aldfrith. The last thing either wanted was his restoration to favour.

However, Wilfrid welcomed him as if he were the prodigal son. To his annoyance Aldfrith ignored him and greeted Colman first.

'I was sorry to hear of Finan's death. He was a holy man and he is already being recognised as a saint. Congratulations on your election to succeed him.'

The two had met on Iona a few years previously and each respected the other. He went on to nod towards his two half-brothers, who acknowledged him, even if they didn't get up to greet him. Before he could pay his respects to Kyneburga or speak to either Catinus or Conomultus, Wilfrid tried again to welcome him.

'Aldfrith, it is a pleasure to meet such a renowned scholar at last.'

'Thank you, but I don't think we've met before?'

'Abbot Wilfrid of Ripon,'

'You are a long way from your monastery, Father Abbot. What brings you to my father's court?'

'I also act as the spiritual advisor to the queen and to King Alchfrith.'

'Strange; I thought they had their own chaplains for that, and surely it is the job of the Bishop of Northumbria to care for his flock. I'd have thought that you would need to stay at your monastery to look after your monks and the good people of Ripon?'

Wilfrid went red in the face. This wasn't going the way he'd expected, so he decided to change the subject.

'If you are not here to visit your father and brothers, perhaps you are travelling somewhere?'

'Indeed; not that it need be any concern of yours though, father abbot. Cyning, may we talk somewhere in private?' he asked turning back to his father.

'Will you not join us and have something to eat first? You must be hungry after your journey.'

'Thank you, but this is too rich a feast for me. Perhaps just a little bread, cheese and water?

As they were eating Conomultus and Catinus introduced themselves and Aldfrith briefed them on the latest situation in Dalriada and Ulster. Domnall Dhu had established himself as the undisputed King of Dalriada but relations with all his neighbours were poor. He had reportedly repudiated his allegiance to Oswiu as Bretwalda of Caledonia and had come out against Eochaid and Lethlobar, supporting instead the claim of Blathmac mac Máele Cobo to be King of the Ulaidh.

Catinus sensed Ruaidhrí stiffen at this. The boy was standing beside Leofric as they were acting as servers for him and Colman and he had clearly heard what Aldfrith had said.

'Is Eochaid still king then?'

'Yes, Blathmac and Lethlobar are fighting over the succession. I imagine that Eochaid will be allowed to live out his remaining days as king, in name if not in fact.'

'Aldfrith, I think I had better introduce you to the boy who is serving Father Colman. He is Ruaidhrí, Eochaid's son and Lethlobar's half-brother.'

'I'm sorry Ruaidhrí, I didn't mean to be insensitive. However, I understand that not a lot of love is lost between Lethlobar and yourself?'

'That is true, lord. However, I care for my father deeply and I'm very relieved to hear that he will be allowed to live out his time as king.'

'I'm curious, what is an Irish princeling doing so far from home?'

'I accompanied Ealdorman Catinus from Larne and I am acting as Bishop Colman's servant until I can return to Lindisfarne to start my training as a novice.'

'Do you wish to be a monk then?'

'I don't think so, but I have yet to experience the life so I can't be certain. However, I think I would prefer to be a warrior.'

'I see. You don't mind acting as a servant then, despite your birth?'

'No, I have no aspirations to be a prince, despite what Lethlobar believes.'

'What about you, Prince Aldfrith? Why is a renowned scholar of the Celtic Church journeying from Iona to Cantwareburg, the seat of the archbishop who leads the Roman Catholic Church in England?' Colman asked.

'Not prince, just Aldfrith please.'

Colman smiled at the mild rebuke. He approved of Aldfrith's aesthetic lifestyle and humility, as well as admiring him as a scholar. He felt a little guilty now for indulging himself at the feast and suspected that he would pay for his gluttony later.

'I'm researching the life of Saint Columba so that I can record it for posterity. Most of the information I need is either on Iona or in Ireland, but there are some books in Cantwareburg that may be helpful.'

'That is indeed a noble enterprise. I wish you God speed on your journey.'

'I wish I could go with you,' Ruaidhrí said wistfully.

'You know that's not possible,' Catinus told him. 'You father wishes you to be educated at Lindisfarne. You will have time to travel later, when you're a man.'

Ruaidhrí scowled at Catinus, frustrated because his journey to the south of England in the company of a man he liked and respected, even on so short an acquaintance, was to be denied him. Aldfrith had that effect on a lot of people. They instantly took to him and trusted him. It was a gift that would stand him in good stead in the future.

CHAPTER EIGHT – STRATHCLYDE

662 AD

Oswiu was visiting Bebbanburg again when the messenger from Elfin of Strathclyde reached him. He had delayed coming north to visit his provinces of Bernicia, Goddodin and Rheged until he was satisfied that his new son, Ælfwine, would live. It had been a long and difficult labour for Eanflæd and she swore after she'd recovered that she would have no more children.

The baby had struggled to breathe initially and had coughed a great deal. He had failed to thrive until Eanflæd took him away from his wet-nurse and breast fed him herself. Because her milk hadn't dried up before this, she took it as a sign from God that He wished her to feed the boy herself. Immediately the coughing stopped and he started to put on weight.

Now that Ælfwine was a plump nine-month-old baby who had started to crawl and get into mischief, Oswiu decided that the time had come to deal with Domnall Dhu. He had wasted no time in expanding the boundaries of Dalriada to include the area to the west of Loch Lomond. The north of this area was part of the Pictish Kingdom of Hyddir and the south belonged to Strathclyde. King Elfin, in particular, was alarmed as it meant that Domnall was now perilously close to his stronghold of Dùn Breatainn. Oswiu was afraid that the whole of Caledonia would return to its former state of instability unless he acted quickly.

Garnait, the High King of the Picts, had been strangely silent about Dalriada's encroachment but a messenger from Hunwald, who Oswiu had made Eorl of Prydenn when he had inherited the kingdom from his nephew, Talorgan, arrived two days later which explained why. Oswiu read the letter from Hunwald with mounting disquiet.

Cyning,

I fear that I am the barer of sad tidings. You will remember Ròidh, Aidan's friend and Bishop of Ardewr. I regret to tell you that he died peacefully in his sleep just over two months ago.

Oswiu looked at the bottom of the letter and saw that it a dated two weeks previously, so Ròidh had died in February. He went back to reading what Hunwald had to say.

Fergus relied on his elder brother's advice a great deal and, by all accounts, was grief stricken at his loss, especially as it happened only a month after their mother's death. Although Fergus married the daughter of the king of neighbouring Penntir, they had not been blessed with children. That left Fergus' illegitimate son, Morleo, as the only other surviving member of the royal house.

Queen Genofeva hated her son's bastard, but he was Ròidh's servant and he protected the boy. When Genofeva died, Fergus wasted no time in proclaiming Morleo as his heir and he brought him to live in the king's hall. Unfortunately it seems that his wife wasn't pleased by this and presumably still had hopes of a child of her own. In any event she tried to poison Morleo, but one of her women betrayed her to Fergus and he forced her to drink the poisoned goblet intended for his son.

Her brother, now King of Penntir, accused Fergus of her murder and the situation between them deteriorated. He invaded seeking revenge and there was an indecisive battle on the River Deveron a month ago. Unfortunately both kings were killed in the battle.

Morleo was immediately hailed as King of Ardewr but the heir to the crown of Penntir was a young boy, Bruide. Morleo rallied his men and invaded Penntir, defeating their leaderless warriors at Turriff. Morleo installed Bruide as king with himself as regent.

Obviously this has worried Bran, the King of Cait to the north, and Garnait, the High King. Morleo has emerged as too powerful for the High King's liking and I'm told that he has called a council of the Pictish kings at Kinross in Pobla.

I haven't been invited to attend but I understand that the council is to meet in the middle of April.

Oswiu paced up and down deep in thought after reading Hunwald's letter. It explained why he'd heard nothing about the reaction of Garnait and Drest to the threat from Domnall; they'd been too busy dealing with the situation in the north-east. He was far from indecisive normally but, at the moment, he wasn't at all certain what he should do.

As he was pondering the best course of action, his chaplain came in to remind him that it was Sunday and time for divine service.

'Ah, Conomultus, you are familiar with Ardewr aren't you?'

'I was there some fifteen years ago, yes Cyning.'

'Did you know Morleo?'

'Morleo? Yes, he was the bishop's servant; a by-blow of the king's I believe.'

'Well, he's now King of Ardewr and has effectively taken over Penntir as well. What sort of a man is he?'

'He was an eleven year old boy when I knew him, but he was utterly loyal to the bishop at the time, tending him as he lay dying. I'd say he was devout, honest and fair-minded as well, but it was a long time ago and he was very young. We all change over the years.'

'Worthy of my support would you say?'

'Well, that's difficult for me to say. I liked him then and, if he hasn't been embittered by Lady Genofeva's implacable hatred, I'd say that you could probably trust him to keep his word.'

'Thank you. Well, we'd better not keep the priest waiting.'

~~~

Both Hunwald and Utta were waiting by the quayside at Dùn Dè when the knarr carrying Catinus and Conomultus docked. Whilst his gesith waited for their horses to be unloaded, the two brothers greeted the eorl and the bishop. Neither had met Hunwald before but Utta was known to both of them; he'd been Conomultus' predecessor as chaplain to Oswiu.

'The king sends you his greetings and this reply to your letter, Eorl Hunwald,' Catinus said formally once they'd introduced themselves.

Hunwald nodded and scanned the contents of the letter before handing it to Utta.

'So it seems we need to make all haste to Kinross. I'm to represent Oswiu there as King of Prydenn but you and your brother are to assess whether we should support Morleo or Garnait. Oswiu isn't normally so vague.'

'We both knew Morleo when he was a boy,' Catinus replied. 'My brother rather better than me; if he is still as devout and trustworthy as he was then, then Oswiu will support him. If not, then we four are to make a judgement as how to best act in Oswiu's interests.'

'I see. And where is Oswiu now?'

'He and his warband are making for Dùn Breatainn to join forces with King Elfin and force Domnall Dhu out of the territory near Loch Lomond that he has invaded.'

'Domnall must be a fool if he thought he could invade Strathclyde and get away with it.'

'Not just Strathclyde. He has also seized part of Hyddir as well. Because that's Garnait's territory we should be able to use Oswiu's action to recover it in our negotiations with him and Drest.'

Hunwald smiled. 'Good. I wasn't sanguine about Garnait listening to us, or even allowing us to join the council, but that should do the trick.'

When they arrived, backed by the twenty well-armed men of Catinus' gesith and Hunwald's fifty mounted Picts there was some alarm in the camp by the side of Loch Leven near the settlement of Kinross. Drest, Garnait and Bran formed their men up on foot in a defensive line whilst a smaller group, presumably Morleo and his men from Ardewr and Penntir drew off to one side. The ever indecisive Ainftech, King of Uuynidd, hung back to see what would happen.

It had started to drizzle earlier in the day and Hunwald was cold, wet and tired. He was in no mood for games.

'Is this a way to greet a friend, Brenin?' he greeted Garnait, calling him king in Brythonic. 'I bring you tidings of the invasion of Hyddir by Domnall of Dalriada.'

As he expected, this was news to all those present and there was immediate consternation, especially amongst the men of Hyddir who had left families behind.

'King Oswiu would have come to this council himself,' the eorl went on, 'but he is hastening with his warband to join Elfin of Strathclyde to repulse Domnall on your behalf. He has asked me and Ealdorman Catinus to represent him here.'

He paused for a moment to let what he'd said to sink in.

'Now can we all get out of this damn rain? As soon as my old bones have warmed up a bit I'll come and find you and the other kings and tell you more.'

It was subtly done and Catinus had to restrain himself from chuckling. Hunwald had left Garnait with no option but to agree.

'You know everyone I think, except Morleo of Ardewr and Bruide of Penntir.'

Hunwald nodded to the man in his late twenties who nodded back and then smiled at Catinus and Conomultus. Evidently he remembered them from the time when they had visited the crannog on Loch Ness. The boy beside him looked to be about ten. He didn't respond except to scowl at them.

'I'm Hunwald of Prydenn and these three are Ealdorman Catinus of Bebbanburg, Bishop Utta and Conomultus, King Oswiu's chaplain.'

Utta smiled at the young boy, displaying his pointed teeth. Most youngsters would have been frightened but not Bruide; the scowl disappeared and he grinned back.

When Hunwald and Catinus had told the council all they knew about the situation in Hyddir, Garnait thanked them and suggested that they should now leave.

'Leave Brenin? I thought that this council of the kings had ben convened to discuss the situation in Penntir. If so, King Oswiu wishes us to represent him in your deliberations, both as King of Prydenn and as Bretwalda of the North.'

'But you are not a king,' Drest spluttered. 'If Oswiu wanted to take part in the council he should have come himself.'

'You seem to forget, Brenin, that he has other more pressing matters to attend to at the moment. Or would you have preferred him to allow the Dalriadans free reign to capture more of Pictland?' He tried to hide the scorn in his voice but failed.

Drest reddened with anger and the argument was about to get out of hand until Garnait thumped the table with his fist.

'Enough! We aren't here to bicker like children. I'm prepared to allow someone to represent the King of Prydenn, but only one man, not four. Now, which is it to be?'

Catinus glanced at Hunwald who nodded.

'I will, Brenin, as it is me that Oswiu briefed.'

'Very well. Now we all know of the tragic circumstances that has robbed us of two of our number. Fergus was precipitate in executing his queen for trying to poison his bas... son,' he corrected himself just in time when he saw Morleo grasp the hilt of his sword. 'But what is done is done.'

'Morleo has been properly elected as King of Ardewr and we must all accept that.'

'Well I don't,' a treble voice piped up. 'He's a bastard and has no right to be king.'

Morleo was visibly enraged by what Bruide had said but there was little he could do about it. He would look a fool if he challenged a ten year old boy. Instead he leaned across and whispered in his ear.

'If you wish to live to celebrate your eleventh birthday I suggest you apologise and mind what you say in future.'

The boy's face reddened in anger, then he looked down at the table for a second or two before raising his head. He looked straight at Garnait.

'I'm sorry, Brenin, that was crass and rude. I withdraw what I said.'

'Very well, but I suggest you think more carefully before you speak. Young princes should watch and learn, preparing themselves for the day when they'll be old enough to rule without guidance. Until that day, keep your thoughts well-guarded.'

He looked around the table before continuing.

'The main matter we have to discuss is how best to provide the guidance and training that Bruide needs.'

'It's not just a matter of mentoring the boy, though is it Garnait?' Bran pointed out. 'Someone has to rule his kingdom in the meantime. He needs a regent as well as a guardian.'

'Quite so. When I heard that Morleo intended to fulfil both roles I was concerned. It would effectively mean one of us ruling two kingdoms. No high king would tolerate giving so much power to one of his sub-kings.'

'You are ignoring the fact that your family holds the high kingship and rules both Hyddir and Pobla, I presume.'

There was a stunned silence. Ainftech was normally content to stay in the background but it was he who put into words what many of the others thought.

'But that just strengthens my position as high king and that makes the Land of the Picts strong. Dividing our land into two factions would mean an end to peace and prosperity for us all.'

'You say that but it wasn't so long ago that you tried to absorb Prydenn as well. If it wasn't for Talorgan and Oswiu you'd control half of the land of the Picts, and I'll wager that it wouldn't be long before you tried to make it all one kingdom.'

Garnait couldn't believe what he was hearing. Ainftech ruled the smallest and least powerful of all the seven kingdoms. Uuynnid lay sandwiched between Northumbria, Strathclyde and Hyddir. His people were poor fishermen and shepherds in the main and he had no warband to speak of. Normally his attitude was placatory, so someone must have put him up to this. Out of the corner of his eye he saw Morleo nod imperceptibly at Ainftech. It seemed as if the new King of Ardewr might be more of a threat than he'd thought.

'Why don't the chieftains of Penntir nominate a council of regency and choose a guardian for Bruide,' Drest suggested brightly.

'Because that would only cause infighting as they struggled for power amongst themselves,' Catinus said, speaking for the first time. 'I have a better idea. Boy kings are vulnerable and if you leave him in Penntir I doubt very much whether he'll live to celebrate his fourteenth birthday, let alone be old enough to rule on his own. I suggest you send him to Lindisfarne to be educated until he's fourteen, then he can be trained as a warrior as part of King Oswiu's warband. When he returns he'll be old enough, and educated and experienced enough to rule on his own.'

'And who will rule Penntir in the meantime?' Morleo asked quietly.

'I suggest you ask King Oswiu to appoint an eorl so that it can be governed as Prydenn is now. He has no interest in feathering his own nest in Pictland, only in maintaining peace along the border with Northumbria.'

'I for one agree,' Morleo said to everyone's surprise. 'The only reason I intervened to make myself ruler of Penntir was to avoid having a hostile neighbour.'

'It makes sense to me,' Bran said, getting up from the table to indicate that, as far as he was concerned, the meeting was over.

'Me too,' added Ainftech.

Garnait realised he'd been outmanoeuvred but he made one last try to retrieve the situation.

'Wait, we don't know what Bruide thinks.'

'Provided that Oswiu swears that'll he'll return my kingdom to me when I'm sixteen, I think that Catinus has made the best proposal. Guret didn't trust his council of regency when he was the King of Strathclyde as a boy. They failed to control him as they wished and he had to have them killed before they did away with him.'

Catinus wondered who had told him about Guret; that had been decades ago. He realised that it must have been Morleo. If so, it only went to show that he was as honest as Conomultus thought he was. If he had been planning to do away with Bruide quietly at some point so that he kept control of Penntir, he would hardly have warned the boy how vulnerable he was.

If he had only known then what a devastating effect Bruide was destined to have on the future of Northumbria he would have engineered his death, not offered him sanctuary.

~~~

Oswiu arrived at Dùn Breatainn, the grim citadel of the King of Strathclyde perched on top of its rock, with a warband of eighty, all mounted, made up of his gesith and Alweo's horsemen. The rest of the army he had hastily thrown together were one or two days behind him. In all he had mustered another two hundred, all trained warriors, from Goddodin, Bernicia and Rheged.

He would have raised a much bigger army had he called out the fyrd or allowed the time for warbands from Deira and Elmet to join him. However, he disliked being this far north for too long. Wulfhere of Mercia was behaving himself at the moment, but he didn't want to give him the opportunity to get up to mischief whilst he was away.

He camped beside the wide waters of the Clyde estuary about a mile from Elfin's stronghold, which dominated the surrounding countryside. It stood where the River Leven ran into the Clyde and looked impregnable. However, Oswiu knew that it had fallen twice to his knowledge: once to him twenty four years and once recently when Elfin had captured it with the help of Catinus and Lethlobar.

His men were still setting up the encampment when four men appeared through the small gatehouse at the base of the hill on which the fortress stood. He called Ceadda and Alweo to his side and went to meet them. Although all four wore mail and helmets they carried no shields and were only armed with swords and seaxes.

'Are you emissaries from King Elfin,' Oswiu called out when they were within earshot.

'Not exactly,' the tall man in the lead called back. 'I'm Elfin. King Oswiu I assume?'

'Correct. I'm afraid they're still erecting my tent but they shouldn't be long; then we can get out of this incessant drizzle. Is it always so miserable here? I remember it rained a lot when I was growing up on Iona and at Dùn Add, but not like this. It started just after we set out and hasn't stopped since.'

Oswiu was used to hardship but he was getting old. Now he was over fifty his bones ached in the damp.

Elfin laughed. 'Not always, Bretwalda, just most of the time. The good news is the water in the Leven is much higher than normal so Domnall can't cross it via the ford to raid along the north bank of the Clyde. As it is fed from Loch Lomond it forms an effective obstacle against him.'

'Can he go around Loch Lomond to the north?'

'Not really. It is very mountainous country and it's where the Kingdoms of Cait, Ardewr, Pobla and Hyddir all meet at Glen Fallon. Their kings may be away but the local Picts would keep harassing them if he tried. He'd lose a lot of men for little gain. No, he seems content to hold onto what he's conquered for now.'

At that moment a servant came to tell Oswiu that his tent was ready and he led the way into the shelter of the waxed leather pavilion. He took off his wet cloak and handed it to Nerian and Elfin did the same before the two kings sat down in the only two chairs available. The others were forced to remain standing, their cloaks dripping onto the rushes that had been scattered on top of the mud.

'Where is he? Do you know?'

'Yes, there's an old hill fort four miles to the north, on the other side of the Leven. He's re-building the palisade at the top; evidently he intends to make it into a stronghold to defend the territory he's taken from me.'

'Well, if he can't ford the Leven at the moment, the same applies to us presumably? How do we get at him?'

'I have ships. There's a knarr and three birlinns moored at the mouth of the river under my fortress. He has a commanding view of the surrounding countryside from the old hill fort so we'd have to cross at night.'

'Good. It'll take some time to ferry everyone across, but once we have enough men on the far bank to defend the bridgehead we can carry on in daylight, if necessary.'

'Cyning, it makes no sense to leave the horses behind. I accept that it would take too long to load them onto the knarr and unload them again, but horses can swim, even if my men can't.'

Alweo was pleading with Oswiu to let him try to cross the Leven with the horsemen upstream from where the rest of the combined army would be ferried across.

'You'd sit on them whilst they swam across? I'm not sure that would work and I don't want to risk losing men trying – or horses come to that.'

'No, Cyning. The men would hold onto the saddles and the horses would drag them across. Let me at least try it out tonight.'

'I don't want to risk losing you, but you can't very well ask someone else to volunteer. It'll look as if you're scared to do something you're asking your men to do.'

Oswiu thought for a moment. It was true he wanted his mounted warriors with him when they attacked the hill fort, not because horsemen would be of any use in the actual assault, but they would be invaluable during the pursuit afterwards. He had no intention of letting Domnall slip through his fingers only to cause more problems later.

'Very well. You can try out your theory tonight.'

'Thank you, Oswiu.'

After he'd left the king turned his attention to another problem. The contingent from Rheged had marched north through Strathclyde and were now encamped on the south bank of the Clyde. But that wasn't the difficulty. They would be ferried directly from there to the west bank of the Leven. No, the problem was that Strathclyde and Rheged had been enemies ever since the latter had been driven out of the region to the north of the Solway Firth a century ago.

Consequently the men of Rheged had taken the opportunity to get revenge on their old foes and raped and pillaged their way north. Despite hanging a few as an example to the rest, the Eorl of Rheged had been unable to control his men. Unsurprisingly Elfin was furious and wanted compensation. He had also demanded that Oswiu place them in the front ranks for the attack on the hill fort, the place of most danger.

This made no sense; for the most part they had no armour and carried small shields, therefore their unprotected bodies would be vulnerable to Domnall's archers during the long approach up the hill. Although Oswiu was irate with them, he didn't see the point in sacrificing men needlessly. He had planned to use those who had chainmail byrnies and large circular shields to lead the attack and he was still determined to do so. However, Elfin was in no mood to listen to reason.

'No, I'm sorry, Oswiu. They despoiled my lands and they must be punished.'

'You're not thinking logically, Elfin. Yes, your subjects have suffered and you need to give them compensation and justice; any good ruler would. However, what you are proposing would only stoke the fires of resentment in Rheged. I've offered to return all the plunder and pay you a chest of silver in recompense. I will, of course, recover the silver through extra taxation in Rheged so ultimately they will pay. I also propose to ask them to produce ten volunteers to lead the assault on the hill fort. That way I will be going some way to meeting your request without stirring up further trouble between our peoples. It is enough.'

'No, I disagree.'

Oswiu's patience was wearing thin and he decided that he'd had enough of trying to negotiate with a man he saw as being pig-headed.

'Disagree all you like; that is what I've decided and, as the bretwalda, you can either accept my judgment or repudiate my leadership. In which case, I and all my men will depart and leave you to sort out this mess.'

Elfin's eyes flashed dangerously. He disliked being challenged and for an instant he had decided to withdraw his allegiance to Oswiu when the bretwalda spoke again.

'Don't decide now, in the heat of the moment. Let me know your answer in the morning. In the meantime Alweo will conduct his trial swim across the Leven tonight.'

Elfin stormed out of Oswiu's pavilion, knocking Nerian out of the way as he did so. The servant looked after him in surprise and shrugged before entering.

'King Elfin seemed a little out of sorts,' he commented.

Over the twenty years that they'd known one another an easy familiarity had developed between the two men, though Nerian was careful not to overstep the mark. He knew from the dark look that Oswiu gave him that this was not the moment for jocular remarks.

'I need to collect your byrnie and helmet for polishing,' he muttered and, collecting them, he made haste to leave.

His master seemed to be depressed lately and he wondered if it was the aches and pains of old age or the never ending difficulties he faced that had caused him to mope and exhibit an impatience that had grown worse in recent months. Perhaps it was a combination of the two.

Nerian was right about one thing. Oswiu was depressed, but it had nothing to do with political problems or even the growing antipathy between the Celtic and Roman churches that had caused it. He had agents everywhere and they enabled him to stay one step ahead of the game. However, the latest report from a blacksmith in his pay in Loidis had worried him. It seemed that rumours were circulating that Alchfrith was conspiring against him. The blacksmith wasn't certain, but he thought that Abbot Wilfrid might be encouraging his son.

It wasn't so much that Alchfrith was ambitious; he understood that. It was the fact that he was apparently a traitor who planned to have him assassinated so that he could seize the throne for himself. Not only that, but he intended to have both Ecgfrith and baby Ælfwine killed as well. Presumably he didn't imagine that his other half-brother, the scholarly Aldfrith, was much of a threat.

His son's treachery had wounded Oswiu deeply. He wasn't close to him, and he was honest enough with himself to acknowledge that it was his fault. He'd paid little attention to him when he was growing up and he regretted it now. Nevertheless, he'd assumed that Alchfrith would be loyal to him just because he was his son, and because he'd made him Sub-King of Deira. It seemed that he was wrong.

He never doubted the blacksmith's report. The man had never failed him in the past and Oswiu knew that he would never have dared make such a report unless he was fairly certain that the rumours were based on fact. He wasn't worried about his own safety but he was concerned about his two young sons. Perhaps the answer would be to give the fifteen year old Ecgfrith his own gesith; they could then guard him and his baby brother. It would be an unusual thing to do, but that in itself might warn Alchfrith off.

Elfin returned the next morning to say that he'd reluctantly agreed to what Oswiu had suggested.

'Good. Thank you for that. Now we can get on with the attack on Domnall's stronghold. You'll be pleased to hear that Alweo's experiment worked well last night. His horse swam both ways with him hanging onto its mane. The last of my contingents has just arrived and so I suggest we launch the attack at dawn tomorrow, provided we can get everyone across the river in time.'

'I suggest you speak to your man who has just arrived first, Bretwalda. It seems the Picts are on their way.'

'Man? What man?'

Just at that moment Catinus appeared in the entranceway to the tent.

'This man, Cyning.'

Oswiu, whose face had creased into a frown at the slightly sarcastic way that Elfin had said *Bretwalda*, immediately changed to an expression of welcome.

'Come in Catinus. You know King Elfin, of course.'

The two men smiled at one another and each clasped the other's wrist in friendship.

'What happened about Ardewr?'

'Morleo has been accepted as king and you are invited to appoint an eorl to rule Penntir until such time as Bruide is old enough to rule himself.'

'I see, and where is Bruide now? Is he to remain in Penntir.'

'The council thought that might be rather dangerous for him so I've brought him with me. He is to go to Lindisfarne until he's old enough to be trained as a warrior.'

'Hmm, he'll be joining Ruaidhrí then.'

A germ of an idea was beginning to form. Bruide and Ruaidhrí were too young as yet but if he gathered together several sons of nobles who were starting their training to be warriors, they could become Ecgfrith's companions without it seeming odd.

'Is Garnait on his way back to Hyddir?'

'Not exactly, Cyning. He and Drest are leading the warriors they had brought with them to the council through Pobla heading for Glen Falloch. I understand that from there they will head south down Loch Lomond and recapture the territory Domnall has seized.'

'Good. But that doesn't help us here, where the bulk of Domnall's forces are.'

'Well, it may, if you can drive him out of the hill fort.'

'What do you mean?'

'Garnait has agreed to advance as far as the isthmus between Loch Lomond and Loch Long, which is the border between Strathclyde and the Land of the Picts in any case, and hold it against Domnall. If he flees north to get back to Dalriada he'll be trapped between us and the Picts.'

A grin lit up Oswiu's face. Even Elfin had stopped scowling and was now smiling broadly.

'Catinus, you're a genius! Perhaps I should make you Eorl of Penntir as a reward?'

'That's very kind of you, Cyning, but I'm very happy being Ealdorman of Bebbanburg.'

Not only did he not want to exchange his comparatively comfortable and secure home for the wilds of the Pictish kingdom, but he knew that the appointment would cease once Bruide reached maturity. However, Oswiu seemed to know what he was thinking.

'Don't worry. You will can remain lord of Bebbanburg whilst you look after Penntir for the next what, five or six years? You can appoint a custos to look after my fortress whilst you're gone.'

The subtle reminder that Bebbanburg wasn't truly his, but was a royal fortress, wasn't lost on Catinus.

'Very well, Cyning. Thank you.'

'We can sort the details out later. For now we need to concentrate on the attack on Domnall Dhu's fort.'

CHAPTER NINE – THE BATTLE OF LOCH KATRINE

662 AD

Wilfrid was frustrated. Alchfrith had obviously got cold feet. The Abbot of Ripon saw Oswiu as the main obstacle to converting Northumbria to Roman Catholicism and he thought that he'd convinced Alchfrith to get rid of his father and seize the throne. He was under Wilfrid's spell and, once he was on the throne, he would get him to expel the heretical followers of the Celtic Church.

But his ambitions didn't end there. Alchfrith had just given a vill he owned just outside Hexham to Wilfrid so that he could found a new monastery there. The grasping abbot wasn't thinking so much about the spiritual welfare of the folk who lived in the area so much as the income he would get from it.

He detested the devout Colman. The man was abbot of Lindisfarne, a richly endowed monastery, and Bishop of Northumbria, yet the man continued to live like the humblest member of his flock. He gave away all his wealth to the poor and the disadvantaged. It was something that Wilfrid just couldn't comprehend.

Oswiu was the same. He should have been the richest of all the monarchs in Britain, but he too gave alms to the poor and had endowed several monasteries without taking a penny in income from them.

Thinking of Colman made him annoyed for another reason. It was stupid to locate the bishop of such an enormous part of England on a remote island in the far north-east. The bishop should be located at Eoforwīc, where the king was normally based. He knew that he would make a far better bishop than Colman too. The man was an ignoramus, theologically speaking, who had spent all his life in Celtic monasteries. He didn't even speak English very well and, although he knew Latin, he had never learned Greek.

By comparison, Wilfrid had studied at Cantwareburg, at prestigious abbeys in Frankia and in Rome. There were few scholars who were his equal; even Deusdedit, the Archbishop of Cantwareburg was a nonentity by comparison. He was the first native-born Saxon holder of the archbishopric and that was about his only claim to fame. The Roman Church had lost ground during his time and Wilfrid despised him in consequence.

'Now is your opportunity, Cyning, whilst your father is away in Caledonia,' he told Alchfrith. 'He is old, older than all his eorls except for two. Most kings had the grace to die on the battlefield before reaching their fifties, but he cannot have long to live now.'

'Then I can wait until he dies,' Alchfrith replied stubbornly.

'And let Ecgfrith steal your throne?'

'He's just a boy.'

'He's nearly sixteen and he'll be old enough to rule if Oswiu lives a couple more years.'

'I thought you just said that he was on the point of death?'

'No, I said that he can't have much longer to live, given the fact that he's now in his fifties. Perhaps he might even be killed in Dalriada, who knows. But he might survive until Ecgfrith is old enough to rule.'

'Why him, even if my father does last another few years. I'm older and already King of Deira.'

'Sub-king; there's a big difference. You mother was from Rheged whereas Ecgfrith's mother is the sister of Edwin, the first King of Northumbria, and is from the Royal house of Deira. It is, of course, for the Witan to decide in due course, but Ecgfrith has the better claim. You need to act before he comes of age.'

'I know what you're saying, but I can afford to leave it for a year or so. If my father dies naturally whilst Ecgfrith is too young to succeed I will be the obvious choice.'

'Perhaps, but time may not be on your side after all.'

'Why? What do you mean?'

'There is a rumour going around that you are plotting against King Oswiu. I've no idea how these things start, but it does mean that you'll have to act quickly before it reaches his ears.'

'I don't suppose you started it did you?'

'Of course not! I'm not a scandalmonger. Like you, I'd have liked a little more time to plan properly.'

Alchfrith knew that the abbot was lying but he couldn't prove it and, in any case, it didn't change the situation. After a few minutes thought he made up his mind what to do.

'I'm going to ride north, to this place Dùn Breatainn, and throw myself on my father's mercy. I'll say that I heard the rumours and came to reassure him that there wasn't a grain of truth in them.'

Wilfrid swore softly under his breath. It wasn't what he wanted at all, but he acknowledged that it's exactly what he would have done in the same circumstances. He forced himself to smile.

'Good idea. That'll put him off the scent and give us more time to plan.'

Alchfrith smiled back but, like Wilfrid, his smile didn't reach his eyes.

After Wilfrid had left him, he called Rægenhere to come out of the alcove where he'd been hiding. The son of the disgraced former Eorl of Hexham was now twenty one. He had been sent to Lindisfarne when he was eleven and had stayed on there as a monk. Now he was Alchfrith's chaplain and confidante.

'You heard?'

'Every word, Cyning.'

'Well? What do you make of it?'

'My brother is ambitious and that makes him dangerous. I know you like him but I remember him from when I was a boy. Believe me, he's not your friend, however much he makes out he is. Obviously Wilfrid started the rumour that you want your father's throne. However, he is right about one thing. You need to go and profess your innocence to King Oswiu before he decides to act against you.'

~~~

Catinus had been accompanied from Kinross by his mounted warriors and so they had joined his friend Alweo for the river crossing. Although it hadn't rained for two days it was still fast flowing and quite deep. The River Leven had nothing to do with Loch Leven near Kinross, where he'd just come from. It was a stretch of water six miles long that connected Loch Lomond to the Clyde Estuary.

'I've done this before so I'll cross first,' Alweo told him. 'The current is quite strong so it'll take you downstream by a couple of hundred yards. There is a small sandy beach just before the river bends sharply to the left. The current will take you close to it and your horse will be able to regain its footing quite easily. You'd better pass that on to your men.'

Catinus nodded and, after giving the fast flowing river a doubtful look, went off to brief his warband. In the end it was easier than it looked. Only one horse and its rider was swept past the beach but, when the river turned back to the right they managed to get out of the water. Unfortunately they emerged on the wrong bank. Once rested, they tried again and made it out successfully on the second attempt.

'According to my reckoning it's about two hours until dawn. I suggest you post a couple of sentries and let your men get some sleep.'

Alweo had been worried about men getting lost in the pitch black but Catinus had suggested that the men grab the tail of the horse in front and lead their own horses. It had worked and, now that the moon made an occasional appearance from behind the dark clouds, he could make out the hill with the fort on its summit looming above them about a mile away.

Their task sounded simple. To capture Domnall. If they managed to kill a few of the routed Dalriadans, so much the better, but they would eventually run into the Picts on their way home so killing them wasn't important. However, identifying Domnall might not be easy, especially if he fled on foot.

Meanwhile Oswiu and Elfin were watching the small fleet ferry the bulk of their combined army over the Leven by the light of the new moon. Oswiu wasn't sure if they could be seen from the old hill fort in this light but, if so, Domnall did nothing to oppose them.

About half way up the hill Oswiu realised that he wasn't as young as used to be. He was in the second wave surrounded by his gesith with Elfin to his right. Ahead of him those members of both king's warbands who possessed byrnies pressed on towards the summit and its palisade.

'Strange that they are sending so few arrows our way,' commented Redwald, panting nearly as hard as his king.

'Yes, perhaps they only have a few.'

The two men said nothing further, keeping their breath for the rest of the climb. As they neared the top they saw that there were only a handful of men manning the palisade, then suddenly they disappeared. Oswiu realised that something was badly wrong just before Domnall launched his attack.

The King of Dalriada had kept the great majority of his army hidden in the wood at the bottom of the hill. He'd waited until the first two waves were committed to the assault on the hill fort before leading his men out of the trees to attack the rest of Elfin's men, who had only just started the ascent as the third wave.

They were the least experienced and worst equipped of the Strathclyde army and they stood no chance against the Dalriadans' overwhelming numbers. Within a few minutes they had broken and fled.

Oswiu realised almost straight away that they had walked into a trap; it took Elfin a little longer. Of course, their best warriors were now at the rear and the least experienced and poorest armed of those who were left were forced to face the victorious men of Dalriada. Oswiu started to push his way to the front with his gesith but that just led to chaos as his bewildered men tried to understand what was happening. Elfin ordered his men to turn about but then seemed content to remain at what was now the rear. Whilst this was going on, Domnall re-formed his men ready to renew their assault on the disorganised army facing them.

Catinus and Alweo watched as a few dozen men ran down the hill from the hill fort.

'Are they just a few cowards or do you think something is going on,' Alweo asked a puzzled Catinus.

'I'm not sure. Perhaps we should intercept them and take a few prisoners to question?'

Alweo nodded his agreement and the mass of horsemen moved into a long line to cut off the fleeing enemy. The ends of the line moved into a canter so that the formation looked like the horns of a bull. The men from the hill fort realised that they were trapped and most threw down their weapons and stood sullenly waiting to be taken captive. A few put up a fight but they were quickly skewered on the horsemen's spears.

Catinus surveyed the ranks of the thirty or so captives and picked on the youngest, a boy of perhaps fourteen. Two of his men went and dragged him before Catinus and Alweo, both of whom had dismounted and now stood grimly waiting to question the boy.

'Now you can survive this little encounter intact or I can cut off your ears, hands and your feet in turn and leave you a helpless cripple, that is if you don't die from blood loss; the choice is yours.'

Catinus took the lead as he spoke Brythonic. The yellow liquid flowing down the lad's bare legs showed how terrified he was. He tried to look behind him to his comrades - either for re-assurance or guidance – but Alweo punched him on the jaw.

'Look at us when we're talking to you.'

Alweo didn't speak his language but the message was clear.

'Now, how many men are left in the fort?'

The boys stubbornly clamped his lips shut until Alweo drew his seax and lifted the front of the boy's filthy tunic with the point, exposing his manhood. He sobbed and his shoulders drooped.

'I'll tell you what you want to know,' he almost yelled at them.

Someone called out to him telling him to button his lip if he knew what was good for him. Immediately one of Alweo's men stepped forward and thrust his spear into the stomach of the man who'd called out. He dropped to the ground screaming in agony and there was no more interference from the captives. The man continued to wail and that unnerved the boy even more.

'There's no-one left.'

'Where's the rest of Domnall's army then?'

The young Dalriadan clamped his mouth shut but when Alweo cut the skin at the top of his left ear and started to saw, he changed his mind.

'They're hiding in a wood ready to attack your fucking army from the rear. It's too late, you'll be wiped out,' the boy shouted triumphantly.

Just at that moment Catinus heard the faint sounds of battle coming from the far side of the hill. He and Alweo had to act and act fast.

'Let them go! Mount up,' he bellowed at his surprised men.

A minute later they were heading around the side of the hill at a gallop. The sight that greeted their eyes as they came around the hill was not an encouraging one. Oswiu and Elfin had the benefit of height but their army was in chaos and many were trying to get away from the scene of carnage. With the weaker warriors either dead or fled, the more experienced and armoured men were now able to strike at the Dalriadans. Few of these had any armour, or even leather jerkins, to protect them and the advance of Domnall's men was now slowing down. However, they were able to envelope the flanks of the Northumbrians and the men of Strathclyde due to their superior numbers.

Seeing the danger Catinus yelled across at Alweo: 'if you charge them from the flank I'll take my men and wheel around and strike them from the rear.'

Alweo nodded back and gave the signal to form into a wedge. His eighty men charged into the Dalriadan flank, scattering men as they went. Alweo thrust his spear into the throat of a large Scot wielding a double-handed axe, sending the giant hurtling back into his comrades. He drew his sword just as a man, braver than the rest, ran forward and tried to impale him on his sword. Alweo batted it away with his own sword and then he was past him and faced by another man trying to get out of his way. He swung his sword and cut into the man's shoulder breaking his clavicle and biting into his scapula. He man fell away, screaming in agony and Alweo had difficulty in holding onto his sword as he tried to pull it free.

He managed to cut off the point of a spear aimed at his throat just in time. He felt a bang on his shield as someone embedded an axe in it and then he was free. With a start he realised that the men now facing him were Northumbrians. He'd fought his way through the entire Dalriadan warband. Gradually his men joined him as the enemy retreated to regroup.

Meanwhile Catinus and his gesith lined up facing the youths and old men in the rear ranks of the enemy. He thought about using the wedge formation but his men weren't trained to fight on horseback. They normally used their mounts to ride from one place to another quickly and dismounted to fight; not today though. He needed the shock of a cavalry charge to break the enemy quickly.

His men started the advance at a walk so that it was easy to keep in line, a hundred yards from the enemy they started to trot and then canter. Now the cohesion of the line was lost but it didn't matter. If they weren't used to fighting on horseback, unlike Alweo's men, those facing them had never faced a mounted charge either. As soon as the ragged line changed to the gallop the ranks facing them began to break up as the young and the old panicked and started to force their way through the ranks of those behind them.

The rear third of Domnall's army were now in disorder. They were also vaguely conscious of the havoc that Alweo's trained cavalry had brought to their comrades in the first two divisions. Suddenly the whole lot broke and ran in all directions, throwing away their spears and shields as they went. Catinus chased after them, cutting them down as he rode amongst the routed enemy. His men did likewise and they effectively destroyed the rear division without losing a single man.

He frantically signalled to his gesith to halt as they broke clear and were faced by the second division. However, they too had been badly disrupted by Alweo's charge and they stood there, bewildered.

Most of the battlefield was spread out beneath Oswiu as he stood halfway up the steep hillside. Immediately below him stood the first division of Domnall's army surrounding his and Elfin's remaining men. Beyond them Alweo's men faced two ways on the flatter ground, trapped between the first and second divisions of the Dalriadans. However, the latter was much smaller than it had been. At the bottom of the hill Catinus and his twenty men sat on their horses facing the rear ranks of the second division.

Suddenly Catinus gave the order to charge and his men kicked their horses into a canter and then a gallop as they struck the remnants of the second division of Dalriadans. It wasn't something that they had trained for but they seemed to perform the charge well enough before releasing their spears as they turned and trotted back. Once more they charged but this time they hacked down at the enemy with their swords. A few seconds later Alweo also charged into the enemy second division, trapping them between the two mounted forces.

It was the decisive moment of the battle and Oswiu waved his sword forward, looking at Elfin, who waved his own sword back. The Northumbrians and the men of Strathclyde charged down the hill into the first division, ignoring the men who were trying to encircle them.

Domnall realised that he had gambled and lost and he fought with his gesith to extricate himself from the first division, cutting down his own men in the process. Once he was clear, he rode at the gallop heading north. When some of his men spotted the group of horsemen disappearing around the hill with the banner of Dalriada still flying proudly over their heads, they lost heart and the news of their king's abandonment of them spread quickly through the ranks.

The fight went out of them and fifteen minutes later it was all over.

'Alweo, you had better keep up the pressure on Domnall. He should run into the Picts at the Isthmus of Arrochar and then you'll have him trapped.'

'Yes, Cyning.'

Without another word he led his somewhat depleted force of horsemen off to the north, following Domnall's clear trail.

'Well done Catinus. It seems I owe you and Alweo for saving me from an ignominious defeat.'

There didn't seem much that Catinus could say in reply to that. He could hardly agree and to demur would be false modesty. So he merely smiled and nodded in acknowledgement of the compliment.

'What happens now, Cyning?'

'We lick our wounds, bury our dead and wait for tidings of Domnall's death.'

However, it was not to be. Six days later Alweo returned with disappointing news.

'Cyning,' the weary man reported. 'The Picts failed to stop him at Arrochar. It seems that he has escaped to Dùn Add.'

'You mean that treacherous cur, Garnait, let him pass?' he asked incredulously.

'So it would seem. The rumour is that Domnall bribed him.'

'Very well. It seems that I shall have to deal with Garnait before I turn my attention to Dalriada. Thank you Alweo.'

The ealdorman left his tent with a backwards glance. He studied the brooding king for a moment, wondering what he would do now, were he in Oswiu's shoes which, thankfully, he wasn't.

~~~

Alweo reined his horse in on the col between two hills from where he had a perfect view along Glen Fallon to the north-east and down to Glen Fyne to the west. So far his scouts had found no trace of the Picts and he was beginning to wonder if he was on a fool's errand. Oswiu seemed certain that Garnait was hiding from him somewhere in these mountains but, if so, he'd seen no sign of even a moderate sized force having passed this way.

There had been the detritus of his camp on the isthmus near Arrochar and he'd followed the trail as far as Alt Arnan near the north end of Loch Lomond but then the trail had disappeared. There were signs of a few horses and men in the boggy area near Alt Arnan and then nothing. It was if they had disappeared into thin air. Evidently they had taken to the many streams and burns in the area where their passing left no trace. His men were now following the most obvious of these as they must have left the water courses at some point, but thus far they had found nothing.

Oswiu and Elfin, with the two hundred and fifty men who were unwounded after the battle near the old hill fort, were camped near the headwaters of Loch Lomond awaiting news of Garnait.

Meanwhile Oswiu had sent messengers to the other four kings asking them to convene at Stirling in three months' time. They, together with the Eorl of Prydenn and Catinus, as Eorl of Penntir, would need to elect a new high king as well as agree on who should rule Hyddir now that he had declared Garnait a traitor. He believed that that would give him enough time to hunt Garnait down and then advance into Dalriada to depose the slippery Domnall. It would have to be. He didn't want to be trapped in the mountains when the weather deteriorated later in the year.

He had also sent messengers to Alchfrith and to the three eorls in Goddodin, ordering them to join him with their warbands. However, it would take at least three weeks for the latter and a lot longer for the former to reach him. Redwald wondered if Oswiu wasn't being a little obsessive in his determination to control the north at the expense of his southern border. At the moment Wulfhere was behaving, at least as far as Northumbria was concerned, but withdrawing Alchfrith and his warband and leaving just the eorls, their warriors and the fyrd to protect Northumbria might just be too tempting a situation for him to resist.

Two weeks later his scouts found Garnait. He and his cousin, Drest, had taken up a position on the narrow neck of land between Lochs Katrine and Arklet. The scouts estimated the numbers at five hundred, mostly on foot but about a tenth were mounted on the surefooted mountain ponies that the Picts rode.

Only the three eorls from Goddodin had joined him so far, bringing the combined Northumbrian and Strathclyde army to about the same size as that of the Picts. There had been no communication from Alchfrith so Oswiu had no idea when he and his men would arrive, or even if they were on their way. He seethed with anger at Alchfrith's silence. He should at least have let him know when he expected to join him.

He would have preferred to have waited, but he was conscious that he still had Domnall to deal with and the date set for the council of the Picts was now only two months away. He therefore decided to march with the men he had.

Three days later he sat on his horse on the lower slopes of Beinn á Choin and looked down at the narrow neck of land between the two lochs. The Picts were camped along the south bank of Loch Katrine, below a mountain called A' Bheinn Mheanbh but, as soon as Oswiu's army made an appearance, they rushed to take up their positions on the high ground to the south of the isthmus.

'If we attack head on, we'll be forced onto a narrow front by the two lochs,' he said thoughtfully to Elfin and Redwald.

'I'm not certain, Cyning,' Redwald replied, 'but the ground just beyond the isthmus doesn't look quite right. But then, my eyesight isn't what it was.'

'No, you're right,' Elfin agreed. 'I'd be willing to bet that they've dug pits and covered them with frames made from thin branches, then put sods cut from the surrounding grassland on top. They must have done it a little while ago because the grass is yellowing.'

'Yes, and there are bare patches of earth to the south of that small loch where the sods must have come from,' exclaimed Redwald.

'Well spotted. That rules out a frontal assault then. Do any of your scouts know this area well, Elfin?'

'One or two do. I'll send for them.'

That night, whilst Alweo, Catinus and their horsemen remained behind to keep the campfires on the southern slopes of Beinn á Choin burning, a few scouts led the rest on a long night march to the north of Loch Arklet and then along the east bank of Loch Lomond until they turned along a steep sided valley that eventually led them to the south west slopes of A' Bheinn Mheanbh.

His men were tired and dawn was fast approaching so Oswiu decided to camp beside a small lake called Loch Ard. Let Garnait and Drest wonder where he'd gone to when they awoke. The more unsettled they were, the better.

'Where in the name of God have they disappeared to?' Garnait asked his equally bewildered cousin the next morning.

Even Alweo and Catinus had moved back along the northern arm of Loch Katrine so that they were out of sight behind the bulk of Beinn á Choin. Garnait and his cousin were left looking at the smouldering remains of the campfires. The smoke still rising made it look as if the occupants of the camp had only recently left. Then it started to rain and the smoking ashes were quickly reduced to a dirty black mess.

Catinus had taken up a position behind some scrub growing on the lower slopes of Beinn á Choin to keep an eye on the Picts and it wasn't long before he saw a score of warriors lope away to scout out the surrounding countryside. It wouldn't take them more than a few hours to find both Oswiu's camp and his own. There wasn't much he could do about the other patrols, but he would at least make sure that the scouts crossing the isthmus didn't report back.

There were four Picts heading along Loch Arklet before turning up the re-entrant and heading for the summit of the mountain. From there they would be able to see Alweo and his men camped on the shore of Loch Katrine. Catinus had brought three of his own gesith with him and two of those had bows. As the scouts worked their way up the re-entrant to where he lay he signalled the two archers to take care of any who tried to run back down the mountain.

Suddenly he and one of his gesith, a man appropriately named Beorn, which meant warrior, rose up when the two leading Picts were ten paces away. Before the two men had realised what was happening, Catinus and Beorn cut them both down. The other two were ten paces behind them, so they had time to turn and run as soon as they had recovered their wits. Like most Picts, they were clad in nothing but saffron coloured tunics, though one did have a helmet on his head. Two arrows chased them down the steep slope, one hitting its target in the middle of his back, killing him instantly, but the other was struck in the right shoulder. It spun him around and he gasped in pain, but seconds later he was running again, clutching his right arm with his left hand to stop his injured shoulder from moving too much.

Catinus and Beorn ran after him. Beorn, being younger than Catinus by a decade, quickly overtook his eorl and he was the one to deliver the fatal blow, half severing the man's head from his body. The helmet rolled away and Beorn picked it up.

'Worse than useless. It wouldn't stop a blow from your son, lord,' he said throwing it away.

'We'd better get back down the hill and keep an eye on the five who went up the loch towards Alweo's encampment.'

Beorn nodded and, collecting the two archers, they ran down the hillside towards their camp. As they crested a ridge they saw the five Picts below them up alongside a small stream. The Picts saw them a split second after that. There was a hasty discussion before the five men spread out to meet Catinus and his men as they charged towards them.

Suddenly the archers stopped and nocked an arrow to their bow. They couldn't aim immediately, not until they had their breathing back under control but, when they did, the two Picts at either end of the line dropped; one with an arrow through his neck and the other with one in his thigh. The archer who'd aimed at him cursed his poor aim, but it didn't matter. The arrowhead had nicked his femoral artery and he quickly bled to death.

That left the other three to face Catinus and Beorn. When Catinus had announced his intention of leading the group to keep watch up the mountain, Alweo had told him he was mad.

'You're an ealdorman who has just been made an eorl, albeit temporarily. You don't have to prove anything. Send Beorn by all means, he's young and dying to prove that the faith you showed in him by making him a member of your gesith was well placed. You've got a wife and children. They need you alive.'

'If I thought like that I'd be killed in my next fight. I need to commit myself one hundred percent, not hold back and let others die in my place. That's not me, and never will be. A brave man frightens his enemies and he survives – in the main anyway. A coward is soon killed. Can't you see that?'

Catinus thought back to their exchange now as he faced the three Picts. One was glowering at him, intent on killing him but the man next to him, scarcely more than a boy, looked terrified. The third one he discounted as Beorn was already racing towards him. As the first Pict thrust his spear at him Catinus batted it away with his shield and brought his sword down onto his opponent's small shield. The blow unbalanced the Pict and he stumbled. Catinus stepped forward and thrust his sword into the other man's exposed chest. It was a fatal wound and he fell to the ground.

Catinus' sword was trapped in the dying man's ribcage and he struggled to pull it out. It was the boy's chance to stab him with his spear but he hesitated. By the time he thrust it at Catinus, the latter had pulled his shield into place to block the thrust and, letting go of the trapped sword, he pulled his seax from its scabbard.

The boy crouched down, looking for a second opportunity to stab Catinus but he'd lost his chance. Catinus brought his seax down, chopping at the part of the shaft just behind the bronze point. Had it been his sword it would have cut through the it, but the seax was shorter and the blow lacked power. Nevertheless it cut part way through the shaft and the next time the boy thrust at Catinus he blocked it with his shield and the shaft snapped.

The boy looked down aghast at the useless length of wood in his hand and tears of frustration formed in his eyes. Beorn made to finish the boy off but Catinus shook his head.

He went back to the body and finally managed to free his sword. Walking back to the boy, whose escape was now cut off by the other three members of his gesith, he swung his sword, cutting the remnants of the shaft in two.

'Surrender or die; your choice boy,' he said in Brythonic.

Now openly weeping the lad threw down his small shield and the last part of the shaft, followed by the cheap dagger he wore at his waist.

'What's your name?'

'Llyffant,' he replied sullenly.

Catinus laughed. 'Frog? Your father must have had a sense of humour.'

'You've just killed him.' He pointed to the man with the fatal wound to his chest.

'He shouldn't have brought you to war. How old are you?'

'I have eleven summers.'

'You look younger. You're a brave lad, Llyffant. Tie his hands and put a halter around his neck Eadstan, we'll take him with us. He may be able to tell us something.'

The leader of the gesith nodded to Beorn who took the rough lengths of rope that the Picts had worn around their waists as belts and used them to tie Llyffant's hands together and then fashioned a length of rope just long enough to serve as a lead. He gave it to one of the two archers to hold as they descended the mountain, which proved to be a mistake.

On a particularly steep section Llyffant gave a sudden tug on the rope and the man holding the end lost his footing and went sliding down the mountainside. The boy took off running back up the mountain. He looked ungainly with his hands tied behind his back but he was still making reasonable progress when an arrow whizzed past his ear and struck the ground in front of him.

The other archer had deliberately missed and the warning wasn't lost on Llyffant, who halted and turned around. A second arrow was aimed at his chest and he reluctantly started back down again.

'You seem to have some spirit, boy, but you lack common sense. Don't try that again. The next arrow won't be sent as a warning, understand?' Eadstan told him.

The boy nodded and the man he'd escaped from gave him such a belt around the head that he was almost knocked from his feet. Grabbing the end of the rope again he gave it a strong yank so that the boy almost lost his balance again. He was docile the rest of the way.

'Now, what do you know that might be useful to me?' Catinus asked after the boy had been fed and allowed to relieve himself.

'Nothing. No-one tells me anything, I'm just a boy,' he replied sullenly.

'What was your father?'

'He was a hunter, that's why he was used as a scout. Ever since my mother's died he's grumbled about me costing him money to feed and clothe. He said it was time he taught me to hunt so that I was of some use.'

Catinus looked at the boy's tattered tunic and worn shoes and thought that it hadn't cost the man much to clothe him and, judging by how small and thin he was, he hadn't spent much on the boy's food either.

'What were the rumours running about the camp?'

'Rumours?'

'Yes, why did your men think Garnait had let the Dalriadans escape? Did Drest agree with his cousin? Were the men behind their leaders? That sort of thing.'

When the boy sullenly refused to answer Catinus decided to change his tactics.

'Look Llyffant, I've kept you alive because I thought you might be of use to me. So far you have been as much help as a horse fly in a latrine. What do you think will happen to you now?'

'I don't know,' he replied, looking crestfallen. 'What are you going to do with me?'

'What I should have done at first, cut your throat.'

'Wait, I'll tell you what you want to know, but I need to know what you'll do with me afterwards.'

'What would you like me to do with you?'

'Let me go back to my people.'

'No. That's not an option. In any case, your father's dead. Who would look after you?'

The boy thought for a moment. 'No-one would want me, you're right.'

'So what else?'

'Could I stay with you and serve you?'

Catinus studied the boy to see if he was being serious. Should he trust him? Leofric was now nineteen and he had been thinking of freeing him for a while. The young man would make a good warrior and he knew that's what Leofric wanted. He decided to take a chance and called for his body servant.

'Take this urchin down to the loch and scrub him clean. Then give him an old tunic of yours to wear. It'll be far too big so you'll have to alter it. Then bring him back here.'

'Yes, lord,' the puzzled servant replied, wondering what was going on.

An hour later Leofric returned with Llyffant. The boy looked quite different. Instead of being dirty brown, his hair was a dark reddish bronze that shone in the light. Without the layers of dirt his face was quite comely and, when the boy smiled tentatively at him, he found himself smiling back. The tunic was an old blue one that Leofric had cut to size and sewn roughly back together but it would do for now. He'd even given the boy an old leather belt to replace the length of rope around his waist.

'Good. You look almost human now, but I refuse to call you Frog. From now on you have a new name, Hefydd.'

It meant bronze in the Pictish tongue and the boy looked pleased by his change in name.

'Thank you, lord. What was it you wanted to know?'

'What do his men think about Garnait's action in letting Domnall and his Dalriadans escape?

'They mainly grumble because the enemy king bribed him with gold, but he kept all of it for himself instead of distributing it to his warband. But that isn't their only complaint; they also want retribution. The miserable dogs had invaded a part of Hyddir and killed all the Picts who lived there and they should have been made to suffer for that.'

It was what Catinus suspected and he concluded that the boy was trustworthy.

'What about Drest and his men. Do they support Garnait?'

'I don't think so. My father said that King Drest and the high king had argued and the men from Pobla didn't want to fight for Garnait.'

'Good. Now I want you to run an errand for me. I want you to take a message to Drest. Can you do that?'

'I can try,' the boy said doubtfully, 'but I don't think they'll let me in to see him.'

'No, I don't suppose they will, but you can get close to his tent can't you?'

'Yes, I'll need my old tunic back though. I should be able to pass unnoticed in that. Why?'

'Here's a dagger. Cut a slit in the tent wall and slip inside when it's deserted and leave this pouch where Drest is bound to find it. Can you do that?'

'With any luck, yes.'

'Then, when you return, you can replace Leofric as my body servant. You'll have to train him first, Leofric, but then you can become one of my warriors.'

'Thank you, lord, I don't need to tell you how grateful I am.'

'It's no more than you deserve for serving me faithfully for the past eight years. I shall free your sister as well, though I expect she'll want to continue in service to the Thegn of Bebbanburg.'

He was being diplomatic. Everyone knew that, in addition to managing the thegn's hall, she also shared his bed. Before Leofric became too euphoric he added a proviso.

'That is always supposing that the boy makes it safely back here, of course,' he said in English.

In the event it was simpler than Catinus had expected. Hefydd had passed through the camp that night without a problem and discovered that the only guard on Drest's tent was at the entrance. He cut a slit in the leather at the rear and slipped inside. From the snores he guessed that there were three people sleeping inside. After letting his eyes adjust to the gloom, he was just able to make out the shape of two men asleep near the entrance, presumably servants. The king himself had to be the man in the bed of furs near the rear wall. He placed the message in its pouch on the man's chest and returned the way he'd come.

He'd been challenged when he was leaving the camp but he'd called out that he needed to answer a call of nature and ran off before the sentry could grab him.

'You did what?' Oswiu was not pleased when Catinus told him what he'd done.

'I didn't have time to find you and get your agreement first, Cyning. I acted in what I thought was the best interests of us all, and you in particular.'

In truth, Catinus was more than a little annoyed at the king's reaction when he told him what he'd done. The message left for Drest by Hefydd had promised him the support of Oswiu and the Pictish kings loyal to him if he refused to fight alongside his cousin in the coming battle. With Drest hopefully neutralised, Oswiu would outnumber Garnait by two to one.

'Well, what's done is done but I refuse to be held by a promise that you had no right to make on my behalf.'

'Then you had better find someone else to look after Penntir for you. I can hardly be its eorl if I'm forsworn.'

'Get out! Get out before I take Bebbanburg away from you too.'

Catinus bit back the retort on the tip of his tongue, bowed curtly and swept out of the king's tent, nearly knocking down the sentry standing outside on his way. He was learning that the favour of kings could be somewhat fickle.

'You're right, of course, Catinus had no right to compromise your choice of the next high king,' Elfin said later when Oswiu told him what had happened. 'However, he's given you victory on a plate, and without costing you men in battle that you can ill afford to lose if you want to pursue Domnall next.'

Oswiu saw the sense in what Elfin was saying, but he refused to accept it. He was still furious with Catinus for what he saw as his high handed action.

When he formed his army up on the north slope of A' Bheinn Mheanbh overlooking the Pict's camp he saw that the part of the camp that had been occupied by Drest's men was deserted. Only the smouldering remains of their campfires and patches of dead grass where their tents had stood showed where they had been. Catinus' ploy had evidently worked.

Garnait had looked up at the massed ranks of Northumbrians and their allies and decided that his only hope was to escape. Abandoning his men he and his gesith headed north on horseback, wending their way through the traps they had dug. Just when he thought he was clear, Alweo and Catinus appeared around a spur of Beinn á Choin where it came down to meet Loch Katrine. They and their men took up position facing Garnait and his bodyguard, who had halted in dismay.

Some tried to flee back the way they had come but, in their panic, they forgot about the concealed pits and fell into them, dying on the pointed stakes at the bottom. The others stood their ground and met the charge head on.

Catinus found his quarry and lined his spear up, aiming at Garnait. One man tried to get in his way but he took the man's spear point on his shield before his heavier horse barged the pony that the Pict was riding out of the way. Garnait knew he'd met his nemesis and didn't even try to defend himself as Catinus' spear struck his chainmail covered chest. The point skidded across the surface, ripping the links apart before entering the king's head under his jaw. The point carried on up through the back of his mouth and into his brain before emerging through the back of his skull, knocking his helmet flying.

Half an hour later, whilst the victorious Northumbrians were building a compound to confine the two hundred and fifty Picts who had surrendered, Catinus took the mangled head of the former high king and presented it to Oswiu.

'I suppose you think that now I'll forgive you?'

'I was rather hoping you might, Cyning. If Drest isn't the man you want to succeed his cousin, then perhaps I should go and kill him too, just to prevent myself from becoming forsworn.'

Oswiu's eyes narrowed for a moment, then he burst out laughing.

'That won't be necessary, Catinus. At least not yet. Let's see if he can be more loyal than his late kinsman.'

CHAPTER TEN – THE SUBJUGATION OF DALRIADA

662 AD

With Garnait dead, Oswiu now advanced into Dalriada. He puzzled over Garnait's motivation for some time but didn't really understand why he'd allowed himself to be bribed to allow Domnall and his routed army to pass. He had discussed this with his chaplain, as he had spent a little time with the Picts when he was younger, but Conomultus was as mystified as his king was.

It wasn't until he spoke to Catinus that he understood.

'Garnait obviously assumed that the Dalriadans had inflicted significant losses on you when you defeated them, or perhaps that was what Domnall had told him. I suspect that he saw an opportunity to drive you out of Caledonia and took it. Had you and Elfin really been weakened by the battle at the old hill fort then he might well have been able to succeed. Presumably that's why his cousin joined him, and then changed his mind when he saw how strong we were in reality.'

'Helped, no doubt, by the promise you made for me.'

Oswiu frowned at the recollection. He obviously hadn't completely forgiven Catinus for offering his support for Drest's bid to become high king.

'Is there no message from your son, saying when he plans to join us?'

'No,' Oswiu replied curtly, his frown deepening. 'He'd better had a very good reason for disobeying me.'

'Perhaps Mercia is causing him concern?'

'No, I would have heard. Now stop chattering and leave me in peace.'

Catinus dropped back to ride beside Redwald, the hereræswa of the army.

'The king doesn't seem to be his usual self,' he said quietly after glancing around to make sure they couldn't be overheard.

'No, he's worried that Alchfrith is turning into another Œthelwald. It's eating away at him.'

The co-incidence that both Œthelwald and Alchfrith had been made Kings of Deira by him didn't help. Œthelwald had been Oswiu's nephew, King Oswald's only son, who had betrayed him by siding with Penda of Mercia. Oswiu had given Catinus the unpleasant job of killing Œthelwald after the Battle of the Winwaed, where Oswiu had defeated and killed his nemesis, Penda. The fact that Catinus had killed Œthelwald in a fair fight didn't do much to ease the former's conscience.

'Then why doesn't he leave Dalriada for now; he's done what he came to do: drive Domnall out of the territory he'd invaded.'

'You don't know the king very well, do you?'

'I thought I did.'

'He's ambitious. He loved his brother Oswald but he hated it when he became King of Northumbria and he had to make do with Rheged. Then he was apoplectic with rage when Oswine became King of Deira instead of him. He schemed to re-unite Northumbria because that's what Oswald had done and he killed Oswine to achieve that. Then he wanted to exceed his brother's success and so he became Bretwalda of Caledonia. It was something Oswald hadn't done and I suspect he felt great satisfaction in his accomplishment.

'Now he's determined to hang onto his position here in Caledonia, come what may. I've tried to convince him that he only needs allies up here to secure the northern border of Northumbria from attack, but he sees himself king of all of Britannia north of the Humber.'

'You're saying that he'd risk everything he has already just to rule over Caledonia as well as Northumbria?'

'That's about the size of it. I just hope that Wulfhere isn't temped to invade whilst Oswiu is weeks away from his southern lands. I have to say that I support Alchfrith's decision to stay and guard the south, though I've more sense that to tell Oswiu that to his face.'

'Why are you telling me all this? I might betray you to Oswiu.'

'I suspect he already knows what I feel; besides, I need your help me to persuade Oswiu to get this over with as quickly as possible and return to Eoforwīc.'

'Why, if Wulfhere is behaving himself at the moment and Alchfrith has the nobles, their warbands and the fyrd at his disposal? What's the rush? Is it that you don't trust his son?'

Redwald sighed and was lost deep in thought for a moment.

'Can I trust you, Catinus?'

'I don't know if you can trust me, but Oswiu certainly can. I owe him everything. I'd still be a Mercian shepherd if it weren't for him. He rescued me and Conomultus from that life and made me a warrior, a member of his gesith, and then an ealdorman. That allowed me to marry a nobly born Angle girl and sire fine children. I am entirely loyal to him.'

'Yes, I appreciate all that. But what I'm about to tell you is secret. It will give you power over me and I'm not sure that I'm ready to do that. I'd prefer it if I knew something about you that would balance what I'm about to say.'

'Very well. I'll tell you something that only one man, other than Oswiu, knows about me. It's something that troubles me to this day but I acted with as much honour as possible in the circumstances.'

'Go on. I swear your secret, if that's what it is, is safe with me.'

'Oswiu charged me with killing Œthelwald quietly so that he disappeared. I did so, but I couldn't do it in cold blood. I killed him in fair fight and buried him in the woods where no-one would ever find his grave. Slaying him bothers me, but not so much as the fact that he was buried in unhallowed ground with no priest to shrive him and send him on his way. The men with me that day are all dead now, only my brother knows what I've just told you.'

'Thank you. I did wonder what had happened to him. Very well; it's not Alchfrith that Oswiu needs to worry about. Oh, he might well betray his father, but he is being manipulated by another, as is the queen.'

'Who? Oh, Abbot Wilfrid?'

'Yes. The man is as sly as a snake and as charming as a courtesan. He is a fanatical Roman and despises the Celtic Church. But his aim isn't just to drive them out of Northumbria. He wants to be bishop with his seat at Eoforwīc. He'd be only too happy if Lindisfarne slid into obscurity; it really infuriates him that it's the centre of Christianity in Northern Britain.

'But it isn't just spiritual power he craves. He regards the banishment of his father, the former Eorl of Hexham, as totally unjust. I suspect that he harbours a deep hatred for Oswiu as the man he holds responsible. But he seeks power, temporal power, as well as a life of luxury so he keeps his hatred in check, for now. He's a complex individual which makes it so difficult to guess what he'll do next.'

'How do you know all this?'

'Because you don't stay as the right hand man of the most powerful king in Britain without making sure that you know what's going on. I have agents in the right places and I keep my ears open and my mouth shut. No-one else knows what I've just confided to you.'

'Not even Oswiu?'

'Least of all him. If I tried to turn him against Wilfrid I'd lose his favour. His wife dotes on the man and Oswiu really suffered when they were estranged. He'll not risk that again.'

'So what do we do?'

'We watch, we listen and we tell each other everything we learn. I'm fairly sure that Wilfrid plots to depose or kill Oswiu and put his puppet, Alchfrith, on the throne. We must prevent that at all costs.'

'Yes, I agree. However, Oswiu is no longer young. Many men are dead by his age. Who knows how much longer he'll survive; what then?'

'Ecgfrith will soon be seventeen. In a year or so he'll be old enough to rule.'

~~~

Wilfrid was feeling pleased. He'd managed to persuade Alchfrith that to abandon the border with Mercia and scuttle off to the far north would be suicidal. Not only that, Eanflæd was now convinced that Alchfrith was correct not to desert Deira at this time. If that didn't drive a wedge between the two of them and Oswiu nothing would. He would be angry with his son when he returned and, when his wife backed Alchfrith up, he could just imagine the king's reaction. He just hoped that this time the rift would be irreparable.

Not only that, Alchfrith saw the sense in moving the seat of the bishop to Eoforwīc. He was fairly certain that Colman would refuse to move from Lindisfarne. He was that much closer to achieving his aim of becoming a bishop. Now he would concentrate on getting the Roman Church accepted as the true Christian faith.

It was all going so well and then disaster struck. The plague returned and this time the centre of the outbreak was Eoforwīc. Wilfrid was many things but one thing he wasn't was a coward. Besides, he was confident that God would protect him. He organised a makeshift infirmary for those who succumbed to the disease and got the garrison to organise the burning of the bedding and clothes of the victims. Unlike most who thought that the disease was transmitted through the air, he believed that it travelled through contact.

The bodies were buried in lime pits as soon as possible after they died and Wilfrid worked tirelessly until the worst was over. His popularity increased and some of the local people were now calling him a saint, something that he relished in private but which he modestly declined to agree to in public. That just made him even more respected.

It was what he needed. His agents spread the idea that he should be made a bishop so that he was able to care for the souls of the people of Eoforwīc as well as their bodies. He thought that the idea would please the queen, but he hadn't appreciated that, whilst she might support his ambition, she didn't agree with the means he was using.

'Wilfrid, I'm told that the people are calling for you to be made their bishop,' Eanflæd said brusquely when he came to make one of his regular reports about the plague. 'Don't they know that they already have one in Colman of Lindisfarne?'

Wilfrid wasn't certain whether the queen was genuinely puzzled or subtlety rebuking him for not discouraging such talk.

'Síþwíf, Northumbria is now a vast diocese. Colman can't be expected to be everywhere,' he replied cautiously.

Everyone knew that, unlike his predecessors, Colman rarely strayed far from Lindisfarne. Really, Wilfrid thought, he's playing right into my hands.

'That's as maybe, but it's not for the common people to decide who should or should not be their bishop. It's a disturbing development and I'll have to talk to the king about it when he returns.'

She sniffed disdainfully to indicate what she thought of popular demands before turning to the purpose of his visit.

'Has the epidemic died out now?'

'There were only three new cases yesterday, Síþwíf, all in the same family. A couple and their six year old daughter. We must pray for their recovery and that the outbreak is now all but over.'

'Yes, indeed.'

She shuddered. The king's hall had been put into quarantine as soon as the plague appeared in the town. Only Wilfrid was allowed to come and go. Provisions were left at the gate for the servants to bring in once the suppliers had left. Eanflæd wasn't about to risk two-year old Ælfwine catching it. She was only thankful that his elder brother, Ecgfrith, was away looking after his estates elsewhere in Deira. He'd wanted to take his warband and join his father, but Alchfrith had forbidden any of his nobles to leave, for which she was grateful.

~~~

The fortress of Dùn Add was surrounded. Oswiu was surprised that the settlement around it seemed to be smaller than it was when he was last here. Even some of the huts that still stood had been abandoned. It was obvious that the population had dwindled since he and Oswald had lived here with their mother. No doubt the various wars and the plague had taken its toll.

When he awoke on the first morning after arriving the place was eerily quiet. It wasn't until he looked outside the tent and saw the mist which enveloped everywhere that he understood. The moisture laden air absorbed sound like a sponge. He worried that Domnall might have taken advantage of the poor visibility to flee but, when the sun later burnt off the mist, he saw that his banner was still flying above the dun. He shivered in the chill air and went back into his tent to allow his servants to dress him.

Two weeks later the situation hadn't altered much, except the weather had changed to alternating days of warm sunshine and heavy rain. Now the noise from the camp reflected the increase in the number of besiegers. He had taken a gamble and had summoned the Sub-kings of Islay, Lorne and Mael Duin of Cowal, Domnall's brother, to meet him there with their warbands. To his intense relief all three had come and had formally acknowledged him as their overlord.

That left Domnall isolated but Oswiu didn't have the time to continue a siege of Dùn Add until starvation forced it to surrender. He was due at the Council of the Pictish Kings in three weeks to elect the new high king.

'What will you do?' Redwald asked him. 'You've been away from Northumbria for too long as it is.'

'Don't start that again. I know you're right but reminding me all the time isn't helping.'

Oswiu paced up and down inside his tent, lost in thought. He had two alternatives: a direct assault, but that could be costly in terms of casualties, or leave Redwald and Elfin here to conduct the siege whilst he, Catinus and the Eorl of Prydenn, accompanied by their respective gesiths, rode to Stirling to attend the council. However, he was loathe to do that in case the miscellany of men that made up the besiegers melted away in his absence. The only common loyalty they had was to him as their bretwalda.

He looked up at the palisaded fortress sitting on top of its mound and wondered again how he might best attack it. The mound on which it stood looked like an enormous burial barrow with a circular mound raised above it about two-thirds the way along. There were two palisades: a circular one twelve feet high around the king's hall on top of the upper knoll and an outer one that was constructed as an ellipse near the top of the lower hill. Inside the outer defences stood the warrior's hall, another hall for the married men on duty in the fortress and other huts which were storerooms and the like.

He considered using fire arrows but the intermittent heavy rain had made that impractical. The thatch on the roofs would be still be sodden. There was a steep path up to the main gates in the outer palisade furthest away from the king's hall and a small postern gate at the other end of the mound. This had a narrow path which zig-zagged up to the gate from the level ground below where the rest of the settlement stood.

Both exits had been closely watched ever since their arrival so, in addition to the evidence provided by the banner, he was confident that Domnall was still bottled up inside. He was still debating what to do when there was a development. Mael Duin asked for a private audience.

Redwald, Catinus and Alweo all counselled against it.

'Suppose he tries to kill you?'

'Why does it need to be in private? What is he going to say that your nobles can't hear?'

'I smell something fishy here,'

They had all tried to speak at once and Oswiu held up his hands for quiet. The three stopped speaking but the king sensed their agitation in the silence that followed.

'I know you don't trust him, but he's the only alternative unless I try and make one of the other two sub-kings the King of Dalriada. As they dislike one another I hardly think that would work. However, they have both indicated that they would accept Mael's rule.'

'Very well,' Redwald said at last. 'But I'll search him for weapons first.'

'Tell him that I too will be unarmed.'

The three filed out of the tent into the rain leaving Oswiu alone for a moment. Shortly afterwards Mael entered after giving up his sword and dagger to the sentries. He shook the water from his cloak onto the earth floor of the tent. It had been covered in straw but that had been trodden into the mire long since and so it didn't make much difference to the amount of mud in the entrance way.

'Why the need for privacy?' Oswiu asked him without preamble.

Mael licked his lips nervously before replying.

'I have a proposition to put to you but I had rather my fellow Dalriadans didn't get to know about it.'

'Go on.'

The sound of the rain hitting the taut leather surface of the tent got louder as Mael hesitated.

'Provided that you recognise me as king and promise me that you'll execute my brother, I'll appeal to his men to surrender. As you've taken the wives and children of the garrison captive the threat of executing them will force them to surrender. Hopefully, if the married men capitulate, the single warriors will do the same.'

'Hmmm, I can see why you didn't want your suggestion that I kill your women and children broadcast. It would end any chance of you being accepted as king. But I don't understand how you intend to keep this from the other two kings and your own people from Cowal. Surely they would be appalled by such a threat?'

'Which is why you need to send someone into the fortress to take the warning to the married men without Domnall or anyone else knowing. Once they are convinced it'll be up to them to get the single men to agree.'

'But it's bound to come out later.'

'Yes, but I can claim it was just a ploy by you which I knew nothing about.'

'It's hardly likely to make me popular is it?

'Provided you have my loyalty, does that matter?'

Oswiu ignored that and changed tack.

'And how does this messenger get into the fortress?'

'The same way as Catinus got into Dùn Breatainn a couple of years ago. There is a garbage chute on the far side of the hill above a near vertical gully. There is a small hatch in the base of the palisade from where the rubbish is thrown out. It's kept secure by a wooden bar but a seax inserted between the hatch and the palisade should be able to lift it out of the way.'

'So all I have to do is to find someone who speaks the variety of Gaelic spoken by you Dalriadans and is also foolish enough to risk his life?'

'Yes, and also someone who is small enough to fit through the hatch; preferably a boy.'

'Who would listen to a boy?'

'They don't have to. I'll send a written message to be given to someone inside who I believe is loyal to me.'

'I see. So you have someone in mind?'

'Yes, you can leave that part to me. All I need from you is your agreement and for you to put the threat in writing.'

'Very well. It's worth a try. Have you told this messenger? Is he willing to risk his life for you?'

'Yes, he is. It's Eógan, my eldest son.'

Eógan crept towards the hill on which the fortress was built, waiting until the moon went behind a cloud before moving again. He was small for fourteen but he'd completed his training as a warrior and, in the manner of young warriors, he was fearless. He didn't regard this mission as dangerous; it was exciting and he relished the trust his father had placed in him.

The night was far from still. An owl swept overhead, its wing startling him, seeking its prey. Small nocturnal animals scuttled about and a wildcat hissed at him as he passed it before continuing to devour the meal it had just killed. The small noises he made went unnoticed amongst the rest. The air was dry but the ground was wet and he nearly slipped as he climbed up the hill beside the gulley full of detritus from the fortress.

It stank, but that was a good thing. It meant that sentry patrolling along the walkway didn't loiter when he reached that point. Eógan nearly lost his footing again on the wet grass beside the hatch but he managed to grab the base of a prickly bush just in time. His hand and arm were lacerated by thorns but it didn't matter. He was there.

He cautiously inserted the blade of his seax between the left hand side of the hatch and lifted it until he felt resistance. He pushed the blade up with all his might but at first it didn't move. Then suddenly the bar lifted and the small door swung inwards.

Seconds later the boy was inside the inner palisade. Carefully he shut the hatch and placed the bar back in position. Now all he had to do was find his contact. He knew that he would be in the hall occupied by the married warriors and, having been there once before when he was younger, he made his way through the darkness to where he thought it was.

He had just reached the hall when he heard a movement behind him. Before he could react, a hand clamped itself over his mouth and a dagger pricked his neck, drawing a trickle of blood.

'Now what are you doing sneaking around here, lad. You are hardly a married man so you have no business here. I'm going to remove my hand so you can talk but if you do anything else but whisper the answers to my questions I'll slit your throat. Nod if you understand.

'Good, now who are you and what are you doing here?'

Eógan knew it was useless to give a false name. Many warriors in the fortress would recognise him as Mael Duin's son.

'I'm Eógan mac Mael and I have a message for one of the warriors in the hall.'

'Eógan? The King of Cowall's son? What message? Who is it for?'

'That's my business, not yours.'

'Don't get coy with me laddie. King's son or not, you have my dagger at your throat.'

'Do you have family down there?'

He pointed towards the settlement outside the fortress.

'Yes, my wife and three children. Why?'

'If I fail in my mission they will all be killed by Oswiu tomorrow morning.'

'What? He'd never dare! He'd be reviled throughout Dalriada and beyond.'

'Then let's hope I'm successful. Now let me go.'

'Very well. Wait. You can't go bumbling around in there in the dark. You don't even know where the man you seek will be. Tell me his name and I'll fetch him out to you.'

Five minutes later Eógan handed the message over but there wasn't enough light to see by. The two went inside the hall where a torch burned by the entrance to guide those who needed to go outside to piss during the night. Neither noticed that the man who had first discovered Eógan had disappeared. The man paled when he read the message.

'Do you know what this says?'

The boy nodded. 'Hopefully you'll be able to persuade the garrison to surrender and then this won't be necessary.'

Just at that moment the first man returned but he wasn't alone. King Domnall and four armed warriors were with him.

'What's going on? Give me that letter.'

The king snatched it away and quickly scanned the contents.

'Well, it seems we have a couple of traitors here, one of them being my nephew,' he said with a triumphant gleam in his eye. 'Disarm them and bring them up to my hall.'

'Wait! Aren't you going to tell your warriors the dire warning the letter contains?' Eógan's contact asked.

By now all of the warriors in the hall were awake and many were on their feet.

'It doesn't concern them,' the king replied tersely. 'Do as I say and disarm them, then gag them.'

'Oh, but it does concern them if their wives and children are all about to be put to the sword.'

At that even Domnall's escort paused.

'What's he saying, Brenin?' one of the men in the hall asked.

There was a murmur from the rest and one or two picked up their weapons.

'He's trying to fool you,' Domnall blustered.

'I've known him all my life and I've never known a truer man. Tell us what's in the letter or give it to me.'

The man who spoke stood head and shoulders above the rest. He had sworn an oath of loyalty to Domnall, but the mention of a threat to his wife and two daughters gave him the courage to stand up to the king.

Domnall realised that the mood in the hall was turning against him. Despite what the man had demanded he doubted if any of them was able to read. The only one who could was the former monk to whom the message had been sent.

'Very well, can you read it? No, I thought not.'

'No, but I can.'

Domnall panicked, which was his undoing. He drew his seax and stabbed the ex-monk in the stomach. He collapsed on the floor, screaming in agony. The king's action had been unexpected and no-one moved for a moment, then Eógan realised that his mission now faced failure. He was furious and, without thinking, he pulled out his own seax and slashed it across his uncle's throat.

The king gurgled and fell to his knees as the blood from his carotid artery spurted across the floor and all over Eógan. His escort went to kill the boy in retribution but the big warrior stepped in front of them holding his axe.

'Leave him be. Domnall's dead and the boy who slew him is the eldest son of the man who's likely to be the next King of Dalriada. Kill him and the first thing he'll do is hang you.'

It wasn't the outcome that Oswiu had expected, but when Redwald fetched him from his tent the next morning, he went outside just as the gates of the fortress were opened to allow the garrison to troop out through the incessant light rain and swear allegiance to King Mael.

CHAPTER ELEVEN – THE SYNOD OF WHITBY

663 to 664 AD

'Why didn't you do as I ordered?'

Oswiu and his son glared at each other. They were standing in the king's hall at Loidis, a comparatively mean building compared to those at Eoforwīc and Bebbanburg. The small dimensions crowded in on the two kings and their respective gesiths. The place reeked of old wood smoke, which had stained the timbers black with soot over the years, and it smelt damp. Oswiu noted with annoyance that the rain was leaking through the thatch at several points. At least Alchfrith might have had the sense to keep his home in good repair.

'Because I'd have been stupid to have left Deira wide open to attacks from the Mercians.'

'I didn't ask you to bring the fyrd. They would have been enough to deter Wulfhere from doing anything stupid, especially as he's at odds with Wessex again. No, you deliberately disobeyed me.'

Abbot Wilfrid, who's been talking to Alchfrith when Oswiu had stormed into the hall with his men, coughed discretely.

'Do you think we should take this conversation into the king's chamber where there is more privacy?'

Oswiu looked around him, as if realising that there were others present for the first time, then nodded and followed his son through the door into his sleeping chamber. When Wilfrid went to follow him Owsiu held up his hand to stop him.

'Private I think you said, abbot. I don't need you.'

'Well? Don't you think I'd considered the situation with Mercia before I summoned you?' he asked his son as soon as they were alone.

'I think you were obsessed with regaining Dalriada to the exclusion of everything else,' his son retorted with some heat.

Oswiu took a deep breath to retain control of his own temper.

'If I can't depend on you as my vassal then you're no use to me.'

'What are you going to do? Depose me?'

'Yes, if you continue with that attitude.'

'Let's face it, father, you've never had any time for me and now you seek to replace me with that pampered fool Ecgfrith, as soon as he's old enough'

Oswiu was taken by surprise. He had indeed been considering doing just that.

'Your brother is neither spoilt not stupid, and he is loyal to me. I'm beginning to doubt that you are.'

Alchfrith realised that he'd miscalculated, and badly so. He'd expected his father to deny that he'd ever thought of taking away his throne. Now it seemed that he was considering doing exactly that. His first reaction was resentment but then his instinct for survival kicked in and he realised that he needed to extricate himself from the situation, not dig himself in deeper.

'Father, I'm sorry. I realise now that I should have trusted your judgment and come to your aid when you needed me.'

'Yes, you should. As it was I managed without you, thanks to Drest's abandonment of his cousin and Mael's eagerness to sit on his brother's throne.'

'Can you forgive me?'

Oswiu sighed. When he was younger he'd have deposed Alchfrith or even have had him killed, but he had mellowed with time and he found himself pardoning him instead.

'Disobey me again or show any sign of disloyalty and I will take Deira away from you; you understand? And get your damned roof fixed,' he added as a cold drop of water hit the back of his neck.

~~~

'I'm glad that you managed to find it in your heart to forgive Alchfrith.'

'Are you? You do realise that Ecgfrith would have replaced him?'

Oswiu was sitting in Eanflæd's chamber in the women's hall at Eoforwīc where she'd been living whilst her husband was away.

'Yes, but that would only have sown dissention amongst your nobles. You've told me that you want Ecgfrith to succeed you as King of Northumbria in due course, when Christ calls you to his side. That's enough for me.'

'You're forgetting about Ælfwine.'

'But he's only two; he's still a baby.'

'Babies grow up to be men all too quickly. I need to do something for him when he's older.'

'There's plenty of time for that. Let him be a child first. You know that Ecgfrith's wife had retreated to her monastery again?' she said, changing the subject. 'That marriage was a mistake; you'll never have a grandson at this rate.'

'What do you expect me to do about it?' he asked, annoyed at the change in direction that the conversation had taken.

In truth, he felt some guilt about arranging his son's marriage to a devout woman who seemed determined to retain her virginity at all costs.

'Get Wilfrid to annul the marriage so our son can marry again.'

'Wilfrid's not a bishop, it would have to be Colman.'

'You know full well that he wouldn't do it. For him 'til death do us part means exactly that. Besides he never leaves Lindisfarne these days. Why don't you make Wilfrid Bishop of Eoforwīc? Then he can look after this part of Northumbria.'

'Bishop of... Did Wilfrid put you up to this?'

'No, it was Alchfrith's idea if you must know, but I do think it's a sensible one.'

'Well I don't agree. Wilfrid's a Roman Catholic for a start, and Northumbria follows the Celtic Church.'

'But I don't, and neither does Alchfrith. The rest of England recognises the Pope as their spiritual leader; it's only Northumbria that doesn't.'

'I'm not the king of the rest of England.'

'Even you must admit that celebrating Easter on two different dates is ridiculous. I and half the court are still observing Lent whilst you're feasting and celebrating the festival.'

'I agree that's awkward but I don't understand what you expect me to do about it.'

'You know that it's the universal practice of all Christians from the Holy Land to Mercia to observe the same date for Easter; only the Ionian community lays down a different date.'

'Even if I agreed with you, I can't see how I could change it.'

'Call a convocation and invite Bishop Colman and representatives of the Roman Church to explain their arguments to you, then make a decision.'

Oswiu thought for a long time about his wife's suggestion before finally nodding his head in agreement.

~~~

Much as he wanted to be reunited with his wife and children again, Catinus had headed directly from Dùn Add to Penntir to take over as the new eorl until Bruide was old enough to rule. He was still smarting from an argument he'd had with his brother before he'd departed. Conomultus hadn't been privy to the threat to kill the women and children and, when he'd heard about it he had been horrified.

He was all for going to tell Oswiu exactly what he thought of him for agreeing to such a plan but Catinus had thankfully been able to stop him. They had argued and eventually Conomultus calmed down. However, when he found out that his brother was aware of the ploy he made no effort to hide his disgust.

'It was only a ruse to get the fortress to surrender, Oswiu had no intention of carrying it out.'

'And since when have you ever know him to back down once he'd made a threat to do something? What would he have done if the garrison hadn't capitulated?'

He paused but Catinus didn't reply.

'No, I thought not. He would have seemed weak if he'd relented and both his pride and his need to keep his vassals in awe of him would have given him no option. He'd have had to start killing them in the hope that they would have then given in. If they hadn't he'd have killed them all.'

'I'm sure you're wrong.'

'Well then, you don't know Oswiu as well as I do.'

His brother had stormed off and they hadn't spoken again before Catinus left. Thankfully though, Conomultus didn't accost Oswiu. He left a message for him instead, saying that he was retiring to Iona for a while. He needed to spend time in meditation as an anchorite.

Catinus knew that Oswiu would be angry at the priest's desertion without obtaining his permission and he suspected that he would now seek another chaplain. He just hoped that the next time he saw his brother he would be in a better frame of mind.

Then another thought sprang unbidden into his mind. If Conomultus had lost the king's favour, might he not also take it out on his brother? It was unworthy and he tried to push it aside but it nagged at him. He had risen far from his humble origins and many resented that. Perhaps they could now turn the king against him as well? It was his greatest fear, far more so than falling in battle.

He decided against travelling from Dùn Add to Elgin overland. It was one hundred and fifty miles as the crow flies and on horseback though the mountains it would probably have taken Catinus some three weeks to accomplish it. As it was, Mael Duin asked the King of Islay to loan him three of his birlinns and two knarrs. By sea around the top of Caledonia was half as far again as the land route, but ships travelled faster and further each day. The voyage wasn't without its small dramas but it only took five days, even putting into the shore each night.

As the small fleet approached the beach at the nearest point to their destination, the inhabitants of the small fishing village fled. The king's hall was at a place called Elgin, some five miles due south of where they had landed. There was no harbour nearby and, as far as Catinus knew, Penntir didn't possess one, nor did it have any ships. It would make communication with Bebbanburg difficult and he decided that one of the first things he would do would be to build a small port near the mouth of the River Lossie, both for ease of trade and connection with the outside world.

It took some time to unload the horses and their equipment so they camped that night near the deserted fishing village. In the morning Catinus bade the Islaymen farewell and they set off on their voyage home.

Without a local guide he was dependent on the little knowledge he'd been able to glean from Bruide before he'd disappeared to Lindisfarne. All he knew was that Elgin lay on the south bank of the River Lossie, which ran south from the coast and then turned west towards its source in the hills to the south west. He only hoped that they'd disembarked at the mouth of the correct river.

When it got light the next morning Catinus awoke to find that the land was covered in a sea mist. He could hardly see ten yards in front of him and he realised that to set out in these conditions would be madness. They'd get lost before they'd gone more than a few steps.

It was then that he spotted a boy not five yards away furtively creeping through the camp clutching a sword. If his filthy appearance and simple tunic made from coarse wool hadn't told Catinus that this wasn't one of his retinue, the stink of fish confirmed it. This must be a local boy who'd decided to risk the opportunity provided by the mist to steal a weapon.

He was just about to disappear again into the greyness that enveloped everywhere when Catinus made his move and jumped on top of him. The boy wheezed in pain as the man's heavy body squeezed the air out of his lungs and for a moment he lay there fighting to breathe. By the time he'd recovered sufficiently to move the man had whipped off the rope belt around his waist and tied his hands behind his back with it.

'Now what's your name and what are you doing here?'

The boy had trouble understanding what the man was saying, but he got the gist. He replied in the local dialect but Catinus had to get him to repeat it several times before he understood him. By this time several of his gesith had gathered around him.

'What's he saying, lord?'

'I think he's saying that his name is Uurad and he's the son of the headman of the nearby fishing village, which I think is called Kinneddar.'

Catinus had experienced no problems in talking to Bruide and he'd assumed that it would be same when he came to Penntir. Now it seemed that the locals spoke a different dialect.

'Well, at least we've found a guide,' Leofric suggested brightly.

'I wouldn't wager on it. He's probably not been more than five miles from his village in his life, not on land at any rate.'

'Perhaps someone from his village has though?' Eadstan, the leader of his gesith, suggested. He had previously been the leader of the garrison at Bebbanburg but when Catinus had formed his own gesith he'd become its leader, handing the more sedentary life guarding Bebbanburg over to an older warrior.

'Good point. We'll have to wait for this mist to clear first though.'

Whilst they were waiting Catinus explained slowly to the boy who he was and assured him that he meant him and his people no harm. After Uurad had given him his word that he wouldn't try and run, he was given something to eat and drink and he scoffed it down as if he hadn't eaten in a week. After he finished he belched loudly and then grinned at Catinus, who he now seemed to think was his best friend.

By noon the mist had just about gone and Uurad took Catinus to where his father was hiding. It took a little time to convince the headman that the new arrivals were friendly but, when he understood that the strange man with black hair was their new ruler, he agreed to take him to Elgin himself. Uurad assumed that he too was invited along and had a heated argument with his father when he told him to stay at the village.

'I think you've found yourself an admirer,' Eadstan told Catinus with a grin.

The eorl gave him a startled look and then smiled.

'Just a bad case of hero worship I suspect, though God alone knows why.'

'Isn't it obvious? He was shit scared of you and then you treated him nicely. His fear changed to relief and then you gave him the best meal he'd ever had. I'm willing to bet his father shows him little attention and he's starved of affection as a result. You can do no wrong in his eyes.'

'Really? If only it was as easy to inspire devotion in grown men.'

'You don't do too badly in that regard. Men respect you; that's far better than puppy love.'

Catinus looked at the boy running beside his horse and the boy beamed up at him. He had to admit it made him feel good. He only hoped his relationship with his own son would be like that when he was a little older. Oswiu had certainly failed to achieve that with his offspring. He needed to make sure he didn't make the same mistakes with his.

Elgin came as something of a disappointment. Catinus knew that it wouldn't be like Bebbanburg but he hadn't expected it to be quite as bad as it was. The settlement around the king's hall was little better than a collection of mean hovels; even the church was little more than four wattle and daub walls with a turf roof. The altar was a crude table and the crucifix on it looked as if it had been made by a young child.

The hall was little better. There was no separate warriors' hall, nor did the married warriors seem to have huts of their own. They all lived together and even the king had enjoyed little privacy, having a bed in one corner it seemed. Catinus' heart was in his shoes. He could hardly bring Leoflaed and the children here. His wife would have a fit, especially with a new baby due soon.

He decided there and then that he would have to build a new hall, and one that was protected. This one didn't even have a palisade around it. He started to think where to site it but then he had another idea. If he was going to go to the trouble and expense of constructing a new hall, he might as well locate it on the coast, perhaps at the mouth of the river, and create a harbour there as well. It needn't be anything elaborate, just a simple jetty with deep enough water for ships to tie up there at any state of the tide.

He would build two halls, one for him and his family and one for his single warriors. Once the married men had built their own huts their families could join them. The more he thought about it, the more enthusiastic he became.

Once he had made his mind up what he was going to do he explained to the headman that he planned to base himself across the river mouth from his village, but the man shook his head.

'There is bad ground there; swampy,' he explained. 'Better to build it on our side of the river. We can move the huts that would be in your way further down the beach. That way you can also protect us from raiders.'

Catinus didn't understand why anyone would want to attack a settlement of poor fishermen, but he didn't question what the man had said. It was only later that he found out that the men from Cait and the Orcades were in the habit of raiding them from time to time for slaves.

The inhabitants of Elgin weren't quite so pleased by Catinus' plans. However, once they had got used to the idea, the reeve and several of them decided that they would also move to the coast and form the nucleus of the new settlement at Kinneddar.

Two months later the two halls were finished and Catinus moved his base to the mouth of the Lossie. Work had just started on a church and on the palisade that would turn the place into a fortress and Catinus decided that the place was now fit enough to invite his wife to move there. Three weeks later she arrived, bringing with her their new baby boy.

'What shall we call him?'

'You haven't baptised him yet?'

'No, I wanted you to be there. Have you chosen a name?'

'I had thought of Conomultus after my brother, but I think he should have a proper Anglian name so I decided on Osfrid - that is, if you approve?'

'Gentle friend, not the name for a warrior then.'

'No, we named our eldest son Alaric, meaning noble ruler. He will be my heir so I hope that this one will become a monk or a priest.'

She nodded. 'Very well, Osfrid it is.'

Two days later the headman came to see Catinus again.

'It's my youngest son, lord. He wishes to serve you as a servant, if you'll have him.'

Evidently the boy hadn't got over his hero-worship of the new eorl. Catinus was about to dismiss the man's request when something made him pause. Hefydd was no longer a slave, though he was still his body servant. He knew the boy desired to become a warrior and he was of an age to be trained as one now. This might be an opportunity to allow him to do that.

'Very well, send him to me tomorrow, but he is to scrub his body and his hair clean and Hefydd will give you a clean tunic for him to wear. If I get one whiff of fish when he arrives I'll send him straight back to you. Hefydd will train him for a week. If he doesn't learn what he needs to in that time I'll send him back to you. Understand?'

'Yes, lord. Thank you. He's a good boy and I'm certain that he'll serve you well.'

'We shall see.'

Things settled down over the next few months and by the start of summer the jetty and deep water access was finished, as was the church and the new huts. Penntir's bishop was also the abbot of the monastery that Saint Aidan had founded years ago further along the coast. He occasionally visited but mainly left the spiritual welfare of Kinneddar, as the new capital of Penntir was now called, in the hands of its priest.

Uurad proved to be as efficient and loyal as Hefydd had been. Every day the boy thanked God that he now enjoyed a relatively easy life as the eorl's body servant instead of suffering the hardships of a fisherman.

Penntir was prospering under Catinus and, finding him a fair and just ruler, most of the people overcame their distrust of foreigners and he became popular. Things seemed idyllic, but it couldn't last.

Tidings of the upheaval that was about to hit Northumbria came with a merchant who brought a message from the reeve of Bebbanburg. In essence it said that the dissention between the Celtic Church, led by Bishop Colman, and the Roman Catholics, led by Abbot Wilfrid, had grown so serious that Oswiu had decided to call a synod of all church leaders in his domain to resolve the issue. The synod was to convene at the monastery of Whitby during the last week of August, which was only a month away.

Catinus decided that he wished to attend. It would give him the opportunity to check on things at Bebbanburg on the way as well. So he set off in a hired knarr with a small escort a week later. He took Uurad with him but Hefydd had started his training to be a warrior, so he was left behind with the rest of his gesith to guard Catinus' family. For a moment Hefydd regretted that he was no longer the eorl's servant as he watched the knarr sail over the horizon. He enjoyed learning how to fight, but it was hard work and lacked any real excitement. Sailing down to Whitby to attend the great synod would have been a lot more interesting.

~~~

Catinus nervously paced up and down in the nave of the church. Oswiu had sent for him but he was being kept waiting, perhaps deliberately. He worried that he shouldn't have come to Whitby; he had no real excuse to be there, other than curiosity. Oswiu seemed more irascible as he got older, perhaps he would punish Catinus for deserting his post? The thought made him depressed. He'd achieved a great deal in this life and his dearest wish was to pass Bebbanburg onto his elder son. The thought that his impetuosity might have put that in jeopardy was unbearable.

It didn't help that some of the few nobles who were present seemed to take pleasure in his evident discomfort. Even Abbot Wilfrid had laughed when he had glanced towards him. Obviously he was making snide remarks about him to whoever he was talking to; he had no evidence of that, but his body language gave him away.

Suddenly the great west door was opened by a sentry and a young man stalked into the church. He took off his brown leather gloves and beat them against his dark green tunic to get rid of some of the dust that covered it. Next he did the same to his trousers before taking off his cloak and handing it to a nearby servant, who bowed as he took it.

If Catinus hadn't recognised Alchfrith he'd have still known that he was a high-born noble from the heavy gold embroidery around the neck, cuffs and hem of his finely woven tunic. To his surprise the king's son made his way over towards him, nodding pleasantly to those he passed on the way.

'Well, Catinus. I didn't expect to see you here.'

'Nor, apparently, did your father, Cyning. I've been summoned.'

'And you think you're in trouble? I doubt it; he probably just wants a first-hand report of how things are in the Land of the Picts.'

'I could be in trouble in that case. I hardly know what's going on in the rest of Prydenn, isolated as I am up there, let alone able keep abreast of events in the other kingdoms.'

He realised that he spoken with some asperity, caused by his nervousness.

'I'm sorry, I didn't mean to speak so sharply. I just wish that I was back in Bebbanburg. I feel that I'm wasted up there; anyone could look after Bruide's kingdom for the next few years.'

'Hmmm, I doubt that. Look, we don't know each other well but I know my father thinks highly of your abilities, both as a commander and as a noble. If he wants you based amongst the Picts, he'll have a good reason. He's had enough trouble in the north over the past few years. I suspect that he's relying on you to keep the country peaceful. Perhaps you need to get out a about a bit more if you feel you're cut off in Prydenn.'

When Ecgfrith walked away he realised that the prince was right. He'd been too busy looking after the people and improving their lot to do what he should have been doing. A few minutes later a priest he recognised approached him and told him that the king would see him now. He was surprised to be summoned by him. The man was Romanus, the queen's chaplain. Evidently his audience was to be with both the king and queen. His sense of foreboding increased.

He was led into a side chapel, separated from the nave by a wooden screen. Oswiu sat at one side of the altar table and Eanflæd the other. Alchfrith stood behind his mother with a scowl on his face and Ecgfrith behind his father. He could tell nothing from the expression on the faces of the other three.

He bowed to both the king and his queen before standing waiting patiently before them. He hoped that he'd managed to keep his face as expressionless as they had.

'Ah, Catinus, good,' Oswiu said, smiling briefly.

Catinus allowed himself to relax a little, it didn't seem to be the greeting normally given to a man who was about to be disciplined.

'I assume that you're here to brief me about the situation in Pictland, but that will have to wait. There are more pressing matters at the moment; that is, unless some disaster had occurred?'

'No, Cyning. All was quiet when I left.'

'Very well. Alweo was to have gone into Mercia to escort Agilbert, the Bishop of Wessex, here. He has been chosen by the Archbishop of Cantwareburg to present the case for the Roman Church. Unfortunately he's had a hunting accident and can't ride at the moment.'

'Is it serious, Cyning?'

'No, just a few fractured ribs I believe, but he finds riding painful and travelling a long distance is out of the question. I was going to ask one of the eorls to go but you know how they are; they'd think it beneath their dignity and make a fuss.'

'Whereas I'll do as I'm told,' Catinus interrupted with a smile.

'I wasn't going to put it quite like that, but you've never been one to stand on your dignity.'

I'd be happy to go and escort the bishop here, naturally, but I've only brought a few of my gesith with me as we had to buy places on a merchantman. Prydenn has no ships of its own at the moment, something I'm in the process of rectifying.'

'Perhaps I might accompany Eorl Catinus, father? I've fifteen men in my gesith who can ride well enough.'

Oswiu looked round at Ecgfrith in surprise. If the eorls though escort duty was beneath them, he would never have expected one of his sons to volunteer.

'Really? Very well, if you're sure; I'm certain Catinus would welcome the company.'

'What's the real reason you wanted to come with me,' Catinus asked him quietly the following morning as they rode south west at a gentle pace.

'I wanted to get away from the glowering looks my elder brother keeps giving me,' he replied flippantly.

Catinus gave him a pained look.

'Oh, very well. My father is getting old and, whilst I hope he'll live a good few years yet, it's evident that there will be a struggle between Alchfrith and me for the throne as soon as he dies. I would be lying if I said I'm not ambitious, but I'm also convinced that Alchfrith will make a weak king. He's under the influence of that weasel, Wilfrid, for a start. Now there's a man who craves power and glory if ever I saw one.'

'So you want to sound me out and find out where my loyalties would lie, assuming I outlive the king, of course.'

'I see that subtlety is not one of your qualities.'

'No, but loyalty is. I will support whoever the king wants to succeed him and whoever the Witan elects.'

'And if they are different men?'

'Then God help the kingdom. We need to remain united in the face of our enemies.'

~~~

Three days later the synod convened. The debate was to be conducted by Bishop Colman, Abbess Hild of Whitby and Abbot Eata of Melrose on behalf of the Celtic Church, whilst Bishop

Agilbert, Abbot Wilfrid of Ripon, the aged John the Deacon and the Queen's chaplain, Romanus, spoke for the Church of Rome. Oswiu invited Colman to speak first and he kept his arguments short and to the point.

'Cyning, we who were educated on Iona follow the teachings of the blessed Saint Columba of blessed memory. He instructed us to eschew the trappings of this world and to embrace poverty. The Romans, on the other hand, love wealth and temporal power. As for setting the date of Easter, we follow the method laid down by Saint John the Evangelist, which is to coincide it with the Jewish Passover.'

Agilbert spoke next but Frankish was his native language and his English was so heavily accented that no-one understood him. Therefore Wilfrid was given permission to speak on his behalf and under his direction. He contested Colman's claim to use of John the Evangelist's method of calculation, saying that they didn't adhere to it properly. But that was irrelevant in any case; the Roman Church celebrated Easter using the method of calculation laid down by Saint Peter. He reminded everyone present that it was Saint Peter who held in his hands the keys to the Gates of Heaven before going on to point out that every Christian on the Continent and even the Orthodox Churches in the East followed Saint Peter's directive. It was only the Irish and the Caledonians who clung to the mistaken method of calculation advocated by Colman.

After the others had rehearsed similar arguments Oswiu asked Colman if it was true that Saint Peter held the keys to Heaven. When he reluctantly admitted that this was so, Oswiu reached his decision.

CHAPTER TWELVE – ALCFRITH'S REVOLT
664 AD

Catinus was loaned a birlinn by Ecgfrith in which to return to Kinneddar and he made haste to depart Whitby immediately the synod was over - before Oswiu remembered that he wanted an account of the situation in the north, Catinus' ostensible reason for being there.

It was therefore only sporadically that tidings reached him about subsequent events in Northumbria. These reports were often unclear and conflicting so it was only much later in the year that he understood what had transpired.

Colman had had a blazing row with the king as soon as Oswiu had announced his decision in favour of the Roman Church's method of calculating Easter. He hadn't said that he had accepted the Pope as the ultimate spiritual authority, but everyone thought that was a foregone conclusion, given time. Colman had immediately left Lindisfarne for Iona in high dudgeon taking most of the monks there with him, including the Master of Novices. This left both Bruide and Lethlobar's half-brother, Ruaidhrí, without a mentor.

After the dust had settled Tuda, the prior, became bishop and abbot in Colman's place but his term of office was cut short by another catastrophe - the plague returned.

Bruide and Ruaidhrí had become good friends during the two years that they'd been at the monastery and the two debated what they should do in the circumstances.

'I don't want to stay here, not with the plague striking down those who are left, do you?'

'Of course not,' Ruaidhrí replied. 'I'm not an idiot. Besides, what's the point? There is no-one to teach us and in any case our two years is nearly up. But what should we do?'

'Well, I don't know about you but I intend to return to my Kingdom of Prydenn. I might as well train as a warrior there as anywhere, and when I'm sixteen I shall claim my throne.'

'Won't that depend on King Oswiu?'

'If he tries to stop me, I'll fight him,' the boy said fiercely.

Ruaidhrí spluttered with laughter whilst Bruide clenched his fists ready to hit his friend.

'I'm sorry, it was just the image that sprang to mind of you challenging the Bretwalda of the North to a fight.'

Bruide lowered his fists but continued to glower at Ruaidhrí.

'My accession is two years away, anything could happen before then. Oswiu might die.'

'True, but I suspect that whichever of his sons inherits will want to keep his hold on Caledonia.'

'Hopefully my fellow kings will join me in fighting for their independence.'

'Perhaps, but I honestly don't think they are going to listen to a sixteen year old boy, king or not. Besides Oswiu has brought peace and prosperity to Caledonia; why would they want to put that in jeopardy?'

'Because we are Picts, not the slaves of some Anglian.'

Ruaidhrí gave up. They'd had this argument before and all Bruide saw was his dream of a Pictland that was free to do as it wished; presumably start fighting amongst themselves again, thought Ruaidhrí gloomily.

'How do we get to Prydenn then? I'm not even sure I know where it is.'

'You'll come with me?'

'I might as well train as a warrior there as anywhere,'

'Good. Well, we can make a start by trekking across the sands at low tide and making for Bebbanburg. Hopefully there are ships there that ply between the fortress and my kingdom as that's where its ealdorman is.'

'Will Lindisfarne survive as a monastery then?' Catinus asked the two boys soon after their surprise arrival at Kinneddar.

'The rumour when we left was that Eata was to become the new abbot and that he was bringing his prior, a man named Cuthbert, and several other monks over from Melrose. However, he was going to let the plague run its course first,' Bruide replied.

'So he's also the new Bishop of Northumbria?'

'No, I don't think so. It was all rather confused, but the monks were saying that King Alchfrith had made Abbot Wilfrid the new bishop.'

'Alchfrith? Not Oswiu?'

'No, Oswiu is ill, close to dying some say.'

Not for the first time Catinus cursed being so far away from the centre of power.

'So where will Wilfrid be based? He can hardly live on Lindisfarne. That wouldn't work, even if Eata and he didn't hate the sight of each other.'

'Some say he's going to Frankia to be ordained bishop,' Ruaidhrí put in.

'Frankia? Why?'

Both boys shrugged, then Catinus recalled that Wilfrid had spent some time there when he was studying. Perhaps he had a mentor there who he wanted to consecrate him? Still, it all seemed a little odd; there were several bishops in the south of England, not to mention the Archbishop of Cantwareburg himself, if he didn't want a Celtic bishop to officiate.

The true reason was that Wilfrid had managed to persuade Alchfrith to take advantage of the king's illness and seize power. However, he was far too wily to be around if it all went wrong. Afterwards he could return when it was safe to do so as the ordained Bishop of Northumbria.

~~~

Ecgfrith had been wrong footed. By the time he'd heard about Oswiu's illness Alchfrith had already taken possession of the town and declared himself his father's heir.

However, he hadn't hesitated. He set off immediately from his estate with his small gesith and as many of his warband as were able to ride. Once close to the town he sent out scouts who told him that there was a camp beside the River Ouse which looked as if it contained between five hundred and a thousand men. Ecgfrith sucked his teeth at that. He had no more than forty of his own men with him.

The local inhabitants seemed happy to tell him what he wanted to know and they confirmed that the town was in his brother's hands, but not the king's hall. That was defended by Oswiu's gesith and warband and Queen Eanflæd had secured the gates against him. So far he seemed loathe to attack.

'Presumably he's waiting for my father's death,' Ecgfrith said to himself.

He waited out of sight until just before dusk, when the gates would be shut for the night, then led his men at a canter towards the town on the side away from Alchfrith's camp. The sentries made haste to close the gates until Ecgfrith called out to them.

'Hold, in the name of King Oswiu. I'm Prince Ecgfrith and I demand entry to see my father.'

The sentries on the gate hesitated, uncertain what to do. They were Deirans and under Alchfrith's orders, but many of them regarded him as a foreigner because his mother had been a Briton from Rheged. In contrast, Ecgfrith was the son of Eanflæd, a Deiran princess. In the end they did nothing and Ecgfrith rode into Eoforwīc unopposed.

Men watched from the side alleys but only one tried to stop them. He sent an arrow towards the prince, which ricocheted off his helmet. Almost without pausing, one of his gesith thrust his spear into the man's belly and, letting go of it as the dying man collapsed, he turned his horse back onto the main street and rode on.

Ecgfrith yelled who he was as they approached the palisade around the king's hall and the gates swung open. Alchfrith's men, who were supposed to be blockading the hall, were taken by surprise and they scattered out of the way of the cantering horsemen. Less than a minute late the gates crashed shut just after the last servant boy leading a packhorse had entered.

Hearing the commotion outside and her son's voice, Eanflæd rushed out to embrace him.

'What's the situation, mother,' he asked once greetings had been exchanged.

'Four of the seven eorls of Deira have already accepted your wretched half-brother as the king's heir, but I don't know what's happening elsewhere in Northumbria. Even worse, there are rumours that Wulfhere is mobilising his army ready to attack us.'

'And father, how is he?'

'He still has a fever and is delirious; the physician thinks that it will either break soon or he will deteriorate and die.'

'I'd like to go and see him, please.'

He was shocked by the change in Oswiu. The virile, bear of a man he was used to had lost quite a lot of weight and he looked like a corpse as he lay on a bed of furs being bathed with cloths soaked in cold water. His complexion was pale, almost translucent and he was mumbling incoherently. Ecgfrith openly wept at the sight of the pathetic old man.

He left the bedchamber and pulled himself together. Privately he thought that his father was near death's door, but he didn't say anything as his mother was obviously hoping that her constant prayers would bring him back to health.

'We need to send out messengers to the three eorls in Deira who are loyal and to those who are nearest in Bernicia, such as the Earl of Hexham, Ealdorman Alweo and the like. It's a pity that Catinus is still stuck up in Prydenn. It would have been useful to have him here now.'

'What about Alchfrith's army who are camped outside the town? Won't they intercept the messengers?'

'Hopefully not if they ride out after dark. He's not actually besieging us yet.'

'No, but he does control the town.'

'Then we'll have to send some men in small groups to one of the gates to seize it for long enough. Hopefully it can be done without bloodshed.'

The next morning Oswiu seemed a little better but the fever still raged. Ecgfrith had just come from seeing him when he was told that a small birlinn was coming up the River Ouse. Taking his gesith, he walked unhindered through the town and out of the river gate. He stood on the wharf, impatient to find out who the new arrivals were. To his surprise the only passenger who alighted was a monk; then he recognised Prior Cuthbert of Lindisfarne.

'Cuthbert! What brings you here?'

'The king does, lord. I dreamt he lives still. I hope the vision wasn't false?'

'No, but he is very ill and likely to die, I fear.'

'You need more faith, Ecgfrith.' The monk smiled to rob the mild rebuke of any offence. 'May I see him?'

'Of course, but prepare yourself. He isn't the man you knew.'

Cuthbert knelt by the bedside and ran his hands over the wasted body, praying as he did so. Whether co-incidentally or not, Oswiu stopped his delirious mumbling and fell into a deep sleep.

'Leave him to rest. When he awakes the fever will have abated, but he's not out of danger yet,' he told the amazed crowd around the bed. 'He'll need broth when he's conscious so he can build up his strength again. I need some sleep but I'll come back in a few hours.'

The crowd parted to let Cuthbert through and a servant guided him to the priest's house near to the church. Once he'd rested the monk went into the church and prayed for an hour before returning to the king's hall.

Eanflæd rushed up to him as soon as he appeared.

'Brother Cuthbert, we are all in your debt. You have saved the king's life. His fever has gone and he is awake and lucid. I can never thank you enough.'

'It wasn't my doing, Síþwíf, but God's. Thank him, not me. I'm merely His instrument.'

The next morning the Eorl of Hexham arrived with his warband as did Alweo with his horsemen. They camped well away from Alchfrith's men and the two contingents eyed each other warily. Alchfrith became alarmed later in the day when four more eorls arrived with their men and joined the other camp. Then the news came that the king was on the road to recovery.

'What will you do, lord?' Rægenhere asked.

'I don't know. Why isn't your brother here when I need him,' he asked.

He was referring to Wilfrid, who was safe in Frankia. His chaplain already knew that Alchfrith wasn't a particularly strong character but he hadn't expected him to go to pieces quite so quickly.

'If you want my advice, you'll go into voluntary exile before King Oswiu demands to know why you raised an army to seize power.'

'I only did it because I thought he was about to die and I wanted to prevent my bloody brother from getting his hands on the throne which is rightfully mine.'

He stopped, realising he was ranting. He needed to think, but the more he thought the more he convinced himself that Rægenhere was right. He needed to put himself out of the reach of Oswiu and Ecgfrith. He could then bide his time, build up alliances secretly, and return when his father was truly dead.

Not for one moment did he think about his wife, Kyneburga, in all this. She was under the misapprehension that her husband loved her but when he abandoned her without asking her if she wanted to accompany him - not even saying farewell - she realised that he didn't love anyone but himself. Bitterly resentful at the way that she'd been treated, she entered a Mercian monastery as a nun. There her previous love for Alchfrith turned into a very unchristian hatred of the man and, by association, of all Northumbrians.

~~~

Oswiu's recovery was a slow process. The threat from Mercia never materialised once news of his miraculous recovery spread, as did Cuthbert's fame as a healer. Now the ill and maimed flocked to Lindisfarne in the hope that he would cure them. It wasn't what he wanted or had expected and he retreated to one of the small islands of the Inner Farne to escape them as much as to meditate.

Oswiu formally deposed the absent Alchfrith as King of Deira and appointed Ecgfrith in his place. He also declared Wilfrid's elevation to bishop null and void. Instead he appointed a priest named Chad to be Bishop of Northumbria. It was a move that was destined to lead to serious internal strife within the Church and eventual loss of face for Oswiu.

CHAPTER THIRTEEN – THE FALL OF ARDEWR
666 to 667 AD

Catinus had breathed a sigh of relief as he watched the sixteen year old Bruide walk down the aisle of the new church at Kinneddar towards Utta, the Bishop of Prydenn, who was standing in front of the altar. Morleo, Bran of Cait and the Eorl of Prydenn stood beside him in the front row of the congregation with Leoflaed and their children behind him. His daughter Hereswith, now aged nine and six year old Alaric stood quietly by her side, craning their necks to try and see what was going on. Osfrid was only two and considered too young to witness Bruide's enthronement as King of Penntir.

He'd been disappointed that the high king, Drest, hadn't come, nor had the other two kings. It was evident that Drest was plotting something but Catinus had been unable to find out any details. He suspected that Bruide and Morleo knew but, if so, they hadn't confided in him.

Tomorrow he and his family, gesith and servants would leave by ship and return to Bebbanburg at long last. It meant that he no longer ranked as an eorl, but he couldn't care less. There were far fewer eorls in Northumbria in any case. The three who had supported Alchfrith had fled abroad with him and their lands had been distributed to five new nobles who'd been given the title of ealdorman.

Oswiu had continued his reorganisation and, when Kenric died, his son, Beornheth – Cuthbert's younger brother – had become an ealdorman. The Eorl of Dùn Èideann was now termed the Eorl of Lothian and the former British kingdom of Goddodin had been divided into a total of six shires, each with its own ealdorman under the eorl's leadership.

Elmet too had been divided into shires under its eorl, as had Rheged. It was only a matter of time before the same structure would be applied to the rest of Deira, and to Bernicia.

Catinus' thoughts were interrupted when a shout went up acclaiming Bruide as king. As his chieftains went up to swear their allegiance he was struck by the look of triumph on Bruide's face. Suddenly their eyes met and Catinus almost recoiled from the coldness in those of the young man. It wasn't exactly hatred but he didn't know quite how to describe it; whatever it was a cold shiver ran down his spine. However friendly Bruide had appeared to be on the surface, it patently hid his true feelings. He was an enemy, and an implacable one at that.

The boy's gaze shifted to Morleo and Catinus realised that he harboured nothing but animosity for his fellow king, presumably because Morleo's father had killed his own. As far as he was concerned the Picts could do what they liked to each other, just so long as it didn't affect him and his family.

Four days later he was back at Bebbanburg and within a week it was as if he'd never been away. There were changes, of course, the reeve had died the previous year and his place had been taken by his son, Godric, and several of the garrison and servants were new since he'd left.

One of the first things he'd done had been to ride around his shire visiting his thegns. Leoflaed's father had died and her brother was now the Thegn of Bebbanburg Vill. Before he went to Wooler he rode to Lindisfarne to enquire whether Octha was there. The scared nine-year old boy he'd first encountered when he'd slain his father was now a strapping eighteen year old with no trace of a limp.

'Do you remember me, Octha?'

'Yes, lord. Of course I do.' He said with a smile. 'You saved me from a miserable life; how could I not remember you, and with gratitude.'

'I'm going to Wooler tomorrow and wondered whether you are now ready to become its thegn?'

The young man shook his head.

'No, lord. I'm content to remain here as a monk. God spared me from the plague and I wish to repay his mercy by serving him all my life.'

He paused before continuing.

'However, I wonder whether I might request that Abbot Eata become the thegn in my place?'

'You want to transfer title to the monastery?'

'Yes please, lord.'

'Very well. Does Abbot Eata know?'

'No, lord. I thought it proper to ask you first.'

'Very well. I'll leave it to you to tell him. But he'll either need to confirm the reeve in place or appoint a new reeve.'

~~~

Bruide gave the first indication of his ambitions in the early spring of 667. He had spent the year since he was crowned building up and training his warband. He had abandoned Kinneddar and moved back to Elgin; the last thing he was about to do was accept the legacy that Catinus had left him. He led his men along the coast to the mouth of the River Ness and then down the loch towards Morleo's crannoch.

Snow still lay on the tops of the hills that lined the glen in which the loch lay. Down at sea level the track was muddy but the air was crisp and dry. However, on the second day, as they set out, black clouds swept across the sky and they hadn't gone more than a mile before it started to hail. At first the hail was merely a nuisance but the hailstones got larger and were painful when they impacted on bare skin. Then one warrior was knocked out and the rest took shelter under their shields as they continued along the lochside.

The Picts may have been Christians but they were also superstitious. Whispers circulated that God was angry with them and was making his displeasure known. Bruide had enough sense to know that he had to do something to restore their morale or he would be heading for disaster.

'How long can this hailstorm last?' he asked Ruaidhrí, who had stayed on with Bruide to become his unofficial counsellor.

'I've never seen anything like it, but hail doesn't normally last very long.'

'Warriors, never fear.' He called out, trying to shout above the noise of the hail. 'This has been sent to hide our approach. It will soon cease.'

Minutes later the intensity of the hail decreased, as did the size of the lumps of ice. As suddenly as it had begun it petered out, leaving the ground white as if it were covered in snow. Because the ground was now slippery, Bruide was forced to slow down or risk broken legs, or worse. However, the ice soon melted and the warriors were able to move more quickly again. As they did so their mood improved.

The settlement halfway down the loch had also been surprised by the hailstorm and everyone had quickly sought shelter, even the sentries at the end of the walkway over the water to the king's hall, a structure on stilts out from the shore called a crannog. When they emerged they discovered that the small horses that were kept in a compound had evidentially panicked and had broken out of their enclosure and scattered.

It was purely fortuitous that three of the men who were sent to round up the horses spotted the warband of some three hundred making their way towards the crannoch. It was obvious that they were hostile and the three ran back to warn Morleo.

Given time, he might have raised twice the number of warriors as the attackers but, as it was, he had no more than eighty warriors to hand. Thirty were in his warband and the rest were men of the settlement who were able to fight. They would be no match for an army four times their size; he doubted if he would even be able to hold the crannog for long against such odds. He therefore decided that the sensible thing to do was to flee and gather an army to confront whoever the invaders were in due course.

'The place is deserted, Brenin,' one of his men told Bruide after they had searched the crannoch and the settlement.

'No matter. They won't have gone far.'

That evening his chieftains joined him for a feast to celebrate his success in capturing the capital of Ardewr so easily. He stood up to make a speech but, after the usual praise and congratulations, he managed to surprise them.

'I'm going to make you Mormaer of Ardewr to rule it on my behalf,' he told the eldest of them. 'I'll leave you the best part of the warband for now so that you can subdue the rest of the kingdom. Give the men the option of acknowledging you as their new leader or being killed after being forced to watch their family being slaughtered in front of them first. Few will choose the latter. Do you understand?'

The man nodded, elated at his good fortune. He knew that mormaer literally meant great steward and the appointment gave him power and a status that he hadn't thought possible, so he thanked the king for his confidence in him; but Bruide had already turned his attention to his friend.

'Ruaidhrí, I want you to take thirty of my best men, hunt down Morleo and kill him. Don't come back without his head.'

Ruaidhrí swallowed hard. He was seeing a side of his friend that he hadn't even suspected was there.

'Don't let me down,' he told him in a tone of voice that left Ruaidhrí in no doubt what would happen if he did. 'I want my men back by mid-summer.'

Gradually the inhabitants returned, once word got around that they and their families would be safe if they submitted to the new mormaer. Those few who resisted paid the price. Morleo tried to raise an army to oppose the invaders but everyone had been cowed by Bruide's threats. Instead, he found himself a fugitive with a price on his head.

Fleeing to one of his fellow kings didn't appeal; they would probably betray him for the reward. The irony was that this would come from the chests of silver and gold he'd left behind when he'd fled. He especially distrusted the high king, Drest. The man had never liked him. And so he and the few warriors who had remained loyal to him made their way south east towards Prydenn where Oswiu's eorl, Hunwald, ruled. The problem was that his fortress of Dùn Dè lay over a hundred miles away through the mountains. To make matters worse, they were on foot and they had no guide.

What he didn't know was that Ruaidhrí wasn't far behind him. One of his men was an excellent tracker and foolishly Morleo and his men had make no attempt to hide their passing.

~~~

Wilfrid prostrated himself in front of the Pope. Vitalianus was now an old man, and looked it. Wilfrid thought that he must be at least ninety. Very few men lived to be as old as that.

He had been about to return to Northumbria after his ordination as a bishop when he heard that Chad had been appointed in his place by Oswiu. He rapidly came to the conclusion that the only option open to him was an appeal to the Pope. However, it had taken him a month to secure an audience.

Vitalianus looked down at the man kneeling before him and beckoned with his hand for him to rise and kiss the ring on his hand. He sighed; it seemed that England brought him nothing but problems these days. When Archbishop Deusdedit of Cantwareburg died in 664, shortly after the Synod of Whitby, the King of Kent had secured the agreement of both Oswiu and Wulfhere to appoint Wighard, a Saxon priest and a native of Kent, to succeed him. He had been part of the late archbishop's household and had been nominated by the monks at Cantwareburg. As archbishop he'd gone to Rome in person for the Pope's confirmation of his appointment.

Vitalianus had been about to confirm his appointment when Wighart caught the plague and died. The Pope was now faced with two problems: who should lead the Church in England and the conflicting claims over the diocese of Northumbria. For a moment he thought that appointing Wilfrid as archbishop might kill two birds with one stone, but then he realised that if Oswiu, the most powerful man in Britain, let alone England, didn't want the man as his bishop, he certainly wouldn't accept him as archbishop.

'So, if I've understood you correctly Abbot Wilfrid, Sub-king Alchfrith chose you to become bishop whilst his father was ill and then when King Oswiu recovered he chose another man in your place? Is it normal in Northumbria for kings to choose their bishop?'

'Yes, Your Holiness; ever since Saint Aidan was sent from Iona the king has approved his successors. However, he has consulted the monks of Lindisfarne in the past.'

'But now that the seat of the bishop has moved to Eoforwīc that is no longer the case?'

'No, because the Abbot of Lindisfarne is not the bishop as well.'

'I see. And why do you think that you are more suited to be bishop than this priest, Chad?'

'Chad is a priest of the Celtic Church, Your Holiness, whereas I have always been a devout member of the Roman Catholic Church.'

'Not quite. You were a novice monk of the Celtic Church on Lindisfarne and at Melrose were you not?'

Wilfrid was surprised at the old man's knowledge of his background. Someone on his staff had evidently been digging into his past.

'Yes, your Holiness, but only briefly. I completed my training at Cantwareburg and then I studied there, in Frankia and in Rome before returning to become Abbot of Ripon.'

'And of Hexham, I think?'

Wilfrid took a deep breath. This wasn't going as well as he'd expected.

'Yes, and of Hexham; a new monastery I built on land given to me by King Alchfrith.'

'It's a pity that you aren't as close to King Oswiu as you evidently are to his son. You call him King Alchfrith but I understood that the Sub-king of Deira is now another son, Ecgfrith?'

'That is true, Holiness, but Alchfrith is the elder and should inherit.'

'And how does Ecgfrith regard the Roman Church. Does he support us or the Celtic Church?'

'He does what his father tells him.'

'And Oswiu? He has aligned the date of Easter with our calculation but has he accepted my ultimate authority as leader of Christendom?'

Wilfrid shifted uncomfortably from one foot to the other.

'That isn't clear, Holiness. I believe that he still regards himself as being in charge of the Northumbrian Church.'

'Is that so? Well, I think we'd better show him who's master, hadn't we? I'll consecrate you as bishop myself and appoint you to the diocese of Northumbria. We'll see what he does then.'

~~~

Ruaidhrí's scouts came running back to tell him that Morleo and his men were less than two miles ahead of them. Ruaidhrí nodded his thanks and thought about how he should go about capturing Morleo. The problem was that he had liked Morleo when he'd met him at Bruide's enthronement and he was far from sure that he wanted to either kill him or take him back to be executed, probably in a very unpleasant manner.

The more he thought about Bruide's conduct since the invasion of Ardewr, the less he liked the young man he'd been friends with. Bruide had skilfully hidden his dark side as a novice monk and initially when he'd become king although, now he thought about it, his ruthless ambition had been there all along; he just hadn't seen it.

However, even if he decided to let Morleo go, the warriors with him would probably kill him as well as the former King of Ardewr. There had to be a way to save Morleo and himself. The band of warriors had crowded around him, waiting for their orders to cut Morleo off and capture him. He sensed their impatience. He had to come up with something.

'Right, it's too late in the day to attack them now. We'll camp shortly and when it's dark I'll take two of you with me to scout their camp. All being well we'll attack at dawn.'

His men nodded at the sense of this plan and followed the trail for another half an hour until dusk, then they made camp. After they'd eaten Ruaidhrí picked the two best trackers to accompany him and they set off in the direction that Morleo had been heading. It was clear night and the partial moon gave them enough light to move quickly. Half an hour after they'd set off the leading scout crouched down and waved his hand for the other two to do the same.

'They've camped by a small stream just head of us. There's one sentry about a hundred yards to our right and another over the other side of the stream. They don't have the common sense to stay still,' he whispered.

'Show me,' Ruaidhrí whispered back. 'You stay here,' he told the second scout.

The first man seemed surprised but he did what Ruaidhrí asked. They crawled forward flat on the ground, hidden from sight by the bushes that grew over them.

'There, can you see the man walking to and fro?'

Ruaidhrí pretended to look, moving his position as he did so. However, he wasn't interested in the sentry, he was trying to surreptitiously unsheathe his seax. He got to his knees, still peering towards the sentry.

'What are you doing?' the scout hissed at him. 'Get down….'

He never got to finish the sentence as Ruaidhrí's seax sawed across his throat. He collapsed with a slight gurgling sound as his blood spurted out, half of it covering Ruaidhrí's byrnie and arms. Leaving him where he lay, Ruaidhrí made his way back to the second scout.

'What's going on?' Then he sniffed the air. The dark splodges of blood weren't visible in the dark, but he smelt the coppery tang in the air. 'Why are you covered …'

He got no further before Ruaidhrí stabbed him in the chest. Unlike him, few of the Picts had chainmail, or even a leather jerkin. The seax slid through the man's rough tunic and into his heart. He fell to the ground, jerked once and lay still.

Ruaidhrí checked that he was dead and then made his way back to Morleo's camp. He walked openly towards the nearest sentry and, when the man suddenly became aware of his presence, he called out that he'd come in peace to talk to Morleo. The sentry was suspicious and levelled his spear at him.

'Don't bother. If I'd wanted to kill you, you'd have been dead long since. Sentries should hide and stay still; moving around just makes it easy for an enemy. Now tell Morleo that Ruaidhrí of the Ulaidh wants to talk to him.'

'Hello Ruaidhrí, what are you doing here? Have you been following me?' a voice from the darkness asked suspiciously as Morleo appeared out of the gloom.

'Yes, Bruide wants you dead. Is there somewhere private we can talk?'

'I would take you aside but I'm not sure how far I can trust you. I thought that you were Bruide's man?'

'I was, but not anymore. If you look closely you'll see blood on me. It belongs to two of my scouts. You can trust me; look, I'll leave my weapons here.'

Once they were out of earshot the two men stopped and Morleo asked him what was going on.

'Bruide sent me after you with a warband who are camped two miles away. The plan is for them to attack you at dawn. I suggest I return to them, say that the two scouts were killed by your sentries and then lead them into an ambush. How many men have you got?'

'Fifteen. I had more but a few deserted.'

'Hmmm, there are almost thirty of Bruide's men. Even caught unawares in an ambush we'd be outnumbered by two to one. That's not going to work.'

'You say you killed their best scouts?'

'Yes, that's why I chose them. There are some hunters left but they aren't nearly as good at tracking as those two were. Perhaps if we made our way down the stream we might be able to lose them, especially if we can find a rocky place to exit from.'

'Yes, I agree. However, there is another problem. We don't know where we are exactly; we need a guide.'

Ruaidhrí swore under his breath. He was beginning to wonder whether he'd made the right decision.

'You mean that I've joined a group of men who are lost and who have no idea where they're going? Wonderful!'

He paused in thought for a moment. He only had a hazy idea of the geography of the country outside Penntir but his knowledge of the coastline was much better.

'Look, I know that there are several ships at Kinneddar. Bruide may have abandoned it as his capital but it's still his major port. When we left there were two birlinns there. It makes more sense to find the major glen that runs north east through Ardewr and up to Kinneddar and steal a ship there. Then we can sail down the east coast to Bebbanburg. I know Catinus will give us shelter.'

'I suppose that's a better plan than trying to find Prydenn overland.'

'It is without a guide. Can any of your men sail?'

'Several are fishermen so they can row and handle a small sail.'

'Good. I know how to helm. If we stay within sight of the shore but far enough out to avoid the rocks we should be alright.'

'But we still have to get to Kinneddar and steal a ship.'

'Do you know where this big glen is?'

'If we head south east we can hardly miss it.'

'Right. Time for you to tell your men I think.'

Morleo had been shy and withdrawn as a boy, mainly due to the animosity of his father's wife. It was only when Fergus recognised him as his heir that he gained some self-confidence. This had been reinforced when he became king but underneath he was still the same introverted, scared little boy. Having to flee for his life had brought his insecurities to the surface again. Now, with the ebullient Ruaidhrí by his side, some of the confidence that he'd had as king returned.

The young men who had deserted him, despite being oath-sworn to serve him unto death, had done so because he seemed beaten and they lost respect for him. Now the morale of those who were left improved immeasurably.

The next day they found the big glen and turned north east, keeping to the higher ground. By this stage their provisions had run out and they had to rely on foraging. In the main this meant killing one of the sheep that roamed the hills every day or so. The shepherds and the boys who looked after them wisely didn't try and challenge a group of well-armed men, but they spread the word and the local thegn rounded up enough men to confront them near a settlement called Aviemore.

It lay inside Ardewr but was remote from any of the centres of population and so Morleo gambled that word of Bruide's coup hadn't reached them yet.

'Greetings,' he called out to the man who was obviously the leader. 'It is good to see that you have come out to welcome your king.'

This was said with a lot more confidence than he was feeling.

'King? King Morleo?' the thegn asked bewildered.

He had only met Morleo once, when he'd attended his crowing and pledged his loyalty to him.

'I beg your forgiveness, Brenin, I didn't recognise you at first. I was told that there was a party of outlaws in the area stealing our sheep,' he said smoothly.

'I confess that we are the guilty party. I am touring my kingdom but have run short of provisions. I did try and pay for the sheep but your shepherds ran away.'

The only clue that he wasn't telling the truth was the rapidly blinking eyes. Ruaidhrí drew in a sharp breath and had to resist the temptation to glance at Morleo. It took skill to deceive so convincingly and he wondered just how far he really trusted his companion.

If the thegn didn't entirely believe Morleo's explanation, he wasn't about to argue with him, especially as he saw an opportunity to profit from the king's unexpected arrival.

'Perhaps you would let us off the taxes we owe for this year in exchange, Brenin, would that be acceptable?' he asked licking his lips, not sure if he was pushing his luck too far.

'Perfectly!'

Morleo smiled. He had no idea how he'd have paid for the stolen sheep if he'd been asked to. The only one of them who had any money was Ruaidhrí and he wanted to keep that for buying provisions for the voyage south.

'Good. Will you stay tonight, Brenin? We'd like to throw a feast in your honour.'

'Yes, of course. Perhaps I can also talk to you about another matter on my mind?'

The next morning Morleo, Ruaidhrí and their men woke up with thick heads. Whatever the women of Aviemore brewed it had a powerful kick. After washing in the stream he and Ruaidhrí felt a little better and went to find the thegn, whose eyes were as bloodshot as theirs.

'Thank you for your hospitality last night. I have to confess that I wasn't entirely honest with you when we arrived. We are having trouble with raids from Penntir and we clashed with a group of them a few days ago. I need to make good my losses and I'm hoping to recruit any of your young men who would like to become warriors.'

Ruaidhrí did his best to hide his surprise at the new story that Morleo had concocted but they had discussed the need for more men to operate a birlinn. Ruaidhrí knew that even the smaller of the two birlinns at Kinneddar required a crew of at least thirty to man it properly. Not counting Morleo, they had sixteen.

The Thegn pursed his lips before replying.

'I suspected as much, Brenin. Are you still chasing them?'

'No, we lost them two days ago.'

'I see. How many are you hoping to recruit?'

'As many as possible but at least ten.'

'Ten! I doubt that as many as that would want to leave their families, though young men also seem to think that life will be more exciting somewhere else. Besides, I'm not sure I can spare so many. There are a few orphan boys who you are welcome to though.'

'Useful as ships boys,' Ruaidhrí whispered to Morleo.

'How many boys?'

'Six I think, I can find out. However, they range in age from quite young to nearly old enough to train as warriors.'

It transpired that there were six orphans from nine to thirteen and all were eager to join Morleo. Another seven unmarried youths also volunteered. That made thirty of them in total, but even the thirteen year old was quite small and so they only had enough men to man twenty two oars. It would have to do.

The new recruits had few weapons to speak of, just a few poorly made spears and shields that would fall apart after one good blow. Morleo gave the biggest of them the two swords and the two seaxes that Ruaidhrí had taken from the scouts he had slain. All of them, including all but the youngest boy, at least had a dagger of some sort and three had hunting bows.

Later that day they set off again up the wide glen heading to where they would need to branch right towards a place called Rothes. At least now they had several guides who knew the immediate area through hunting. Morleo and Ruaidhrí relaxed a little. They still had to get around Elgin and steal the birlinn, but the two were more hopeful now.

However, they were tempting fate. Their new recruits were beginning to suspect that the yarn they had been spun wasn't entirely true. Why were they heading north east along the border with Penntir for a start? They had expected to be heading north-west towards Loch Ness.

Furthermore, unbeknownst to them, the rest of Ruaidhrí's original group hadn't given up the chase. Their new leader, Lutrin, knew that returning without Morleo's head would be tantamount to signing their own death warrants. It was pure luck that one of them found a scrap of cloth on the thorns of a bush just where their quarry had exited the stream. Sometime later the faint trail left by Morleo's men led them to the wide glen.

It took them a little time to find tracks leading north east but then they cornered a young shepherd in the hills who was only too willing to tell them about the men who had slain his younger brother not two days previously. When asked where they'd gone, the boy pointed towards Aviemore.

'I swear to you that we haven't seen King Morleo or his men,' the thegn licked his lips and refused to look his questioner in the eye, a sure sign that he was lying.

'The fugitive Morleo is no longer king,' Lutrin sneered. 'King Bruide now rules Ardewr. Now stop lying. Which way did they go?'

The thegn looked helplessly towards his wife, who was standing a few yards away with their two children, a boy of nine and girl of six. Lutrin nodded his head towards the three and his men dragged them in front of him.

'You have until I count to ten to start talking or I'll kill the girl first, then your son and, if you still don't talk, your wife.'

'Alright, alright.' The thegn's shoulders sunk dejectedly. 'I'll tell you, just let them go.'

'One, two, three..'

'Stop! Very well. They set off along the glen, heading north east.'

'When?'

When he hesitated the man started counting again.

'Four, five..'

'Yesterday,' he said quickly, cold sweat glistening on his forehead. 'Late morning.'

'So they've a day's start on us,' Lutrin said to himself.

Without any warning he thrust his seax into the thegn's belly and sawed it to and fro. The man collapsed with a shriek, trying to stop his intestines escaping from the slit that had been cut in his body.

'Come on, we'll need to move fast.'

His men got ready to leave but one called out 'shouldn't we fire the settlement? They're traitors.'

'No time. Get moving.'

But he took the time to chop of the head of the thegn's young son before he left.

'Boys grow up into vengeful men,' he muttered, almost in apology to the distraught mother.

Meanwhile Morleo's group were moving at a much more leisurely pace. When they stopped at a stream to drink and chew on some of the hard bread they had brought with them from the settlement, two of the new recruits who had been acting as scouts approached him nervously.

'Brenin, where are we going? Do you seek another settlement to recruit more men? If so, we are going in the wrong direction. If we carry on we'll soon be in Penntir.'

The speaker shuffled from one foot to the other as Morleo glanced at Ruaidhrí. He seemed to be depending more and more on the Irish youth as time went on. The latter nodded back, almost imperceptibly.

'Gather round, I need to tell you something.'

He swallowed, took a deep breath and then spoke briefly about Bruide's invasion and confessed that they were making for a port in Penntir where they would be able to steal a ship to take them south into Northumbria. To his delight the new members of the group seemed to think it was all a big adventure and were quite excited, chatting amongst themselves. He had worried needlessly about how they would take the news. What no-one noticed was that one of the group seemed less enthusiastic than the rest.

'One of the new men has gone,' Ruaidhrí told him the next morning.

'Gone? You mean deserted?'

'I'm afraid so. He will have high tailed it back to his settlement no doubt.' He shrugged. 'Probably good riddance.'

The young man felt he'd been cheated and, in any case, he was missing the girl he'd bedded recently. He'd tossed and turned, wracked with indecision the previous night, and then made his mind up to desert. He'd waited until it was his turn on guard and then slipped away. It was mid-morning before he ran into the men chasing Morleo. He should have been paying more attention to his surroundings but it was raining hard and he had his cowl over his head, trying to keep as much water from running down his neck as possible.

'Describe the leader to me,' Lutrin asked brusquely.

'Uh, the thegn said it was King Morleo.'

'You're certain?'

'Er, yes. That's what Ruaidhrí called him. The others addressed him as Brenin.'

'Ruaidhrí! So he has turned traitor. I wouldn't want to be in his shoes when we drag him back to face King Bruide.'

His men laughed dutifully, but the truth was most of them had liked Ruaidhrí. Not that it mattered much, they were scared to death of Bruide.

'Now, make yourself useful and guide us back to where you left the bastard Morleo and his men. Don't try any tricks or I'll cut off your manhood.'

~~~

King Oswiu was less than pleased when he heard that Wilfrid had returned to Northumbria and was claiming that the Pope himself had ordained him a bishop and appointed him to the diocese of Northumbria. Bishop Chad was equally upset.

'What does the man think he's playing at? I agreed to change the way we calculate Easter and other matters to coincide with the way the Romans do things, but I didn't acknowledge the supremacy of the Pope.'

His voice rasped. Eanflæd made haste to soothe him. He had complained of chest pains a few weeks ago and, for a time, he'd lost the use of his left arm, his face had fallen on that side and his speech had become slurred. He was a lot better than he was but the peculiar sound of his voice and his constant irritability didn't seem to be improving.

What he did next was an indicator of how much he'd changed since his collapse. Wilfrid had returned to Ripon pending his installation as Bishop of Northumbria so he was surprised to find Ealdorman Alweo at his gates one morning demanding to see him. Alweo was not alone. He had brought his twenty-five strong gesith with him. However, only Alweo was allowed into Wilfrid's presence.

'Brother Wilfrid,' Alweo began without preamble, 'the king has decreed that you are to leave Northumbria.' This was said with a certain amount of relish. The two men had never liked each other.

The other man's eyes narrowed. 'I'm not Brother Wilfrid. You must have the wrong man.'

'The king has deprived you of your monasteries here and at Hexham; how else should I address you?'

'I am an ordained priest but, more importantly the Pope himself has consecrated me as a bishop.'

'Well, then. As he's the Bishop of Rome I suppose I should address you as bishop, but I'm not sure of where. Certainly not Northumbria; that post is more than adequately filled by Bishop Chad.'

Wilfrid drew himself up. 'Not any more. Pope Vitalianus has deposed him.'

'Vitalianus doesn't rule here, Oswiu does. You are to go into exile; the king doesn't much care where.' Alweo tried to keep the sneer out of his voice and almost succeeded.

'And if I refuse?'

'Then I am to arrest you and take you back to Eoforwīc where you will be imprisoned.'

Wilfrid was soft and enjoyed the good things of life. He shuddered at the thought of being incarcerated in a cell with only the rats for company.

'Very well. You may escort me to Mercia. I'm sure that King Wulfhere will welcome me.'

Alweo scowled at the arrogance in his voice. He was tempted to punch him in his fat belly.

'Be ready to leave in an hour.'

With that he stalked out of the gates.

It was only much later that Oswiu heard that Wulfhere had indeed welcomed him; not only that, he'd given him land on which to build a new monastery.

'He's welcome to him,' Oswiu grunted. 'He'll soon find out that he's harbouring a viper in his bosom.'

~~~

Morleo and the rest of the group had settled down for the night by the time that Lutrin's forward scouts found them. They were not as adept at moving silently at night as the two who Ruaidhrí had killed and one of the sentries heard them on the far side of the stream. Puzzled, he waited, wondering who or what was making the noise. At first he thought it might be a large animal, but then he heard another twig snap ten yards away from the first just as he discerned at stealthy movement in the region of the first noise.

It had been raining earlier but now only the occasional drop of water descending from a leaf to the ground remained as a reminder. The clouds were still that dark grey colour that indicates further rain to come however, and so the darkness was all but complete. It had been too wet to light fires and so they had eaten a cold meal before lying down to sleep so not even the embers of a campfire illuminated the gloom. Nevertheless the sentry was certain that there were two shadows that were slightly darker than the background.

He cautiously withdrew from his position and tried to find Morleo. However, he found Ruaidhrí first and whispered in his ear what he'd heard and seen. The Irish youth tapped the sentry on the arm and gestured for him to return quietly to his original post. He silently drew his seax and sword from their scabbards and disappeared into the darkness.

His big problem was not in finding the two scouts but in crossing the stream quietly. In the end he decided that brazenness was the best policy. He walked openly up to the stream's bank and unloaded the contents of his bladder into it. As soon as the splashing sound started he stepped into the stream and, whilst still pissing, moved to the far bank. Once safely across he waited without moving to see if the scouts gave any indication that they knew he was now on their side of the stream.

After a minute or two he detected a very faint whisper, then silence. He cautiously made his way towards where he thought the sound had come from and circled around behind it. He knew how disorientating the silence of a pitch black night could be and, for just a moment, he thought he had miscalculated; then he heard a faint movement near where he was.

He waited, his mouth dry, trying to hear any sound from the other man the sentry had reported. He had just decided that they had gone when a man rose from the ground not five yards in front of him. He very nearly moved in for the kill but he needed to know where the other scout was. It was nearly his undoing.

A sixth sense warned him just in time and he jabbed at the shadow behind him. He felt his sword enter somewhere on the body of the scout, but he didn't have time to find out what damage it might have inflicted. The second man cut at him with his sword; it was a mistake. Had he thrust instead he would have beaten Ruaidhrí's defences. As it was, he was able to let go of his sword and bring his seax up to meet the descending blade.

The other man wasn't expecting it and he lost his balance. As he stumbled, Ruaidhrí kicked him hard in the groin. The man doubled over in agony and Ruaidhrí slashed his seax across his throat. With a soft gurgling sound the scout fell to the ground and lay still.

Ruaidhrí was about to relax when he heard a movement behind him. He instinctively ducked and a blade whistled over his head. He'd made the mistake of thinking that the first scout was incapacitated. However, the effort was too much for the wounded man and he stood there in pain, trying to recover.

At that moment the clouds parted and the scene was illuminated by the silvery moon. By its pale light Ruaidhrí saw the other man clutching at his bloody side. Evidentially his sword had struck his ribs and had been deflected downwards to cut deeply into the side of his abdomen. The man had pulled the sword out but now he was bleeding copiously.

Ruaidhrí kicked out with his foot at the hand holding the sword and the man let go of it; it went spinning away just as another black cloud covered the moon. Ruaidhrí thrust his seax at where he thought the man was but it met no resistance. Now plunged into the inky darkness again, Ruaidhrí was worse off than before the moon had put in its brief appearance. He had lost his night vision.

He stood and listened for the other's breathing but he heard nothing. Suddenly he felt a searing pain in his calf. The man had obviously collapsed but had the strength to stab him from the ground, though what with he didn't know as the man had lost his sword.

He put his weight onto his other leg and stabbed down with his seax. This time he felt it enter flesh and he kept stabbing until he was certain that the man was dead. He sat down heavily and cursed. The rush of adrenaline had left him cold and weary and his leg was beginning to really hurt. With a wound in his calf he would slow Morleo and his men down and they would need to move fast from now on. It was obvious that that the warriors that Bruide had given him were not far away.

He ripped a length of material from the dead man's tunic and bound his wound with it as best he could. He waited for the moon to put in another appearance and then looked for his sword. With a grimace at the irony of it, he found it clutched in his attacker's hand. The scout had evidently found it on the ground and used it to stab its owner.

He hobbled painfully back through the stream to the camp. He didn't call out in case there were other enemy close by but whispered to the sentry to go and wake Morleo. Five minutes later he was being carried by two of the strongest men as the group quietly left the clearing and made their way through the trees.

When dawn lit the hills to the east they stopped and one of the men who claimed to have a little knowledge of healing bathed the wound and sewed the edges together with catgut before bandaging it again. The stronger men took it in turns to carry Ruaidhrí on their backs; luckily at seventeen he was still quite slim and didn't weigh as much as many his age. By the time that they stopped for a five minute rest and a quick breakfast of rye bread and water they were a good ten miles from the campsite. Morleo hoped that their pursuers had waited for the scouts to report back before moving on; in which case they'd probably waited until dawn before setting out. That meant that they had a start of several hours on them; they would need it with Ruaidhrí slowing them down.

This time Morleo sent out his own scouts - two ahead of them and two more to the rear - to give them warning if they saw their enemies behind them. It wasn't until the day was drawing to a close that the ones in the rear came running up the trail to say that they had seen a group of about thirty men come over a ridge behind them.

'How far behind us?'

'No more than two miles, Brenin.'

Morleo might have been deposed by Bruide but his men still accorded him the title of king.

'We need to slow them down. I want those of you with bows to take out those in the lead. Don't tarry though. As soon as the rest of them have taken cover, run and catch us up. If we keep doing that we should slow them down as well as cutting down their numbers.'

The five men with bows and Morleo hid as soon as they reached the next area of trees. He'd decided to remain with them to bolster their resolve, though he was as nervous as any. They waited apprehensively for the enemy to appear, which seemed to take an age; then, just when Morleo was wondering if they'd gone another way, the first half a dozen appeared.

He thanked God that they hadn't sent out scouts. Now they'd be able to do some damage.

'Now.'

Five arrows sped across the sixty yards that separated them and three men fell, one with two arrows in him. From the screaming at least some were only wounded. Morleo smiled. Hopefully, they would slow the rest down. The enemy stood there stunned for a second. It was enough to get a second arrow off but this time only two were hit.

'Run,'

It took them half an hour to catch the rest up and by then they were exhausted. Morleo sent two men to watch their back trail whilst they got their breath back. By the time that night fell there was still no sign of their pursuers.

~~~

Wulfhere sighed when he heard that Wilfrid had requested another audience. He was beginning to regret having given the man sanctuary and, even more, to have appointed him as abbot of the new monastery at Medeshamstede on the River Nene.

Wilfrid strode into the king's hall as if he owned the place and made straight for the raised dais on which the King of Mercia sat with his new queen, Ermenilda, and a man in his early twenties that he didn't immediately recognise. Then he realised with a start that it was Wulfhere's younger brother, Ethelred. The last he had heard he was still a guest at Oswiu's court. Later he found out that Oswiu had released him a few months previously on the occasion of Wulfhere's wedding, which he'd attended.

'What can I do for your now, Abbot Wilfrid,' Wulfhere asked, trying to keep the irritation out of his voice.

'I fear that the masons you have sent me are just not up to the job, Cyning. Oh, they can cut a block of stone and lay it in place well enough, but they can't carve anything I'd be prepared to allow to be seen.'

'Carve? Why do they need to carve stone?'

'Because all the new abbey churches in Frankia have round columns, not square ones. Even Ripon, Whitby and Hexham have round columns. And the window frames need to be carved.'

'You have already had twice as much money for your new abbey than I had expected; I'm afraid you'll have to make do with what you have.'

'You should know by now that my brother isn't to be cozened out of silver as easily as that fool Alchfrith.'

Wilfrid glowered at Ethelred. The two had disliked each other when they were both at Eoforwīc. Now that he had returned to Mercia Wilfrid realised that the prince was going to make his life as difficult as possible.

He had thought that Wulfhere wanted to dispose of his younger brother but, perhaps because he'd failed to sire children so far, the two had become reconciled. He realised that he wasn't likely to get what he wanted with Ethelred dripping poison in the king's ear. Perhaps the time had come to find somewhere that appreciated his talents more. He bowed stiffly to Wulfhere and left.

'Have you heard, brother, that pain in the posterior, Wilfrid, has left Medeshamstede; apparently for good,' Ethelred asked him a few days later.

Wulfhere stared at his brother in surprise.

'Left? And gone where? Not back to Northumbria surely?'

'The rumour is that he's travelling down to Cantwareburg to see the new archbishop, Theodore of Tarsus.'

'Why would he do that? Not to complain about funding for the new monastery surely?'

'No,' his brother laughed, 'a fat lot of good that would do him. No, I suspect that he still has ambitions to be Bishop of Northumbria. Perhaps he wants to enlist Theodore's support.'

'Would that help him? The man at Cantwareburg might call himself archbishop but he's not universally acknowledged as having authority over the other bishops in England.'

'From what I hear about him, he is a formidable man and I'm sure he wants to change that.'

'Well, if he manages to knock Oswiu off his lofty perch I for one will enjoy that.'

~~~

Lutrin was worried. So far he'd lost five men dead, including his two best scouts, and had three wounded, one seriously. One was the man who had betrayed Morleo and he felt no sympathy for him, but the other two were men he'd known for years. He hardened his heart; he could do nothing for them.

He had taken over when Ruaidhrí had deserted them but he had no real authority and now men were beginning to challenge his leadership. They had been badly shaken by the sudden ambush and no-one was willing to put themselves in danger at the head of the group. He sighed. He'd obviously have to lead by example and, taking his younger brother forcibly by the arm, he faced his men.

'Very well, if you lily-livered weaklings are too scared to scout ahead my brother and I will do it. But be sure that King Bruide will hear of your cowardice. Follow on fifty yards behind us, and make sure you come running if we encounter Morleo's men.'

'What about the wounded?'

'Leave them. They'll only slow us down and we need to move fast. We'll come back for them once we've caught Morleo.'

Of course, none of them believed him. He was leaving them to die. Much as they all hated doing it, they all acknowledged to themselves that it was the only sensible thing to do.

An hour later they found where Morleo had camped the previous night beside a small loch known as Indorb. Lutrin was puzzled. The track they were following was heading north-east into an area known as Moray, which was part of Penntir. Why would Morleo be sticking his head into the wolf's den? Surely he didn't plan on attacking Elgin whilst Bruide was away? It was only defended by old men and boys, but there were enough of them to deal with Morleo's small band.

He puzzled over the conundrum as he headed after them. Then it struck him. They weren't headed for Elgin; they were making for Kinneddar. Once they'd stolen a ship they could head south for the coast of Northumbria. Now he knew where his quarry was headed Lutrin decided he had a chance of getting there first. Morleo would have to give Elgin a wide birth, whereas he'd save time by cutting straight through it.

He'd been so lost in thought that he hadn't been concentrating on the path ahead. His brother grabbed his arm and was about to yell a warning when two arrows hit him, one in the leg and the other in the throat. Lutrin watched aghast as his brother fell at his feet. He was so shaken that he didn't think of his own danger. By the time that he did, it was too late. The three arrows all struck him at the same time. His eyes glazed over and he collapsed on top of his brother's corpse.

When the rest of the group reached him he was still alive, but barely so. However, he did manage to whisper 'Kinneddar' before his lost consciousness and, shortly afterwards, died.

The twenty survivors withdrew a safe distance, just in case Morleo's men were still about, and went into a huddle to decide what to do. No one was in favour of continuing the quest.

'But if we go back to Bruide having failed you know what he'll do to us; Lutrin told us. He'll kill us.'

The group was silent for a little while before someone spoke again.

'Perhaps our best bet is to join Morleo.'

'Are you mad? He'd kill us too.'

'No, he won't. He's short of followers, isn't he? Whatever he plans to do he'll need warriors.'

At first most were against the proposal but, the more they debated it, the more it seemed like a good idea. A few minutes later they ran off to the north-east leaving the corpses of Lutrin and his brother as a feast for the crows.

~~~

Morleo breathed a sigh of relief as Kinneddar came into sight. They'd made it. Now all they had to do was to steal a birlinn. Just as he was congratulating himself three warriors stepped into the middle of the road a hundred yards ahead of them. They were followed by over a dozen more and he realised that they must be the group who had been pursuing them, something that Ruaidhrí confirmed when he limped over to his side a second or two later.

He took a tight grip on his spear and Ruaidhrí drew his sword and seax as the archers strung their bows, preparing to kill as many as possible of their enemy before they covered the distance between them.

Then one of the enemy held up his hand before dropping his spear and shield into the dust. He slowly walked towards Morleo, swallowing nervously.

'We've had enough Morleo. We want to follow Ruaidhrí's example and join you.'

As he spoke he nodded a greeting towards his former commander.

'Why should I believe you? How do I know that this isn't some sort of trick?'

'Because Lutrin, the man who led us after you, er ... departed, is dead. But he'd already warned us that Bruide would execute us if we returned without your head. We have no option now but to throw in our lot with yours.'

Morleo thought for a moment. He was tempted to ask Ruaidhrí what he thought but that would make him appear weak in front of both groups. For his part Ruaidhrí stayed impassively quiet. He too was wondering how far he trusted his former warriors.

'Very well, I agree.'

At that point Ruaidhrí whispered something to him and he nodded.

'Would you be prepared to swear an oath of loyalty to Prince Ruaidhrí? If so you would become his gesith.'

The tension in the stance of the spokesman for the other group vanished and he relaxed. The men behind him seemed pleased as well.

Two scouts walked ahead of the combined warband as they entered Kinneddar, checking each narrow alley as they past. The place had become surprisingly run down, almost derelict, in the year since Morleo had attended Bruide's wedding. Even Ruaidhrí was surprised at how neglected it had become over the nine months since Bruide had moved his capital back to Elgin. Rats scurried about in the shadows and filth and excrement, both animal and human, lay in piles, adding to the stench of the place. The settlement appeared deserted but the odd pair of eyes peered out of the huts, watching their progress. Morleo was unable to shake off a sense of foreboding as they approached the jetty.

Ruaidhrí had insisted on walking on his own, leaning heavily on a spear, when they entered the place and, as he limped painfully alongside his friend, he noticed with disquiet that there were no masts visible above the huts in front of them. As they emerged onto the space by the jetty his fears were confirmed: not a single ship was tied up alongside. Without them they were trapped.

CHAPTER FOURTEEN – THE RETURN OF WILFRID

667 – 668 AD

Archbishop Theodore was no fool. He saw Wilfrid for what he was but he knew he could be useful to him.

'What do you expect me to do, Wilfrid?'

'Well, I had hoped that you would explain to King Oswiu that I have been ordained Bishop of Northumbria by the Pope himself and he has no right to prevent me taking up my appointment.'

'And Bishop Chad? What do you expect me to do about him?'

'There are other vacant dioceses, my lord archbishop.'

'That is true, but Chad might not wish to exchange the vast province of Northumbria for any of them. Let me think on it.'

Theodore of Tarsus was a Byzantine Greek born in Tarsus who was 12 years old when he'd fled from the Persians after they captured the city. He'd studied at Antioch in Syria and at the Byzantine capital of Constantinople before travelling west to Rome where he joined the monastery of St. Anastasius. There his knowledge of medicine, astronomy and theology and an outstanding intellect had brought him to the attention of the Pope. He was sixty six by the time he arrived at Cantwareburg, but he still had the vigour of a man much younger.

The Synod of Whitby had brought the practices of the Church in Northumbria in line with that of Rome but there were many priests, abbots and monks who still clung to the Celtic Church. Abbess Hild of Whitby, the king's cousin, was one such, Bishop Chad – for all his professed acceptance of Roman doctrine – was another.

'What will you do?' Abbot Hadrian asked him after Wilfrid had left.

Hadrian had been a fellow monk in Rome and had travelled with Theodore to take up the vacant post of abbot of the monastery at Cantwareburg.

'Move Chad to somewhere far less important and install Wilfrid in his place. It's not a question of what so much as how,'

'I don't have to tell you that Wilfrid only wants to be bishop because of the prestige, power and wealth that it will bring him.'

'No, you don't. He's also an intellectual snob. He thinks he's a scholar who knows more theology and religious doctrine than anyone else. Well, he's wrong. It would be arrogant of me to claim that I know more than he does, but you certainly do. However, he will advance the cause of Rome and show obedience to the Pope, which will bring the whole of the North into line with the rest of England. That's my priority for now.'

'But you don't know how to persuade Oswiu to accept him?'

'Not yet, but I've an idea or two which I need to develop.'

~~~

Morleo knew he had to act quickly or his men would lose faith in him as a leader.

'Go and find someone who can tell us about the movement of shipping,'

'Perhaps a tavern keeper,' Ruaidhrí suggested.

Morleo nodded.

'Go and see what you can find.'

Whilst he waited Morleo started to bite his finger nails, then stopped when he realised what he was doing. It was a sure sign of the tension building up within him. Ten minutes later Ruaidhrí returned with two men and a boy of about ten being dragged along by six members of his new gesith. Morleo wondered why they'd brought the lad along, he'd hardly know where the ships were and when they were expected back.

'Have you questioned them?'

Ruaidhrí shook him head. 'No, but one's a tavern keeper and the other man is his brother. He's in charge of the port so he should be able to tell us what we want to know. The boy is his son. I brought him along in case he needs encouragement to talk.'

'Well, where are all the ships?'

'Lord, King Bruide sent for them. They were to go to the mouth of the River Ness; that's all I know.'

Morleo looked at Ruaidhrí, a puzzled frown on his face, but the other man looked as perplexed as he did.

'Boy, run to the fishing village and ask the headman to come here; I need to speak to him. Don't think of doing anything foolish, remember I've got your father here.'

The boy nodded, swallowing hard, and ran off. When he returned he was followed by thirty fishermen, all carrying a weapon of some kind, from wicked looking gaffs to homemade spears.

'You all know me,' Ruaidhrí called out. 'I swear in the name of God the Almighty that we mean you no harm.'

'What do you want with us, lord?' the headman called out from a safe distance. 'Why have you brought so many armed warriors with you? Is aught amiss?'

'We need the loan of your boats and men to crew them for one night. We will pay you, of course.'

'Why? Where do you wish to go?'

'We'll tell you once we are out at sea, but you will be back before dawn.'

'How much are you willing to pay for this journey to nowhere, lord?'

'Four ounces of silver.'

'Make it ten.'

'No, that's too much, six?'

'Eight and we won't ask any more questions.'

'Very well. How many fishing boats do you have and how many extra men can they carry?'

'Each will need two men or a men and a boy to sail them. They vary in size but, to be safe, we can probably carry an extra twenty men in total.'

'It's just enough to crew a small birlinn or a knarr,' Ruaidhrí said quietly to Morleo, who nodded.

'You'll be carrying eighteen men and four boys,' he called back.

'Very well. When do you want to depart?'

'We'll come to the beach where your boats are just after sunset.'

The fishermen walked away, talking animatedly amongst themselves just as one of the men who had been left to watch the two roads into the settlement came running up.

'Someone managed to escape on a horse, Brenin,' he told Morleo. 'He headed along the coast road.'

'How long will it take him to get to the mouth of the Ness?' he asked Ruaidhrí.

'Probably about three hours, but hopefully he'll make for the crannoch on Loch Ness.'

'That'll take another hour or so. It'll be after dark before he gets there. By then we'll have left here.'

'Half of us will. What about the other half?'

'I'm no sailor. You lead the group to get the ship; I'll lead the rest to the beach ten miles to the west of here. We'll meet you there as soon after dawn as possible.'

'What happens if Bruide sends warriors there to reinforce whoever he's left with his fleet?'

'I doubt he will. He'll head here as fast as he can to try and trap us,' Morleo replied. 'I'll set out for the beach as soon as you leave to make sure we don't encounter him on the way. The beach is two miles from the road so we should be safe there.'

'Very well. Good luck. If all goes well, I'll see you early tomorrow.'

~~~

Theodore bowed as he entered the king's hall at Eoforwīc. He was ten years older than Oswiu but he looked younger. The king looked pale and his face was haggard. He hadn't left Eoforwīc for some time now, leaving the running of the kingdom to Ecgfrith, who he'd made King of Deira a few years ago.

The latter was reported to be away in Goddodin trying to discover the truth about the situation in Ardewr. The rumour was that Bruide had invaded his neighbour but no-one seemed to know whether he'd killed Morleo or whether his takeover was still being disputed. Drest hadn't intervened and it seemed that none of the other kings were keen to get involved either.

'Thank you for seeing me, Domine.'

Theodore spoke in Latin as his English was poor and he knew that Oswiu was proficient in the language, if not exactly fluent.

'Archbishop, to what do we owe the pleasure of your company?'

Theodore paused and let his eyes run swiftly over those on the raised dais around the king. His wife sat on a smaller chair beside him studying Theodore intently and in front of the couple a boy sat on the steps. He appeared to be about seven or eight so he assumed that he was Ælfwine, the king's youngest son. The child was quite striking in appearance. His elfin shaped face was framed by long hair so fair that it was almost white and he had piercing ice blue eyes that appeared to look into his very soul.

He shuddered slightly before tearing his gaze away to look at the two men standing behind the throne. One was dressed in a long black robe like a priest with a large bronze cross suspended from a cord around his neck. He assumed that he was Bishop Chad. The other was clearly a warrior. He later found out that he was Redwald, the Hereræswa.

'I have come to make the acquaintance of the Bretwalda of the North. Is it so strange that I should want to meet the most powerful ruler in my new ecclesiastical province?'

'I have accepted Roman doctrine instead of that of the Celtic Church in which I was raised, but that doesn't mean that I accept your authority or that of Pope Vitalianus.'

Theodore nodded and appeared to think for a moment.

'Lord king, may I be permitted to rest my old bones before we continue with our discussion?'

'Of course. Forgive me. Bring a stool for the archbishop, and refreshments.'

'Thank you, a little water would be welcome.'

When he had sat down Theodore replied to Oswiu's bald statement.

'You are familiar with Saint Peter, of course?'

'The disciple of Christ who was executed by the Emperor Nero? Yes, of course.'

'Do you recall what Jesus said to him before he was crucified?'

'About him denying him three times before the cock crowed?'

Ælfwine, who was watching the archbishop intently, had to stifle a giggle at the flash of annoyance on the old man's face. Theodore, who found the boy's intense stare disconcerting, had to take a moment to recover his composure.

Oswiu gave his son an affectionate glance. He was closer to his youngest than he was to any of the others, even Ecgfrith. For a moment he thought of the other two and regretted not making time for them when they were young. It was said that Alchfrith now led a band of mercenaries in Austrasia and his eldest, Aldfrith, was back on Iona the last he had heard.

'No, not that.' Theodore replied a trifle brusquely. 'I was referring to Jesus' statement about Saint Peter being His rock on which He would found His Church. He also said that He would give him the keys of the Kingdom of Heaven. This means that souls of the dead are admitted through the Heavenly Gates at his discretion.'

He paused to let Oswiu digest the import of what he was saying. It was similar to the argument that Wilfrid had advanced at Whitby. When he saw the king growing thoughtful he recommenced his verbal attack.

'Saint Peter was, of course, the first Pope and there has been a continuous chain linking all subsequent popes back to him. They are his descendants and the authority that he wielded they wield.'

'You're not suggesting that Vitalianus now controls entry to Heaven?'

'No, of course not.'

For a king who was meant to be devout and who had been taught by the monks of Iona and by Saint Aidan, Oswiu seemed to be ignorant of important aspects of the Church's teaching.

'I am saying that the authority in spiritual matters that Christ bequeathed to Saint Peter has been passed down over the centuries to subsequent popes.'

'Not according to the Celtic Church.'

'They are mistaken. Their Church was founded by Saint Patrick who was converted to Christianity by a vision. His religious education was patchy and derived from ignorant priests and monks who were taught by descendants of those who lived in Britain at the time of the Romans. Much important doctrine was lost over time. Although pious and a great missionary, Patrick was not what I would call an educated man. Their philosophy is thus littered with misconceptions and assumptions.'

'So you say, but there is much more in common between the two Churches than there are differences, apart from your insistence on the rule of the Pope. The authority of the Celtic Church derives from the scriptures, not a mortal man.'

Theodore changed his opinion about Oswiu. He was more learned that he had initially thought. He certainly hadn't expected such an exacting debate. He decided to appeal to the concern that most men felt about death, something which had to be on Oswiu's mind, given the state of his health.

'Are you willing to gamble your place in Heaven on your assertion that the Pope does not derive his authority direct from God and Jesus Christ? Would it not be better to take the safe route and accept the Pope's decree than to find out when you die that you were in error?'

Oswiu rubbed his chin whilst he pondered what Theodore had said.

'What do you say Chad? You've been unnaturally quiet during our discussion.'

'Cyning, I cannot deny that Saint Peter holds the keys to the Gates of Heaven, though I doubt that Our Lord intended to hand spiritual power over all Christendom to one man, however holy. Of course, the Pope is not all powerful in any case. It's not only the Celtic Church that refuses to accept his imperium; the Eastern Churches do as well. They have their own patriarchs.'

'Thank you. Archbishop, you have given me much to think about. I suggest that we meet again in a few days and continue our discussion.'

'Of course, lord king. Until then may the blessing of God Almighty be with you.'

'It's no good asking you what you think, Eanflæd, you were brought up by Roman priests.' He said to his wife after Theodore has left. 'I wish Conomultus was still here for me to discuss what I should do with him. My present chaplain will say only what he thinks I wish to hear.'

'Father, you haven't asked me my opinion, but I think that he's dangling the keys to Paradise in front of your nose. No doubt he believes that is the deciding factor.'

'When did you get to be so cynical, Ælfwine, and so clever?'

'I just asked myself what my brother would say if he was here.'

'Ecgfrith would say anything to keep Wilfrid away. He can't abide the man. To be honest, if the Pope wanted to impose anyone else on me as bishop, I'd probably agree.'

Chad coughed politely. 'Where does that leave me, Cyning?'

'That is something else I need to take into account.'

~~~

Ruaidhrí knew that that there would be trouble as soon as he told the fishermen where they were headed. They may have been paid half the silver in advance with the promise of the rest when they reached their destination, but they were terrified what Bruide would do to them and their families once he found out that they had taken his enemies to where his ships were beached.

It was only by threatening to cut the throats of the younger man or boy crewing each boat, usually the son or nephew of the older man, that they were persuaded to continue. With a sinking heart Ruaidhrí realised that he'd have to kill them anyway once they had played their part; otherwise they'd betray them before they had a chance to steal a ship and make good their escape. He racked his brains trying to think of another way to keep them quiet but at that moment he couldn't.

The fishermen took them in towards a beach some six miles from the mouth of the River Ness. The sand looked silver in the bright moonlight and Ruaidhrí could clearly see across the water to the far side. There were no ships anchored anywhere as far as he could see. The coast on the other side of the inlet didn't look as if it was suitable for beaching ships either, so where were they?

'Is there anywhere else for ships to anchor or be beached?' he asked the man at the tiller who merely shrugged.

However the twelve year old boy with him spoke without thinking.

'There's a large inlet to the west of the river mou...'

His father cuffed him around the ear to shut him up, but it was too late.

'Why didn't you tell me that? You wanted to strand us here, miles away from where we need to be.'

Ruaidhrí supposed that he couldn't blame the headman. He was obviously scared of what Bruide would do to his people; this way he could claim that he'd tricked his king's enemies and hoped that would suffice to get him out of trouble.

'Take us to this other inlet and we'll take two ships so that we can take you and your families south with us. That'll put you out of the reach of Bruide's vengeance.'

The man thought for a moment and then nodded. He rowed across to each of the other boats in turn and told the other fishermen what he had agreed. Some were dubious, but there was little other option.

The flotilla of small boats were too visible on the open water so they sailed back to the narrow entrance into the first inlet and crossed to the western shore. Lost against the blackness of the land, they rowed back down to the entrance to the other inlet. Once they had passed through the narrows Ruaidhrí saw three ships: two birlinns and a knarr, anchored close to the southern shore. The seashore appeared to be rocky with the odd stretch of shingle; there were no silvery stretches of sand here.

Two fires burned on land near where the ships were moored and it was obvious that most of the crews were camped ashore. The small flotilla clustered around Ruaidhrí's boat and he explained what he intended. A third of the boats then set out towards each of the ships. Ruaidhrí heart was in his mouth. He expected someone on watch to spot them any second but the eerie silence continued, broken only by the murmuring burble of oars entering and leaving the water and of night birds hunting their prey.

Ruaidhrí's boat, together with three others, glided softly against the hull of the knarr and two boys stood precariously on the shoulders of men as their craft rocked beneath them, threatening to spill their occupants into the dark waters of the firth. The boys grabbed the gunwale and dragged themselves up and over the side, dropping onto the deck. They threw down a rope and the men climbed up to join them.

The ship was quiet except for the sound of snoring coming from the aft section of the deck. The men left on watch thought they were safe and had drunk themselves into a stupor. They didn't even return to consciousness as their throats were slit. Ruaidhrí looked across at the two birlinns and saw someone waving a white piece of cloth on both vessels – the agreed signal for success. He told someone to do likewise and then they threw the four bodies over the side whilst the fishermen and those amongst his men who had sailed before hauled up the mainsail, then he cut the anchor rope.

All three ships were near the entrance to the inlet before the dozy sentries on land realised that something was wrong. By then it was far too late and an hour after dawn they beached the three craft on the beach where Morleo awaited them. Once they had collected the fishermen's families they had a total of eighty men and boys old enough to be useful as well as forty women, girls and young children on board. They would need all three ships to transport them south.

They spent the rest of the day back at Kinneddar loading provisions and those possessions the fisher folk didn't want to leave behind. All of the latter, together with the women and children, would travel on the knarr. There were thirty seven men who knew how to row and several who were capable of manning the helm, although only Ruaidhrí had handled a birlinn before. The rest would have to learn how to man an oar and no doubt would have worn the skin off their hands before they were proficient; it couldn't be helped.

All went well, despite the occasional minor mishap, and only one man had been lost overboard by the time that they reached the entrance to the Firth of Tay on the fifth day. They had stayed a couple of miles offshore but had kept the coast in sight up until then. As they left the firth behind the sky grew darker and the wind picked up. Off to the east what looked like a grey curtain was approaching rapidly across the sea.

'Squall,' Ruaidhrí yelled. Get the sail in and get ready to row like you've never rowed before. We'll have to keep her head to wind. Those of you who aren't rowing, tie yourselves to something secure.'

The other birlinn and the knarr had also seen the danger and made haste to do likewise. The knarr was least well equipped to deal with it; it was broader in the beam and only had five oars a side, unlike the birlinns that were smaller and had a dozen oars on each side.

They had all stowed their sails and turned into the wind from the east when the squall hit them.

~~~

Chad had been quietly moved to the diocese of Lichfield in Mercia to make way for Wilfrid. The latter gave the briefest of bows when he entered the king's hall to greet his scowling king for the first time since he had taken up his new office. He walked up to the dais on which Oswiu sat on his throne beside a smiling Queen Eanflæd and, mounting the first step, bent forward and offered his ring for the king to kiss.

'If you think my father would ever kiss your ring, you must be a fool,' the boy sitting at his father's feet told him.

From his tone of voice the boy might well have been talking about the man's fat posterior instead of the ostentatiously large bejewelled gold ecclesiastical ring on his plump finger.

'The boy is right. I only agreed to accept you as bishop because Theodore persuaded me, against my better judgement. Don't push your luck Wilfrid.'

Eanflæd gave her husband a sharp glance and smiled at the bishop.

'Well I, for one, am glad to welcome you back, Wilfrid.'

Nevertheless she refrained from taking his hand and kissing his ornate ring. To do so in front of her husband would only enrage him needlessly.

'Cyning, I'm pleased that my monastery at Ripon is to be returned to me but another is claiming to be Abbot of Hexham. I was elected to be its abbot and I have not relinquished my right to it.'

'You've got what you wanted, now be content with what you have.'

'King Alchfrith gave me title to the land, as Queen Eanflæd can attest. I spent my own money in building the church and the abbot's lodgings and I want what is mine.'

Oswiu grew red in the face. 'Alchfrith is a traitor. If you mention his name in my presence again I'll have you whipped, bishop or no bishop.'

'Some people never learn, do they father,' Ælfwine chuckled from his perch near his father's feet.

'Why you insolent puppy.'

For a moment Ælfwine thought that the incensed prelate was going to kick him and his smile broadened. If he goaded the man into doing something really foolish, perhaps his father would have an excuse to exile him once more, if not imprison him.

'Be quiet, Ælfwine, you are not helping,' his mother told him with some asperity.

'You are here to learn boy, not make comments, however accurate,' Oswiu said, supporting his wife whilst, at the same time, showing his son that he agreed with him.

Wilfrid stood his ground. Let no-one say that he lacked perseverance.

'Hexham, Cyning? If you return it to me I'll complete it at no cost to you. The man who's there now has done nothing since I left and I'm told that the monks live in hovels.'

'Oh, very well. You'll have to find a suitable post for the present abbot though, and I'll need to approve it.'

'I understand that the Abbot of Abernethy in the land of the barbarian Picts is close to death. I'll write to Bishop Conomultus tonight to suggest the former Abbot of Hexham as his replacement.'

He knew that mention of Conomultus would annoy Oswiu and he was correct. He hadn't forgiven his former chaplain for deserting him. The king grew even more annoyed when he imagined Wilfrid figuratively rubbing his hands together with glee. It might cost the bishop quite something to finish the building work, if he did what he'd promised, but the income from the vills that the monastery owned would more than make up for that.

'Cyning, there's a messenger here from King Ecgfrith.'

Oswiu waved a hand in dismissal and Wilfrid made a curt bow, passing the mud splattered messenger on his way out. The man pulled a sheet of vellum from the leather cylinder he was carrying and handed it to the king. He broke the seal and read the contents with mounting disquiet. He skipped the usual flowery greetings and scanned the rest of it before reading it again more slowly.

Father,

Stories are beginning to reach me here at Dùn Èideann that cause me considerable concern. Some time ago it would seem that Bruide, King of Penntir, invaded Ardewr and drove Morleo out of his kingdom. No one is certain what has happened to him, but he is probably a fugitive in his own land. Bruide seems to have shown considerable cruelty, disturbing in one so young, in suppressing all resistance to his rule. He appears to have terrorised the population of Ardewr into accepting him as their king, ruthlessly eradicating all opposition, so he now effectively rules the largest kingdom in the

Land of the Picts, other than the sparsely uninhabited Cait in the far north.

There are rumours that he intends to oust your eorl from Prydenn next. If he succeeds he will be powerful enough to remove Drest and take the high kingship. My suspicion is that he intends to unite the Picts under his rule, not as high king, but as king of a united Pictland.

We know that he hates Northumbrians, and us Anglians in particular. If he succeeds we will have lost control of Caledonia because I doubt that Strathclyde or Dalriada will be able to stand up to him. That will, of course, make Goddodin and Rheged vulnerable to attack.

My instinct is to strike now and kill Bruide before it's too late, but I will, of course, be guided by you.

Your loving son,

Ecgfrith of Deira

If only Oswiu had supported Ecgfrith the history of Britain might have been very different, but he was old and worn-out. He told his son to have patience until the situation was clearer; only if Bruide attacked Prydenn would he intervene.

~~~

One minute the sea was calm and there was scarcely a breath of wind; the next moment it was as if the ancient furies had emerged from the underworld and attacked them. The wind struck the ships, causing them to shudder to a halt and then move backwards, despite the efforts of their rowers. The sea was whipped into spume laden peaks and deep valleys that came at them from all directions, causing the ships to heal over first one way and then the other. Seawater crashed into the three craft, threatening to swamp them. Men baled furiously with anything that came to hand – leather buckets, helmets, even the piss pots that the rowers used so that they wouldn't have to leave their posts.

The rowers heaved on their oars one moment and backed them the next to try and keep the bows head on to the lashing wind. Ruaidhrí struggled to keep the steering oar under control but he was tiring fast. The damned thing appeared to be alive and fighting to escape his grasp. Then two men came to his aid and together they managed to tame it.

Seconds later an ominous crack was audible above the howling of the wind and the top portion of the mast fell over the side, enveloping part of the ship in tangled rigging. Leaving the two men to steer, Ruaidhrí picked up a war axe from under one of the rowing benches and started to hack at the cordage. Twice he was nearly swept off his feet and over the side, but he recovered and, with his long hair whipping into his eyes and lashing his face, he eventually cut the last rope so that the ship sprang free of the wreckage.

The wind died as suddenly as it had arrived. Once minute it was so strong that a man could scarcely stand upright against it and the next it was calm again; not so the sea. The waves no longer had spume streaking from their crests but now an oily sea lifted the ship onto the top of a wave just before it plunged down again into a trough thirty feet below. The planking of the hull flexed and water found its way through the gaps, despite the caulking.

Ruaidhrí looked to the west where the squall had disappeared to and saw that the coast was now less than half a mile away. The waves were crashing against the spit of sand that jutted out three miles from the southern shore at the entrance to the firth. They had two options, to try and make enough sea room to clear the spit, or run into the Firth of Tay and seek shelter at Dùn Dè. He decided on the latter as they would be able to make repairs there. He looked across the sea towards the other two craft and saw Morleo in the bows of the other birlinn. Both ships looked in better shape than his birlinn, but the crews were still having to bail energetically. He pointed towards Dùn Dè and Morleo waved back, indicating his agreement.

They arrived at the port to find the eorl and his fully armed warband waiting for them. He had evidently heard the stories coming out of Ardewr and was understandably suspicious at the arrival of three of Bruide's ships. He knew Morleo but was apprehensive when he saw Ruaidhrí. When he last saw the latter he had been Bruide's right hand man. Perhaps Morleo was a prisoner and they were trying to trick him. It took some time of shouting to and fro across the intervening distance before the three ships were allowed to come and tie up alongside.

Three days later they were underway again, having re-caulked the planking and repaired most of the minor damage. However, Morleo and his original warriors from Ardewr weren't with them. He was reluctant to go into exile far from the land he had lived in all his life, so he had volunteered to help the eorl to defend Penntir, if it came to that. Furthermore it gave him the opportunity to build up enough support to challenge Bruide for Ardewr in due course.

The others had also left the birlinn with the damaged mast behind. Not only had the top part broken off, but the squall had also sprung the soleplate on which it was mounted. It would take some time to repair and, without Morleo and his men, the rest would just fit into the other two ships.

They reached Lindisfarne without further incident and Ruaidhrí watched the isle he'd left with his friend Bruide not eighteen months earlier slide past. He reflected sadly on how things had changed. Less than an hour later they beached the two ships on the sand below the fortress of Bebbanburg.

Catinus had been playing with four year old Osfrid, watched by Leoflaed and his eleven year old daughter, Hereswith, when his other son, Alaric, ran in to say that two strange sails were in sight to the north-east.

Alaric was now eight but he showed more inclination to become a cleric, like his uncle Conomultus, than he did a warrior. He even preferred reading the bible to riding or playing with the other boys. He'd been talking to the priest, who was taking his daily stroll around the battlements after the midday meal, when the ships had appeared around the north-east point of what was now being called the Holy Island of Lindisfarne.

He followed his father down to the beach with Eadstan and several members of his gesith, including Leofric, and his body servant, Uurad, who was carrying his master's helmet and shield just in case they were needed.

'Ruaidhrí, what are you doing here?' Catinus called out in amazement when he recognised the youth who had jumped down onto the sand before the gangplank was run out.

'Greetings lord, it's good to see you again, but I fear I'm not the bearer of good tidings.'

CHAPTER FIFTEEN – BROTHER AGAINST BROTHER

669 to 670 AD

Catinus cursed as he tried in vain to keep the driving rain from trickling down his neck as he rode south for the wedding of his daughter Hereswith to his friend Alweo. At first he wasn't sure that it was a sensible idea. After all, she was thirteen and he was thirty nine, only two years younger than Catinus himself. However, it was a good match. She would be the wife of not only an ealdorman but an atheling of the Mercian royal house.

Because neither Wulfhere nor his brother Ethelred had so far produced any children, there was a chance that her son, his grandson, might even become King of Mercia. Since Catinus had started life as a poor Mercian peasant the thought made him proud of what he'd achieved.

He looked across at his wife and daughter, who were riding beside him. They looked as miserable as he felt.

'Cheer up, only a few more miles to go and we'll be at Alnwic.'

It meant the settlement on the River Aln and it was where Alweo had built his hall. Unlike the mighty fortress of Bebbanburg, it wasn't built so much with defence in mind, but with comfort. True it had a palisade around it with a gateway set between two towers, but an agile child could climb over it. It was meant to delineate the ealdorman's home more than to keep out a determined foe.

As they rode through the next stretch of woodland Catinus noticed how early the leaves on the trees were changing colour this year. It had been a cold, wet summer and it was turning into a cold, wet autumn. He worried that his people would starve this winter. The harvest had been poor, though he had some grain stored from the previous summer when there had been a bumper crop.

Animals would have fared poorly as well and there was now less meat than usual on both livestock and those they hunted. It meant that hungry packs of wolves would come down out of the hills looking for food and he would need to find and kill them first, always a risky undertaking, though it was good experience for young warriors. With these thoughts at the forefront of his mind he was in a gloomy mood when the settlement of Alnwic appeared through the rain a little while later.

The next day was overcast but at least it wasn't raining. All the women had a muddy brown hem around the bottom of their gowns by the time they reached the small church. Catinus sensibly wore leather boots over his red trousers. His woollen tunic was dyed blue and decorated with silver wire embroidery and his knee length cloak was secured by a large round silver buckle embedded with gems.

He looked positively distinguished compared to Alweo, who appeared in a garish multi-hued tunic encrusted with golden stars, bright green trousers tucked into brown woollen socks with a crimson band at the top and tied from ankle to knee in criss-cross yellow ribbons. Instead of boots he wore leather shoes stained black, which had turned back to brown in the mud.

Hereswith looked radiant in a cornflower blue surcoat worn over a cream gown. On her head she wore a crown made from woven stalks of wheat into which leaves of every colour from green to dark brown had been stuck. To get over the mud problem she was carried to the church in a chair carried by four warriors from Catinus' gesith. On her way back to the hall for the feast their place would be taken by members of Alweo's household.

When he entered the church beside his daughter to escort her to the side of her husband-to-be he almost didn't believe his eyes. He came to a faltering halt and Hereswith had to restrain a laugh. She was privy to the secret of who was to conduct the marriage ceremony but everyone had kept it a secret from her father.

A broad smile lit up Catinus' face as he almost left her behind in his eagerness to reach the altar rail.

'Conomultus, you don't know how good it is to see you again brother.'

'And you too, Catinus. We'll have plenty of time to talk later, but now I have a couple to wed.'

'Why did you leave Iona?'

'Oh, I was happy enough there, I suppose, but I felt that life was passing me by. One day was much like the next. I got older but a feeling of frustration started to grow. In the end I was getting depressed and so, after years there, I made up my mind to leave.

'However, before I did so we learned that Utta had died and Drest had sent to Iona for a replacement. He wanted a Pict or a Briton; not another Anglo-Saxon. The abbot chose me and I was on my way to Bebbanburg to beg a ship from you to take me the rest of the way to the Firth of Tay. I had travelled with a merchant as far as Alnwic where Ealdorman Alweo told me about his forthcoming marriage to my niece, so I offered to stay and officiate. I was going to send a messenger to tell you, but Alweo persuaded me to surprise you.'

'The last I heard Utta was the Bishop of Prydenn and was Oswiu's nomination. Why has Drest got involved in the appointment of his successor?'

'Because Drest wants one bishop to be responsible for all of Pictland. In the same way that there is no longer a separate Bishop of Rheged, but just one for Northumbria, he sees it as a way to exercise more control over Pictland.'

'Where will you be based? Not in Prydenn presumably.'

'No, at Abernethy, Drest's new capital. He has established a monastery there and I'm to be abbot as well.'

Catinus nodded. Then a thought struck him.

'Does the king know you're in Northumbria?'

'I doubt it, I'm an insignificant priest, there's no reason why he should. Besides, what happened at Dùn Add was years ago now. Hopefully he'll have forgotten.'

'Forgotten that his chaplain deserted him because he disapproved of his threat to murder women and children? I doubt it. And what about Wilfrid? He hates you as much as he does Eata for humiliating him when you were all novices together on

Lindisfarne. He's now the bishop here. He'll find a way of harming you if he discovers that you're in his diocese.'

'You're not making me feel very welcome, brother.'

'It's not a laughing matter. Alweo might well be in trouble for harbouring you too.'

'I hadn't thought of that. But I don't think it matters. I'll be leaving with you in a few days.'

'Wilfrid would still make trouble for Alweo and me given half a chance.'

'I'm sorry. I didn't think.'

'Very well,' he sighed. 'I intended to stay for a few days, but the sooner you're on your way the better. Oswiu is still Bretwalda of the North, and therefore Drest's overlord, but I don't think he'll risk upsetting the Picts once you're safely ensconced at Abernethy. We'll leave together tomorrow.

'In the meantime let's forget that you're about to become a sober bishop and a pillar of the community and celebrate both our reunion and my daughter's wedding by seeing how much of Alweo's ale we can drink before we collapse.'

~~~

Morleo halted on the ridge above the settlement in the valley. He had spent the past year training his men and another fifty or so that he'd recruited to help the eorl by patrolling the north-eastern and north-western borders of Prydenn where it adjoined Ardewr and Penntir. All seventy men had been trained to ride and were mounted on small hill ponies. They weren't fast but they were sure-footed and had stamina.

Below him the River Dee glistened in the sunshine, marking the boundary between Prydenn and Penntir. He watched as a party of some fifty men made their way along Glen Muich that ran from the Dee south into Prydenn. Behind them came as many women and children as there were warriors, then several laden pack horses led by boys. Half a dozen more warriors brought up the rear. A favourite tactic of Bruide was to encroach into areas with little or no inhabitants, establish farmsteads there populated by his subjects, and then claim the land as his. Morleo had already defeated three such incursions and yet here was another one.

The difference between this one and the others was the size of the party of invaders. Whereas the others had contained a dozen or so men, this incursion was over three times the size. Including the families was a new development too.

Vara, his oldest and most experienced warrior, watched the column for several minutes.

'This time I'm not so sure it's a straightforward attempt at a land grab.'

'Why, what else would it be?'

'That is a lot of warriors to tie down in holding an unimportant area of wilderness. No, he's after something else.'

'Such as provoking a major skirmish to give him the excuse to launch a reprisal raid?'

'Which might turn into a full scale invasion? Yes, possibly.'

'In which case we are going to need to be a lot more careful this time. All of the people down there are going to have to disappear. Without any witnesses Bruide won't have the pretext for a dispute.'

'Quite, but how do we do it?'

'A straightforward ambush is out of the question; some would escape and we would lose men, perhaps a lot of men, something I want to avoid.'

'Hit and run tactics then?'

'Partly. But in the end we'll have to surround them first so none can escape and then eliminate them one way or another; either kill them or sell them into slavery.'

Glen Muich ran between two brooding ranges of mountains: Lochnagar to the west and Fashielach to the east. At the end of it lay a loch three miles long. On a day like today it lay blue and inviting under the bright sun; normally its grey hue reflected that of the cloud laden sky above. It was a good strategic place to hold because, from there, there was a long glen that ran south all the way to the coastal plain – an easy invasion route.

'If they set up their base on the side of the loch - north or south it doesn't matter – they would be left with only three escape routes,' Morleo mused as Vara and his other senior warriors listened intently. 'If they camp on the north side of the loch, they can't very well go west either unless they want to end up in a treacherous bog. So we need some men on the slopes of Lochnagar to stop them escaping that way, and then use main body as a blocking force on the route they came along.'

'What happens if they camp on the south side of the loch?' someone asked.

'Well, then we have a greater problem because then they can go east, south over the hills or back the way they came and we don't have enough men to block everywhere. However, the north bank is a better place to camp so just pray that their leader does the obvious.'

When the invaders emerged from Glen Muick the warriors headed along the northern shore of the loch and Morleo breathed a sigh of relief. He waited with a dozen men in the trees near the northern end of the loch until the families had passed and then his archers started to pick off the rearguard whilst he led the rest in a charge at the boys leading the packhorses.

His men had clear instructions to knock the boy handlers out or otherwise disable them. He wanted them alive if possible; selling them in the slave markets of Northumbria or Mercia would give him the funds to recruit more warriors.

The archers brought down four of the six members of the rear guard and the rest of his men were waiting further up Glen Muick to dispose of the other two as they fled. Only one of the five boys was killed and the other handlers were rendered unconscious. The operation had been a complete success and the timing couldn't have been better. It was all over in seven minutes and, by the time that the main body realised what was happening, dusk was beginning to fall.

Only one of Morleo's men had been injured and he'd only suffered a minor flesh wound to his leg. It wouldn't stop him riding. The boys they'd captured ranged in age from twelve to fifteen and would fetch a good price. For now they were shackled together and three men were left to guard them.

That night Morleo led his men on foot from their base beside a small lochan two miles north west of Loch Muick to attack the enemy camp. It was easy to find their way in the dark as all they had to do was follow the burn that led from the lochan into the main loch and then move along the shoreline to the camp.

To his ears the sound of feet on grass or slithering over slippery stones by the water's edge sounded unnaturally loud but the flap of owls' wings and of other nocturnal birds seeking a meal was louder. The new moon and the stars gave just enough light to illuminate the path. It had been a fine day and now it was a clear night. It wouldn't last, Morleo thought gloomily. In his experience rain was more usual than sun in these mountains.

Morleo halted and waited with the bulk of his men two hundred yards from the camp whilst his scouts went forward to deal with the sentries. That done, he sent some of his men to cut off anyone fleeing back into Glen Muick then led the rest forward.

The only sounds in the camp were snoring and the occasional moan of pleasure as a few couples had sex, oblivious to the others around them. Without the packhorses everyone had been forced to sleep in the open.

Each of Morleo's forty men picked a sleeping warrior and then, when he gave the signal, they started to slit their throats. It was unfortunate that the second man that Morleo went towards was one of those busy pleasuring a woman. The man wasn't aware that anything was amiss but his partner saw Morleo looming out of the darkness with a seax in his hand and she screamed. The man rolled off her and with, with surprising alacrity considering what he'd been doing a moment before, he came to his feet, oblivious of his naked state, and picked up his axe.

The scream had woken all those except a few who were too drunk to be roused. Soon Morleo's men found themselves in a desperate hand-to-hand fight. This wasn't how he'd planned it and he only had himself to blame. He just hadn't been quick enough to silence the pair. The warrior confronting him swung his axe at his head but he easily ducked out of its way. As he straightened up, he thrust the blade of his seax into the man's bare belly.

He pulled it clear with a grunt and looked for another adversary, but he'd foolishly forgotten about the woman lying at his feet. She had found a dagger from somewhere and now plunged it into his thigh. He managed to slash down and partially sever her head from her neck, but then his leg gave way under him and he fell to the ground. His head hit something hard and he lost consciousness.

When Morleo came to he found a worried Vara bending over him.

'Thank the good Lord for that. I was beginning to think that you'd left us for good and I'd have to start taking decisions, not my strong point.'

'What happened?'

'To you? Well, you took a nasty blow to the head and you've lost quite a lot of blood from that wound in your thigh. It's been washed clean and stitched up whilst you were unconcious so, although you won't be able to walk on it for a while, it should heal alright.'

'I meant did we kill the men and stop the women escaping?'

'Difficult to say as it's only just getting light but most of the women and children are distraught, which must be a good sign. We killed all the warriors who fought us, but we lost three men with a few more wounded, but not too badly. They should recover in time. The rest we rounded up and tied their hands and feet together. The group you sent up the glen returned a little while ago to say that ten had tried to escape that way during the night and had been killed or captured.'

Morleo nodded and then, with Vara's help, managed to get to his feet, holding his left foot clear of the ground so that he didn't put any pressure on his injured leg. One of the older boys handed him a tree branch which he'd fashioned into a crude crutch and, after tucking it under his armpit to support his weight, he nodded his thanks and then scanned the slopes of Lochnagar. As the sun rose it illuminated the summit with its halo of cloud. It promised to be another fine day. He felt a moderate breeze on his cheek, though he scarcely noticed it over the pain in his throbbing head. Slowly the blanket of light worked its way down the mountainside like a tide of ants on the march. When it reached the halfway point he spotted movement.

There were four separate peaks in all and they stood between two thousand eight hundred feet and three thousand eight hundred feet tall. It would take the fugitives some time to reach one the shallow saddles that linked the summits and, even after they'd made it to the far side of the line of hills, the River Dee lay miles away over difficult terrain. He picked out his four best runners.

'Go after them. I saw two, but check thoroughly in case there are more. Don't bother to bring them back, kill them and leave them to feed the crows.'

When he questioned the women captives later he was told that two of the girls were missing, sisters of thirteen and fourteen. They buried the warriors they'd killed in a common grave well away from the lochside where no one was ever likely to find them. Just as they'd finished the men he'd sent after the runaways came back.

'We only found the two girls. We left the bodies behind as you instructed but we brought back their heads.'

The man held up his grisly trophies, grinning like a madman. Morleo shuddered in revulsion but he forced himself to thank the men for their efforts. They had no doubt raped the girls before killing them and the thought made him feel sick. However, that aside, they'd done what he'd ordered and a good leader knew what conduct to punish and what to ignore.

The next day they set off with their captives on the long march down Glen Clova back to Dùn Dè. The weather had finally broken and fine drizzle managed to permeate their clothing, however tightly they wrapped their lanolin impregnated cloaks around them. Every step of the way Morleo was in pain. He might be riding but the pony jarred his leg all the time on the uneven path. Not for the first time he wondered what the hell he was doing there. He was no longer sure that recovering Ardewr was as important to him as it had once been.

~~~

Rægenhere read his brother's letter with dismay. He and Wilfrid might have had the same mother and father but they were nothing like each other. He was devout and tried to live a good life whereas the only vice the Bishop of Northumbria wasn't rumoured to indulge in was fornication.

One might have thought that, having achieved his ambition of becoming bishop of his native land, his brother would be satisfied. However, he was now scheming to replace Oswiu on the throne with Alchfrith when the former died; an event that he didn't think would be long delayed now.

He wanted Rægenhere to act as an intermediary between himself and the exiled former King of Deira. As he was Alchfrith's chaplain, Wilfrid seemed to think that Rægenhere was in a perfect position to represent him as communication between him and his only living relative shouldn't arouse any suspicions. Rægenhere wasn't so sure. They had never been close - in fact they loathed each other – and Ecgfrith would be a fool if he wasn't suspicious of correspondence going to and fro between the bishop and the continent, and Ecgfrith was anything but a fool.

He watched the smoke curl up from the bronze dish as the parchment burned to a cinder. As it turned to ashes he wondered if he'd done the right thing. If Wilfrid wrote directly to Alchfrith when he didn't get a reply from his brother he wasn't sure how he was going to explain why he didn't pass on the letter. In the end he decided to tell Alchfrith the contents and say that he'd destroyed the letter to save it falling into the wrong hands.

Alchfrith listened to what his chaplain had to say intently. Rægenhere could picture him piecing together the bits of information he'd just given him with what he already knew, like a girl trying to repair a broken pitcher. This Pict, Bruide, had evidently kicked over a hornets' nest and no-one seemed to know what to do about him. Morleo had taken refuge with Oswiu's eorl in Prydenn and now Bruide was demanding that he hand him over for slaughtering the men of one of his villages and selling the women and children into slavery.

Of course, the eorl had refused and denied any knowledge of the group in question. Bruide couldn't produce any evidence, apart from the fact that they were apparently missing. How he knew that Morleo was involved was a bit of a mystery, unless he had spy amongst Morleo's men of course.

'Your brother seems to be suggesting that I employ an assassin to kill Ecgfrith whilst he is still in the north. Ælfwine is far too young to be considered a threat so that would make me the only possible heir.'

'Apart from Aldfrith, of course.'

'Aldfrith? But he's a bastard and a monk. In any case he must be ancient.'

'He's a scholar but not a monk; he never took his vows. I believe that he's in his mid-thirties now.'

'Really? Well, he's still not a contender.'

'You wouldn't really consider committing the sin of fratricide, would you?'

'It was your God-fearing brother that suggested it.'

'Not quite. Even he isn't that wicked. What he said in his letter was that if Ecgfrith should meet with an accident, then your chances of succeeding Oswiu would improve immeasurably.'

'It sounds like a pretty clear suggestion to me.'

Rægenhere wished his brother had never put pen to paper now. What was he thinking of? If that letter had fallen into the wrong hands Oswiu would execute Wilfrid, whether or not he'd been consecrated by the Pope.

'I've done what Bishop Wilfrid asked. May I retire, lord?'

'Yes, yes. I suppose so. I was hoping we could discuss our options, but I suppose a sanctimonious priest wouldn't want to sully his hands. It would be more useful if Wilfrid was my chaplain. Well, what are you waiting for? Get out.'

Rægenhere didn't sleep well that night. He couldn't stop worrying that Alchfrith would do something stupid like actually sending someone to kill Ecgfrith. He tried to convince himself that

Alchfrith would drop the idea once he'd thought it through. He'd have been even more worried had he known that, far from abandoning the idea, that was exactly what he was planning.

~~~

The sleet swept across the dark, grey waters of the firth. Ecgfrith saw nothing in front of him except for the white curtain that stung his face, but the helmsman seemed to know where he was going. January 669 had been unusually mild but February had swept in like a vengeful demon. Ecgfrith thought that perhaps he should have waited before moving from Dùn Èideann to Dùn Dè in Prydenn but he wanted to take Bruide by surprise. If these miserable conditions were the price he had to pay, so be it.

The temperature dropped as the sleet changed to snow. At first the flakes melted as they struck the wet deck, but then, as the surface cooled, the snow started to settle. The rowers cursed as they struggled to propel the birlinn against the steadily increasing wind. Everyone would be glad when they turned out of the Firth of Forth and started to head north. Then the easterly wind would allow them to hoist the sail.

Slowly the snow petered out and Ecgfrith looked astern to make sure that the rest of the fleet followed in his wake. He could only see the next two ships, which carried Beornheth and his gesith. Previously he'd been the Ealdorman Dùn Barra but had now become the Eorl of Lothian following his childless predecessor's death. The rest of the fleet transported Ecgfrith's warband and that of Lothian, the English name which had now replaced the British one of Goddodin. It wasn't a large force – merely two hundred men at the moment – but the addition of the warband of Prydenn and Morleo's men should double the size of the army for the invasion of Ardewr.

During the autumn messengers had worn a path between Dùn Èideann and Abernethy. Drest wasn't willing to confront Bruide but he had at least agreed not to interfere if Ecgfrith aided Morleo in the recovery of his kingdom.

The black clouds scudding across the sky gradually lightened in colour until, just as they entered the Firth of Tay, a window of light blue appeared. By the time that they had beached the ships ready to disembark the sun had put in an appearance. It did little to warm anyone but it did cheer them up.

Two days later they set out in bright sunshine. The column of marching men, baggage carts and horsemen snaked back down Glen Clova for half a mile. As they reached the small loch under the brooding mountain called Lochnagar the sun vanished and a cold wind sprang up which chilled the bones of everyone from king to servant boy alike. By the time that they entered Glen Muick it had started to hail. The small lumps of ice stung bare flesh and the warriors used their shields to protect their heads.

The ponies and horses started to get skittish and, just when Ecgfrith thought that he'd have to call a halt, the hail stopped as suddenly as it had started. In the aftermath of the hail rattling as it hit any hard surface the glen now sounded eerily quiet. Only the distant bleating of sheep far away up the hillside broke the silence. By dusk they'd reached the river and camped on the Prydenn side. Tomorrow they'd cross into Ardewr.

Some of Morleo's men had watched the flanks and scouted ahead of the main body but no one had thought to watch the rear. As the tents were erected and fires were lit in the twilight two men sat on their horses and watched from the flanks of Creag na Gall, the mountain to the north west of the army.

~~~

That night the two men crept down on foot towards the camp. A bitter wind swept along the glen in which the dark oily river ran and the black clouds obscured the moon. As they made their way along the valley floor their shoes caused the grass to rustle slightly but the sound was hidden by the wind. An owl hunted its nightly meal some distance away and small animals scurried out of the way of the two men.

They paused once they neared the camp and waited patiently for the sentries to reveal their positions. Unlike novices, these warriors knew better than to move about, giving their positions away. They sat or stood still facing away from the campfires so as to preserve their night vision. The two assassins, for that was what they were, knew that they faced a difficult task. Getting inside the camp's perimeter would not be easy. Then they had a stroke of luck. The watch changed and two of the new sentries obviously lacked the experience of their older fellows.

They chose the one who changed his position regularly, rubbing his cold hands together and huddling into his cloak when he stopped. He kept looking in towards the campfires that were slowly dying down to glowing embers, evidently wishing he was near one instead of freezing to death. That ruined his night vision and so he was oblivious of the two men as they crept towards him.

Suddenly he heard a twig snap somewhere out in the inky blackness that surrounded the camp. He looked nervously towards the place where the sound had come from and the second assassin took advantage of the distraction created by his companion to cross the final five yards. As he came up behind the young sentry one of his hands clamped itself across his mouth whilst the other drew a seax across his throat. Satisfied that the lad was dead, his killer lowered him silently to the ground.

Once inside the camp the two men walked boldly through it as if they had every right to be there. No one challenged them, indeed the only person they saw was an elderly man on his way to relieve his bladder. They ignored each other.

However, when they neared Ecgfrith's tent, distinguished from the rest by its size and the banner of Deira – a blue spread-eagle on a yellow background - flying outside it, they halted and melted into the shadows. There were two guards outside the entrance and another patrolling around the back. The obvious target was the man at the rear and they used the same diversionary tactic with him, this time throwing a pebble off to his right.

It was a lucky throw and it pinged off an empty cauldron outside one of the other tents. The man turned in that direction and one of the assassins ran towards his exposed back whilst the other threw a knife at his chest. It was a good throw and the man collapsed into the first assassin's arms with no more than a grunt of pain before he died.

The knife-thrower recovered his blade and used it to cut a slit in the tent. To his annoyance he found that the tent was double skinned; an outer layer of leather and an inner one of woven wool. He cut a second slit before poking his head through the two slits to look inside.

He could tell from the soft snores that the man lying on the heap of furs in one corner was asleep. The second occupant had the slight build of a youth – a servant presumably – but he was making no sound. The two men crept into the tent and approached the bed cautiously. They had ignored the servant which proved to be a mistake.

As one clamped his meaty hand over Ecgfrith's mouth, the other raised a dagger ready to plunge it into his heart. It started its descent but it never reached its target. The man with the dagger suddenly felt a paralysing pain in his back and he collapsed on top of the king, his blade falling harmlessly onto the furs beside them.

The other man whipped around to see the servant tugging at a sword, trying to free it from his fellow assassin's back. He went to pull his seax free of its scabbard but, just as his hand curled around the hilt, he felt his hand spasm open involuntarily. The king on the bed was trapped by the dead body but he'd managed to free an arm and had grabbed the fallen dagger. He'd used it to plunge the point into back of the man's right hand.

Ignoring the pain, he reached across with his left hand for his seax but the noise and the cries of the servant had been heard by the two sentries and they came rushing into the tent.

'Don't kill him,' Ecgbert yelled at them. 'I want to question him.'

With two spears levelled at his throat he knew when he was beaten. His life was precious to him and he'd been able to preserve it in the past when caught by offering his services to his captor.

Once the body was removed and Ecgbert had dressed the interrogation began.

'Who paid you?'

When it was obvious that the man didn't understand either English or Brythonic, he tried Latin but, although he knew a few words, it wasn't enough. Then Ecgbert's chaplain thought to try Franconian, the language of the Franks. Relieved, the man responded in a rush of - to Ecgfrith - unintelligible gibberish until he kicked his kneeling body to shut him up.

'Ask him who paid him.'

'He says a man in a tavern. He doesn't know his name but he'd seen him before.'

'So? Where?'

'In the entourage of the Northumbrian prince, Alchfrith. He thinks that he's the captain of his gesith. He's offered to go back and kill Alchfrith if you let him go, Cyning.'

Ecgfrith laughed. 'Why should I trust the word of a paid assassin? No, take him outside and kill him. Throw the two bodies into the river; let them feed the fish. And you had better check the sentries. I suspect that we've lost more than the man guarding the back of my tent tonight.'

The next morning the small army crossed the swollen river at a well-used ford. Because of the recent rain the river was deeper than usual but the horsemen took a rope across for those on foot to hold onto. The last man had crossed before it started to rain again, but by midday the sun had put in an appearance and the wet cloaks started to steam as the water evaporated. By nightfall everyone had dried out and they had reached Aviemore without encountering any opposition.

The settlement was deserted but it showed signs of recent occupation. In one of the vegetable patches outside a hut a pig was digging up turnips with unconcealed delight at this unexpected treat. A hen ran hither and thither squawking its disapproval of the new arrivals and in one hut a cauldron containing the peasants' staple diet of root vegetable and lentil stew thickened with barley bubbled away merrily. Presumably the people had taken fright when they saw so many armed men approaching.

They stayed at Aviemore overnight and Morleo left behind payment for the slaughtered pig, chicken and two goats they'd found eating straw in the stables. Instead of retracing the steps that Morleo had taken when he fled, they followed a track through the mountains via several more settlements – all of which had been deserted in haste, like Aviemore – until they reached the mouth of the River Ness at nightfall.

Ecgfrith now deployed many more scouts. He had no intention of being caught in a trap. At first all was normal as they advanced along Loch Ness, but then the plethora of bird calls faded away and an eerie silence descended on the woods that lined the loch.

Ecgfrith halted and deployed the warriors on foot into a long line to sweep through the trees whilst the horsemen cantered over the grass covered hill side above them to cut off any escape. The so-called Mormaer of Ardewr had laid an ambush, expecting his enemies to walk into it. Instead, he was caught out.

The mormaer's men were hidden fifty paces back into the woods in a line parallel to the lochside. Ecgfrith rolled them up like a rush mat whilst Morleo's horsemen charged into the routed majority who tried to flee over the hills or back to the crannoch. The upshot was that the mormaer and two hundred of his men were killed and another one hundred captured, many of them wounded.

Morleo strode along the walkway back in the deserted king's hall on its platform above the water with a mixture of emotions: exultation that he'd won back his kingdom so easily mixed with sadness and regret. In Prydenn he'd been happy whilst this place would always be inhabited by the ghosts of Genofeva who had hated him and his father who'd only had the courage to recognise him after Genofeva was dead. The place was also tainted by Bruide's cruel treatment of Morleo's people. Sorrow for those who had died lay on his heart like lead. Perhaps Ecgfrith was right when he said that he didn't have the streak of ruthlessness you needed to be a good king.

~~~

After a long time when he could do very little, Oswiu felt some of his original vigour returning. He would have dearly loved to have gone on a stag hunt to celebrate but Eanflæd was adamantly opposed to that idea.

'Are you mad? Do you want a relapse?'

'I'll just watch. The young men can take all the risks.'

'No. I've been married to a living corpse for the past two years. If not exactly virile, you are more like the Oswiu I used to know. I won't allow you to put that in jeopardy.'

Not many things depressed Oswiu but his wife's description of him and her comment about their enforced celibacy due to his ill health struck home.

'No,' she continued, 'if you want to get out and about we'll take a leisurely tour around the kingdom. You can show your face and counter the rumours about your imminent demise. However, you'll travel sitting in a chariot.'

'I will not,' he replied equally vehemently. 'That's for women and small children, not grown men. Besides, you always complain of being jolted half to death in them. I'll ride a horse and I'll not be dissuaded.'

After a leisurely journey north Oswiu and Eanflæd arrived at Whitby in the late summer to see his daughter Ælfflaed, who was now sixteen.

'I'm too old to carry on ruling Northumbria, Hild,' he told his cousin who had been the abbess since the monastery's foundation.

As he spoke he chewed on the hard brown bread that had been served with an equally hard cheese as the evening meal. He found the absence of half his teeth a distinct disadvantage and eventually gave up, resigned to going to bed hungry.

Hild was only a year younger than Oswiu but she had retained the vitality of someone much younger. She also had most of her teeth.

'Will you retire to a monastery?'

'No, I'd like to go on a pilgrimage to Rome and meet this Pope Vitalianus.'

Eanflæd, to whom Oswiu had said nothing of this, was speechless for a few moments, then she reacted with anger.

'Have you taken leave of your senses? Even this short journey has tired you out. You'd be lucky to make it to Frankia.'

'Not if I go by sea.'

'By sea? How?'

'You are well educated, wife, but it seems that geography isn't a strong point. I can sail down past Frankia and Iberia and through the Pillars of Hercules into the Middle Sea. Rome is only twenty miles or so from the port of Ostia, so I'm told.'

'And how far is this sea voyage?'

Oswiu was on less certain ground now.

'It should take no more than a month, with favourable winds.'

'And you feel up to the privations of life on board a ship do you?'

'Mind what you say, woman,' Oswiu retorted, conscious that he was being hen pecked in public.

Once on their own in a small hut that had been set aside for their use, Eanflæd returned to the attack.

'You are no more up to making a pilgrimage to Rome than I am of swimming over the Firth of Forth.'

'I didn't know you could swim,' he said, trying to stave off the tirade he knew was coming.

'I can't! That's my point. Now you can forget this nonsense. I won't allow it,' she stormed at him.

'You won't allow...' he began in an incredulous voice but he didn't get any further before he clutched at the centre of his chest and sat down heavily in the only chair in the hut.

The pain grew more intense and then spread to his shoulders and down towards his stomach. He felt dizzy and started to pant. At the same time he broke out into a cold sweat.

'Oswiu? Are you alright,' she asked before realising it was a foolish question. Plainly he wasn't.

She screamed for her slaves and sent one of them to find Hild and the other to find the infirmarian. The latter confirmed what she had feared.

'The kings' heart is worn out, Síþwíf.'

He'd merely confirmed what she'd feared.

'Will he recover?'

'Some men do, others don't. Every case is different.'

'It may be best if you pray to God but make provision for the worst,' Hild told her gently.

'Yes, you're right, of course. I must let my son know.'

'Where is Ecgfrith?'

'Somewhere in the north, I don't know where exactly.'

'It's important that he returns as soon as possible, just in case the worst happens. It might take longer for a messenger to reach him and for him to return than it will take Alchfrith.'

A look of alarm crossed the queen's face. She'd almost forgotten about her stepson. If he became king she didn't think that either Ecgfrith or nine year old Ælfwine would survive for long.

'You're right. Send for Redwald.'

At that moment Wigmund, Prior of Whitby arrived.

'I'll let my cousin, Alweo, know that the king is seriously ill. It may be sensible to advise the other nobles.'

The queen nodded and the prior bustled away to be replaced by Redwald. He took one look at Oswiu and sighed deeply.

'I'm sorry, Síþwíf. Is there anything I can do?'

'I don't honestly know. I'm out of my depth.'

Suddenly she chuckled, which drew a strange look from the Hereræswa.

'I'm sorry, Redwald. I'd just remembered what the king said moments before he fell ill. He was reminding me that I couldn't swim.'

Redwald was no wiser but he smiled dutifully nonetheless.

'We must guard against our enemies taking advantage of this situation. With Ecgfrith hundreds of miles away we are vulnerable if Mercia seeks to take advantage.'

'Don't forget Alchfrith.'

'Alchfrith?'

'Yes, he was said to be gathering an army and a fleet earlier in the year but for now they seem to have dispersed again. No doubt he could quickly re-assemble them.'

'For that he'd need money,' she scoffed.

'Yes, well, he appears to be getting enough of that from somewhere.'

'From someone on the Continent? Do we have enemies over there?'

'Not on the Continent, no. I was thinking of someone a little closer to home.'

Eanflæd looked startled.

'Who?' Her voice trailed away, then her eyes narrowed. 'You don't mean Bishop Wilfrid? You can't do!'

'He hates Ecgfrith and he was Alchfrith's protégé.'

'And mine,' she snapped. 'Don't be ridiculous. Now get out and do something useful.'

He bowed and left, sighing over how blind people could be sometimes.

Ecgfrith arrived back in October. His mother was relieved to see him, now he could take the burden of running the kingdom off his father's shoulders and perhaps Oswiu would then have a chance to recover.

However, the person most delighted to see him was the nine-year old Ælfwine. He worshipped his elder brother and had been bitterly disappointed when he refused to take him north with him.

'Now you're back you can tell me all about it.'

'I will, little brother, but not now. The kingdom can't be governed from Whitby. I need to leave for Eoforwīc tomorrow, now that I've seen father. Taking all the scribes and other administrators with me will ease the burden on the monastery too.'

'Can I come with you, please?'

'It might be a good idea. He's bored here and I can't devote much time to him. I need to spend as much time with your father as I can,' Eanflæd said.

'Very well, but you're to behave. I've heard what you've been up to here,' Ecgfrith told him as the excited boy jumped up and down.

He was referring to his exploits in the monks' hall where they ate communally, an innovation suggested by the prior a year or so ago. Previously monks had lived in huts in threes or fours and cooked for themselves. They still slept in the small huts but ate together listening to extracts from the bible.

The hall was heated as usual by a fire in the centre and already the beams above had become coated with soot. When Ælfwine had appeared one day with his tunic and trousers covered in black marks it didn't take a genius to work out that he'd been climbing up into the rafters. It wasn't the ruination of his expensive clothes so much as the risk of him falling to his death that had got him into trouble.

The two came back again to Whitby to celebrate Christmas. Oswiu seemed quite a lot better and even managed to attend mass and the meal that followed. The monks and nuns prayed together but lived separately so Eanflæd joined Hild and the rest of the women whilst Oswiu and his sons ate in the monks' hall.

Oswiu didn't manage to eat much and retired straight afterwards. Nevertheless both Ecgfrith and Ælfwine were encouraged by it. They returned to Eoforwīc two days later with Oswiu confident that he would be able to follow them in a few weeks. However January passed and he was no stronger.

On the tenth of February a messenger arrived to say that Oswiu had suffered another collapse and this time it didn't look as if he would recover. He was unconscious much of the time now and he wasn't eating. He died five days later with his wife and their two sons by his side.

The icy wind blew near horizontal gusts of snow across the monastery compound as they carried King Oswiu of Northumbria, Bretwalda of the North, in his coffin from the simple hut where he'd died across to the stone church. If anything the building was even colder inside than it was out, but at least those attending the funeral were sheltered from the elements. He was laid to rest in a grave dug in front of the altar after a simple ceremony conducted by Hild and her prior, Wigmund; Wilfrid was pointedly not invited.

Afterwards, after the earth was shovelled back in to cover the coffin, the slabs were replaced, one of which had been inscribed with his name and the words Rex Regum - meaning King of Kings in Latin.

Eanflæd had made up her mind to stay at Whitby with her daughter Ælfflæd months before Oswiu's death and now she lost no time in taking her vows as a nun. She was destined to outlive both her sons and to succeed Hild as the abbess.

Oswiu's eldest son, Aldfrith was in Ireland when his father died and didn't learn of his death until nearly three months after the event. They had never been close and, as a bastard, he didn't consider himself a contender for the throne, so it didn't upset him that the Witan of Northumbria had met and chosen Ecgfrith as their next king without considering him.

Alchfrith had gathered his warriors and hired a fleet as soon as the news reached him. It mattered not that the Witan had already chosen his half-brother, though he was furious that he hadn't even been considered. As an Ætheling of Northumbria he had been entitled to attend and state his case. Well, he wasn't to be disregarded so easily. He would eliminate both Ecgfrith and Ælfwine and then the Witan would be forced to select him as the only legitimate survivor of Oswiu's sons.

He set sail from Austrasia in early May 670. The stage was set for Ecgfrith's first challenge as King of Northumbria.

To Be Continued in The Fall of the House of Æthelfrith

Author's Note

This story is based on the known facts, but written evidence is patchy and there is some confusion in the main sources about dates, names and even relationships between family members. The main events are as depicted, even if the detail is invented. The chronology of events has sometimes been slightly altered in order to suit the story but this is, after all, a novel.

ANGLO-SAXON ORGANISATION AND CULTURE

The leaders of the Anglo-Saxons were constantly at war with one another during this period. Borders kept shifting and smaller kingdoms were swallowed up by larger ones. Kings had to pay their warbands and that took money, hence the need to plunder one's neighbours. The peasantry were only there to feed the kings, his nobles and their warriors.

Most kings had a small personal bodyguard of companions – called a gesith – and a warband - that is a permanent army of trained warriors. These were usually no more than a few hundred strong, if that. Nobles and some thegns would also keep a small gesith or warband to protect them, collect taxes and the like. The rest of the army was composed of a militia called the fyrd. It was made up of freemen, or ceorls, who provided their own weapon, and armour if they possessed any. Their standard of training and equipment varied.

When the Anglo-Saxons moved from paganism – about which little is known – to Christianity, being a churchman instead of a warrior became an acceptable career for the well-bred. We know that several kings abdicated to become monks. Most other kings died in battle. Oswiu died in bed in his late fifties, but that was a rarity.

The spread of Christianity started with Augustine in the south and the converted recognised the Pope in Rome as their spiritual leader. In the north it was Aidan and the Celtic church who were largely responsible for the religion's growth. Inevitably the two churches came into conflict, resolved in Rome's favour by Oswiu at the Synod of Whitby.

The Anglo-Saxons were a cultured people, as surviving artefacts testify. The standard of illumination of religious tomes, intricate jewellery and well-made ornaments all demonstrate the high standard of their craftsmanship and their culture.

There was a parliament of sorts called the *Witan*, or more properly the Witenagemot, in most kingdoms. It was an assembly of the ruling class whose primary function was to advise the king and elect a replacement when there was a vacancy. It was composed of the most important noblemen and the ecclesiastic hierarchy, but its membership could be expanded to include the thegns when the most important matters were to be discussed.

Thegns owned land of sufficient size to qualify for recognition by the king as such. A freeman could become a thegn by acquiring more land. Their estate was known as a *vill*, which corresponded roughly to the post-Norman manor.

Apart from members of the royal family, nobles also included the *eorls*, and later the *ealdormen*. They were appointed by the king to administer sub-divisions of the kingdom. Later the word was combined with the Norse jarl (meaning chieftain) to produce the title *earl*. However Anglo-Saxon earls ruled what had been the old major kingdoms of a dis-united England (for example Wessex, Mercia and Northumbria). The function of the earlier eorl gradually became that of the *ealdorman*, who was a royal official and chief magistrate of an administrative district called a shire.

ANGLO-SAXON KINGDOMS

In the early seventh century AD Britain was divided into over twenty petty kingdoms. I have listed them here for the sake of completeness, though only a few of them feature significantly in the story. A few others get a passing mention. From north to south:

Land of the Picts – Probably divided into seven separate kingdoms in all in the north and north-east of present day Scotland at this time. Later they became one kingdom. The names of the individual kingdoms seem to vary depending on the source. The names I have used are listed in the Glossary at the start of this novel

Dalriada – Western Scotland including Argyll and the Isles of the Hebrides. Also included part of Ulster in Ireland where the main tribe – the Scots – originated from

Goddodin – Lothian and Borders Regions of modern Scotland – then subservient to Bernicia and therefore part of Northumbria. Later called Lothian

Bernicia – The north-east of England. Part of Northumbria

Strathclyde – South west Scotland

Rheged – Modern Cumbria and Lancashire in the north-west of England. A client kingdom of Northumbria and later absorbed within it
Deira – North, East and South Yorkshire
Elmet – West Yorkshire. Originally a Brythonic kingdom rather than an Anglo-Saxon one
Essex – Similar to the present day county of Essex
Lindsey – Lincolnshire and Nottinghamshire
Gwynedd – North Wales
Mercia – Most of the English Midlands
East Anglia – Norfolk, Suffolk and Cambridgeshire
Powys – Mid Wales
Middle Anglia – Bedfordshire, Northamptonshire and Warwickshire
Dyfed – South-west Wales
Kingdom of the East Saxons – Essex
Hwicce – South-east Wales, Herefordshire and Gloucestershire
Kingdom of the Middle Saxons – Home counties to the north of London
Wessex – Southern England between Devon and Surrey/Sussex
Kent – South-eastern England south of the River Thames
Kingdom of the South Saxons – Sussex and Surrey
Dumnonia – Devon and Cornwall in south-west England

It's worth noting that the coastline fourteen centuries ago was very different to what it is today. In particular, much of Cambridgeshire, part of Kent and the land around York was under water.

OSWIU, KING AND SAINT

Oswiu became King of Bernicia, possibly as Penda's vassal, after the death of his elder brother, Oswald, who had also ruled Deira. However, Oswine became King of Deira until deposed by Oswiu seven years later. Oswald's son, Œthelwald, then became king but he was a constant thorn in Oswiu's side. After he betrayed Oswiu and sided with the Mercians at the battle where Penda was slain (although for some reason his men didn't take part in the battle itself) he disappeared, possibly going into exile or, more likely, Oswiu had him quietly disposed of. Oswiu's son, Alchfrith, became sub-king of Deira as a vassal of his father.

The early part of Oswiu's reign was defined by struggles with Oswine and then Œthelwald to assert control over Deira, as well as his contentious relationship with Penda. In 655 Oswiu's forces killed Penda at the Battle of the Winwæd. This established Oswiu as the most powerful ruler in Britain. For three years after the battle Oswiu's rule also extended over Mercia, earning him recognition as bretwalda over much of England.

Oswiu was a devoted Christian, promoting the faith among his subjects and establishing a number of monasteries, including Gilling Abbey and Whitby Abbey. He was raised in the Celtic Christian tradition rather than the Roman Catholic faith practiced by the southern Anglo-Saxon kingdoms and some members of the Deiran nobility, including Oswiu's queen. In 664, Oswiu presided over the Synod of Whitby, where clerics debated which of the two traditions - Celtic or Roman Catholic - should prevail. Oswiu decided that Northumbria should follow the Roman Church, a momentous decision which would affect England for the next millennium.

Oswiu is thought to have had children as follows:

1. Out of wedlock by Fin (Fianna in the novels):
   Aldfrith. King of Northumbria 685 – 705.
2. By Rhieinmelth:
   Alchfrith. Sub-king of Deira 655-664.
3. By Eanflaed:
   Osthryth (dau).
   Ecgfrith. Sub-king of Deira 664 – 670. King of Northumbria 670 – 685.
   Ælfflaed (dau). Abbess of Whitby.
   Ælfwine. Sub-king of Deira 670-679.

Like Oswald, Oswiu too was recognised as a saint, though some of his actions weren't very saintly. The first half of Oswiu's reign was spent in the shadow of Penda, who dominated much of Britain from 642 until 655. The once and future Kingdom of Northumbria was again composed of two separate countries for part of Oswiu's reign. The northerly kingdom of Bernicia, which extended from the River Tees to the Firth of Forth, was ruled by Oswiu. The kingdom of Deira, lying to the south of it as far as the Humber, was ruled by a series of Oswiu's kinsmen, initially as a separate kingdom, later as a vassal state.

After Oswiu slew Penda in battle he ruled Mercia for three years as well. The Mercians eventually revolted and installed one of

Penda's sons as their king, but Oswiu remained as lord paramount or *Bretwalda* over most of England and, through an alliance with his nephew, who was High King of the Picts, and his successors, most of Scotland.

BUBONIC PLAGUE

The first recorded epidemic affected the Eastern Roman Empire and was named the Plague of Justinian after Emperor Justinian I who was infected but survived. The pandemic resulted in the deaths of an estimated 25 million to 50 million people throughout the world over the next two centuries.

In the spring of 542 the plague arrived in Constantinople. Travelling mainly from port to port it spread around the Mediterranean Sea, later migrating inland eastward into Asia Minor and westwards into Greece and Italy. The disease spread along the trade routes.

The so-called Plague of Justinian seems to have arrived in Ireland around 544 AD. There is no conclusive evidence that it spread to mainland Britain, apart from one report that the death of King Maelgwn of Gwynedd in 547 was due to the plague. However, information about this period of history is notoriously scarce and unreliable.

An outbreak occurred in England in the late seventh century which Saint Cuthbert succumbed to, but survived. Deusdedit, Archbishop of Canterbury and Bishop Tuda of Lindisfarne died of the plague in 664 and the next archbishop, Wighard, similarly succumbed in 666. The plague must have lasted for decades as Bishop Eata of Lindisfarne is recorded as dying of the disease in 686 AD. There is no evidence that Ælfflaed contracted the plague, but it doesn't mean she didn't. If she did she recovered.

NORTHUMBRIA AFTER OSWIU

When Oswiu died of natural causes in 670 AD, Northumbria was ruled by Ecgfrith with his younger brother, Ælfwine, as King of

Deira. As he was only nine at the time it was probable that the title was purely honorific. Northumbria continued to flourish under the rule of Oswiu's sons and became culturally important. However, its political decline started with the loss of the territory Oswiu had gained in what would become Scotland.

When Oswiu's eldest son, Aldfrith, died in 705 he was succeeded as King of Northumbria by his son Osred, an eight year old boy. When Osred was murdered by a usurper in 716 his brother Osric quickly regained the throne. He ruled for another eleven years. He was the last of his line and the throne passed to another branch of the descendants of Ida, the first King of Bernicia. After Osric Northumbria's decline accelerated. There were ten kings in the space of eighty years who were murdered, deposed or abdicated to become monks.

On June 8th 793 a raiding party of Vikings from Norway attacked Lindisfarne. Monks fled in fear and many were slaughtered. More raids followed until eventually the invaders, mainly Danes, settled. There followed a period of Danish supremacy with England divided in two. The Danelaw in the north included much of Northumbria, but by then most of Rheged had disappeared, swallowed up by Strathclyde. However, the area around Bebbanburg was never conquered by the Danes and remained independent under Anglian rule, though the ruler contented himself with the title of earl.

The story of Northumbria during these turbulent times will be covered in subsequent novels in this series.

Northumbria eventually became an earldom as part of a united England. The last Earl of Northumbria was Robert de Mowbray, a Norman, who was removed from his earldom for joining a conspiracy to depose William Rufus, the son of the Conqueror. Much later there were earls and dukes of Northumberland but the county was defined by the rivers Tweed and Tyne and the county of Cumbria in the west – a pale shadow of the Kingdom of Northumbria that used to be.

Other Novels by H A Culley

The Normans Series

The Bastard's Crown
Death in the Forest
England in Anarchy
Caging the Lyon
Seeking Jerusalem

Babylon Series

Babylon – The Concubine's Son
Babylon – Dawn of Empire

Individual Novels

Magna Carta
The Sins of the Fathers (no longer available)

Robert the Bruce Trilogy

The Path to the Throne
The Winter King
After Bannockburn

Constantine Trilogy

Constantine – The Battle for Rome
Crispus Ascending
Death of the Innocent

Macedon Trilogy

The Strategos
The Sacred War
Alexander

Kings of Northumbria Series

Whiteblade
Warriors of the North
Bretwalda

About The Author

H A Culley was born in Wiltshire in 1944 was educated at St. Edmund's School, Canterbury and Welbeck College. After RMA Sandhurst he served as an Army officer for twenty four years, during which time he had a variety of unusual jobs. He spent his twenty first birthday in the jungles of Borneo, commanded an Arab infantry unit in the Gulf for three years and was the military attaché in Beirut during the aftermath of the Lebanese Civil War.

After leaving the Army he became the bursar of a large independent school for seventeen years before moving into marketing and fundraising in the education sector. He has served on the board of two commercial companies and has been a trustee of several national and local charities. He has also been involved in two major historical projects. His last job before retiring was as the finance director and company secretary of the Institute of Development Professionals in Education.

He now divides his time between giving talks on a variety of historical topics and writing historical fiction. His first novel was the Bastard's Crown about the Norman Conquest.

He has three adult children and one granddaughter and lives between Holy Island and Berwick upon Tweed in Northumberland.